A SILENT UNDERSTANDING

THE KILTEEGAN BRIDGE SERIES - BOOK 5

JEAN GRAINGER

"There is a sacredness in tears. They are not a mark of weakness, but of power. They speak more eloquently than ten thousand tongues. They are the messengers of overwhelming grief, of deep contrition and of unspeakable love."
Washington Irving

Dedicated to my mother, who is never far away.

PROLOGUE

 HE STORY SO FAR...

BEAUTIFUL FARMER'S daughter Lena O'Sullivan is only seventeen when she and Malachy Berger fall in love. Lena becomes pregnant, but Malachy's wealthy father, August Berger, a Nazi in hiding, persuades Malachy to abandon her. Later, Lena marries generous, loving Eli Kogan, a Jew, who treats her son Emmet as his own.

Malachy, heartbroken, leaves Ireland and becomes the wealthy owner of an engineering company in California, but he is never able to forget Lena. He knows Emmet is his son, and once the boy finishes school, he invites him to America to make his own fortune.

Nellie, Emmet's cousin of the same age, follows Emmet to California. She has been miserable ever since becoming pregnant by a married man. Her mother, Lena's sister Emily, is raising the baby boy, Aidan, as her own, but Nellie just wants to get away and forget the whole thing.

In San Francisco, Emmet works hard to get into Stanford but messed-up Nellie turns to drink and drugs and ends up in a cult.

When Emily hears of this, she leaves baby Aidan in Lena and Eli's care while she drives her husband Blackie to Dublin airport, telling him to fetch their daughter home.

Lena and Eli stay with baby Aidan in the flat over Blackie and Emily's shop. When they wake in the middle of the night to find the place is on fire, Lena escapes to raise the alarm while her husband races to save the baby. In desperate scenes, a neighbour scales a ladder to the topfloor window to snatch the baby from Eli's outstretched arms, just as Lena's beloved husband is overcome by smoke and flames.

NOW READ ON...

CHAPTER 1

$\mathcal{N}$ ew York, 1977

MALACHY BERGER SAT in total silence reading the document Rosa Abramson had passed to him, his half-finished T-bone steak and baked potato pushed to one side, a deep frown on his face. Around them, the trendy Manhattan restaurant was a cacophony of clattering plates, clashing cutlery, jazz on the sound system and the countless voices of New York businesspeople having working lunches.

Rosa ate her green salad with grilled chicken slowly, allowing the Irishman plenty of time to take in her proposal and gather his thoughts.

She'd chosen such a noisy venue because it meant he could raise his voice without being overheard, and she was fully expecting him to argue. She was used to it; people always did. She knew the sum she was suggesting must seem shockingly large, and the rich were very fond of their money, however it had come to them.

What did surprise her, though, was that she'd almost forgotten how very attractive this man was. Powerfully built, with thick chestnut hair, bright emerald eyes with long dark lashes, hollow cheeks, a strong jaw.

Rosa had got to the age of thirty-eight and had never married, and of late she'd kind of stopped seeing men as potential love interests. She'd had lots of relationships, some more meaningful than others, but never one that had come close in importance to her career. The law was her life, simple as that. Especially her branch of it. Chasing down people like this Malachy Berger and squeezing – hard.

Romantic entanglements always ended the same way, with some guy telling her she was a workaholic, that there was no room for him. And they were right. There wasn't. So she let each relationship die a death without a struggle and not much regret.

This Irish guy was intriguing, though; she'd give him that.

She had first met him in Ireland, at Eli Kogan's funeral. She'd been at that sad occasion because Eli was her cousin, a fellow Holocaust survivor, and Malachy Berger had been there because... Well, it was complicated, but Eli's widow, Lena, was Emmet's mother, and Malachy was Emmet's biological father, even though Eli had been Emmet's real dad, the man who raised him.

The Irishman reached into his jacket pocket, pulled out a fountain pen, uncapped it and started making notes in the margins. Checking and challenging her math, she assumed. It was always the way in these situations. The long pause while they tried to pick holes in her figures, and then the denial, the usual disclaimers: *Nothing to do with me. I was a child at the time. These things happen in war. If we gave everything back to everyone...* Followed by self-righteous anger: *America rescued you people. Why are you trying to bankrupt me? I'll see you in court...*

She tried to guess which way this guy would jump. Would he sneer at her, belittle her, go straight to threats? When she'd told him back in Kilteegan Bridge that she was preparing to investigate his wealth and its origins, he'd been polite and charming, but that was before he'd seen these figures. He'd inherited a fortune certainly, but he'd turned it into an even larger one, so as far as he was concerned, he was self-made. He was quiet, proper, and she suspected he worked as hard for his money as she did. But he wouldn't have been where he was today without that legacy from his grandparents, which had enabled him to invest in a small engineering firm and build it up into a West Coast conglomerate.

Berger's grandparents had been well-connected Nazi sympathisers. They were wine dealers in Alsace who also dealt in art, antiques and a variety of other things. Due to the meticulous record-keeping of the German war machine, the specialist legal firm for which Rosa worked had gathered irrefutable proof that the Bergers' fortune was grown from the assets of deported Jews. The Bergers had stolen their treasures and sold them on to the highest bidder. One item, a first-edition music manuscript of Beethoven's that was sold to a collector in Canada, was originally the property of a Jewish man murdered in Mauthausen Camp in Austria.

Another windfall for the Bergers had been the wine cellar belonging to the Loeb family, vineyard-owning Jews who had been deported to Auschwitz. It would seem there was some personal connection between the Bergers and the Loebs beyond theft and exploitation; her investigation was ongoing. The older Loebs had been murdered, but they had a daughter, Rebecca, who was used in some kind of gruesome experiment dreamed up by a Nazi doctor to show the inherent inferiority of the Jewish people. Such research turned others' stomachs, but Rosa didn't allow herself those feelings. She was laser-focused on the job, no room for emotions.

Rosa as a child had been liberated from Hitler's death camps and sent to America as an emaciated little girl who couldn't speak a word of English. A very distant cousin of her father's had been found, the link so tenuous it barely existed, but the woman had been prepared to borrow the money for Rosa's visa. Elise and Joel Hersh of the Lower East Side of Manhattan, between the Bowery and the East River, had taken Rosa Abramson in, tacked her onto the end of their own brood of five boys and raised her as their own. Within weeks she was playing baseball in the street and yelling at her brothers in a New York accent.

Elise had never sugar-coated anything. She'd told Rosa the whole truth from the start. Rosa's papa and *mutti* were dead, as were all the members of her immediate family. Rosa's great-grandmother and

Elise's grandmother were cousins, but they'd never met nor had any contact. Still, the Hershes were Jews and were as close to family as she was ever going to get. She had nobody else, so they would take care of her and she was welcome to take their name, Hersh.

At seven years old and eager to fit in, she had been delighted to be called Rosa Hersh. They were her new family, hard-working New Yorkers through and through. Joel had a fur shop, selling coats and stoles, and Elise did book-keeping for him and other small businesses. They were upwardly mobile working class, and Rosa was treated as the boys were, fed and clothed and educated and loved. She would always thank God for them.

Later, as a student at Harvard, she started calling herself Rosa Abramson again – she felt she owed it to her murdered family – and as a result, Lena's stepfather, Klaus Rizzenburg, who researched Holocaust survivors, had tracked her down and she'd discovered a first cousin in Ireland, Eli Kogan, and Eli's mother, Sarah, and Uncle Saul in Wales.

Now, in this expensive Manhattan restaurant, Rosa Hersh Abramson went back to studying Malachy Berger's handsome face. His expression was unreadable, and he was still writing on her report in a neat schoolboy hand. Rosa's adoptive father, Joel, always remarked on people's clothing and taught her to spot a well-cut jacket or a properly tailored shirt from fifty yards, so she could tell he was wearing a Saville Row suit and the shoes on his feet were handmade, Italian probably. Understated, neutral colours, except for a gold tie, but he exuded wealth. Maybe he would be the 'see you in court' type of guy.

Finally, the engineer capped his pen, took a sip of water, wiped his mouth and raised his eyes to hers. They really were the most extraordinary green. She imagined they were the colour of the Irish grass, so vibrant, so verdant. His copper hair would curl if it was allowed to, but he was immaculately groomed, his hair cut expertly and held in place with some kind of product.

'So you've calculated what I received from August Berger's estate?'

Rosa thought it was interesting that he didn't refer to August

Berger as his father. 'That's correct. We sourced our information from publicly available documents, such as your father's...' – she noticed an angry flash in his green eyes – 'I mean, August Berger's will.'

He smiled slightly and inclined his head. 'But not the percentage of my business I owe to that legacy?'

'Correct again. We do not take the growth of the original capital into consideration, even though there is an argument for doing that. As you know, I work for a legal firm here in Manhattan seeking Jewish reparations, and my role is to find the original money taken from Jews, whether that was in cash, assets, buildings, art, wine, whatever it might be, and try to get some of it back for the survivors or their descendants. We are simply about retrieving the money stolen, not the profits that money might have generated in the interim.'

'And your conclusion is that I should pay ten percent of my personal wealth into your firm's reparations fund – is that it in a nutshell?'

Rosa nodded. 'Upon the death of your father in 1959, you inherited cash and assets to the tune of approximately 200,000 pounds. Some of that, the property in Ireland for example, came through your mother's line and is therefore exempt, but the considerable cash inheritance, in the region of 120,000 Irish pounds, came from the Berger line –'

'And which you're telling me was stolen from Jews,' Malachy finished for her.

'Exactly. Your grandparents were quite wealthy before the war, of course, but their assets and wealth expanded, exploded you might even say, in the period from 1937. They dealt in expensive wines, paintings, jewellery. They had a voracious appetite for acquiring anything, it would seem. And these items that have resurfaced – a fraction, no doubt, of the things that passed through their hands – have almost all been verified as belonging to Jewish families.'

'And if I refuse to pay?' Malachy asked, his eyes holding hers.

Rosa sighed inwardly. It was strange, but somehow she'd hoped this man would be different from all the others, that he would at least recognise the justice of the claim. But of course he was just another wealthy businessman determined to hold onto his money. She plastered on a bright, hard smile. 'If you refuse, then we will sue you and pursue the retrieval of the money through the courts. And I warn you, Mr Berger, I will win. I always do.'

'I don't doubt it,' he said, a faint answering smile playing around his lips.

She was taken aback – this wasn't the usual response – but her face was trained to remain impassive.

'I believe you that my grandparents were thieves and conspirators.'

She stared at him. 'Did you know them, as a child?' she heard herself ask. Normally she wouldn't get into the emotions, the relationships; she was strictly about getting the assets back. But something about this man...

He shook his head. 'August Berger met my mother in Dublin, before the war. Then he went back to fight. He was a committed Nazi, and he joined the Waffen-SS. When he returned to Ireland, he told everyone he'd fought for the French Resistance. It's even on his headstone. He told me his parents lived near Strasbourg but that he had very little contact. Of course, he was a pathological liar, so he could have spoken to them every week and I wouldn't have known.'

'You didn't get along with your...August Berger?' Rosa asked, knowing she shouldn't. She was a lawyer and could yet face this man across a courtroom, but she couldn't help herself.

'No. I hated him.' His handsome mouth was set in a determined line. There would be no further revelations, she could see. Clearly he had nothing more to say on that subject.

'OK.' She took a sip of sparkling water to give herself time to think.

'So how does this work?' he asked, picking up the document again and flipping through the pages.

'That depends. If you accept my firm's findings, you can simply make the reparation in one or more payments, and efforts are made to return the money to the nearest descendant if the original owner is dead. In your case, we have failed to find surviving relatives. That's often the case.'

He raised his eyebrows. 'So then...?'

'The money owed will go into a trust, and one of a number of charitable institutions will benefit.'

'It goes to charity?'

The faint confidence she'd begun to feel, that this man would be different from all the rest, drained away. Clearly he was hoping that if there were no descendants, then there was no need to give anything back. 'Can you outline your objections to that?' she asked sharply, back in lawyer mode.

He shook his head. 'I have no objection. I'll give all the money back, willingly. I'm just sorry it took you to bring my attention to the wrongdoing. I should have guessed or investigated it myself, but as I say, I hated my father, so I left him and everything to do with him in the past. Returning the money now won't help the victims of my family's greed and lack of morals, but if it does some good for others in need, I suppose it's better than nothing.'

Rosa inwardly sighed with relief. If only it was always this easy. 'Mr Berger...' she began.

'Malachy.'

'Malachy. Thank you. That saves me a lot of time and energy. To say nothing of court fees.'

He signalled the waiter for the check and waved at her to put her purse away. 'Let me get this. There is one more thing, though, Rosa. Could we talk about which charity is selected?'

She spoke calmly, fearing it was too good to be true. Did he have a charity of his own in mind? One where he'd recoup the money he returned? 'Well, it would be one of our approved charities. There's a committee that gets applications from various organisations, and they assess the merits of each and decide, so there wouldn't be much to talk about.'

'Still, I'd be interested. We could meet again, for lunch. Or even dinner.' He gestured around him with a rueful smile. 'Though somewhere quieter this time.'

She was used to men hitting on her, but she wasn't sure about this one. Was it the destination of his money that he was concerned about, or did he want to see her? He was enigmatic, but she found to her surprise that she liked him. 'Well, if you really want to... Most people aren't interested in what happens after they've settled the bill, so to speak.'

'But I am.'

'Well, then, I'll call you.'

As she shook his hand and they parted on 7th Avenue, him into Penn Station to be swallowed up by the New York City subway and on to JFK for his flight back to San Francisco, her to catch a cab down to Wall Street and her office, she thought Malachy Berger might be one of the most fascinating men she'd met in a very long time.

CHAPTER 2

$\mathcal{K}$ilteegan Bridge, 1977

LENA SAT at the library window, an unread book in her hand, gazing down the avenue at the gate lodge that was now a working doctor's surgery again. She saw the patients come and go, some on foot, others on bicycles, a few still by pony and trap, more and more people in cars that they parked in the avenue.

Yesterday she'd told her gardener, Joseph Murphy, to take down the brass plaque saying 'Dr Eli Kogan, General Practitioner' and replace it with the one she'd had inscribed with 'Dr Michael O'Halloran, General Practitioner'. Then she'd asked her sister Emily to take her shopping to buy a new winter coat so as not to be there when the changeover was happening. Though as they drove home through the gates, the new coat that Emily had selected without any input from Lena was on the back seat of the Morris Austin, Joseph for some reason had only just got around to unscrewing the original plaque.

Emily had been furious. She would have eaten the head off the poor man if Lena let her. But it didn't matter. It didn't upset her that much to see Eli's name being taken down. Not really. People always thought it was those big things that hurt the most, giving his clothes to charity or contacting the electricity company to tell them he was dead. But those things happened as if she were on autopilot; it was mechanical stuff that just needed to be done, the business of getting on with life, putting one foot in front of the other.

It was the sudden, out-of-the-blue things that left her breathless with grief. Her son Pádraig asking his friend Oliver Lamkin if his father could drop them both to the football match, when Eli should have been there to take them. The smell of turf fires on the street of the village that he'd said was unique to Ireland and he'd never smelled anything as sweet. A phrase she'd heard some old local saying that she longed to relate to him; he found Irish phrases and sayings hilarious. The faint scent of his aftershave, Old Spice, coming off their son's cheek when she kissed him. His favourite tune on the radio, 'Here Comes the Sun' by the Beatles; Eli would always sing along with it, rather badly for an honorary Welshman.

Those were the things that burst the stitches of her grief wide open, her acceptance of his death pumping out like blood from a fresh wound. And that sentence again drumming inside her eyes.

Eli is dead. Eli is dead.

He'd left her alone. She was alone.

After a while, the surgery doors closed, and ten minutes later, the receptionist, Margaret, left, pulling on her coat with a glance up the avenue towards the big house. Five minutes after that, Mike O'Halloran himself emerged, rolling his wheelchair down the ramp constructed for that purpose.

Dr Mike O'Halloran had caused a bit of a stir at first, a doctor who used a wheelchair, but like everything, it was a five-minute wonder. His cheerful good nature won the people of Kilteegan Bridge over easily. He'd had Joseph turn the spare examination room into a little bedsit for himself, and though it was small, he assured Lena he was perfectly comfortable there, with everything on one floor and easy to access. Kilteegan House had steps and uneven floorboards and old stone flags and an upstairs bathroom; he couldn't have lived there.

And the village was a nuisance to get in from every day. Joseph Murphy drove him to the shops and generally helped him with things he couldn't manage, but Mike was a resourceful man.

Lena was grateful that Anthea O'Halloran had suggested her son, Mike, as Kilteegan Bridge's new doctor. Lena had been dreading having a stranger on the premises in Eli's place, but Mike was as good as family because he was the godson – and the biological son – of Lena's godfather, Doc, who had been the local practitioner in Kilteegan Bridge before Eli. So there was something right about it. Eli had taken over from Doc; now Mike had taken over from Eli. She knew Doc would have been pleased. Mike's surgical training had been interrupted sixteen years ago when he broke his back, but since then he'd returned to college and retrained as a general practitioner, and he said he would stick around for as long as Lena would have him.

Even so, her heart sank as he turned the new electrical wheelchair towards the house and came buzzing up the avenue. She really didn't feel like a visit from anyone. Sarah was up at the farm with her cousins, Ted and Gwenda's girls, and Pádraig was out playing Gaelic football, and Lena had been glad of the time to rest. She was so tired all the time, so lethargic, so lost. It was such an effort keeping going, just getting through the day-to-day, making sure the children did their homework, had all their clothes for school. Trying to show an interest in their daily activities.

And however hard she tried, she often caught a sad, confused look in their eyes, like they were at a loss as to where their cheerful mother had gone. She knew Eli would be cross with her for not being a better parent to them, but she couldn't help it. She was able to function, but she was powerless to come back emotionally. There was nothing she could do. She tried; she really did. Each night that she would crawl between the sheets, longing for the merciful release of sleep, she would promise herself that tomorrow she would try harder. But tomorrow came and all she wanted to do was be alone.

At least she was functioning, which was more than could have been said for her own mother, Maria, after Lena's father died all those years ago. And there were lots of other adults around to help. Annie

Gallagher, the housekeeper, who cooked the children's meals. Emily, when she wasn't too busy in the shop. Skipper and Jack at the farm. Even Maria, who was so much better now that she was on lithium.

Emmet had threatened to leave his engineering degree at Stanford and study medicine in Cork so as to be near her and help out as well, but as much as she would have loved to have her son come home from California, she'd told him that if he did, she wouldn't open the door to him. So she was doing her best for everyone. She was doing her absolute best. Emmet and Sarah and Pádraig would be all right; they'd survive.

She heard the back door open. Mike had arrived, using the shallow ramp they'd installed at the back of the house. Maybe he was only looking for Joseph, who sometimes sat in the kitchen with Annie to have his tea. She hoped he didn't want anything from her; she hadn't the energy for a conversation.

The next thing, she heard the wheelchair crossing the hall.

'Hi, Lena.' He stuck his head around the library door. He was in his forties now, his beard still flame red and his blue eyes had the same old twinkle. As ever, he wore a purple shirt and light-blue trousers.

'Hi, Mike.' She said nothing more, not to invite him in or anything. She found if she didn't volunteer a word, people gave up eventually. She used to be the kind of person who couldn't bear a silence, dreaded the awkwardness of it, but increasingly now she was the creator of that discomfited pause, and she didn't care. She didn't start conversations, and she didn't participate unless asked a direct question.

'Can I have a word?' He wheeled in and parked his chair facing her, next to the armchair where Eli had often sat reading reports on his patients from the hospital or researching some new drug.

She nodded, though she longed to scream at him to get out.

'Lena, about the plaque,' he said very gently.

She said nothing.

'You really didn't need to have it changed on my account. That place is Eli's and always will be.'

'No. It's yours.' Her voice was cold, flat.

'I think we should change it back again.'

'We have to move on.'

'But Eli might not want –'

'Eli is dead.'

There was a long pause. Rooks gathered in the old sycamore outside the window, cawing softly. The sun was softening behind pink clouds. At last Mike spoke. 'Lena, as your friend, and as one of your family, I hope, and as your doctor, I'm worried about you,' he said gently. 'I know you're heartbroken, I understand that, but Eli –'

'Don't.'

'Lena, I just –'

'Mike, I had the plaque changed to prove to all of you that I'm moving on. Is that such a bad thing? Everyone keeps telling me to cop on, to shake it off, to think of the children, that I'm not serving his memory. So I am copping on, and I wish everyone would just give up walking around me like they're on eggshells.'

'Or rolling around,' he murmured with a twitch of his lips.

She paid no attention to his self-deprecating joke. 'And I don't want to hear how Eli would or wouldn't want me to feel about this or that, or how I should act because "that's what he would want". I won't hear that, I won't listen to it, because it's all rubbish. Eli is gone, dead. He is never coming back. He's not watching over me to see what I will do. His charred body is above on the hill, and what he would or wouldn't want has nothing to do with anything.' Her voice shook, and she heard it rise in both volume and pitch. 'I know you mean well, but please, just don't. I'm doing the best I can, and I'm doing just fine. I'm moving on. I can't do any better than that, I just can't, so please...just leave me alone.'

He looked at her with such sympathy, deep compassion in his blue eyes. 'I'm a doctor, Lena. I'm all about science. But if it's any help, I strongly feel we'll all meet again one day in a better place.'

'Mike!' Fury rose within her as she hit the arm of her chair with her fist. 'Stop it! We were raised with all of this God and heaven and all the rest of it, but there's nothing. It's all rubbish. We live and we die, like a flower or an apple, and that's all there is to it. I don't want to believe it, but it's true.'

She was sick of being told otherwise. Her mother, Skipper, Emily, Jack, even Blackie, had tried a ham-fisted effort to talk about how Eli was watching over her or something, but every time she sent them away with a flea in their ears. And afterwards the feeling of being lost and alone just threatened to engulf her. A year ago, she'd had a moment of hope. Vera Slattery had told her to look in the drain by the back door, and there was the wedding ring Eli had lost.

Since then, she'd worn it on her thumb, stroking it, twisting it. Asking for another sign. But none came. It had been a stupid coincidence, that's all.

She said more gently, 'I don't want to think I'll never see him again, Mike, but that's the truth. Every single morning, I wake up in an empty bed, and every single morning, I have the crashing realisation that he's left me here alone, and I honestly can't bear it...' She saw the fat tear land on her blouse before she knew she was crying. 'But he's gone, Mike, and that is that. And please don't change the plaque back again.'

'Well, Lena, it's your decision. I just wish –'

'Goodbye, Mike.'

He hesitated, then said kindly, 'Goodbye, Lena. We all love you. Try and hold onto that.' He started up the chair and rolled away with a faint hum, like there were bees in the room.

She sat mulishly, staring out the window, watching him drive down the avenue back to his own little house. Was he lonely there? she wondered briefly, but then she dismissed the thought. He was always so cheerful, so happy. That's why he wanted her to be more like him, bright and breezy and enjoying life.

It wasn't going to happen. She was never going to stop hurting.

Only three days ago, Maria had sat here beside her at this window, the September breeze rattling the windows. She and Eli had been planning on replacing the windows last summer.

'When I lost Paudie, Lena,' her mother had said suddenly, 'I lost me too. Everything that should have been bright and colourful – my children, nature – went suddenly grey, monochrome. People think grief is crying all the time, but it's not, or at least it wasn't for me. For me it was a dark, bitter lump in here.' She pointed to the base of her sternum. 'I could never get away from it. I could never stop it. Some things masked it for a while – medications, a hug from one of you – but it was never far away. It became my constant companion, my grief. I almost needed it. It became me, if you know what I mean?'

Lena nodded. 'I do.'

'You almost don't want to smile again, because that's moving on, and you won't ever move on, or move away, or forget. But time is a healer in some sense. Not the way people say it, like an old platitude they trot out because it's too uncomfortable to sit in the pain with you, but time teaches you how to live with it.'

Lena had looked dully at her mother. Maria's blond hair was almost all grey and silver now, and her long bony fingers clasped her knees.

'You don't ever move on, Lena love. This is with you now until the day you draw your last breath. It will take up a part of who you are and who you'll always be. But I promise you this – it won't always hurt this much.'

Lena didn't believe her.

And the truth was, she didn't want the hurt to stop. She didn't want to smile again and be happy. She wanted to be left alone, to wallow in her loss, to try to remember what his arms felt like around her, to hear his voice, his tuneless whistle as he got dressed in the mornings.

But she never could hear him, or feel him, again. Because he was dead.

His missingness, his goneness, was a huge black hole in her life, and she was only existing around the edges of it.

CHAPTER 3

'*A*idan Crean,' Emily warned as her toddler made for the sugar in the base of the dresser for the second time. 'Do not open that cupboard again or I won't be responsible, do you hear me?'

The dark-haired, blue-eyed boy chuckled, knowing she was only joking. He was a ray of sunshine, and everyone adored him.

To Emily's immense pride, he was a fast learner in everything. Nellie had taught him all the noises animals made, and he loved to recite them, taking particular delight in roaring like a lion at his mock-terrified mother. He could say 'Mama' and 'Dada' and stand on his own two feet by the time he was one; at eighteen months, he was walking and even running. He was still a bit wobbly, but he was making the most of it.

Now he toddled back to the cupboard and put his hand on the door. Emily chased him, and he squealed with laughter. It didn't matter if he ran around; there were no stairs to fall up or down. After the fire in the shop, when Eli had died saving Aidan's life, the Creans had not moved back into the flat above but had used part of the insurance to build a bungalow just outside of the town. It gave them a bit of distance from work, and also from the terrible memory of the fire.

There was a clatter of feet down the hall, and Nellie emerged, dressed for her job as a nursing assistant at the Star of the Sea nursing home on the western end of town. She was wearing a starched blue dress, a white cap and dark tights with flat shoes that the old Nellie would have run fifty miles away from.

Aidan saw her and ran to her. She swooped him up in her arms, spun him around and tossed him up in the air as he shrieked with joy.

It warmed Emily's heart to see how much Nellie loved the little boy, but she was also glad to see it was the love of an older sister for her little brother, rough and cheerful, not the panicky tenderness of a mother. Emily was Aidan's mother now, that was the reality, and Nellie's life was no longer in danger of being ruined just because of some ignorant boy who had liked her enough to get her pregnant but not enough to stick around.

These days Nellie seemed to love being back at home, and she was so happy in her work, fetching and carrying for the old folks and listening to their stories. The Sisters of Charity who ran the home were always saying how wonderful she was, how the old people loved her exuberance and wit and how kind she was.

It wasn't what Emily and Blackie had envisaged for Nellie in a million years. She had been such a wild child, all make-up and short skirts, but her experiences over the last few years seemed to have changed her irrevocably. She was still bright and bubbly, but she dressed much more conservatively now, hardly ever wore make-up and kept her blond hair tied up in a ponytail almost all of the time.

At first the dramatic transformation had worried them; she'd been so quiet and subdued when she came back from California. But as time wore on, they realised she just needed time to come to terms with all that had happened. Becoming pregnant, having the baby, going to America and falling prey to a religious cult… It was a lot, and Nellie needed space to recover.

Gradually she'd opened up to Emily with her feelings about the pregnancy, about how hard it had all been, and on several occasions, she ended up crying herself to sleep in her mother's arms. But as the weeks became months, the light began to glow inside her, and Emily felt her child heal and everything settle down into the new normal.

Between spending time with Sarah and Pádraig and Ted and Gwenda's girls, Nellie was becoming herself again, although a less rebellious, more calm version for sure. Emily exhaled with relief when she heard her daughter tease Blackie, or when she had everyone laughing with how she could wind a story.

The job at the Star of the Sea nursing home had happened by chance, but it was perfect for her. A young nun had spoken to Nellie in the cemetery when she was visiting her Uncle Eli's grave. Somehow they'd hit it off, and now Nellie was working for the sisters and wearing her assistant's uniform with pride.

'I thought it was your day off?' asked Emily, suddenly remembering.

'Yeah, I wasn't supposed to be working this morning, but I said I'd pop in. It's Whacker Keating's ninetieth, and he's always trying to give me a squeeze. He's a harmless old divil, but I promised him a kiss on the cheek for his birthday, so I'll keep my promise.'

'That's so kind of you. I remember Whacker. When I was a child, he had this mad old donkey that nobody, including Whacker, could manage, and we used to be giggling as kids to hear him cursing and swearing at this animal. The whole place thought it was hilarious.'

'I know.' Nellie had set Aidan down and made herself and her mother a cup of tea. She handed Emily's to her. 'Sister Carmel is forever giving out about him cursing, but he doesn't take a tack of notice of her. But he's absolutely fascinated by Sister Martina – he thinks she's some kind of walking saint, and he's on his best behaviour for her. It's gas.'

'He probably loves being around all you young ones.' Emily smiled, then sipped her tea. Aidan was peacefully playing with his blocks on the floor for once.

Nellie nodded. 'Sister Martina's not that young – she's twenty-five. But she's really normal, you know, not fierce holy or serene or anything like that, more like an ordinary person who happens to be a nun. She's amazing on the piano, and she plays for the patients in the afternoons, all the old songs, you know. But last week we were up at the church when it was empty, and she asked me to sing, and we did a duet of "Strawberry Fields Forever", her playing the organ. She knows all the Beatles stuff. Can you imagine? A nun knowing the Beatles?'

Emily laughed, amused both by the idea that eighteen-year-old Nellie thought twenty-five was 'not that young' and at the thought of a nun playing pop music on the church organ. 'Well, it's a far cry from how nuns were in our day, but I'm glad you two get along so well.'

'We really do, and she's so interesting on the whole God thing. Like, we all go to Mass and all the rest of it, but she asked me a lot about the holy crowd I met in San Francisco. Nobody else asks – I think they're terrified – but she asked me why I went with them.'

Emily had never really spoken to her daughter about the details of her time with the cult; Nellie seemed to find it even more difficult to talk about that than about Aidan. Even now, after her daughter had raised it first, Emily felt nervous to ask. 'And do you know why you did?'

Nellie's brow furrowed as she thought about it. 'Well, I think I do. Like, I know everyone was all, "Oh, it's terrible, they are terrible people," but they weren't all mad. The leaders were up to no good definitely – I can see that now – but the girls were almost all lovely. They wanted a better world, and what's so wrong with the concept of people living peacefully, spreading love, not hate? I mean, the way they talked, it made me realise I was a bit, I don't know, hollow inside or something, and finding a sense that there is more to it all, that there's a divine plan that we don't see or understand, was comforting.'

'Oh.' Emily wasn't sure what she felt about this. To her, God was someone you could keep on the right side of by doing what the priest told you; she'd never worried about the lack of a divine plan. Life was just life, and what happened after that was a mystery to be discovered.

Nellie took another wooden block from Aidan, who had toddled over to her and was offering her them one by one. 'We're all taught that we're following the right rules,' she said. 'Catholic rules are right, and everyone else's rules are wrong, and I'm sure other religions say more or less the same. But if God made us all and we're all His children, then He loves us all surely? And if you're born in India or Ireland or Alaska or whatever, it shouldn't matter, should it?'

Emily thought about it in surprise. 'No, I suppose it shouldn't.'

'And so maybe there's a new way, a way to believe in a loving God, but not in the whole "we're right and everyone else isn't" way. Just trying to do good, be kind, love one another kind of idea, but without the crazy, in whatever church is handiest.'

'So do you like the Church now, Nellie?' Emily asked cautiously. 'You weren't that interested in it before. I remember having to drag you to Sunday Mass.'

'No, I wasn't. And it might sound funny, but spending time with those people in San Francisco changed me. Not the crazy stuff, but I realised I was looking for something, Mam. I was looking to see what was the point of it all. Like it seemed a bit meaningless, just drinking and partying, and having babies I wasn't ready for, and hanging around with people that were no good for me.' Seeing the expression on her mother's face, she laughed. 'Not Emmet, obviously. He was amazing, and I was being a brat. His friends are lovely, especially Wei, who rescued me...'

'Oh, I know. Blackie told me all about her. She's a saint.'

Nellie laughed merrily. 'Not really, but maybe you'll meet her one day and find out for yourself. Right, I'd better go.' She paused as she put her hand on the door handle. 'Mam, would it be OK if I asked Sister Martina to come for her tea one evening?'

'Of course you can.' She picked up Aidan, who was trying to follow Nellie.

'Great.' Nellie looked very satisfied. 'And we'll bring Nana as well. I was telling Sister Martina about Nana's painting, and she suggested that I ask her to come up and do a painting class with the patients. Do you think she would? She's not that confident about it, though she's an amazing talent.'

'I think she'd be delighted. She can't refuse you anything anyway.'

'Then I'll pop in later and ask her. She's in the middle of that huge piece for the library – have you seen it? It's incredible. It's like a walk through Kilteegan Bridge but also through time. I don't know how she does it.'

'I haven't. I must call up to her. Her house is so nice, and whenever

I go up there these days, Aidan does wreck. She says she doesn't mind, but he's too small to know not to touch all of her precious things, so I'm on the edge of my seat all the time.'

'Ah, Nana loves him.' Nellie returned for a moment to tickle her little brother under his chin while he wriggled and giggled. 'Doesn't Nana love you, Aidan?' she cooed. 'She wouldn't mind about stuff like that.'

Emily hoisted the boy higher as he tried his best to slip down out of her arms. 'I know, but for so long she had nothing. Everyone looked down on her, pitied her miserable life with Dick and Jingo. And now she has her little cottage and everything is just so. I hate messing it up on her.'

'No, Mam, you're wrong there. She loves to see you coming. And I know she had nothing nice with them, but she had no family either. She loves having you up, and she said to me the other day how much she missed you calling, so you should. Don't worry about Demolition Dan here.' And she kissed the baby's cheek and left.

Emily shook her head as she gazed after her daughter walking happily down the front garden path. Nellie had grown up so much; she spoke so wisely compared to only a year ago. Maybe she was too grown up, though. She met her old friends when out and about but had not gone to a dance or a party or even to the cinema since she'd come home from America. *Oh well*, Emily thought. A tea with her parents and grandmother and this nun wasn't exactly rock and roll, but it was a start.

CHAPTER 4

*E*mmet was confused and shaken.

'Why, though?' he kept asking.

Wei, usually straightforward to the point of being rude, was being uncharacteristically evasive. 'Because I need some space to work something out. I told you.' She wouldn't meet his eye as they sat on the grass around the Oval on the Stanford campus. All around them groups of students chatted or read. One couple were engaging in fairly passionate kissing for a public place, and Emmet still had to remind himself that this was America and it was the 70s. Not Kilteegan Bridge.

The warm Californian sun burnt his fair Irish skin, so he had to sit in the shade, and he and Wei had a favourite oak tree they usually met at. They often sat and studied together under its branches, but today all was not harmonious, and Emmet had no idea what had gone wrong.

'Are you breaking up with me? Is that it?' He hardly dared ask, he was so afraid of the answer. They'd recently started sleeping together, the most wonderful thing he'd ever experienced in his life, and he was head over heels in love with his tiny, quirky, spiky girlfriend. She was Singaporean and had some customs and ways of being that he found strange, but so did he to her, and they were gradually learning each other's foibles and had been getting closer. Or so he'd thought.

'No.' She sighed, like he was being stupid.

'No? Just no? I don't understand, Wei. Maybe I'm being thick, but is it to study or what?' He tried to lighten the mood. 'You always beat me anyway – there's no fear of me overtaking you.' There was a healthy rivalry between them, as they both studied civil engineering and were routinely numbers one and two in the class, she usually being the number one despite suffering from serious exam nerves.

She exhaled in frustration. 'I know that. Emmet, I just need some time. It's just for a month or so, I promise. I'm not breaking up with you. You have to trust me – nothing is wrong between us. I just need some time to fix something. What's so hard about that to understand?'

A thought occurred to him, unnerving but at the same time, not the worst thing in the world. 'You're not pregnant, are you? Because if you are, I don't mind...'

She laughed at him – in horror, not in amusement. 'You think I'm dumb enough to get pregnant by accident?'

'Well, it happens, even to brainiacs like you, y'know,' he said, slightly hurt by the disgusted expression on her face.

'I'm not pregnant, Emmet. Which is just as well, because if I was, my father would kill you.' Wei's father was the chief of the Singaporean police and, by all accounts, a man not to be trifled with.

'OK, I know. But then, why?' This was hopeless; he couldn't understand why she wouldn't tell him. A month's absence with no explanation? Whatever it was, something bad was going on. 'Wei, please, let me in. Tell me what's the problem. I swear I'll do whatever you want, but I can't just walk away and not know. I'm worried about you.'

She softened a bit then, her golden -brown eyes with tiny flecks of amber meeting his. She was so beautiful, she took his breath away. They made such a contrasting pair, him at six feet tall and broad-shouldered, with dark-red hair and green eyes, and she a tiny four foot eleven, with silky black hair and smooth brown skin, but it was love. From his side at any rate. He'd never said the words to her, not while she was awake anyway, but he felt it. He hoped fervently she felt the same, but it was hard to tell. He was used to being an object of female interest, but Wei wasn't like other girls. She was tough and smart and sometimes ruthless, and he loved her with all of his heart.

'Emmet, there's no need to worry. I'm going to be perfectly safe.'

'Then why can't you tell me? Am I even going to see you in college? What about your classes?'

'Emmet.' Her eyes were like flint now. 'I said I need space. I'll be in class, but I need you to not talk to me or contact me outside college either. I have some personal things to attend to, and I don't want to discuss it with you. It's private. Do not worry, I'm fine, and I'll get in touch with you when I've done what I need to do. If that's not enough for you, then...' She shrugged, and he felt the icy frost of her exclusion. He knew her well enough to know not to push it.

'Fine. See you in a month.' He stood up and walked away across the grass and down Palm Drive without looking back. He longed to beg, to plead, but he knew it would do no good, and besides, he wasn't going to crawl on his belly for her no matter how much he loved her. He wasn't her pet, to come and go when she clicked her fingers. When he reached the parking lot – he made his friends laugh when he called it a 'car park' like they did in Ireland – he ran across it and jumped into his Corvette, gunning the engine and grinding the gears in frustration.

How was he going to cope if Wei was finished with him? He had two more years to go for his degree, two more years of seeing her and not being able to speak to her...to touch her hair...to take her in his arms. He loved engineering and construction and was so glad he'd chosen his career well; he had taken extra credits and had excelled at everything. Life had been going perfectly until...

Stop it, he told himself sternly. *She said she isn't breaking up with you, so she's not, OK? She's not a liar. She never lies – she's too brutal. She's just being...well, she's just being Wei. Independent, headstrong, single-minded. Impossible sometimes. But isn't that why you like her? Maybe so, but this is just miserable.*

He let himself into the home he shared with his father on Los Robles Avenue, Palo Alto, and found Malachy on the phone, standing at the glass dining table, the tubular steel and leather dining chairs pushed in neatly all around. It was late afternoon, and the house was flooded with sunlight that gleamed off white walls, some of which were curved, and the tiled mezzanine that reflected the Spanish influence one saw all over this part of California.

As usual, the place was immaculate. Sometimes Emmet longed for the cosy messiness of his childhood home, but the housekeeper, Juanita, was relentlessly tidy, as were Jorge and Miguel, who took such care of the garden and the pool that not a leaf was astray ever, either lying on the perfect lawn or floating on the pure, still water of the pool.

Malachy waved at Emmet and continued talking. 'That sounds ideal. I'm really excited to get started on this.' He smiled. 'That might well be necessary.'

He took his diary out of his briefcase resting on the table and leafed through it as the other person spoke.

'How about this weekend? I could pick you up if you wanted to fly out. I could show you the site, and maybe we could have dinner? And I could show you how we live out here without cream cheese, bagels and hot dogs...' Again he chuckled. 'OK, let me know times and I'll be there.' He smiled again. 'Me too!'

Emmet pulled a face as he headed for the black-marble kitchen. He poured himself a glass of milk from a container he took from the huge chrome refrigerator that contained beer, champagne and a series of re-heatable meals prepared by Juanita. Was Malachy having more luck with his love life than he was? It sure sounded that way, and when Malachy finished his conversation and followed him into the kitchen, Emmet raised an eyebrow at him.

'What's that for?' asked Malachy suspiciously.

'Who was that on the phone?'

Malachy laughed but didn't answer the question. 'Well, I'm glad you're home. I want to talk to you about something.'

'What?' Emmet drained his milk and refilled the glass.

'I've just bought a piece of real estate, a half-acre lot in San Jose, downtown.'

'OK.' This wasn't *new* news; Malachy was always buying and selling land.

'I thought you might like to come and look at it with me, see what you think about what we can build there.'

'Sure. That would be great.' He appreciated it when Malachy expressed an interest in his opinion.

'Maybe you'd like to help out with the design, as your first project?'

Now Emmet stared in amazement. Was Malachy being serious? For the first time since Wei had demanded 'time and space', his heart lifted.

He loved being on-site. He'd spent a lot of his weekends on building projects with Malachy, learning all he could about the business from top to bottom. Engineers needed to understand the work of electricians, plumbers, plasterers, bricklayers and carpenters as well as the technical side of construction. Malachy had a team of ten who reported directly to him, managing at least two but often more projects each, and he insisted that every site foreman had at least a working knowledge of all trades.

But to help out with the design? He wasn't even qualified yet.

'I know you're still in college and so on,' said Malachy, seeing his hesitation, 'so I know you can't be involved every step of the way, but this is a special project for me and I'd love to have someone to discuss ideas with, someone who could bring fresh eyes to the project, here on the ground in California. Someone who... Well, the thing is, as your father's son, I just think it would interest you, because it would have interested him.'

Emmet was confused. Of course he was interested in engineering, just like Malachy, his biological father. But then he realised Malachy was referring to the man Emmet thought of as his real father, the man who had raised him, the man he called Dad, Eli Kogan. 'Why would Dad have been interested? Is it a doctor's surgery or something?'

'No. It's something I've been in discussion about with your father's cousin Rosa Abramson. It's a sort of community centre. It was her I just came off the phone with, actually, so now you know.'

'OK...' Emmet's brow furrowed. 'For the city, is it? A public contract or something? And why is Rosa involved?' He had a vague memory of his father's cousin at the funeral, a tall, narrow-faced, dark-haired woman with red lipstick.

Malachy shook his head. 'No, none of that. It's for the survivors of the Holocaust and their relatives, a space for them to tell their stories, to educate, inform and connect with each other. And you and I will be working on it pro bono, and I will be funding it personally.'

Emmet stood silently, letting this information sink in. His dad was a Jewish refugee child from Berlin; his Granny Sarah, Granduncle Saul and Eli's cousin Rosa Abramson were all refugees. Everyone else in their family had perished in the death camps. Emmet wasn't Jewish by birth and had no blood tie to the Kogans, but through the man he called Dad, he had a very strong emotional connection.

'Well...I mean... Well, I think it's a wonderful idea, and you're right, Dad would have been very interested. But why are you involved? And why are you spending your own money?'

'Because that money never belonged to me. It was stolen.'

'What? How do you mean, stolen?' Emmet stared at him; it wasn't like Malachy to be opaque.

Malachy pulled out two stools from the black-marble kitchen island and indicated for Emmet to take one, then sat down facing him. He was grim-faced, no longer smiling and lighthearted as he'd been on the phone earlier.

'I hate to tell you this, Emmet, because it concerns your own blood relatives, but Rosa Abramson is a lawyer who works for Jewish reparations, and she has discovered that the money I used to set up my company, inherited from my father, was stolen from Jews in Europe during the war. My grandparents, your biological great-grandparents, were from Alsace, and they traded and dealt in the treasures – wine, paintings, jewellery, furniture, anything valuable actually – that were confiscated or stolen from Jewish families.'

Emmet allowed the words to sink in. So the life Malachy and he enjoyed was somehow funded off the misery of the Jewish people of Europe. He remembered his father's grief over his murdered family; it made this very hard to hear.

'Did you know?' he asked, his voice sounding colder than he intended.

'No. I didn't. But that's not a good excuse, because maybe I should have known. I never met my grandparents, but I knew they were wine dealers in Alsace, French with German connections, and wealthy. And I knew August Berger was a Nazi –'

'My grandfather was a Nazi?' Emmet felt like he'd taken a blow to the gut. He raised his green eyes to Malachy's, the exact same eyes as his own. 'No, wait, it says on his grave he fought for the French Resistance...'

'That was a lie, Emmet. He was in the German army, and not just as an ordinary soldier like Klaus but as a member of the Waffen-SS.'

'No. He couldn't have been...' His mind floundered for clues in his past. He was sure nothing had ever been said to him about this, by anyone. 'Did Mam and Dad know?'

'They did, but they wanted to protect you from the truth until you came of age, and... I'm so sorry, Emmet. I shouldn't have told you suddenly like this. I just thought now you were eighteen...'

'No, don't be sorry. It's good for me to know the truth.' He fought to mentally clear the myriad of thoughts and emotions that crowded his mind. 'My actual grandfather was a Nazi? Our house, where Dad lived, was once the house of a Nazi?'

'Yes, unfortunately that's true, Emmet. But you and Lena and your family are not implicated in any way, neither financially nor morally, and nor is your mother now that the house has passed to her,' Malachy reassured him. 'Kilteegan House belonged to your Irish grandmother, Hannah Fitzgerald, and her parents and grandparents before that, so it has nothing to do with Nazis or anyone else. The tainted money is all from my father's side. Rosa estimates ten percent of my personal wealth is ill-got and contacted me a while ago to ask if I would be interested in volunteering to make reparations.'

'So you've been meeting Dad's cousin about this?'

Malachy nodded.

'And you are paying back all the money?'

'Of course. I think it will actually work out at maybe twice what is calculated, but I'm taking into account the profits I've made from the use of the money. I might have to sell this house, but the firm will survive just fine.'

Emmet exhaled, a long shaky breath. He didn't mind the idea of Malachy selling this big steel and glass house if that's what it took to make this right. 'I'm so glad. But why not just give it back to the relatives?'

'Normally a cash payment would be made to the survivors – or their immediate relations if they'd died – but they were all murdered. So instead, the money will go to a trust, and the board of that trust has already decided on a charitable project. In my case, because I can offer free expertise, it has been decided to build a community centre for survivors, somewhere they can gather and meet. The idea isn't fully fleshed out yet – Rosa and I are still working on the concept – but that's where we've got so far.'

Emmet nodded, slowly recovering from his shock. 'I like the idea of the centre, and I think my dad would have been proud of you and Rosa for thinking of it. He often said the biggest disease was loneliness, feeling isolated. As a country doctor, he saw a lot of it, people coming to him just for a chat, so he would be in favour of something like this.'

'Thanks, Emmet, it means a lot to me.' Malachy's voice sounded a bit choked, and Emmet realised his biological father was very touched. 'So that brings me back to my original question. Do you want to be a part of this project?'

'Oh!' He'd almost forgotten Malachy's offer in the shock of all these revelations. 'I'd love it, really, really love to, but...I don't want to make a mess of it...and I... Do you think I can be of help?'

Malachy nodded. 'Well, you won't be on your own – you'll have me with you every step of the way. And even if I let you off on your own for a bit, I'm going to give it to Johnny O'Hara's crew. He's the best foreman I've ever worked with, and he won't try to make a fool of you the way the others will. Builders like to think we're unnecessary, and they love a chance to show an architect or engineer up as a rookie, but Johnny's OK. He'll be gentle with you.'

'And you'll check everything I do?' Emmet knew Malachy would, he was sure of it, but he was also full of nerves, as bad as Wei before an exam.

'Everything.' Malachy nodded. 'I do want you to learn how to be in charge, but I won't let you fall.'

Emmet felt a glow of warmth at Malachy's reassurance. 'Then thanks, Malachy, thanks so much. I'd love it. And my dad... He'd be so proud of us.'

'Emmet,' said Malachy seriously, 'I think he'll know.'

Emmet nodded. 'I do feel he's watching over me,' he said truthfully. He did often feel the hand of his father on his shoulder, keeping him from acting rashly, advising him against stupid decisions. It was the only reason he'd just walked away from Wei and not broken it off with her then and there for the sake of his pride.

'And by the way,' added Malachy with a wide smile, 'if Wei wants to be involved as well, then she's very welcome.' Wei had often joined Emmet on-site, drinking in the knowledge that Malachy handed down, and Emmet knew Malachy liked how very ambitious Wei was and even how she could be calculating in getting what she wanted.

But at the sound of her name, he felt cold again, and shrugged. 'Wei told me today to back off for a month and not to contact her.'

'Oh...' Malachy's smile dropped. 'I'm sorry to hear that, Emmet. I know how close you two are.'

He shrugged again, trying to appear casual, like Malachy always did around women. 'I'm all right. She just says she needs time and space to do something, and she won't tell me what – she only says she doesn't want to see me for a while.' He couldn't help adding, 'I don't know. It feels wrong to me.'

Malachy stood up to get two beers from the fridge and sat down again, pushing one across the table. The legal drinking age in the U.S. was twenty-one but in Ireland it was eighteen and since Eli and Lena didn't mind him having an odd beer Malachy followed suit. 'Do you want to talk about it? Not that I'm any expert on relationships, but I can make sympathetic noises in the right places.'

Emmet smiled wryly. It was true; Malachy was terrible at relationships. He never dated anyone for long, though loads of beautiful women made less-than-subtle plays for him. He seemed to enjoy the company of women, but once things got too serious, he always backed off. Even a few of Emmet's college friends tried flirting with him one evening when they were all gathered at the pool in the garden. Malachy didn't bite, thankfully, but had he crooked his finger, Emmet knew those girls would have gone in a flash.

It was the complete opposite of Emmet's parents. His parents had been inseparable, so much so that his mother was like a shadow. He'd got letters from Sarah and Pádraig telling him how she was there but not there, and how it was as if the spirit of her, the fun, irreverent, kind Lena they loved, had gone away with Eli, leaving just the shell.

Malachy had more or less admitted to Emmet in a quiet moment that the reason he had never married was because he was still in love with Lena and always would be. But Emmet was sure his mother would never consider another man. Not long ago, Wei had wondered aloud if Malachy would make a move now that Eli was gone for a year. Emmet had been so upset – it was their worst fight actually – and she'd been at first confused and later contrite. For someone so brilliant, Wei was a bit emotionally stupid sometimes.

'No, it's OK. I don't need to talk,' he said now. 'I'm just going to wait it out and see what happens. But how about you and Rosa?'

'Oh, Rosa.' Malachy smiled to himself, sipping his beer. 'She's a nice woman. Fun.'

Despite Malachy's nonchalance, there was an expression in his eyes Emmet hadn't seen there before – a spark of happiness at the thought of a particular woman.

Maybe Malachy was capable of getting over Lena after all, which was good to know. Emmet had always felt sorry for the man sitting opposite him. He'd never thought of him as his father, not really, but Malachy was still someone he loved and cared about, and he'd been wanting for a long time to see him happy in love, instead of restless and always on the move from woman to woman.

CHAPTER 5

'What was that?' Skipper asked as he stood at the sink in the farmhouse rinsing his coffee cup before bed.

'What?' Jack looked up from the paper.

'Someone ran across the yard.' Skipper went to the nail on the door to grab his waxed jacket, then stuck his feet into his cowboy boots that were always on the back porch, plonking his Stetson on his head.

Jack followed him, grabbing his coat as well. There had been some reports of horses stolen recently, so they were on high alert. Fourteen, named in honour of Paudie O'Sullivan's faithful Border collie Thirteen, didn't stir from her basket by the fire, but her sister Fifteen jumped up, excited at the idea of a midnight stroll.

Jack took a long torch for himself and handed Skipper their only shotgun as they went out into the miserable night. The Montana cowboy was raised with guns on the ranches he worked on back in the States, so he was the better shot of the two. It was dark and cold outside, and the rain was falling vertically for once instead of driving sideways. Skipper often said he'd never before seen sideways rain like in Ireland.

'Which way were they running?' Jack asked, his face instantly wet as his hatless head got soaked.

Skipper shook his head, sending droplets from the brim of his Stetson. 'Towards the stables, I think.' He made off in that direction with the gun, while Jack paused to shine the torch down the lane, looking for a vehicle of any kind.

'There's no van or car in the boreen,' he shouted over the clatter of the heavy downfall as he caught up with Skipper. 'Whoever it is must have walked here.'

The stables were empty apart from several valuable horses. In the barn next to the stables, Jack shone the torch all around and Skipper brandished his weapon, but it was empty as well except for the bales of hay they were storing as feed. On one wall was a series of hooks holding saddles, bridles and lead reins, and everything appeared as it should be.

Fifteen ran over to the pile of hay and barked, but there was no room for any hulking horse stealers to hide back there, so it was probably a mouse. Skipper followed him and poked in among the bales, then told the collie to be quiet and returned to Jack. 'I think –'

But before he could finish his thought, bright headlights came up the lane on the far side of the yard and a car roared up to the door of the farmhouse and stopped. Sergeant Flannery, the local policeman, got out.

'Ah, Skipper, Jack, 'tis yourselves.' He greeted them as they trudged towards him through the rain. 'I'm sorry for the intrusion so late and on such a desperate night, but Mother Ignatius here is looking for someone – well, two someones actually – runaways from the orphanage, a big girl and a smaller one she took with her, and the Mother needed my help. So I don't suppose you've seen any kids around here? The girls are gone for two days, and we've been checking every place around Mary Immaculate Convent. A woman who saw them yesterday thought they ran off in the direction of Kilteegan Bridge, so they might've crossed this land if they went as the crow flies.'

Jack stooped to nod hello to the the nun in the passenger seat. She sat stiffly and didn't acknowledge his presence. Her head was covered by her veil, and a long black coat covered her habit. She had cold pale eyes, a pinched nose and a hard thin mouth. He knew this woman of old. She had come to the farm one time and told Jack's father that it would be best if all his children went to the orphanage because his wife couldn't cope and him being a man meant he would have no idea how to rear children. Paudie had put the run on her, telling her that he and Maria were both perfectly capable of raising their family, thank you very much.

Jack straightened up and shared an unspoken conversation with the man he had lived with for over fifteen years. If it had been two little girls running across the yard, he didn't want to betray them to this hard-faced woman, and anyway, they were gone now and could be anywhere. 'We've seen nobody, have we, Skipper?'

'No, not a soul,' Skipper agreed promptly. 'Nothing moving at all.'

'Righto so,' the sergeant said gratefully. 'We'll be off then.'

The nun spoke then, looking out the window and pointing one long finger at the shotgun. 'Why were you two out in the rain so late with a torch and your sheepdog if there was nobody here, and carrying that?' She pointed at the shotgun.

Jack hesitated, searching his head for a good reason, but Skipper stepped in. 'Checkin' on a foal born today. Young'uns, horse or human, need care, don't you agree, ma'am? And the gun here was because we are wary of the horse stealers that've been here of late, and the foal is a valuable one, born of the stallion Right to Live Free.' The American locked eyes with the sour-faced nun.

'Fair enough, Skipper, 'tis true for you, a valuable property, a racehorse,' the sergeant agreed. He enjoyed a flutter, and Skipper was always good for a tip. He had an uncanny knack of being able to read horses. 'We'll let ye at it so, and, Mother, we won't be bothering these good people again.' He turned to get back into the car, but the nun opened the passenger door and set one flat black shoe on the wet ground.

'I think we should just check the barn there, since we're here.' She said it quietly but with complete conviction that her instructions would be obeyed.

'Well, Mother, I don't think really... If they saw nobody...' The sergeant was in an awkward position now.

'Look for them, Sergeant Flannery. Now.' The woman was not for turning.

Flannery gave the two farmers a look, one that said, *This old bat won't be happy till I've searched everywhere.*

'Be my guest, Sergeant,' said Jack calmly in reply, and Skipper made a grand gesture, indicating that both the policeman and nun should accompany them back across the yard, as another splosh of water tipped from the broad brim of his hat.

Once they were inside the barn, Jack again shone his torch round the large space. The air smelled sweetly of damp hay, linseed and leather. Nothing moved, not a whisper, not even a sign of the mouse Fifteen had spotted earlier. The dog began to move towards the heap of hay, but Skipper called the dog to heel and turned to the sergeant with a broad smile.

'See? Nothin' here. Now if y'all don't mind, I'm gonna hit the hay myself.'

'Where is this foal you were talking about?' asked the nun, looking around suspiciously.

'In the stable, ma'am. We were only in here to fetch it a blanket.' Skipper picked up a soft, clean horse blanket from a folded pile and tucked it under his arm.

'Well, that explains it all. Thanks, Skipper and Jack, and sorry again for disturbing ye.' The sergeant backed out of the barn door, then hurried across the wet, dark yard towards his car.

Instead of following him, the nun stepped in front of Jack and Skipper. 'If you do see the girls, both of them need to be returned for their own safety.' She fixed her hard eyes on Jack, and he held her gaze. Her intention was to be intimidating, but he was not going to give her the satisfaction of looking away. 'The older girl is not of sound mind and could possibly be dangerous,' she added, intoning the words with no inflection or accent.

'Well, myself and Jack here sure do find girls and little children right scary, ma'am, so we'll be sure to turn her in if she shows up.'

Skipper chuckled.

'It's "Mother Ignatius",' said the nun coldly.

'What?' The cowboy was clearly confused.

'You addressed me as ma'am, but I am a Reverend Mother. You will address me as Mother Ignatius.'

Before Jack could intervene to stop him, Skipper grinned broadly at her. 'I ain't got but one mama, ma'am, and she's in heaven and I sure ain't fixin' to get me another one, so I'm afraid "ma'am" will just have to do.'

The nun glared at him contemptuously, then turned on her heel and walked back to the car without another word. Moments later she and the sergeant drove off, and the two men went into the farmhouse and closed the door.

Jack watched at the kitchen window until the car was gone down the lane, then turned to Skipper. 'What on earth did you say that for?' he asked. Most people wouldn't ever speak out to the clergy so frankly, but the Montana cowboy wasn't most people, which both amused Jack but also alarmed him; the way they lived together, they couldn't afford to bring the Church down on top of them. The other man ignored the question, his blue eyes fixed on the dark yard outside.

Jack loved Skipper with all his heart, but sometimes Skipper was infuriating. 'Are you planning on going searching again? I don't think there's anyone –'

'Wait here,' the cowboy said to him. He went out into the wet night once more, this time without the gun or dog, just with the torch, while Jack stood in the kitchen.

Maybe five minutes later, to his shock, Skipper reappeared from the direction of the barn with a very small girl clinging to his right hand. She was wearing a coat and hat that were much too large for her. An older girl, a rake-thin slip of a thing dressed only in a grey dress and broken shoes, no stockings, coat or hat, trailed along at his other side, looking terrified.

His mind in a whirl, Jack went to fetch dry towels from the hot press as Skipper brought the children in and sat them down at the large dining table. The older girl looked at Jack fearfully as he gave her a towel, her dark-blue eyes huge in a face that was pale and pinched. Her lips were white with the cold, almost as white as her wet skin. She slipped off her chair and went to the younger child, helping her take off the too-big hat and coat and rubbing the girl's fair hair tenderly with the towel, even though it was her own mousy-brown hair hanging in dripping strands to her shoulders that needed drying the most.

The little girl barely noticed what the older one was doing for her; she was too busy staring at the lump of cooked ham that Skipper had just taken out of the fridge.

'All right, I'm going to assume you two are who that nun was looking for?' Skipper asked gently as Jack started cutting wedges of soda bread and slicing tomatoes to make ham sandwiches.

Patting vaguely at her own hair with the second towel, the girl looked warily from one to the other of the men but didn't reply.

'I think you'd better tell us what's going on here. What's your name and this little one's name?' Jack asked kindly as he cleared a space on the table for the plate of sandwiches and Skipper made a pot of tea; as usual the tabletop was covered with papers and condiments and laundry and whatever else he and Skipper landed there.

There was a long pause, and those dark-blue eyes hardly blinked.

'OK, can you start by telling us how old you are?' Skipper suggested.

The smaller girl started to say something this time, but the older jabbed her in the side with a sharp elbow and she fell silent again.

Jack sighed. 'Look, we're on your side, I promise, but you gotta talk to us. We can't help you if we don't know anything about you.'

After another long pause, the older girl whispered, 'I'm fourteen.' The collie in the basket by the fire looked up at the sound of her name, then settled again.

'All right.' Jack caught Skipper's eye, and Skipper shook his head slightly. It was a problem. At least the girl was older than she looked, but she wasn't old enough to be making her own decisions. If she was in the official care of the orphanage, there wasn't much they could do for her; she would be a ward of the nuns. 'So what's your name?'

She clutched the towel to her sodden dress. 'Katie. My name is Katie O'Neill.' Even though she was still speaking in a whisper, Jack could hear a strong working-class Dublin accent.

'And how come you ran away from the orphanage?' asked Skipper. 'Not that I blame you. That Mother Ignatius, she sure is a pothole, best avoided.' He grinned, obviously hoping he could put them at their ease, but it didn't work. He tried again. 'She's like that scary person in that movie about the flying car – what's it called again? You know, it flies and there's a father and two children...' He was trying, but the two girls just looked at him like he had two heads.

'Chitty Chitty Bang Bang?' prompted Jack. He remembered Lena and Eli had taken the children to see it in the cinema as a treat one Christmas.

'Yeah, that one,' agreed Skipper in relief. 'Well, y'all remember, girls, there was an awful scary thing in that, a child catcher?'

The children still stared blankly – they'd clearly never been to the cinema in their life – and Skipper finished lamely. 'Well, there was a scary child catcher, and the nun reminds me of nothing so much as that.'

'Hold on there, Skip.' Jack had just realised how very cold the older girl was, more than could be solved by the heat of the fire. Even though the kitchen was very warm, she was shivering like a frightened whippet. 'Let's warm this one up before we talk any more. I think there's some clothes of Lena's upstairs in her old room. Follow me, Katie O'Neill, and I'll find you something dry to wear, and then we can go back to talking. Your sister will be fine here with Skipper, I promise.' Jack hadn't been told they were sisters, but the resemblance was clear.

She looked scared again, but she followed Jack up to Lena's former bedroom, and he found her a pair of jeans, a t-shirt and a hand-knit jumper that looked like it might do, albeit too big despite Lena being the smallest person in their family; even Pádraig was taller than her now. He opened a drawer and found some underwear and socks.

'Take anything you want from in there, help yourself, and you can put on those clothes and then come down and eat when you're ready.'

Katie nodded wordlessly, still clutching the towel to herself.

'And if you want to hang your dress up in the bathroom, it will be drying overnight.'

'All right,' she managed finally.

'You're welcome, and once you've had something to eat, you two girls can sleep in that room across the landing. It belonged to my twin sisters once and there's two beds in it, but for now, get into those warm things.'

'Thanks, Mister.' Her voice was hoarse.

'Call me Jack, and the fella that looks like a cowboy is called Skipper.'

Her eyes widened suddenly. 'Is he a real cowboy, like in the pictures?'

'Oh, he's a real cowboy all right.' Jack grinned. 'He's from Montana in America, but he lives here now.'

'I never met anyone from America before.' She gave a ghost of a smile.

'Well, this is a night of experiences for you so. See you below.'

Jack left her to dress, closing the bedroom door behind him.

Downstairs, the smaller girl's mouth was full of ham and bread, and she was telling Skipper in a muffled voice that she was called Maggie and she was seven and Katie was her sister. 'I love my sister. She takes care of me. She gave me her hat and coat when we went for this walk, and it was all right yesterday, it was dry, and a woman gave us some bread and milk, but she told us we had to go back, but we didn't want to go back, so we ran away from her and slept in the woods on lovely dry leaves. But it started to rain, but I wasn't wet at all because of my hat and coat, but I was getting so hungry, but Katie said if I kept very quiet behind the hay, then the fairies would bring us something to eat.' She crammed in another mouthful.

'Of course,' said Skipper. 'This here is magic ham, which means the more you eat of it, the more there is, so don't be worrying – you can have as much as you want.'

The child beamed and reached for a second sandwich. 'My mammy makes lovely sandwiches, and we're going to go home to wait for her, and Katie will get a job in Dublin, and we'll be fine until Mammy comes.'

'Maggie, stop. I said don't talk about Mam,' came a scared voice from the foot of the stairs.

Maggie looked abashed and went back to eating. Katie walked slowly across the room. She looked like she'd rather run away again, but the sight of the food clearly lured her. She slowly took her seat and then a small nervous bite out of the sandwich on her plate. And then a bigger hungrier bite, and a grateful drink of the hot sweet tea Skipper had put in front of her.

Jack moved to the stove and put milk on to heat, then got out a tin of drinking chocolate.

Skipper sat down beside Katie. 'So are you really planning to walk all the way to Dublin? Where's your mama now?'

Katie's head went down and she said nothing, but Maggie piped up again. 'The bad men took her away. The nuns said she was after killing my da!'

'Shut up, Maggie,' snapped Katie, a faint hint of colour coming into her white cheeks. 'Mam didn't kill nobody. She was just protectin' me.' She shot a fierce glance at Jack and Skipper, as if daring them to contradict her. 'Da was *hurtin'* me, he was...' She stopped then, clearly not wanting to say any more.

'Hurting you how?' prompted Skipper, with a startled look at Jack.

The girl scowled and dashed her thin hand across her eyes. 'Never mind what it was, but Ma came at him with the poker and now she's in jail. But she didn't do nothin' wrong – it was my da. But Uncle Thomas is in the guards, and he said he saw it all and he said it was unprovoked. But I don't remember was Uncle Thomas there 'cos it was all black, but if he was there, he was lyin'.'

Skipper nodded. 'So do you know how long your mama is gonna be there for? Do you think she'll be out soon? Is that why you've run away now?'

'I dunno. They never told me. Only when the guards and Da's

brother came for my ma, and the doctors came for my da, they took me and my sister too and gave us to the nuns. We've been in the orphanage for over a year – I've been counting the Sundays – and it's an awful kip. They done things to me there, nuns, and I wasn't going to let them, so I kicked them as hard as I could and they battered me for that.'

'Who battered you?' Jack was finding it hard to get his head around all this.

'The nuns. They beats us, and starves us, and even the small ones, they slaps them so hard they scream.'

Jack swallowed; his throat hurt. How could people of the cloth, people who were supposed to have dedicated their lives to God, behave like this?

Skipper was also grimly silent, but Katie went on in a louder voice, strengthened by food and warmth.

'I could stand it so long as I was there to look after Maggie and steal extra food for her from the kitchen and stuff, but now they want to send me to one of those laundries, and another girl told me you never get out of there, not unless you have hundreds of pounds. And I know my da would never help me, and my ma, even if she got out of prison, wouldn't know where I was to find me, and she wouldn't have the money anyway.'

Jack handed Katie a steaming mug. She stopped talking and wrapped her tiny bony hands around it, sniffing at it suspiciously. 'What is it?' she asked.

'Drinking chocolate.' He smiled.

She took a tentative sip. 'It's lovely.' She beamed, and it was the first time they'd seen her smile properly.

As Jack blew on another mug of chocolate, cooling it down for Maggie, who was watching him impatiently, Skipper resumed his questioning. 'And so you don't know how long your mama is going to be in prison?'

Katie shook her head, her smile turning off like a light.

'And your father is where now?'

'Living with some brasser in Foley Street.'

Skipper glanced at Jack, who mouthed back at him, 'Painted lady,' a term for a prostitute that he'd heard last year at a bar, the Bucket of Guts in Butte, Montana. They'd gone to visit Skipper's brother and his wife.

Skipper went back to gently questioning her. 'So he ain't fixin' to take you back?'

Her eyes darkened. 'Not me anyway, but I heard a nun say something about him maybe taking Maggie back when she's twelve, but I don't want that either.'

'You don't want Maggie to go home without you?'

'Not to him. He's no good.'

'And have you any other family?'

She shrugged her brittle shoulders. 'There's my Uncle Thomas, but he's on Da's side, so I wouldn't go to him even if he'd have me, which he wouldn't. Uncle Thomas did offer to have Maggie while Da was in the hospital, but my da said it was better for the nuns to feed her for free until she was old enough to...old enough to come home and look after him and Thomas.'

Jack exchanged another glance with Skipper. This was a terrible situation, but it was hard to know what to do unless they just hid these two children away... And how long would that work for? They'd be bound to get noticed, and it would look really wrong, two single men, no relations of the girls, taking them in off the street and hiding them.

'Well, Katie...'

She looked up sharply, clearly hearing the tone of apology in Jack's voice. 'Don't send us back, Mister, please don't. Don't send us back. We'll be murdered altogether! We'll keep running away. I don't care what yous do to me, we'll run in front of a car and kill ourselves if we have to, but we won't go back to that auld crow, we won't, I swear!' She was shouting now through her tears, her Dublin accent strong.

'Don't send us back, Mister!' echoed Maggie, bursting into tears.

The small child's tears and the terror in Katie's eyes broke Jack's heart. How could he and Skipper allow her to go back to that place after all she'd told them?

'Please keep us, Mister. I'm very sorry for shouting. You're nice, and we're safe here, I know we are.' She was in floods of frightened tears now, like her little sister. 'Please, I won't shout again. I'm a good girl, really.'

Jack and Skipper shared a despairing look, and Jack said, 'Look, Katie and Maggie, I promise no harm will come to you. We'll sort this out whatever way we can, but everything will be OK in the end, I promise.'

The two girls stopped crying then and drank the rest of their chocolate, then used the toilet, washed their faces and went hand in hand up to Molly and May's old bedroom. Jack had found some night-dresses of his sisters' and left them on the bed, and he filled two hot water bottles for them. When he peeked in on them ten minutes later, they both were fast asleep in one of the little white beds, which he kept made up in case Sarah or Pádraig decided to come for the night, their arms around each other.

He crossed the landing to the room he shared with Skipper and locked the door behind him.

Skipper was sitting up in bed, his hat balanced on the small chest of drawers beside him, reading a farming magazine. When Jack came in, he put the magazine aside and looked at him with his eyebrows raised.

'Everything will be OK in the end, will it, Mr Jack? You're going to sort it all out and everyone will live happily after? And how exactly is all that going to happen?'

'Don't start.' Jack sighed as he pulled off his clothes.

'First thing,' Skipper said slowly, 'we can't have two little girls here living with us and us being two gnarly old bachelors. It just wouldn't look right. You know you can't keep a secret in this place, so once it gets out, we'll be the talk of Kilteegan Bridge and the Monsignor will be here faster than you can say Jack Robinson.'

Jack grinned. Skipper was clearly getting more knowledgeable about how things worked in Ireland. He didn't used to think anyone noticed anything because no one ever said anything to his face, but over time he'd figured out their peculiarities. 'Well, I don't know. We keep ourselves fairly secret, don't we?' He exhaled. 'But you're right, Skipper. I already had a thought about that. I'm going to talk to Ted and Gwenda. Their place is totally off the beaten track, further away even than the Maddens' farm. They've no visitors hardly now the excitement over the house they built has died down, and Katie will sort of blend in with their girls, like she's a friend come to visit from Australia or something.'

'And how about Maggie? It's one thing to have another teenage girl around the place, but –'

'I know, but sure, I'll think about it in the morning. Everything's always easier by the light of day.' And he climbed in between the sheets and turned off the bedside light.

* * *

ONE MOMENT SKIPPER was riding a black stallion across the Ruby Valley in Montana, and the next he was sitting bolt upright in bed, listening intently. Slowly, he relaxed. Nothing to hear. Only the rain pattering on the windows, the wind soughing in the trees and Jack's gentle rhythmic snoring. But just as he was about to settle to sleep again, he heard another faint movement from downstairs.

Pulling on his jeans and a warm sweater Maria had knit for him last Christmas, he unbolted the door and moved quietly onto the landing and listened. The girls were a hump in the small bed, fast asleep, but there was someone in the kitchen for definite. He looked around for a weapon. Finding nothing, he remembered Pádraig had asked Jack to put a strip of metal around the end of his hurley, the stick used in the sport Irish people seemed to obsess about. It was at the bottom of the stairs, leaning against the wall.

He crept down, avoiding the squeaky floorboard on the third step, and found the hurley. It was about three and a half feet long and was much heavier and sturdier than a hockey stick. One carefully aimed swing would disable whoever it was long enough for Skipper to restrain them.

He walked forwards, keeping close to the wall along the

passageway leading to the big old kitchen. He could feel the heat from the range, which they never allowed to go out completely but just banked down with turf overnight. The door was slightly ajar but not enough for him to get a clear view into the room, which was at least twenty feet long and probably fifteen wide. The electric light wasn't on, but there was flickering candlelight coming from behind the door, where they kept a large dresser crammed untidily with all the crockery and tableware. Someone was rustling papers on the dresser. Whoever was rooting around there would need a lot of luck to find anything of value.

He paused just outside the door. He'd have to burst in, take the intruder by surprise and swing the hurley. He kicked the door open, keeping both hands on the stick for maximum strength in his swing...

...and was met by a shrill scream.

'I'm sorry, I'm so sorry, Mister!' She crouched on the floor with her arms over her head, a ghostly little thing wearing Lena's old white nightie. 'I'm so sorry, Mister. I didn't mean to...'

Sighing, he lowered the hurley and turned on the electric light, a single bulb dangling from the rafter. 'It's OK, kid. I didn't mean to scare you either. I thought we was bein' burgled, to tell the truth. I thought y'all were sleepin'.'

'Maggie's asleep, but she sleeps weird up on her knees, so she looks bigger in the bed than she is, Mister.' Katie's dark-blue eyes blinked up at him.

'My name's Skipper. Stand up and don't look so afraid – no one's going to hurt you. What were you doing down here? Were you hungry?' He looked around the kitchen. There was no sign of raiding the larder, but she had lit the candle on the dresser that he and Jack kept there in case of power cuts, and he could tell from the way it had burnt down that she'd been there for some time. Beside the candle, she'd cleared room for a sheet of notepaper, and she'd been writing on it with a red crayon, which was now broken on the floor.

'What's this?' He walked towards the dresser but then stopped because she'd shrunk again into a little ball of terror.

'I'm so sorry, Mister...'

'Katie, I told you, my name's Skipper and there's nothing to be afraid of. Look.' He put the hurley down very carefully on the sofa. 'Can I come closer now and see what you're writin'?'

Still white as a sheet, she gave a scared little nod.

He drew closer and looked at the sheet of paper. In a laborious red scrawl, she had written:

Ma ar you alrite me n M ar

The letters were big and badly formed, and it was hard to work out what she was trying to say.

'You're writing to your mama, are you?'

'There was a pad of paper in the bedroom, but I only took one piece, Mister, and I'll get you a new crayon, soon as I find some work...'

Skipper sighed. 'Katie, you're welcome to as much paper as you like, and nobody cares about a broken crayon. And you've every right to write to your mama. I'll post it for you in the mornin', will I?'

Immediately a sort of shutter came down. Her face went blank, and she crumpled the page up into a ball and stuffed it in the pocket of her nightie. 'Yeah, well, I'm useless at writing. It took me an hour to write this much, and anyway, even if she could understand it, they probably won't let her have it, so there's no point in sending it.'

Skipper's heart went out to the girl. She was small for her age, he could see that from comparing her to Ted and Gwenda's girls or Sarah, who was tall like Eli. Now that her hair was dry, it hung all jagged and without shape, and she was painfully skinny, though at least the sandwiches and hot chocolate had put a faint colour in her pale face.

'What did you want to say to your mama?'

'Just we were alive and...' – she looked at him warily – 'somewhere safe, you know, with two nice fellas who aren't at us like Da was.'

'Well, why not write that? I can get you a proper pen and a new sheet of paper?' he said gently.

'Yeah, well, I just don't want to write anything more now.' Despite her initial fright when he came bursting into the kitchen, she was clearly a tough little thing. He got the impression that she had built walls around herself for protection and wasn't going to let them come down easily, or at all.

'If you want, I can help you with your spelling?'

She reddened slightly, a blush of shame. 'Yeah, well, you don't need to tell me. I know it was all spelled wrong,' she said heavily. 'I can write some letters, but I couldn't learn in school how to put them together. I don't know why. The other kids could do it, but I just can't. Just thick, I suppose.' There was no trace of self-pity despite her horrible bad luck for what seemed like all of her life; she explained it factually, without exaggeration or emotion.

'I don't think it's that,' Skipper replied, hoping he didn't sound patronising. 'Some people just learn differently, I guess. You sure ain't dumb, if that's what you think.'

She gave a mirthless laugh. 'Ah, Mr Skipper, I am, and my schooling is over. Whatever I know now is all I'm going to know.'

While he thought about what to say, he turned away to open up the range, got the milk saucepan that he and Jack used to make hot chocolate and set about heating up some more milk. Katie sat down at the table, watching his every move with her dark-blue eyes.

'Well, you reckon you ain't got no learnin' left to do?' he asked at last.

'Me and school weren't the best of friends, Mr Skipper.'

'Well, school ain't the only place to learn, Katie. I'm like you, kinda raised myself up, and I can tell you one thing for sure – every day you learn somethin' new. My mama died and my old man wasn't no good, so me and my brother had to fend for ourselves. Now, if our mama was alive, she'da whooped our asses and sent us to school, but ain't nobody cared much if we went or didn't, so course, me and Wyatt, after some careful consideration' – he winked – 'decided against it.'

He glanced at her and was happy to see her smile.

'But he's smart, my brother, and he married a really sweet girl, but she got it up here too, y'know?' He pointed a finger to his temple. 'So now they own the busiest bar in town, and her and Wyatt – her name's Laurie Lee – have a really good business, money in the bank. I wasn't like him, so I bummed around for a while, travelled, workin' here and there, but then I got a job working with the horses.'

'It's different for me, though,' she replied reasonably. 'I'm not going to get a job ridin' horses now, am I?'

He shrugged. 'Why not? I did. And then I met Jack and came here, and we do OK. We got this farm, and between that and the horses I get in shape for their owners, we're fine for money. Jack hated school too, reckoned he was too dumb for it, but he runs this place, and not just the farmin'. He does the books, deals with the government and taxes and all that stuff. And he didn't learn none of that in school either.'

'Well, my luck would have to change, that's for sure, to meet someone like Jack.' She sighed, and Skipper heard the sigh of a grown adult with the cares of the world on their shoulders, not that of a young girl. 'But I won't, and my ma, whenever she gets out, won't have a shilling, so I'll have to work at something. It would be better if I could get a shop job or in an office – I'd make more money. But 'cause I can't hardly read or write at all, that's not going to happen.'

Skipper placed a steaming drink of chocolate in front of her, found a packet of biscuits in the dresser and sat down at the table with her.

She fixed him with her eyes as she warmed her hands around the hot mug. 'Will you be able to keep us here for a while, like Jack says, seriously, Mister? Not trying to cheer me up now – the truth.'

He sipped slowly at his own hot chocolate and thought about how honest to be with this tough, sad little waif. He could tell her everything was going to be fine, but if Mother Ignatius found out where the runaways were, she had the law on her side and he and Jack could be in big trouble. He set down his drink.

'OK, you listen up now, y'hear? I ain't 'bout to make no promises I can't keep, but me and Jack, well, we're talkin' 'bout maybe you can stay with these neighbours of ours. They've got two girls of their own –'

'I'd rather stay here, Mister.'

'No, you'd be better there, but you can run across the fields to us any time, though you'd have to be careful and try not to let anyone see you, 'cause I guess if that Mother Ignatius finds out where y'all are at, she'll come to take you back and we might not be able to stop her.'

Katie didn't look shocked or surprised at that thought, just despondent. 'And I suppose once I'm back there, they'll be even worse 'cause I defied them.'

He tried to cheer her up. 'I guess, but your mama might be gettin' out any day now, and she can come and get you?'

'I wish that was true, Mister.'

'Well, maybe it is. We can try to find out. We can talk to a solicitor about her. There's a good man in town, Kieran Devlin – maybe we can even ask him about finding out.' He had to stop talking, he told himself. He was getting like Jack, making rash promises, but the sight of that sad little face was breaking his heart. 'And maybe he can even work on getting your mama out a bit early with a pardon or something...' He really had to stop talking. 'She sounds like a good woman and a good mother, so maybe we'll be able to do something about it, OK?'

She nodded slowly. 'I know, she *is* good, and she'd never do anything that would hurt me and Maggie. She used to sit at night with me and read stories. She pretended it was for Maggie, but she would read slowly with her fingers under the words, and I'd watch and try to read with her. Maggie can read way better than me, but Ma never made a big thing of it. She's just patient.'

Skipper smiled at her. 'She sounds like a great mama, and we'll do everything we can for her, and for you and Maggie too.' He took her empty mug along with his own and rinsed them in the sink. 'Now, miss, you get yourself to bed and try not to worry. We'll sort this out. And don't give me heart attacks creepin' around in the dark no more.'

She stood up immediately and went to the door of the hall. 'Goodnight, Mister.'

'It's Skipper.'

'Goodnight, Skipper.' She gave a faint smile.

He smiled back at her. 'Night, Katie. Sweet dreams, y'hear?'

'Yeah, sweet dreams.' She padded away towards the stairs, a little ghost in her long white nightie.

CHAPTER 6

*M*alachy and Rosa sat in the big picture window of a seafood restaurant on Pier 39 in San Francisco.

'This sourdough is incredible,' she exclaimed, tucking into another piece of the warm bread for which the city was famous. 'How is it I've never even heard of it before?'

He broke off a piece for himself from the basket. 'It's a very San Francisco thing. It became a staple during the California Gold Rush of 1849. The gold miners liked it because it doesn't go stale for ages, and it's easy to keep sourdough yeast going so you can keep making more bread.'

'Well, thanks for the history lesson, Mr Berger.'

'Sorry. Boring, I know.' He smiled. He knew he had a tendency to spout facts when he was slightly on edge. Not that Rosa wasn't easy to be with; he was just quite in awe of her.

She smiled back at him. 'Not at all. I love it when you get technical. And while you'll never tell me any bread stuff is as good as a New York bagel, this comes close.'

He grinned and relaxed. This woman was beautiful and clever, and he realised that for the first time, he wasn't comparing a potential new girlfriend to Lena, his first love.

Lena was his eternal problem when it came to relationships, because none of the women were her. And Rosa was as unlike Lena as it was possible to be. Her edges were much sharper, her emotions fully contained, and she was driven by career, not family. She never appeared in public unless she was perfectly coordinated and her make-up immaculate. She would never sit in a car getting greasy fish and chips all over her hands, or run down a muddy lane to him in red shoes, her heels getting stuck...

Maybe that had been his problem all along, trying to find someone who reminded him of Lena and not succeeding. Rosa had been thrust upon him with the providence of his inheritance, and what had all the promise of a bitter, acrimonious and possibly legally confrontational relationship had blossomed into something else. He wasn't sure what it was, and she was cagey about her feelings too, but they were having fun and he was enjoying it. They'd met several times now, and though the community centre project was always the cover story, with each meeting it felt more like pleasure than business.

As they laughed over Dungeness crab for him and Chicken Creole for her and a nice bottle of Chablis, he found himself enjoying her company immensely. They chatted on and on, about work, her family, his business, and he loved how easy she was to be around. Other women he dated had, he'd always felt, an agenda. But this top-flight lawyer didn't need his money and she certainly didn't seem to be looking for a husband, and it was nice to just be.

He told her how happy Emmet was to be working on the new project, how he really needed it now that his girlfriend had decided to put things on hold or something. 'I'm a bit clueless in terms of giving him advice, so he's doing what I do, burying everything under a ton of work.' He smiled ruefully, surprised that he'd admitted that to her.

'Aw, Malachy, you never told me you had a broken heart?' she said, half serious, half joking.

'Oh, I don't have a broken heart,' he said, but even to his own ears, he didn't sound completely sure of himself.

She looked at him oddly. 'Is there something you want to tell me?'

'No, God, no...'

'Or is there something you *should* be telling me? Like for instance, what is the deal with your son's mother?' She took a sip of her wine, her brown, almost-black eyes fixed on his. She had a way of looking into one's soul. Malachy felt a bit like he was in a courtroom, rather than at a restaurant table.

'Lena is grieving the death of Eli. Emmet says she's really struggling.' He took a bite of the delicious crisp salad that came with the crab.

She raised a perfectly shaped dark eyebrow. 'That's not what I was asking, Malachy. I was asking what *you* feel about her.'

Clearly Rosa felt their relationship had progressed to the point where personal questions were permitted. He tried not to bristle; she was probably entitled to ask.

'She's the mother of my son. You know all of this.'

She put down her glass and laid her fork on the plate. 'What's going on here?' she asked him.

He felt himself stiffen slightly with alarm, his easy enjoyment draining away. 'What do you mean? We're having dinner together.'

'Malachy. Tell me.'

He looked at her warily. 'Tell you what?'

'Tell me, did Lena leave you because she didn't love you, or did you leave her when you found out she was pregnant? Wait.' She held up her hand as he opened his mouth to protest. 'Malachy, you were a teenager. I'm not seeking to allot blame. I'm just trying to understand your feelings for her. Then and now. And before you ask, yes, we do have to do this. We've had endless meetings and conversations about the community centre that we both know aren't strictly necessary, and it always turns to dinner, and now here I am in San Francisco having yet another dinner with a man I've crossed the country to see. But if someone was to ask me what was going on with us, I'd have to say I hadn't a clue.'

'Well, I...' Malachy panicked slightly. Was she planning to call it off between them, whatever 'it' was? 'I like you. I like you a lot actually, and I enjoy our meetings, and I just thought...'

'Malachy, I'm nearly forty years old. I was too busy for a relationship in the early years of my career, so I realise I'm a slow learner when it comes to this, but I'm going to go out on a limb here. I like you too. I wouldn't have come here if I didn't. But I need something now. Enough with the "let's have a meeting" and it turns to dinner and blah, blah. So I'll ask again – what is it I need to know about Lena?'

He gave up trying to stall her; she was too smart for him. 'What do you want to know?'

'What are you prepared to tell me?' she countered.

Malachy thought about it. He could lie about his feelings for Lena. He could brush them off as nothing. And Rosa would know what he was doing, and the chance of a relationship with her would end before it could even start.

He took a deep breath, trying to figure out where to begin. 'OK. The reason we split up was August Berger. He deliberately set out to break Lena's heart, and mine, because he thought her father and my mother were having an affair. And I shouldn't have believed his lies. The idea of Lena... My God...' He shuddered, remembering that terrible time when the old Nazi had pretended to name Lena's many alleged lovers.

'And I didn't even know she was pregnant, but if I had known, I don't know, honestly, maybe I'd have abandoned her anyway because I would have thought the child wasn't mine. Cruel...I was so cruel to her. And then August Berger told Lena that he'd killed her father,' Malachy heard himself say, feeling oddly separated from himself as he spoke. Rosa would probably run a mile from him now, and he needed to stop talking, but it was as if some sort of floodgate had been opened.

'I'm sure he murdered my mother too, though he never confessed to it. And now he's lying next to her in her family grave with "a hero of the French Resistance" written under his name. And it's a lie, just like the lie he told me about my mother committing suicide, and the lies he told me about Lena when he decided to punish us both for what he called our parents' sins. Lena's father and my mother weren't even having an affair – he just imagined they were. Mam was lost and alone with me as a child, and then Berger came back after the war and she found herself living with a man she didn't know or understand, and Paudie just helped her, that was all. And because of that, he killed them both. And he got away with it, made it look like an accident and a suicide, while he died on his couch in the library as an old man.'

His eyes were on the table now. Retelling the terrible events of his past was something he'd not done since arriving in America.

'Look at me, Malachy,' she said, gently but firmly.

He raised his green eyes unhappily to hers.

Her face was full of sympathy. 'Malachy, you went through a terrible, unbelievable time. I don't wonder that you're upset and confused and angry. It must be all mixed up together, the grief about your mother, the grief of finding out what kind of person your father really was, the grief about Lena and having your son raised by another man.'

He sat looking at her, listening to her, amazed by this kindness. 'I've been trying to forget what happened all my life, but I can't seem to get over it,' he said softly, and it felt good to say it, have it out there between them, the truth.

'I'm not surprised. And if I were you, I'd take the name "August Berger" off that headstone and his body out of that grave.'

He nodded, wondering why that never occurred to him before. 'You're right, I *should* do that.' He had been paralysed all his life, thinking nothing could change, his whole existence set in stone like the lie engraved below his father's name, sullying the Fitzgerald headstone, his mother's grave. But it wasn't true. He could change things. He could move forward. 'I can do that. I *will* do it.'

'It would be a good first step, I think. And there are other steps you can take. You can get therapy. And I'm not saying that to stop you from talking to me about this. I think you should tell me the whole dreadful story, and we'll talk it all through, as much as you need, I promise. It's just that a professional therapist can bring something else to the picture, help you untangle all your emotions so you can see all of them separately, your feelings about your mother, Lena, your... August Berger. Your son.'

'Emmet is the best thing that ever happened to me,' he said honestly. 'So at least one good thing came out of all this heartbreak.'

'That is a good thing. But can I ask you another question, Malachy?'

'I suppose while I'm spilling it all out,' he said with a rueful smile. 'You might as well know everything.'

'You say Lena's heart was broken as well as yours?'

He dropped his eyes, ashamed. 'Yes, it was. I know it was. She said as much.'

'I'm sure that's true. I don't doubt you. But within the year, she'd moved on and married another man, my cousin?'

He winced, feeling the pain of the truth. 'Yes. I know it seems fast, but she was pregnant, and of course she needed a father for her child.'

Rosa's gaze became sterner, a slight frown appearing between her beautifully shaped eyebrows. 'Seriously, Malachy? That's the way you look at it?'

'I'm sorry, what do you mean?' He wasn't sure what he'd said wrong.

'Have you told yourself it wasn't true love between Lena and Eli?'

He shifted uncomfortably in his chair. 'I didn't mean to say that...' Though maybe she was right; maybe he had done that. Had he always secretly thought it was only about finding a father for her baby? Was that a part of why he couldn't let Lena go?

'Because I can tell you, Malachy,' said Rosa firmly, 'it was true love. I met Lena when I went to London the first time, to be reunited with Eli and Aunt Sarah and Uncle Saul, and the bond between her and Eli was so obvious. And she was so good to me. It was such a strange experience. I'd been a child in the camps. Eli remembered me from before the war when I was a toddler, but I didn't remember him or his mother or uncle. And to hear people speak about my parents, people who knew them, my grandparents, other aunts and uncles and all of that, it was surreal, to be honest. And Lena understood what I was going through. She was always working to diffuse the emotional tension – she was so fun and clever and kind. And she clearly adored Eli and he her. They had a very happy marriage.'

He sat in silence while she held his gaze, not letting him look away or change the subject.

'Lena moved on, Malachy,' she said. 'Of course her heart was broken, but she was young and resilient. And for her, the story isn't as tied up with August Berger, as terrible and cruel as he was, because he wasn't her father, her blood. For her it was the story of a teenage love affair, which was followed by a lasting solid adult marriage.' She squeezed his hands, let them go and sat back in the chair, a smile on her glossy red mouth. 'Now that's enough about Lena for one evening. How about me?'

'About you?' He was still shaken to the core. Everything he thought he knew was true was being turned upside down by this brilliant, perceptive woman.

'Let me rephrase that. How about us?'

Again, he felt turned inside out. 'Us,' she had said. So she believed there was hope for them yet. 'Um...well...you mean...'

'Do you want to date me, Malachy?'

He laughed at her directness. 'I do.'

'As one of a string of unimportant women, or just me, as an important one?'

He laughed again; he felt like a huge weight had been lifted from his shoulders. 'Just you, Rosa. Is that enough importance for now?'

'Yes, that's enough.' She smiled and raised her glass. 'For now.'

* * *

AFTER DINNER they strolled hand in hand – in itself a new development – along the pier, where the vendors of milkshakes and chocolates were still plying their trade. He bought her some chocolate in Ghirardelli's, which she devoured.

'How do you keep that wonderful figure when you eat so much?' he teased her as she decided she next wanted a hot chocolate with whipped cream.

'I never stop running, Malachy, that's how,' she said lightly. 'I've been running since I was a tiny child, and I don't think I'll ever stop. So I'm a bit like you, you know. My mother was murdered too, and all my family around me, murdered by the German state, which we'd thought was there to protect us, like August Berger was supposed to protect you, except he turned out to be a madman.'

He held her hand tighter as they walked in silence to a bench, and they sat with their hot chocolates watching the ferries come and go across the bay, the folks leaving the city to go home to Sausalito, the ominous hump of Alcatraz Island so close they could almost swim out to it, the Golden Gate Bridge spanning the bay, its top now shrouded in the ubiquitous San Francisco fog.

Rosa was dressed in a sheer black silk dress, with a silver belt, black suede boots and large silver earrings, and her signature red fingernails rested on his leg as she drew nearer to him on the bench, ostensibly for warmth. For the first time in ages, he felt a thrill of excitement rush through him. There was something so intriguing about Rosa. She was a unique mixture of invincible and grounded.

The temperature was dropping – it was always cooler in San Francisco than in Palo Alto where he lived – and he could feel her shivering against him. He stood up then, took off his camelhair Crombie coat and put it around her shoulders.

She smiled at him, and said, 'Now you'll be cold.'

'Which is precisely why I'm going to suggest we get a cab back to your hotel.'

'Are you ready for this night of revelations to end?' She glanced up at him from under her dark curling lashes.

'Maybe the revelations for now, but not the night if you don't want it to.' He pulled her gently to her feet, slipped his hands inside his coat, his arms encircling her waist, and kissed her. The response was passionate and confident. Rosa Abramson was clearly a woman who knew what she wanted. And later that evening, Malachy was pleased to discover that he fit very firmly into that category, at least for now.

CHAPTER 7

'*G*wenda has a new maid, or so Ted says, but she's like a frightened rabbit and scurries away any time anyone comes close. I only caught sight of her by accident myself. I'd never have known she was there at all, but I saw her run past the window when I was having tea with Ted a couple of days ago.' Maria was mixing flour and buttermilk in a bowl, making soda bread to go with the carrot and parsnip soup she had simmering on the hob. Lena's mother was still visiting her daughter from Cork twice a week, and she always cooked delicious food.

Sarah had arrived home half an hour ago from school, and she'd sniffed appreciatively at the warm aroma of cooking and hugged her granny before she kissed her mother's cheek. Lena felt a pang of guilt. Sarah was such a good girl, and Lena always made sure her children had nutritious food, but she knew the meals she cooked for her children since Eli died were all very plain and tasteless. She just couldn't get an interest in it; she'd forgotten about eating purely for pleasure.

'Did you hear me, Lena?'

She looked up with a start. 'Something about a rabbit?'

'I'm talking about that new maid of Gwenda's,' said Maria patiently. 'She's very shy, never comes down to the village. I have a feeling...' She paused, clearly waiting to see if she had Lena's attention.

'I'm listening,' Lena said, wishing she could just go up to her room again and climb beneath the covers and rest. Grief was very tiring; she knew that from before, when her father died, but never more so than now.

Maria deftly turned the sticky dough out of the bowl onto a floured board and began to knead it. 'I have a feeling it's something to do with the orphanage. I think maybe Gwenda is thinking of adopting her out of there. I'm beginning to realise she's got a big heart, that woman, so maybe she's in some kind of secret negotiation with the convent, because when I asked Ted who the girl was, he got all worried and said not to mention her down the town. So don't say anything about her, Lena, will you? *Lena?*'

'What?' Lena looked up again, startled. She'd been far away, sitting in the kitchen rocking chair, turning Eli's ring on her thumb, wishing again that she could hear his voice.

'You're not to say anything about that girl around the town.' She waited until Lena nodded, then went on. 'The nuns out at the orphanage were always hard. I remember Paudie telling me about the boys from there coming into school back years ago, when he was a boy, and they were underfed and terrified out of their wits. Though they all get tarred with the one brush, sure the sisters above in St Catherine's were lovely altogether, so kind and gentle. And Nellie loves it at the Star of the Sea, and they're nuns too, and finer women you couldn't meet.'

'Yes, I suppose so,' said Lena mechanically.

'That's right.' Maria was enthusiastic. 'They are. So I was thinking, and I mentioned it to them – I called in to St Catherine's the other day, brought them a few queencakes I made – that you were finding it all so hard, and they said if you wanted to come up for a few days or weeks even... And I said I'd mention it to you. Might do you a power of good...'

Maria prattled on, but Lena felt like she'd been punched. 'What?' she snapped.

'What?' Maria asked, her blue eyes innocent.

'What did you say? That I should go to St Catherine's?' Lena battled down the urge to scream at her mother to get out of her house. How dare she come in here and suggest Lena be sent to a *mental* hospital? Yes, Eli went on often enough about getting rid of the stigma around mental health, but no matter how he tried to make people see it like any other illness, there was still a shame to it. Her mother had been in and out of there all of her life, but Maria had genuine mental problems, her nerves, manic depression, whatever they called it. Lena was just legitimately grieving for her husband, and now it was all right for her mother to call her unhinged?

'There's no shame in it, Lena. You're having a very hard time, and maybe the people there can help,' Maria said gently.

'I. Am. Not. Mad.' Each word was enunciated slowly and distinctly.

'And neither was I,' Maria said smoothly. She was so much more resilient now on lithium, and things that would have hurt and upset her years ago just didn't any more.

'I do not need a mental hospital.' Hot tears sprung to Lena's eyes, and she spat the words through gritted teeth. 'I cook. I clean. It's not like I leave everything to Annie Gallagher. I make sure the children do their homework, I tend to the garden – Joseph Murphy only does the heavy stuff – I mind Aidan for Emily when I'm needed –'

'I know, I know, darling. You're nothing like I was when Paudie died. You function perfectly. That's not what I was getting at.'

'I never lie around in bed, even though I would love to – I'm so tired all the time. What more can people possibly want of me?'

'Lena, darling.' Her mother looked at her with huge sympathy. 'Of course we want more for you. You never go out with friends, or have any fun. You haven't got your hair done in over a year.'

'Because I'm busy shopping and cleaning and cooking and ferrying the children! I'm doing it all for the children –'

'I know, Lena, and that's the thing. You're going through the motions of minding them, but you never emotionally connect with them. You're just not there in yourself. Sarah and Pádraig are learning to live without their dad, and it seems they're having to learn to live without you too. They want you back, Lena. You need something, love, because this can't go on.'

'*What* can't go on?' She wanted to rush upstairs to cry, but her limbs were so tired, she seemed stuck to this stupid rocking chair. 'Mam, I'm doing the best I can. I'm trying my hardest to be a good mother, a good sister, a good daughter.'

'Lena,' Maria said gently, 'if you're doing so well without anyone's help, why don't you come up to the grave with me?'

Lena looked at her mother in horror. She'd refused to go to the grave since the day Eli was buried. She couldn't face it. And though she used to visit her father and Doc in the cemetery overlooking the town, high up on the hill, fairly regularly, she couldn't make herself go there now. There was a dark hole in her chest instead of a heart. It would suck her in, the whole of her.

'Please, Lena.'

'No, Mam.' She shook her head.

Maria pleaded with her. 'Small steps...'

Again, she shook her head. 'I can't.' Eli's mother, Sarah, and her husband Charlie had asked if they could contribute to his headstone a few months ago, and she'd let them do it completely, even though they'd had to come over from Cardiff. She'd never even looked at a picture of it. It was customary to wait a year before placing a head-stone, but even that had seemed too soon for her, too final.

'His grave is lovely, Lena, just what he'd want. It's a mixture of everything that made Eli, Eli. Please come and see it. It can't make you feel any worse, and it might help, even a little bit?'

Lena swallowed. She knew her mother was right. She should go. Not going was a sign of madness; everyone visited their loved ones' graves. Could she bring herself to do it?

Her mother seemed to know without her saying that she was going to try. Maria went out of the kitchen to the hallstand and brought back Lena's coat and a hat; it was cold outside, and the evenings were closing in rapidly. Barely three o'clock now and the sun was sinking in a pink and purple sky.

Lena allowed her mother to help her on with her coat and

mechanically followed her out to the car. Eli's car, the pale-blue Rover. She opened the driver's door and sat in. She had driven this car many times since Eli died. It was all part of functioning as a mother, driving the children to school if it was raining, taking them to birthday parties, to football training. Pádraig often liked to stay over with the Lamkins, who lived a long way out of town. Sarah could ride her horse to the hunt, of course, but she had her Leaving Certificate exams next June and was getting extra help with maths and science from Kevin Walsh, the retired science teacher who lived three miles beyond the farm, so Lena drove her there twice a week.

It started to rain almost immediately as they drove down the avenue, and the wipers sloshing was the only sound. Lena breathed in the scent of the leather and the open air, and she realised it had been ages since she'd simply left the house on her own account rather than as a taxi for her children. She went to Mass every Sunday but sat with Pádraig and Sarah and left immediately afterwards, where before she and Eli would have stood around chatting with their neighbours. She couldn't bear the looks of sympathy, or the vague disapproval that she'd not shaken herself out of the grief by now nor visited his grave.

* * *

THE RAIN HAD BLOWN OVER, but the graveyard was empty as Lena and her mother made their way through the creaky old gate. The gravel paths were well tended to. A local committee took care of the place, planting flowers and shrubs and generally making it look nice.

Her father and Doc were buried overlooking the sea, very close together, under a chestnut tree. Maria led Lena past their graves to a quiet corner where two stone walls met at a narrow angle. The graveyard was owned by the Catholic Church, and Eli being a Jew would normally mean he couldn't be buried there, but the Monsignor had made an exception for the beloved local doctor.

There in the depth of the corner, protected from the wind, was a polished grey-granite headstone, glowing in the lowering sun. Carved into the stone, along the curved top, was a Star of David, and on either side, also exquisitely carved, were a Welsh dragon and an Irish shamrock.

There was an inscription in the Hebrew language that Lena couldn't read, but she knew from Sarah that the words underneath in English were a translation, and they took her breath away.

Eli Kogan
Dearly beloved husband, father, son, nephew, brother, doctor.
1935–1976
Survivor of the Holocaust, devoted to his family and community, he died a hero.

Beneath the bilingual text was the caduceus, the staff with wings, intertwined with serpents, the symbol of medicine and doctors.

Lying at the foot of the stone was a posy of fresh flowers.

'Isn't it lovely?' Maria put her arm around her daughter's waist. 'Sarah comes up every morning with flowers from your garden. She's growing them on her windowsill in the house now – it's too cold outside – and she rides up here on Second Chance before school to put them on his grave. And Pádraig often comes up in the evening and sits here for hours telling Eli about his matches and his friends.'

Lena didn't trust herself to speak; she merely nodded. She was focused on trying not to feel her sorrow, on getting through this, on learning to be in the same world as Eli's grave.

'Don't be afraid of your feelings, Lena. They're part of being alive.' Maria was incredibly intuitive, always able to tell what was in people's minds. 'You should talk to him when you miss him, Lena. The way you used to talk to your father and Doc before Eli died. Didn't you feel they were with you? Didn't they solve your problems?'

'I thought they did,' she whispered. 'But I've changed my mind. Nobody's here, Mam, not Daddy, not Doc or Eli. It's just empty, a place we put bodies.'

'Of course not. He isn't there in the grave, love. He's with you, and the kids. He would never leave you, not really.' Her mother drew her close, kissing her cheek. 'That's what I believe. They're in our hearts but also in the air, the trees, the flowers and animals all around us.' Maria had never discussed her spirituality with Lena before. The O'Sullivans all went to Mass like everyone, but individual beliefs never came up. 'Sure, didn't he send you his ring?'

Lena glanced down at her hand and twisted the gold band on her thumb. It was engraved with her and Eli's names inside. 'It wasn't Eli sent it to me,' she heard herself say blankly.

'Oh, Lena, don't say that. Didn't Vera Slattery tell you where to find it?'

'That's what I mean, Mam.' She smiled ruefully to soften her words. 'If he talks to anyone, maybe he talks to Vera, but he doesn't talk to me.'

'But if you listened closely?' Maria said softly.

The evening had really darkened now, and the rain clouds hung heavily in the evening sky.

'You really think he's somewhere?' Lena asked, though the black hole where her heart should be felt nothing.

'I do,' Maria said with conviction. 'I'll tell you something I never told anyone.'

Lena looked at her.

'Do you remember I said to you before, after Paudie died, I thought I would take the car, drive it to the cliffs at Sheep's Head and walk off them into the ocean below?'

'And you came back because the car was out of petrol,' said Lena flatly. There was no room in her to feel for her mother's grief.

'That's what I told you, darling, but there was more to it than that.' She took Lena's arm, and they walked very slowly away from Eli's grave towards Paudie O'Sullivan's. 'Remember when you were small, a red deer stag with a white flash on its face used to come very regularly to the gate at the east field and just stand there, and Paudie used to take us to the window upstairs to look at him because he was so magnificent?'

Lena nodded slightly.

'And your father told us he was a Monarch stag because he had sixteen points on his antlers, and he said it was very rare? And about a year or so before Paudie died, the stag disappeared. We thought he'd died. They only live about twelve or fifteen years in the wild, and he'd been around that long at least.'

Lena nodded again. 'I remember Dad talking about him, what a magnificent animal he was. He never allowed the hunt to use our land. He hated hunting. I'm sure he'd disapprove of Sarah riding to the hunt, though she insists it's kinder than poisoning, and the farmers have to do something.'

'I know, I know... Ah, he'd be fine about it. He'd have loved his grandchildren so much, they could never do wrong in his eyes. Anyway, the time I thought about the cliffs, it was a cold and blustery day like this one, with rain on the wind, but when I was driving down our lane, there he was, the stag. Just standing there, no more than ten feet away. We'd not seen him for over a year at that stage. He didn't bolt. He wasn't frightened by the car. He just stood there gazing at me. He had that flash of white on his face, so he was really distinctive, and his sixteen points – I'd never seen one with that many points, before or since. And he stood there until I looked at the petrol dial and told myself the tank was nearly empty, although there was probably plenty enough to get me to the cliffs – it's not far. And only when I turned the car to go back for money did he trot off, and then you were there waiting for me in the doorway and you hugged me... Well, I never again thought of killing myself.'

'You think it was Daddy?' Lena asked.

Maria nodded. 'I know it was. That stag was never again seen.'

Lena stood, looking towards her father's grave and then at Doc's, and then she allowed her mother to walk her back to the church gates. A courting couple were sitting in a car – the graveyard was a local romance spot, being out of sight of the town – and the window was down a crack. They could hear music from the car radio, 'Here Comes the Sun' by the Beatles.

Maria glanced towards the car in surprise and laughed. The young couple stared assiduously ahead as if sitting in a car in the middle of the afternoon was a perfectly normal activity. But Lena stood stock-still and felt a deep throb where her heart once was. Eli always sang if this song came on the radio. Oh, she remembered that now. His voice, it was suddenly in her head. She could hear him, her Eli...

And suddenly she just had to get away, be by herself. She had to get away from other people's voices, her mother, the children, everyone.

'Mam, I'm sorry. If I drop you to Emily's, do you mind? Blackie will see you home. I have to go somewhere.'

Maria looked frightened. 'Are you all right, Lena? Where are you going? Can't I come with you?'

Lena smiled at her reassuringly as they got into the blue Rover. 'No, Mam. And I'm not going to do anything stupid, I promise. I just need to be away from it all for a while, please. It's OK. If you can ask Emily to pick up Pádraig from the training and make sure Sarah's OK at the house – she'll need her dinner and she loves your soup.'

Lena turned the key, and the engine roared to life. It was just after four in the evening now, and nearly dark. She drove down the hill and turned left away from the town, letting her mother off at Emily's new house, the one that had been built after the fire.

In the rear-view mirror, she saw her mother, stricken-looking on Emily's front steps, but she waved and was gone.

The drive to Cork felt good, and she even turned on the radio and allowed the pop music to wash over her. No Beatles, though, so she turned it off again so Eli's voice could once again fill the car, singing...

'Eli, when I said I wanted to hear you, I didn't mean your awful singing.' She laughed aloud. 'I suppose you're going to tell me it's a case of "be careful what you wish for".'

She stopped at the Munster Arms Hotel in Bandon and phoned Emily. 'Tell Mam I'm not gone off the deep end, Em. I just need to get away. I'm going to Cork – I'll stay in a hotel – but I'll be back tomorrow, all right? Tell everyone not to panic – I'm fine.'

To her surprise Emily didn't question it.

Lena was immediately suspicious. 'Mam suggested I go to St Catherine's. Did you know that?'

'What? I...no...I didn't.' Emily blundered over the words. She was a terrible liar.

Lena laughed. 'It doesn't matter, Em. I'm not going there, or anywhere else. I'm just taking a day for myself, and I'll be home then. Can you let them know? And tell Sarah and Pádraig I'll bring them back something nice tomorrow.'

'I will, Lena, of course I will.' Emily sounded nervous.

'Em, I know everyone's been worried, but I'm going to be fine. Maybe Mam was trying to shock me by suggesting I was batty enough to go to St Catherine's, but either way, I know I need to pull myself together. And I will, I promise. But first I need some time.'

'All right, Lena. We'll see you tomorrow evening?'

'See you then, Em.'

She hung up, and as she was walking out of the hotel and back to the car, she was met with the familiar aroma of fish and chips. She'd not had any for a while, but Eli used to bring her back a portion when he'd taken the children to the beach for the day – they loved to get fish and chips after a long cold swim – and he would keep his to eat with Lena. She would pop them in the range to keep warm, and later they would have them on their laps in front of the fire, when the children were finally sleeping.

She walked into the chip shop and joined the small queue of people.

'Fish and chips for one, please,' she said when it was her turn. She took her newspaper-wrapped bundle, along with a bottle of fizzy orange, and walked back to the car.

She drove out of town a mile or two to the banks of the River Bandon, where there was a picnic area, and stopped, unwrapped her feast and sat there, the windows of the car steaming up, the smell of vinegar and fish and hot chips filling the space, and finished the whole lot.

It was night now, and she spoke aloud into the darkness. 'I'm sorry, Eli. I was wallowing, I know I was, and it's not good enough. Something about Mam saying I should go to St Catherine's, well, it shocked me out of it, I suppose. But it wasn't that really, it was… Well, I'm sorry I didn't come to see you before at the grave, and thank you for singing to me after. I'm going to go to Cork now. I'll go to a hairdressers' in the morning and do something with the grey – You never knew I was going grey, did you? You thought it was all natural, you poor deluded man.' She smiled broadly, an expression so unfamiliar to her, it felt strange on her face. 'And I'll buy some new clothes – not black, something colourful. And so the children don't feel left out, I'll get Pádraig some new football boots. I'll ask the man in the shop to tell me what the latest ones are – you'd have known, but I haven't a clue. And I'll buy Sarah a dress. She's been asked to the Lamkins' hunt ball on St Stephen's night, though she says it's only because Isobel Lamkin, one of the younger girls, is still sweet on Emmet.'

On and on she chatted to him, pouring her heart out, and she felt him there, heard him answer her in her head. For the first time since he died, she could hear him, his lovely lilting Welsh accent, joking with her, supporting her, reassuring her. Maybe she was going mad, but she didn't think so.

'I'm going to go home and raise our family, Eli, look after them properly, and look after myself and do you proud. But you need to be beside me, all right? I can't do this without you, but I feel like if you're near me, like you are now, I'll be all right.'

She bundled up the newspaper, climbed out of the car, walked over to the public rubbish bin and deposited it, looking up at the starry sky. Her breath was visible on the cool night air now, and the yellow hunter's moon hung low in the sky.

She wrapped both of her arms around herself against the cold, but still she stood. 'Be with me, Eli, please. I know you had to leave me, but please stay with me now, darling, wherever you are. Just be with us now.'

She looked at her thumb; Eli's wedding ring glinted in the moonlight. She kissed it.

'I'll never stop loving you, Eli, never,' she whispered, 'but I'm going to live now, until I see you again.'

CHAPTER 8

*E*mily placed the joint of roast lamb surrounded by crispy roast potatoes on the table. 'I'll just butter the carrots and peas, and then we'll be ready,' she said as Peggy started a gravy from the meat juices.

'And I'll give the carving knife a quick bit of a sharpen,' Blackie said helpfully. Emily's husband had come home early from the shop on her instructions and had a wash and changed his clothes in honour of their dinner guest.

'Well, be quick then, or it will all go cold.'

They were all three of them a bit in awe of having a nun to dinner, but to be fair, Sister Martina was nowhere near the likes of Mother Ignatius, that ran the orphanage.

Right now, she was happily kneeling on the floor with Nellie, building up blocks and knocking them down again with Aidan. The baby was laughing as the sister made funny faces, on her hands and knees, her large bottom up in the air. Emily and Blackie were used to the floor-length black habits and the enormous wimples of the nuns of their youth, so seeing this young woman, as wide as she was tall, with a knee-length dress, a simple white blouse and a short veil, rolling around on their floor was something to get used to. She seemed to be permanently cheerful, and Nellie and she were giggling together like schoolgirls.

Peggy caught Emily's eye, with a look that said, *This is a nun?*

Emily returned the look, a silent conversation passing between them.

'Martina, dinner's ready,' Nellie announced, and she scooped Aidan up and placed him on his high chair.

Now Emily was seriously shocked. Surely Nellie shouldn't be addressing the nun as Martina? It should be Sister Martina.

'Oh, this looks delicious. Thanks so much, Mrs Crean, I'm absolutely starving.' The nun pulled up her chair to the table with a scrape of the legs. She had a round face and bright hazel eyes that looked huge through the lenses of her thick glasses.

Blackie cleared his throat. He had been warned to say grace before they ate, though they never normally did, but before he had the chance, Nellie and Martina were tucking into slices of meat and lathering their potatoes with butter.

Blackie raised his eyebrows at his wife, not sure what to do, and Emily gave the tiniest of shakes of her head. *Forget grace; eat on.*

'Oh my goodness, this meat is so delicious. Sister Angelica was our cook and she was brilliant, but she's having a hip operation so Sister Anthony and Sister Patrick are managing it between them. But honestly they are not natural cooks, so it's all a bit hit and miss at the convent these days. Last night the stew was watery because they forgot to thicken the stock and the meat was like shoe leather, but God love them, they are trying their best, so nobody said anything, though Sister Benedict's dentures were no match for the meat.' The nun and Nellie guffawed loudly, and everyone else smiled.

'So what part of the country do you come from, Sister?' Blackie asked politely.

'Oh, call me Martina please, Mr Crean. It's my actual name. I asked Mother Kevin when I was a novice if I could keep my name, and she agreed, because I told her the story of how my mam and dad were a late marriage. My nana was a bit of a pill, to be honest, and wouldn't let Daddy marry while she was alive, so he had to wait till she died.

But luckily enough he met Mam at a mass at the neighbour's house – you know the way they have a station mass in the parish, she was the neighbour's niece visiting from Dublin – and they hit it off. Mam was on the shelf a bit too.' Martina laughed again. 'So they married and they went to Rome for the Mass, got a papal blessing and the whole lot, and when they were there, an old nun said they'd be blessed with a child. Sure, Mam was forty then and Daddy forty-five, so they took that with a pinch of salt, but anyway, didn't I come along. And St Martina is the patron saint of Rome, so they named me for her, the little miracle that I was.'

This set Nellie off laughing again.

'They must have been delighted with your vocation then?' Emily asked doubtfully.

'Delighted? They nearly had a stroke!' Martina roared happily. 'They have a fine big farm, and they had great hopes for me marrying a big strong buck and bringing him in, in the hope that the acreage and the road frontage and the milking Friesians would distract the poor boy from my obvious physical shortcomings.' She hooted with laughter at this. 'So no, me becoming a nun was not what they wanted at all. But I persisted, and my poor battered-down father can refuse me nothing – I was spoiled rotten, you see, fed like a prize pig, buns and cakes and sweets – and in the end, they had to give in.'

'And you wanted it that much, to walk away from the farm?' Blackie was clearly fascinated, and Emily kicked him under the table on the ankle for being so impertinent. Even if this Martina was not like any nun she'd ever met, that didn't mean he could be so familiar with her.

Martina nodded, suddenly calmer. 'I did. Like I didn't have a vision or a dream or anything. I just always knew I'd be a nun, always. Mammy says when I was small, I dressed my dollies as nuns all the time and I used to make little rosary beads for them with flour paste. They thought I'd grow out of it, but no. The nuns at home – I'm from Athy in County Kildare – always went to ten o'clock Mass, and I'd kick up all kinds of a fuss if Mammy and Daddy wanted to go to any other Mass because then we'd miss the nuns singing. Nun-obsessed, I suppose you'd call it.' She gave a guffaw again.

'And are you a nurse now?' Peggy asked, gaining the courage to speak for the first time. The Sisters of Charity ran the nursing home, and they had their own chapel and everything so were rarely seen. But the Sisters of Mercy ran the schools in town, and some of them were most disparaging to her when Blackie and Jingo were boys going to school, insinuating that she should have done a better job keeping her husband out of the pub. She was fearful of them. The other order were the Good Shepherds, who ran an orphanage, but they were closer to Skibbereen.

'I am,' Martina said proudly. 'I trained in Dublin, in St Vincent's, and when I qualified, I was sent down here. To be honest, at the start I was fierce lonely altogether. Like I used to go home twice a month when I was in Dublin – it wasn't far – so West Cork seemed like the moon. But the sisters here are so nice, and the patients are lovely, though I have trouble understanding some of them with the accent. Nellie has to be my interpreter.'

'Remember poor old Mrs Kinneally? She was telling Martina that she was having terrible trouble with her tie, and Martina thought she was trying to undo her dressing gown, but sure nobody down here pronounces "th", so I had to explain it was her thigh – she's had stitches after a fall.'

Both girls fell about laughing.

'Our whole day is like that!' roared Martina. 'Sister Anthony calls us the confusion sisters, says...'

And both Nellie and Martina did an impression together of a northern accent, '"You two would confuse a nation."'

'Would you like to do nursing as a career, Nellie?' Peggy asked conversationally as she helped Martina to more mint sauce.

'I would, Nana,' Nellie said brightly.

Emily exchanged an astonished look with Blackie. Since coming home, she and her husband had been slow to press their daughter on anything to do with the future. Nellie had seemed so fragile and broken at first, and they just wanted her to be happy. Though since she'd met this nun and started work at the nursing home, she had become much more like her old self. 'Is that right, Nellie?' she asked her daughter.

Nellie pondered the question this time. 'Yes, I do think I would. I don't know if it would be too hard, though, all the studying and stuff, but I would like to be a nurse.'

'You'd be well able for it, pet,' Blackie said warmly, ever her instant champion. 'Sure, haven't you got your mammy's brains? So it would be no bother to you if you wanted it.'

'Well, you would say that, Dad. You think I'm a genius, but the nuns above in the school wouldn't agree – they thought I was an awful eejit altogether,' Nellie said ruefully. 'I just never really cared about it, you know?'

'Well, isn't that the problem?' Martina replied wisely. 'I'm always telling you that you should talk to Mother Bridget. You could do your training at the Star of the Sea because it's a registered hospital as well as a nursing home, so you wouldn't even have to leave home. You'd be great because you're interested, and you care.'

Nellie beamed but then cast an uncertain glance at her mother. 'I don't know, Mam, what do you think?' In the Crean household, Emily was the final arbiter of everything.

Emily thought about it for a moment, then made her decision, which was easy enough. 'I think it would be marvellous if you wanted to do it. And I think you'd be a wonderful nurse, and you could travel anywhere in the world with a qualification like that.'

'I think my Marco Polo days are behind me, Mam. I've seen enough of the world, for now anyway, and Kilteegan Bridge will do me fine.'

Nellie said it like she was joking, but Emily knew there was a truth to her words. From the age of sixteen, Nellie's life had been turned upside down and inside out, and here she was, back at home, safe and happy, and it was something her daughter would never again take for granted.

'Anyway, I'll have a think,' Nellie added contentedly as she helped herself to another roast potato.

'You should say a prayer to St Agatha – she's the patron saint of nurses – and ask for guidance,' Peggy suggested.

Emily's mother-in-law was a very devout woman, though quietly so, and knew the patron saints of the most obscure causes. Emily used to have to hide her laughter at how Peggy could tell you the patron saint of playing cards was St Balthasar, or she would say a prayer to St Columbanus if someone got a motorbike because he was the patron saint of motorcycles. She even had an icon on the wall of her little hallway of St Gummarus, who was, according to Peggy anyway, the patron saint of difficult marriages. And God knows she needed him over the years with Dick Crean.

'I will, Nana,' said Nellie, so seriously that Emily glanced at her in surprise. 'I was thinking about it in Mass actually, and I was saying a prayer to Our Lady for any bit of advice or guidance, but maybe St Agatha is the right woman for the job.'

'He's so sweet, isn't he?' cooed Martina, who was watching Aidan happily eating peas one by one while squeezing a potato between his pudgy fingers. 'You're so lucky to have a brother, Nellie. I wish I had one.'

'He's adorable, and an absolute menace at the same time, but he has us all wrapped around his chubby little fingers, haven't you, you little rogue?' Nellie stopped talking about saints and started tickling Aidan's neck as the little boy giggled and tried to tickle her back.

'Now, Mrs Crean, Nellie tells me you're the next Michelangelo?' Martina said, turning to Peggy as Emily and Blackie cleared the plates. Blackie got bowls, and Emily fetched a tray of bread-and-butter pudding and a jug of custard.

Peggy coloured. 'Not at all. Nellie, don't be saying things like that. I just do a bit, but only small things and only for people I know who ask...' she mumbled, mortified.

'I don't know, Mrs Crean. Nellie showed me one of your paintings. She brought it up to show the patients, and they thought it was magnificent. I know Nellie asked you before and you said you'd be too shy, but the days are so long for the people in the nursing home and an art class would be just fantastic. We even have paints and brushes and things that someone donated when a newsagent's closed down someplace, so we'd be all set. All you'd need to do is give them a few pointers, nothing too complicated. A bunch of flowers or a bowl of apples or something. We'll leave the live nudes until they have the hang of the basics.'

She hooted again, and this time Emily laughed out loud – this nun really was a tonic – and Blackie and Peggy joined in the merriment.

'Ah, Nana, please do it,' begged Nellie. 'I'd be so proud of you, and they really thought your painting was amazing, not just saying it to please me. And Mrs O'Toole, remember her? She said she used to buy her husband's work socks from your shop years ago – he had huge feet?'

'I do.' Peggy smiled as she helped Emily serve out the pudding. 'Andy O'Toole, God be good to him, had the hugest feet of any man I'd ever seen. We had to get them in specially from England, and during the war, when we couldn't get them, she used to have to knit them and it would take her forever.'

'And anyway,' Nellie went on, 'she was amazed and said if you could have sold your paintings over the years, you'd have had no need messing around with coal and animal feed.'

'I don't know about that,' Peggy said, but her pink cheeks gave away how pleased she was.

'So will you do it, Nana, please? We'll say a prayer together to St Luke even,' Nellie pleaded.

Emily was confused, but Nellie and her grandmother explained together, 'He's the patron saint of artists.'

'Well, you're the right experts on saints anyway, the pair of you,' Blackie said, tucking into the delicious bread-and-butter pudding, covered in custard, with enthusiasm.

'I really like learning who is for what, Dad. Some of them are really interesting, and sure God would be worn out and Our Lady too if every person in the world was asking them for stuff all day long. It makes sense to spread it out a bit. Like what would poor old St Servatius be doing all day, only lying around on a cloud going out of his mind with boredom if he wasn't responsible for mouse and rat infestations. Or St Rita might be cracking up if she didn't have to look out for all the children who were late walkers.' Nellie chuckled.

'You'd better not be blaspheming, Nellie Crean,' Emily warned, worried this might be a reversion to the irreverent Nellie of old and her cheeky attitude to the Church. She'd famously called the Monsignor a lecherous old man one day a few years ago when he'd told her that her skirt was too short.

'I'm not, Mam. I actually do pray to the saints,' Nellie said seriously as she tucked into her dessert, but Emily wasn't sure whether to believe her.

The conversation turned back to nursing, with the two girls regaling Nellie's family with wild stories from the Star of the Sea, which by all accounts was an absolute riot of a place, with jokes and fun around every corner.

'And you should see the scuffle the day Dr Mike comes. They all loved Dr Kogan, Nellie's Uncle Eli. He used to go there on a Tuesday, and the old folks adored him. They'd all get into their best clothes and everything for him. But now we have Dr Mike, and when they saw him coming the first day in his wheelchair, they were all agog – a doctor using a wheelchair just like they do was not what they expected. But they love him, and he's very good with them. He's very like Dr Kogan in that sense – he has time for them and actually listens. And he has great tips on the horses. Mother Bridget would have an absolute hairy canary if she knew. But you know the man that drives Dr Mike?' Martina lowered her voice as if the Reverend Mother might appear any moment from under the table.

'I do. 'Tis the groundkeeper from Kilteegan House, Joseph Murphy, is it?' Blackie said, interested in any bit of news to do with his family.

'Yes, Joseph, well...' She paused for dramatic effect. 'He's running a book, and he takes bets and puts them on for anyone that wants them. It's the Punchestown Winter Festival next week, and they all have been watching the form and having a flutter. Not much now, only a few pence, but they all crowd around the radio when they're commentating on the race, and the excitement if their horse comes in, it's fantastic.' Her eyes gleamed with the sheer joy of it all.

'I can't see the Reverend Mother being happy about the pensioners losing their shirts at the races right enough,' Blackie said, with a faint grin at his wife.

'Ah, it's harmless and a bit of craic, and if you can't have a bit of a laugh at the end of your life, then what's the point of it all?' Martina replied. 'I have a suspicion Mother Bridget knows fine well what's going on, but she chooses not to see it, I think.'

They all chatted amiably until it was past Aidan's bedtime. Blackie offered to bring Peggy home before the whole rigmarole of getting a baby to sleep began, and to drive Martina back to the nursing home, which she accepted gratefully.

* * *

'WELL NOW, what do you make of all of that?' Blackie asked as he settled into bed beside Emily, the whole house quiet. 'Our daughter's best friend is a nun, and Nellie is praying to saints all day like her nana?'

'I don't know what I make of it, Blackie.' Emily was troubled. 'It bothers me a bit, to be honest.'

He grinned as he reached to turn off the bedside light. 'What do you mean, Em? Sure aren't the mothers the length and breadth of Ireland giving out that their kids are losing their religion, and here we have one as devout as anything?'

'That's what worries me. Like, Nellie wasn't a pious child, far from it. I could never stop her fidgeting at Mass and later on caffling down the back with the boys and mortifying me. But since she went to America, and... I don't know, love, I just worry.'

'Ah, Em, she's grand. I know you're her mother and you're more tuned into stuff like this, but she seems absolutely delighted with life. She's happy out with Martina, and surely that's better than her hanging around the town with all sorts of an evening?'

'You're right, I suppose. It's just such a change.' She rested her head on his shoulder.

'It is, but she's changed too. She couldn't have gone through all she did and not be changed by it. She could have gone off the rails entirely, hit the bottle or mad for fellas or whatever, but she's not one bit like that. She's a good girl who works hard and cares about all the old people up there. She even told me she had a nice chat with the Monsignor after Mass about a poor old divil above in the home who has no family – she asked the Monsignor to pay him an extra visit. And she's best friends with the maddest nun I ever met and happy as Larry. I think we should just be relieved and not go looking for problems where there are none.'

Emily sighed. Blackie usually conceded to her in everything – she was the boss, he always said – but she had to remember and respect that he had his own opinions. 'You're right. I know you are. It just feels all a bit too good to be true.'

'Em, love, we deserve some luck, all we've been through. Maybe Mam praying to St Seraphina of Lisbon, or St Ambrose or whoever, did the trick and our lives are going to be all right.'

She laughed and her heart lifted. 'Maybe you're right, Blackie,' she said as she snuggled into him.

CHAPTER 9

'Well, this is a nice surprise, unless you're here with a medical problem?' Mike O'Halloran looked up as Lena knocked on the open door of what had been Eli's consulting room.

She had not set foot in here since Eli had died, but it had been a while now since the brass plaque outside had been changed to read 'Dr Michael O'Halloran, General Practitioner', and today she'd decided it was time to cross that bridge.

She'd watched from the window of Kilteegan House until she was sure Margaret, the receptionist, had gone home for the day, and then she'd walked down the gravelled driveway to the converted gate-house. Then she had stood outside for a full ten minutes in the cold dark evening before getting up the courage to enter.

Once in the empty waiting room, she could see Mike through the half-open door still at his desk, checking patient files and writing up prescriptions. Eli had kept that same desk pushed up against the wall so he could sit on the same side of it as his patients and not intimidate them. But Mike had moved it out into the room so he could sit behind it, which made it harder to tell he used a wheelchair. He clearly preferred his patients not to be distracted by his disability.

Lena stood, watching him work for a while, before she knocked.

He was in his mid-forties and handsome in a kind of big lion or bear sort of a way. He had a huge head of brown hair inclined to curl, and as many Irish men did, a flame-red beard. His body was large and muscular on top, and even though he was paralysed from the waist down, his legs had not wasted. She knew he had regular therapy from the physiotherapist in Kilteegan Bridge who rented Doc's old surgery, and Mike had told her that he'd set up an exercise bar in his bedsit.

Now she stepped into the surgery in answer to his warm smile of welcome. 'I'm fine, no medical problems. I'm just here to see how you are,' she said, smiling back at him.

'Glad to hear it. So have a seat.' He reached into a drawer in his desk and produced a small bottle of Midleton 30-year-old pot still, a very expensive brand of whiskey, and two Waterford crystal tumblers. Without asking her, he poured them each a measure and invited her to take one. '*Sláinte*,' he said, toasting her.

'*Sláinte is táinte*.' She smiled and raised her glass. 'This is a big day for me, Mike. I've not been in here since Eli died.'

He nodded. 'I know it, and I trust you'll come more often now. Your husband was so well loved, and you deserve to hear the patients talking about him.'

Lena was surprised to note that tears didn't immediately spring to her eyes as they normally did when someone mentioned Eli. 'I know he was loved, but thank you. He was a good man and a good doctor.'

He grinned at her. 'Sure there isn't a day goes by when someone hasn't a story about him, about what a saint he was, the best doctor in the world, never been a better one, if only there were more like him…'

She smiled wryly. 'I'm sure it must drive you mad, the saintly Dr Kogan. If it's any consolation, he had to listen to the same about Doc when he took over from him.'

Mike guffawed, that infectious laugh that endeared him to the most fractious child or the most whiney pensioner. 'They are big boots to fill, no doubt, but I'm managing. Haven't killed anyone yet anyway.'

'They love you as well, Mike, though you do create all colours of a scandal by being seen in the bookie's.'

'Ah, I only bet on a dead cert. I have Skipper and your man Joseph Murphy as my consultants, and it funds my expensive whiskey habit.' He winked at her, and she laughed.

Mike O'Halloran was a very interesting man in so many ways. He was a doctor and a very good one, but he smoked and drank and backed horses. He believed life was for living. When she'd asked him how he told his patients off for those exact same vices, he said he didn't, and he explained his philosophy.

'Well, something has to get you,' he'd said, 'so if you never drink or smoke or eat cake or have a flutter on the horses, you'll still be lying in a hospital bed at the end of your days dying of nothing. Nobody's getting out alive anyhow, so we might as well enjoy ourselves.'

'So how are you finding living here?' she asked now. 'Not too lonely for the bright lights of Dublin?' She took a sip of her whiskey, which was smooth and warming.

A slow smile crossed his face. 'I'm not. I love it here, though I do worry about my mother. She can't cook or clean to save her life. I mean, without me to look after her, I worry she might starve to death and be eaten by cats.'

Lena laughed. 'I think Professor Anthea O'Halloran is much more capable around the house than she lets on.'

'I hope so. And I do know she wants me to live my life without her. After the accident she was anxious I'd fall into bad ways if I didn't go back to doctoring. I have fallen into bad ways, of course, and I'm delighted with them, but not to a point where it makes me unprofessional or careless – you do know that?'

'Of course I do. Everyone is mad about you and thinks you're a great doctor and very involved in the community. Nellie was telling me that you've asked Miss Kearney in the girls' school to go up to the nursing home to do keep-fit classes?'

Sarah's PE teacher coached the girls' Gaelic football team. She'd never married; her father died young, and her mother had terrible rheumatoid arthritis so she'd stayed at home to mind her. She had several brothers who seemed to think it was all right for their sister to dedicate her life to old Mrs Kearney's care and didn't do much to pitch in and help. Old Mrs Kearney had died two years ago, but thirty-nine-year-old Jane Kearney was still living in the same house. She was kind and generous and energetic, and all the girls liked her.

Did Lena imagine it or did Mike colour a little at the mention of the teacher's name? To be honest, she was watching for his reaction. A little bird in the shape of Nellie had already whispered to her that maybe it wasn't just the girls at her old school who liked Jane.

Mike cleared his throat and lowered his gaze to the files on his desk. 'Well, physical exercise is proven to be beneficial in even the most infirm of patients. Even if it's just sitting in a chair and doing upper-body work or going for a short walk. The old way of people sitting in chairs or lying in bed all day is all wrong, and luckily Mother Bridget is in agreement with me. So every morning, everyone who can manage it at all there is up and dressed and doing something.'

'Well, Miss Kearney is a great hit apparently. Well done. And she's nice, isn't she?'

'She's very nice,' he agreed, though he didn't quite meet her eyes.

'Am I missing something here, Mike?' He was normally so confident, always full of jokes and fun; this hesitant Mike was strange.

'Well, I don't know... I...'

'Do you like her?' Lena asked him directly.

He blushed deep red now. 'Whether I do or I don't is a bit beside the point, I suppose. I'm not exactly the catch of the county now, am I?'

Lena chuckled at his shyness. 'You're a great friend to me, Mike, so maybe I'm biased, but I'd say you're a good-looking man and you're great craic and you're a doctor, so I'd say you are a fine catch.'

He sighed, not giving his usual jokey response. 'Ah, Lena, come on, what girl in her right mind would want me?' He gestured to the chair. 'Even if anyone did, it wouldn't be right.'

'But you like Jane?' she prodded gently, ignoring his doubts.

'Well, I don't know. Yes, maybe... Look, I...I was in the butcher's a few Saturdays ago, and that Vera Slattery walked past the window. I got my meat and went outside, and she was stopped, talking to Jane.

She beckoned me over and introduced us. Said she knew we'd get on well.'

'And did you?'

'We did, though why Vera thought we would, I don't know. Sure she only knows me to look at – she's never been in to consult me at all.'

'She's what's known as a *bean feasa*, Mike, a seeing woman,' explained Lena. 'It goes back generations in her family, and people listen to her. She's been able to cure things that conventional medicine can't. Even Eli sometimes consulted her on a tricky diagnosis, and she cured his hand of arthritis when no cream or tablet worked.'

'Really? I never knew that. She never said.' Mike was clearly intrigued.

'She's not one to blow her own trumpet. She goes about her business quietly and only offers when asked. She must feel very strongly about you and Jane if she introduced you.'

'Ah, I don't know, Lena. I don't think that sort of thing –'

'But you hit it off anyway?' She smiled encouragingly.

'Well, yes, as it happens. We chatted for a while in the street, and it started to rain, so she said she was about to go into the Copper Kettle for a cup of coffee and asked me to join her, so I did. And honestly, we talked for ages. I thought we'd only been there for about half an hour, but it turned out it was more like two hours. We talked about her mother, and mine, our lives so far, religion, politics, all the things you're not supposed to mention, I suppose, but it was good…nice, you know?'

'And did you ask her on a date then?'

He grimaced. 'I did in my ear – are you mad? She was just a nice woman sharing a cup of coffee with the local crippled doctor. I don't think for a second she'd want to –'

'So you just walked away?' Lena was incredulous. For a smart man, he was being a bit thick.

'Er, no…I rolled away.' He patted the arms of his wheelchair with a grin. With anyone else she would have been mortified at her gaffe, but Mike joked about the chair quite often, so she didn't feel bad.

'You know what I mean.' She rolled her eyes. 'So you "rolled" away, you big eejit.'

'Thanks, very supportive.' He smiled sheepishly.

'And then what happened?'

'Nothing really, only...'

'Mike, just tell me.'

He was bright red behind his beard. 'Well, she came here last Monday, with an appointment – and she... Well, she's just being friendly, of course...but before she went, she invited me to lunch on Sunday at her house, told me the place was made wheelchair accessible for her mother so I can get in there easily.'

'That's great, Mike.'

'But I don't know if I'll go.'

'You don't know?' Lena was exasperated. 'You're telling me that a woman you really like has practically thrown herself at you and you're thinking of turning her down?'

'She's not throwing herself at me. She's just being charitable and would only be horrified to know –'

'That you like her too? For goodness' sake, Mike, give the poor woman a chance to make up her own mind what she wants.'

He refilled his whiskey glass and took a big gulp. 'The thing is, Lena, even if she does like me like that, and it's a big if... I mean, maybe... But even then...is it wrong to encourage her when... Well, I'm never going to walk down the aisle, am I?'

Lena fought the embarrassment at the question that occurred to her, but she remembered Eli saying how many men who had spinal injuries, depending on which vertebrae were damaged, could still have a normal sex life.

'Mike, romancing notwithstanding –'

'Hold your horses! It's just lunch, and like I said, she is probably just taking pity on me.'

'*Romancing notwithstanding...*' Lena repeated purposefully. 'Mike, this is none of my business, I know, but Eli was at a conference a few years ago on men who'd had spinal injuries in war specifically, and the whole weekend was dedicated to restoring as much normal function as possible…' She coloured and knew if her husband were here, he'd be rolling his eyes at what he called her Catholic shame for even owning a body.

Mike smiled, a broad beam that crinkled the sides of his light-blue eyes. 'I'll spare you the embarrassment. Everything works, Lena.' He gave a self-deprecating laugh. 'It's just the wrapping doesn't look too enticing.'

Lena exhaled; at least that was good news. She would love Mike to have a relationship. He spread such good cheer and deserved a bit of it back. 'I don't know about that. I think you underestimate yourself, Dr O'Halloran.'

'You have to say that – you're my sister.'

'Am I?' Her heart warmed with pleasure. 'I do think of you as a brother, I have to admit.'

'Of course we are. Doc was my biological father as well as being my godfather, and he was like a father to you when your dad died, so that makes us brother and sister in my book. I never had a sister before, so what do you think – will you be my sister? I know you have a brother already…'

'To have two brothers will make me very happy.' She clinked her glass against his, then asked another question that had popped into her head. 'Were you ever in love when you were younger, Mike? I mean before…?'

He shook his head. 'I broke my back a long time ago, so when my friends were getting married and having children, I was in hospitals, in rehabilitation clinics, then later I was back in university, completing another medical degree and retraining as a GP. I hid behind the books, if I'm honest. The chair is what people see first, and everything else is through the lens of this. I'm not complaining – it's how things are – but it does tend to change things.'

'Not for everyone, though, maybe.'

He shrugged. 'Maybe, but I won't be getting my hopes up.'

Lena stood up. 'I've a chicken and leek pie ready for dinner, if you fancy coming up to the house to have some?'

He smiled warmly. 'Thanks, but I'm going to the Donkey's Ears.

There's a soccer match on the television, and I know you don't have one in the house.'

'I don't, and I have no desire for one, though the children keep on and on about it. Is Joseph driving you?'

'He is. He's a Leeds supporter, but United are going to hammer them, so I'll win back his wages this week.' He chuckled.

'A doctor with as many bad habits as you, Dr O'Halloran, drinking, gambling on horses, soccer matches, I don't know...' She shook her head mock despairingly.

'Ah, Lena, gambling is only a bad habit if you lose, and I never do.' He winked.

'Well, be sure to win on Sunday so, smarty-pants.' She went around the desk and kissed his cheek. 'See you tomorrow, big brother.'

CHAPTER 10

*K*atie O'Neill, together with her little sister, Maggie, had been hiding out with Ted and Gwenda for nearly a fortnight now, and Gwenda still hadn't had the heart to discuss the future with the older girl. Katie had a way of making one feel like they were kicking a puppy if anyone raised the subject of her and her sister ever moving on.

Every time Gwenda tried to talk about it, the poor child baked a cake, or swept the stone floors of the beautiful house she and Ted had built, or mended all the rips and tears in Sophie and Annamaria's riding clothes, despite their attempts to make her treat them as sisters instead of acting like she was their servant. She only spoke when spoken to and was always warning Maggie to shush, but when she did speak, she was cheerful and grateful.

Every day she got up at the dawn and fed the chickens, mucked out the stables and baked white soda bread with currants before Gwenda had even woken up – and Gwenda woke very early. At lunchtime she would run across the fields, with Maggie at her heels, to Jack and Skipper's farm and insist on making them a meal, a hearty delicious stew followed by an apple tart. Bill Madden had passed by on a tractor today and spotted the two strange children running across the field, and he'd been very curious as to where they had sprung from. Gwenda had had to lie through her teeth and say she was fostering them while their parents were indisposed.

Which was kind of the truth in a very roundabout sort of way – not that the nuns or guards would see it like that if they found out she and Ted were harbouring the fugitives.

Gwenda was at a loss as to how to deal with the situation. She caught a glimpse of her reflection in the oval mirror hanging by a chain from the chimney breast. She looked her age but didn't care. She wasn't carrying extra weight, but she was stocky and strong. Her auburn hair, streaked with gold and grey was in a plait as she always kept it, only taking it out at night, and her tanned face was leathery from years of sun damage.

'Ted, we have to talk to Jack and Skipper about them, we really do,' she pleaded with her husband one evening after all the four girls had gone to bed. 'It won't be long before the truth is out. Our two are as good as gold, and Sarah as well – they've all taken a shine to them both and think it's all very exciting, hiding Katie and Maggie away from everyone – but I had to lie to Bill Madden when he came by on Jack's tractor today.'

'He's not supposed to be up on the tractor. He only got his hip done three weeks ago,' Ted said disapprovingly.

'You try telling *him* that, mate.' Gwenda rolled her eyes. 'He insisted on bringing some of the cross-poles down in the trailer for the girls to set up jumps in the river field because they're too heavy for them.'

Bill and Deirdre Madden had sold their farm to Ted and Gwenda, but they had remained in their farmhouse two fields away and it was impossible to stop Bill from farming, even though he had all sorts of things wrong with him. Bill Madden would have to be taken off the land feet first; the idea of a day doing nothing was anathema to him.

Ted sighed. 'I know. He was with me when I was bringing the cows in yesterday. He ducked behind the ditch when he saw Deirdre driving back from town – she'll murder him if she catches him.'

'But that's not the point, Ted. The point is, he'll be bound to tell Deirdre, and who will she tell?'

'Ah, she's a quiet woman is Deirdre. She keeps things close.'

'Maybe she is, but it's not just her and Bill. You know Maria saw Katie in the yard, and why on earth did you think she would buy that nonsense about her being a maid?'

'It was the first thing came into my head. I'm sorry. I told her not to mention it...'

'Well, maybe she won't, but I think the postman saw Maggie on Friday even though I told her to be careful and keep out of his way, and Emily has already hinted to me that tongues are wagging in the village.'

'Look, love, people always need something to gossip about. It's harmless.' Ted winked, finally putting down the book he was reading by the fire; it was about the care of sheep in a wet climate, which apparently was altogether different from the care of sheep in an Australian dust bowl.

'Except it's not, ya flamin' galah.'

Ted grinned. His wife might have left Australia, but she was Aussie through and through and quick-tempered with it.

'If anyone here knew what a galah was, you might get into trouble for calling people that. Eddie Dulea is totally confused by you.'

'What?' Gwenda's brow creased. Eddie collected their sheep's wool for the mill, and she thought he was a little bit slow.

'He asked you how things were going, and you told him you were "flat out like a lizard drinkin'". He was bewildered, the poor fella.'

Gwenda rolled her eyes and sighed. 'Ted, be serious for a minute.'

'I am being serious! You speak a different language.'

'Whatever you reckon' – she dismissed him – 'that's not the issue here. We have to talk to Skipper and Jack about this. I know they can't have the girls with them. It's not right a girl of Katie's age living with two bachelors who are no relation, even if she's safe as houses with them.'

She knew he'd understand what she meant; the whole family did. They just never referred to it out loud. It was the Irish way, she supposed. 'And don't get me wrong. I was happy to help out when Jack asked us. I know the girls haven't got anywhere else to go, and we sure as hell can't send them back where they came from if even one tenth of what Katie's told us about the convent is true. But we have to do something with them.'

She had Ted's serious attention now; he was sitting with his long legs crossed.

'Sure, but what else can we do, Gwen? We can't just turn the two of them out on the road. And I like them. The girls like them. They remind me somehow of me and Maria when we were small, no proper loving family to look after us, and I only wish someone had stepped in to save us. Now I've got a chance to do a good turn for two children who are as sad and lonely as we were, and I don't want to turn my back on them.'

Gwenda looked at her husband with love. He was such a good man. He wasn't just a hero who had risked his life to help the Allies win the Second World War; he was a wonderful husband and father to his girls, a loving brother to Maria, and he still had enough room in his heart left over for these two waifs and strays.

But, she wondered to herself, did she?

She was a tough woman, a survivor, weather-beaten and wrinkled by desert sun. She had lost her battle against the droughts and then floods in rural South Australia that had first burnt then swept away her family ranch. She'd upped sticks and agreed to make a new life with Ted in his home country, on the far side of the world, and it had been a good move; she wasn't denying it. She'd found her first winter in Ireland a bit hard to cope with – the grey skies that felt like they were just a foot over one's head, and it had been a particularly wet winter – but all in all, she loved it, and it had been a source of delighted astonishment to her how easily everything grew once the spring came. Her daughters had blended into life in Kilteegan Bridge as if they'd been there all of their lives, especially as Skipper kept racehorses and show jumpers that they were allowed to train and ride. Ted loved life here, and he and Maria had become as close once more as they had been as children. And so for the entire family, it felt right. Everything had been settling down, but now this problem had come along, threatening to undermine everything they had accomplished.

When Jack and Skipper had first come to them asking them for help, she'd thought it was only going to be a day or two before it all got sorted out.

'We're at a bit of a loss as to what to do with them,' Jack had said. 'They can't go back to the orphanage – it's awful. But their mother's in jail and it's not right if they just stay with two men – they need a woman in the house. So we're going to find out from Kieran Devlin if the mother is getting out any time soon, or what we can do.'

'Poor kids. Reckon they've gone walkabout for a reason.'

'They have. The nuns were very cruel,' Jack had confirmed.

That had put the tin lid on it as far as Gwenda was concerned, and of course Ted would do anything for his nephew.

Now nearly two weeks had passed, and the only thing that had changed was they now knew there were three more years left to run on the mother's sentence. Jack and Skipper weren't turning their back on the problem; they just didn't know what to do any more than Gwenda did. Her worry was, if people guessed she and Ted were harbouring two runaways from the home the nuns ran, it might end up with her family being isolated in the community. She had only been in Ireland a year, and already she knew such opposition to the institutions of Church and state was generally frowned upon.

'Ted, you're right, we can't turn them out. But the nuns or the guards will find them one day, and then we'll be in terrible trouble, maybe even with the law involved, so we have to come to a decision. If we're going to keep them, this has to be all above board.'

'Right then,' said Ted. 'Let's make it official.' And as if that were the end of the matter, he picked up his book again.

'Ted...what? Don't start reading again! What do you mean, make it official?'

He lowered the book slightly, peering at her over it. 'The father clearly doesn't want them. The mother is in prison. They're in an orphanage. So I agree with you – let's foster them until this mother of theirs gets out of prison. Isn't that what you meant, Gwen, by making it all above board?'

'Foster Katie and Maggie?' Her mind was in a whirl. Four girls instead of two, maybe for years to come. 'But what would Sophie and Annamaria think…'

'They'll be delighted. They're always complaining their family isn't as big as an Irish one.'

'And Jack and Skipper?'

'Sure they'd adopt them themselves if they could.'

'Ted, neither of us knows how the law works in this country. We might need the parents' permission as well as the nuns or something.'

'But we'll give it a try?' He looked at her hopefully over the edge of his book.

Gwenda thought about it, long and deeply. Was she really prepared to double her family overnight, take on two young ones when her own were reared, with all the extra trouble and money that would entail? Was she really prepared to annoy the Church here, when it seemed to have such power, by admitting to having kept two of its wards in secret without saying anything?

At the same time, she thought how nice it would be to see Katie relax and stop acting like a servant, shushing her little sister like making a noise was a crime and hiding away in terror every time a visitor came to the house. And things couldn't go on like this; they were going to get found out eventually anyway. The only alternative was to stick the poor children on a train to somewhere, and then God knows what would happen to them.

She made her decision.

'OK, but we'll have to tell the guards and the orphanage we only just found them in the woods, though how we'll be able to explain how we've got two healthy-looking children now, with flesh on their bones and a sparkle in their eyes, instead of one little seven-year-old wearing her big sister's clothes and another rail-thin waif with bruises on her arms…'

'Good.' Ted grinned and, now that it was all settled, went back to his book.

Gwenda was already making her plans. 'I've to take Annamaria showjumping in Skibbereen tomorrow – I'm bringing Sophie too – and the orphanage is out that way, Coolnagarrane, so I'll call them before I go and explain we found the two girls in the woods and want to foster them. I'll make an appointment to see them, and you come with us, and we'll go into the nuns on the way home.'

'Will we bring Katie and Maggie with us?' wondered Ted, lowering his book again.

'Strewth, no! Katie is so suspicious as it is, she'll think we're delivering her and Maggie back to that hellhole. No, we'll leave them with the two boys. And don't be saying anything to them about this, none of them, not even Jack and Skipper. I don't want any of them getting their hopes up.'

* * *

'Hi, Katie,' Jack called as he and Skipper took their boots off on the porch of the back door. 'That stew smells goo…'

The words died on his lips as he saw who was sitting at the kitchen table. Mother Ignatius and Sergeant Flannery were on either side of a petrified Katie and a weeping Maggie. He stopped dead where he was, taking the whole thing in.

'Mr O'Sullivan,' the nun said imperiously. 'This is the girl I was looking for the night I came here, the night you and that American man said that there was nobody here.'

'And there wasn't,' Skipper said from behind Jack, a hint of steel in his voice.

'Well, whether she was or she wasn't, she is here now, and I've just this morning been informed in a phone call from your aunt, Gwenda Hannigan, these children were found yesterday wandering in the woods between your two farms. When we arrived to collect them from your uncle's farm, no one was at the house, but frankly I'm not surprised we found them here. I knew that night you were hiding them, and I'm only glad your aunt and uncle saw it couldn't go on the way it has been going.'

Jack was stunned, shaken to the core. Gwenda had betrayed these poor girls to the nuns, without a word to himself or Skipper? No. He didn't believe it. 'I don't understand. What did my aunt say to you?'

'That's not your business and neither are these children. They are my responsibility. They are wards of the state, entrusted to my care, and should not be roaming freely about the countryside by day and *living with men by night.*' She spat the last five words as if whatever had been going on was very unsavoury indeed.

Skipper stepped up next to Jack, his temper clearly mounting. 'Well, they sure as hell don't want to live with you, and I don't blame 'em. When they came here, they was nothin' but skin and bone all covered with cuts and bruises, so if y'all were supposed to be caring for them, you sure done one hell of an awful job.'

He took another step towards the table. Maggie made a leap for him but was dragged roughly back by the nun and slapped, while Katie cowered, clearly terrified of a blow. 'I didn't say nuthin', Mother,' Katie whimpered. 'I didn't say nuthin' about what happened. I said yous were all lovely and yous are...'

'Sergeant Flannery,' Jack began, doing his best to keep his own temper while restraining Skipper with a firm grip on his arm. He knew Declan Flannery of old and had never had a problem with him before. 'I don't know what my aunt and uncle said to Mother Ignatius on the phone, but I'd sure like to know before we decide what to do in this situation.'

The guard looked almost as cowed as Katie. 'I'm sorry, Jack, but it's already decided. Mother Ignatius is the children's legal guardian, appointed by the courts. That oldest one is a very difficult child, the Mother tells me. She was placed in a reform school for girls after she confessed she tried to kill her father with a poker, only she was found not guilty by the court because the mother admitted to it instead. The social workers sent her to Coolnagarrane and Mother Ignatius with her sister, Maggie, here.'

'And aren't you a lucky girl' – Mother Ignatius turned with a thin smile to Katie – 'that we were willing to take you in after all the trouble you caused.'

Katie looked despairingly at Jack, fat tears running down her woebegone little face. 'I didn't think you'd take me in, Mr Jack, if I told you the truth about the reform school. And Ma was only trying to protect me, and she wasn't what they said she was. She loves me, and when she gets out, she's going to make a lovely home for us far away from him and everything –'

The nun laughed then, a shrill, cruel sound. 'Your precious mother was convicted on charges of attempted murder and grievous bodily harm, so do not lecture us on the happy-ever-after fairy story you have concocted.' She turned then to Skipper. 'She does this, lies and manipulates, in order to get sympathy. She would rob you blind if she were allowed to stay here. You would not be quite so disposed towards her if you understood the monstrous things she has done, trying to protect her criminal mother, lying through her teeth to the courts. I've had enough of this nonsense. Sergeant, bring the other one.'

She stood up and marched towards the door, dragging Katie with her, leaving Maggie to the guard.

'Don't beat me,' wailed Katie.

'Mary, behave yourself,' hissed the nun.

'Mary? Her name is Katie.' For a wild moment of hope, Jack thought maybe the nun had come for the wrong girl.

'Katie is an unsuitable heathen name,' snapped Mother Ignatius, 'given to her by her mother, who was no better than Cain. There's bad blood in that girl, and if she is to be saved from going down the same path her sinful murdering mother did, only I can help her.'

'Please, Mr Skipper, don't let them take us, please...'

'Let her go,' said Skipper determinedly, standing in the nun's way. His blue eyes glinted with fury. 'She's a child, and I only see one monster here. Now get out of our house and leave her behind.'

Mother Ignatius sniffed in sour amusement. 'And who do you think will stop me?'

'Mr Jack, please...'

'It's all right, Katie,' Jack said quietly, joining Skipper. 'You're not going anywhere.'

Mother Ignatius tightened her grip on the girl's thin arm. 'I insist on being allowed to do my job unencumbered. Now kindly get out of my way.'

'Jack, Skipper, this is not how this should be done. The law is against you, and the Church is against you.' The sergeant was standing with a struggling Maggie held tight in his brawny arms. 'Mary is only fourteen years of age and therefore the ward of the state. Her mother is in prison, and the father is still suffering from his injuries, so he says. Maggie is seven and also a ward of the state, which has placed her with the nuns.' He was trying to sound placatory, but he was a custodian of the law nonetheless there to make them follow the rules. 'They will have to come with us – it's the law. Don't make me call in reinforcements, but I will if I have to.'

'I understand, Sergeant,' said Jack grimly. He could see the writing on the wall, but he decided to give it one last try. 'But just as a favour to my aunt and uncle – they're good people – can we wait until they're back so you can explain directly to them why you're taking the girls away?'

'Your aunt and uncle *wanted* them taken away,' sneered Mother Ignatius. 'They said they were little savages, lurking in the woods, stealing money and food and anything that wasn't nailed down.'

'That's not true! Auntie Gwen an' Uncle Ted wanted to keep us!' bawled Maggie suddenly, trying hard to wriggle down from the sergeant's arms. 'I heard them! They were by the fire. They were going to ask the nuns to fos...fos...'

'They wanted to foster you?' asked Jack in relief, everything suddenly becoming clear. 'Oh, now I understand...' He could have strangled the nun for lying, but instead he smiled at her and said in his most reasonable voice, 'What a good idea, Mother Ignatius, don't you think? So let's all wait and discuss it with them when they get home.'

'There's nothing to discuss,' snarled the black-robed nun.

'But surely you'd rather have these troublesome children off your hands?'

She narrowed her cold pale eyes. 'They are off my hands. Mary is already booked into our sister house in Cork for after Christmas, where she will, along with girls like her, work off what she owes the state and Church for her bed and board, and Maggie is to go back to her father as soon as he's well enough to have her, which won't be long. There's no fostering needed to be done. Now get out of my way.'

'Mother Ignatius, please…'

'Jack, Skipper, you have to move out of the way,' begged the guard as he struggled to keep his grip on an increasingly desperate Maggie. 'The law is on the side of Mother Ignatius. And if either of you put a hand on her or otherwise prevent her from leaving this house with her wards, I'll have to arrest you and bring you to court. And you can be sure there's no judge will look kindly on two strapping men who threaten a nun.'

'Don't let them take me! Don't let them take Maggie!' wailed Katie as the sergeant opened the door widely for Mother Ignatius, then followed her out with the little girl screaming in his arms. He pushed it shut with his big boot behind them.

Skipper whipped the door open again and ran out into the yard. 'We won't give up, Katie. I promise we won't give up!'

As the sergeant's car roared away, Skipper returned to where Jack was slumped at the table, and Jack could see the anger and deep sorrow in his eyes. They sat together in silence. Neither felt like cheering the other up. Jack was trying very hard not to imagine what would be happening to poor Katie now, facing the wrath of the nun after making the brave move to escape. And how was he going to tell Ted and Gwenda when they came home? They would be devastated.

'We'll get them out,' said Skipper, taking his hand. 'We will.'

'But how?' said Jack despairingly. 'It's not just the nuns – it's the police and everything who are against us.'

'There has to be a way. We'll go to Kieran Devlin again first thing in the morning. He'll know what to do.'

'I doubt it. The Church and state run a very tight ship when it comes to those places, Skip. It's a machine. Taking on the mighty Church is bad enough, but adding the guards and the courts to it, well, the odds are against us.'

CHAPTER 11

*M*alachy sighed contentedly as he watched Rosa padding across the room to the bathroom, dressed only in his shirt. The New York traffic was gridlocked outside the hotel on Fifth Avenue, and the cacophony of horns and expletives from the frustrated hoards were a dull hum through the heavily glazed windows. New York was so different to San Francisco. More hectic, and people in New York were less patient, less friendly. Just yesterday an older woman dropped her bag of vegetables on the sidewalk and commuters just skirted around them, looking put out that their progress was being impeded by a carrot or a potato. Malachy tried to help her, but as he went to pick up some of the produce, the woman yelled at him not to touch her stuff, so he backed off. Rosa had pealed with laughter when he told her.

'Welcome to the Big Apple, baby,' she teased as she kissed his cheek.

Still, he liked the pace of the place, the sense of being alive.

Life was good, he thought, lying on the huge bed with his hands locked behind his head, because Rosa Abramson seemed to have broken Lena's spell.

He loved Rosa for who she was, instead of grieving for who she wasn't. They both worked very hard, liked the good things in life, nice clothes, fine dining, vintage wine. She was dark and sultry and incredibly sexy, and when she dressed up, moving away from her austere and formal work suits, she was breathtakingly beautiful.

Last night they'd gone to the theatre, and he'd discovered Rosa was a much more social person than he'd ever been – she knew everyone – and he had to admit it had been fun. As gritty and sometimes ugly as it was, it felt as if New York was the capital of the US, and California just a dreamy summer vacation home. New York was where everything happened.

And with Rosa Abramson at his side, he found himself right in the middle of a Jewish remaking of the city. The Yankees had just won the World Series, and Beame, a Jew, was coming to the end of his term as mayor. Rosa had become so animated as she explained that in 1825 there were fewer than a thousand Jews in New York, a small community occupying a tiny corner of Manhattan, but that had grown, and the Big Apple now had the largest Jewish population in the world, bigger even than Israel. It felt in many ways that the events in Europe under Hitler and the Nazis had set New York up as the new home for European Jewry.

He'd been largely ignorant of the Jewish influence, but given his family's terrible history, he felt eager, even compelled, to learn about it. Rosa had been patient with him, taking him to New York and showing him first-hand how Jewish organisations, all staunch supporters of Israel, were now exercising influence on international matters, how they funded charities, and their role in coordinating political movements had opened his eyes. He was surprised that the fact he was not Jewish didn't seem to matter to Rosa, but thankfully it didn't bother her, it would seem.

She appeared in the doorway of the bathroom, her toothbrush in her hand, her dark hair tumbling down her back.

'So, em... I...' She seemed unsure for once. 'My nephew – well, my foster brother Joe's kid – is having his bar mitzvah today. The whole family is gathering, my five brothers, their wives and kids and my parents. There's going to be food and drinks and things, and you can come if you want to.'

He raised an eyebrow at the peculiar invitation, but he was getting used to her. 'Do you want me to?' he asked, throwing the covers back and getting out of bed.

She thought about it. 'I don't know.'

'OK, well, I'll take a shower and get dressed, and if by then you've decided, you can ask me again.' He smiled and kissed her cheek as he walked past her into the bathroom.

He could see her through the frosted glass of the shower cubicle, doing her hair and make-up, and he wondered what that had been about. She'd met Emmet, of course, and they liked each other a lot, but he had no other family for her to be vetted by. With Rosa it was different; she had a huge extended family. He'd overheard conversations on the phone between her and her adoptive parents and siblings – they called a lot – and she seemed exceptionally close to them all, though perhaps a little suffocated. Taking him to a family occasion was making a statement, he knew that, and what she was weighing up was if he was worth that level of investment.

Time would tell, he thought as he wrapped a towel around his waist and shaved.

She wasn't in the room when he came out of the bathroom, and he wondered for a moment if she had left for the bar mitzvah without him, but her things were still all around the room. She was incredibly untidy, something else that had surprised him, because she was so neat and efficient in her appearance. It reminded him of something Lena had told him once about that new doctor Mike's mother Anthea, how untidy she was yet always so immaculately attired...

He pushed Lena ruthlessly from his mind.

He dressed as he always did, in a dark suit, one he had bought at Saville Row the last time he was in London, but today he decided against a tie and just wore an open-necked shirt, an Yves Saint Laurent in lapis lazuli blue.

Lena had once said that although that colour blue should clash with his green eyes, it didn't and looked good on him, so he tended to select it often...

Stop thinking about Lena.

His hair was inclined to curl but he did like it a little longer than the more conservative short back and sides, so he oiled his unruly curls and was satisfied with the result.

As he splashed some cologne on his face in the bathroom, he heard her return. She pushed open the door, then leant on the door frame, two cups of coffee and a bag from the bagel store down the street in her hands.

'I'm sorry. I sounded like a kid asking someone to the prom earlier,' she said sheepishly.

'You did, but that's all right.' He grinned, accepting the drink and the bagel.

'So I'll try again. I would like it if you came with me, but I'm also kind of nervous, because by taking you to this, I'm telling my family we are together and it's serious, because I would be out of my mind to take anyone I wasn't serious about to such an event.'

'OK.'

'And I suppose' – she blushed, something he'd never seen before – 'I thought this would be just a fling, a bit of fun, but it's turning into something else for me, and I don't know if you feel the same. And so that's why I feel a bit insecure. I don't want you thinking that I think you're mine or anything, when we've not really discussed it, and, well...'

'That's a lot of self-awareness right there,' he said in amusement. He was going to a psychotherapist now, as Rosa had suggested, and he was getting used to the language of self-improvement, though he thought his therapist often overcomplicated things that were easy, finding problems where none existed and coming up with solutions that didn't please him at all and that he certainly was never going to put into practise, or even mention to Rosa. Though to be fair, she never asked.

'Yep, that bit of self-awareness cost me thousands of dollars.' Rosa nodded, coming into the room. 'And I am very *angry* at Adolf Hitler –

that cost another three thousand dollars, that one sentence.' She laughed as she put the coffees and bagels on the table.

He was used to her joking. It was a Jewish thing, he was learning, a kind of darkly wicked sense of the macabre. He enjoyed the comedy of Woody Allen and found elements of his humour in Rosa. She was of the opinion that in order to be funny, one had to also experience tragedy. According to her it was why Jews were funny, and same with the Irish.

'Rosa, I would be honoured to go to the family party, and in answer to your question, this *very uptight emotionally stunted Irishman'* – he put on a bad fake American accent for that bit – 'thinks this might be turning into something else for him too.'

She smiled and came over and kissed him, leaving a lipstick stain on his cheek that she wiped with her thumb. He found the gesture so intimate, more so even than their passionate lovemaking last night, that his heart wrenched, and for a second she wasn't a hotshot well-dressed lawyer, scaring men to death in a patriarchal world, but a little German Jewish girl, on the quayside alone, with no English, no family and no idea what had just happened to everyone.

He took her in his arms. He didn't kiss her as he normally would but cradled her to his chest, his lips brushing the top of her head.

'If you want me to be yours, Rosa, then I am,' he whispered softly.

* * *

SITTING AT THE BAR MITZVAH, surrounded by a cacophony of Brooklyn and Yiddish voices, Malachy watched Rosa laughing and dancing in a circle with her nephews and nieces, the children of her adoptive siblings. It was unusual for him to be in such warm and raucous company. For so long, most of his adult life, he'd been so torn apart with loss and love and guilt and anger that he did nothing but work; it numbed the emotional turmoil inside him. And it had paid off. He owned one of the most prestigious engineering firms on the West Coast, and his personal wealth had him featured in *Forbes Magazine*. But there had been a cost to that, he now realised.

When Rosa approached him in Ireland, it had been devastating to learn the news about his paternal grandparents. The very thought of them repulsed him, and he hated to even think that their or his father's blood ran in his veins. But Rosa had been direct while not judging. She accepted he didn't know how they'd made their wealth; what she cared about was the degree to which he was willing to make a reparation.

And the community centre was such a great idea on so many levels. It was doing something morally good, first and foremost. Secondly, it had brought the beautiful Rosa Abramson into his life. And as an added bonus, Emmet was cutting his teeth on project management and seemed to be really enjoying it, something that bode well for the future.

He and his son never really discussed it – he didn't want to push it – but Malachy's dream was that one day he would make Emmet his partner, and eventually retire while Emmet ran the business. His son had Malachy's natural fascination for construction; he had excellent spatial intelligence and the ability to envision things before they existed. He also had something Malachy had learnt but didn't have naturally – he had his mother's eye for the aesthetic.

Lena knew instinctively how to make a house a home, how to turn a clinical doctor's surgery into a place that made people feel less worried and more comfortable. She had a flair for fashion, colour, texture, and he knew she would have transformed his austere glass and chrome home in Palo Alto by adding books, a rug, maybe an antique hallstand found at a flea market, so that it was a place he looked forward to coming home to rather than a clinical space to sleep, shower and eat a prepared meal made by Juanita.

Stop thinking about Lena.

As the party was in full swing around him, he forced his mind back to Emmet. The boy was up most of the night studying, because he insisted on being on-site during the day. It made Malachy feel guilty about overworking him, but Emmet insisted he wanted to do it this way, and it was keeping his mind off that girlfriend of his – or ex-girl-friend, as she seemed to be nowadays. Also, it gave Malachy such joy to share his love of construction with his son. Before Emmet arrived, he'd been worried about having Lena's son in the house, constantly reminding him of her. And he *was* like Lena, sensitive but tough...

Stop it.

Though it turned out Emmet was very like Malachy as well. He loved talking about the latest developments, from computers to microwave ovens. Malachy bought him a subscription to *Popular Electronics* for his birthday, a magazine that investigated and reported on all the latest innovations in the world of technology, and Emmet loved it and read him articles from it, and the fact that he and his son shared so many common interests was a source of great joy to him.

'So you're Rosa's young man?' A stooped old man wearing a yarmulke sat down beside him, setting two glasses of wine in front of him, as if he intended to stay for a chat.

Malachy glanced towards his girlfriend, twirling on the dance floor. She had kicked off her high heels and was dancing in stockinged feet. 'I guess I am,' he said with a smile. 'Though I'm not young.'

The old man scoffed. 'I'm eighty-one. You're a chicken hardly out of the egg compared to me.'

Malachy turned to look directly at his questioner. He had already been introduced to lots of members of Rosa's extended family, a blur of names and faces. 'Hi, I'm Malachy Berger.' He shook the old man's hand.

'A German name. Interesting. I'm Rosa's Great-Uncle Joachim Stein. Well, I am if you count Rosa as one of Elise and Joel's children, which I do. We all do.' He spoke in a thick Brooklyn accent that Malachy found endearing.

'I know, and she's so happy to be one of you.'

'So you're the one building us a community centre?'

'That's right.' He hoped Joachim wouldn't raise the shame of where the money came from and why he was paying it back. He knew nothing could ever exonerate the wrong done by his family.

'You've decided what to put in there?' asked the old man. 'How to use it for the good of us survivors?'

'It's not decided, but Rosa and I were talking about an intergenerational space where people could hold social events, a café, a library, help with welfare if people need it. Rosa is involved with a foundation that have set up similar intergenerational projects for different communities on the East Coast, and they work really well.'

Joachim nodded and listened, pausing before speaking. 'I'm a survivor, Malachy. I was a husband to a beautiful wife, and the father of four sons and three daughters. I had a mother and father and three brothers and a sister. And I was the only one of my immediate family, of three generations, to survive. What am I going to do in this intergenerational community centre of yours, Mr Berger?'

It was a subject Malachy and Rosa had come back to over and over again, the impossibility of fixing such unspeakable trauma, the arrogance of even trying to help. 'I suppose that's up to yourselves how you wish to approach it.'

'You want us Jews to decide the answer among ourselves, just by talking to ourselves, keeping it to ourselves?'

'Or not even talking, perhaps,' suggested Malachy. He felt judged and found wanting, though he wasn't sure what he'd said wrong.

'Not talking at all?'

'If that's what people want. My son's father... That sounds strange, and he's living with me now, but when he was growing up, his adoptive father was a man called Eli Kogan, a very brave man, a doctor, and also Jewish. And Emmet tells me that his dad never talked about what happened in the war, and nor did his grandmother.'

'And how exactly was their silence supposed to help the world?'

'I don't know, but I can understand? Not personally, I mean. But I have a foreman on the site – he's not Jewish but he was in Europe, the Normandy landings, and all the hard fighting there. He lost all his friends and refuses to ever discuss it, but every Wednesday night, he and other former vets meet and play cards, drink beer and just connect. He tells me they never speak about the war – it's a common thing when people experience trauma that talking about it is too hard – but there is comfort to be had in being around people who get it, a kind of silent understanding. They don't need to talk about it because they all know, but it helps them recover.'

'So you want us Jews to be silent and be comforted by our silence?' He was sparring with him, Malachy knew, but he wasn't sure how to proceed.

'I didn't mean that.' He wanted to protest that the old man was being unfair to him.

Joachim's dark eyes softened. 'I know you think I'm being unfair, but for too long what happened has gone undiscussed. We know about the American soldiers – they're in war movie after war movie. All guts and glory. Where are the German Jews, the Polish Jews, the French Jews? People have to know about us, about the missing. When I talk to Americans, they say, "You're being unfair, Mr Stein. Our boys shed their blood for you in Europe." And I say, "I'd rather have had American visas for my sons and daughters, for my wife and my parents and her parents, than have you sacrifice your boys."'

'Of course, if you want to talk…'

'I don't want to talk. I want to *teach*. I want my children's lives, my wife's life, our parents' lives, to have meaning, to never be forgotten. I want a place where American schoolchildren can come and learn what happened from real people, the eyewitnesses, the survivors. I want them to learn how fascism can creep up on people. I want them to know, if it happens here, and if they see "good" people defending it, their friends even, they still have to speak out or it will come for them too. My people are in mourning, but silent mourning. We need to shout about this, to tell our story, no guts, no glory, just the hard, unvarnished truth. Your people need to listen and learn, or it will happen again.'

'Hello, Uncle Joachim. So you two have met?' Rosa, flushed and gasping for breath, flung herself down in the seat on the other side of Malachy and threw her arm slightly drunkenly around his shoulders. 'I hope you two have been getting along.'

'I don't know. Have we?' asked Joachim, winking at Malachy.

'I think we have,' said Malachy, smiling back at him. 'I think we're getting on very well. And I think we have a lot more to talk about and we should meet again tomorrow.'

'Well, who would have thought it.' Rosa laughed, kissing him on the cheek. 'I thought you and I were the match made in heaven, but it turns out it's you and grumpy old Uncle Joachim.'

CHAPTER 12

a car crunched on the gravel outside as Lena crossed the hall towards the library to find a book she hadn't read, if there was such a thing still in the house. She'd read so many of the ancient volumes on the shelves, trying to lull herself to sleep without Eli beside her. Going to the long window by the front door, she saw Emily's black Beetle pull up.

She opened the door as her older sister climbed the steps. 'Hello, Em. I wasn't expecting you today. What's up? Where's Aidan?' She knew by the set of her sister's jaw that something was afoot.

'Nothing's up. Aidan's with Peggy. I just need tea to go with these cream cakes.' Emily brandished a paper bag from the Copper Kettle and pretended to smile, which didn't really work.

Without questioning her further, Lena led her sister into the kitchen, where Pádraig was reading the sports results from the local newspaper.

'Hi, Auntie Em.' He looked up. 'Tell Mam we need a television for Christmas.'

'Hello, handsome.' Emily smiled more naturally and ruffled his hair. 'And I'll tell her no such thing. They're awful yokes.'

'They're not! They're only brilliant! Emmet wrote to me saying that Malachy bought one, and now they can watch pop music programmes and things like *The Six Million Dollar Man* and *M*A*S*H*, and it gives them something to talk about.'

'Pádraig, that bedroom of yours is like a place bears live. Get up there now and tidy it, and put the dirty things in the laundry basket, not under the bed like last time,' Lena instructed him. It needed to be done, but she also wanted to have time alone with her sister, to winkle out what was wrong.

'Can't I do it later?' he asked, running his finger down the fixtures list in the newspaper. 'Ah no, we're away to Bandon. I was hoping that would be a home game.' He was very interested in the list of upcoming matches and not at all interested in tidying bedrooms.

'No, you can't. I asked you during the week, and you claimed you were too busy with studying. My eye you were, by the way. I didn't come down in the last shower. Your test results are not those of a boy driving himself to distraction with the books, as you well know, so up you go, tidy the room, study for an hour, and if it's done, to *my* standards, not yours, then you can go training.'

'Ah, what? I have to go training! We've a league final in two weeks,' he protested in horror.

'Well, all the more reason to get the jobs done then. No tidying and no studying mean no training. So go!'

Emily slipped him a pound note. 'For all the help you gave Uncle Blackie loading the firewood into the shed.' She winked, and he pocketed it gleefully.

'Thanks, Auntie Em.' He kissed her cheek.

'I didn't see that.' Lena raised an eyebrow. 'He did that to be helpful and because he lives here free, gratis and for nothing.'

'Well, I didn't ask to be born, you know, Mam.' Pádraig laughed, and she did too. It had become a family catchphrase after Sarah shouted it at Eli one night in a teenage tantrum, and he'd shouted back, 'If we'd known it was you we were getting, we'd have thought twice too, you know.' It had been so unusual for Eli to react so heatedly, the entire family had broken down in hysterical laughter.

'Get up those stairs, you pest.' She swiped tall gangly Pádraig with the tea towel, and he expertly ducked out of the way, still laughing but going.

Lena closed the kitchen door after he left and turned to her sister. 'Well?'

'Well, what?' Emily said, putting the bag of cakes on the side and sitting down at the table.

'What's happened? Because something has.'

'Can't I just have a peaceful visit with my sister without facing the Spanish Inquisition?'

'No, you can't, not when you bring cream cakes from Chrissie's. That always means something ominous or big is happening in your life.' Lena moved the kettle to the hottest part of the range and put the cream cakes out on a plate. She must go back to baking, she realised. Before Eli died, the cupboard was always stocked with homemade treats.

Emily sighed. 'OK. Has Sarah said anything to you about anything?'

'Yes, she has. Is this about Mother Ignatius and Sergeant Flannery turning up to take those girls back to the orphanage? Sarah was so upset about it. She'd really got to like Katie, and Katie had a little sister with her as well – Sarah said she was a sweet kid. Ted and Gwenda are miserable, so I feel guilty about saying this, because of course they were doing the Christian thing, but I'm surprised they risked harbouring two runaway orphans in the first place. Ted told Mam that Katie was their new maid, but Mam guessed straight away it was something to do with the orphanage. And I know Mam is amazing at knowing when people are lying to her about something, but if she guessed right, then someone else could as well, so it was bound to get out in the end.'

'I know what you mean, Lena, and there was a rumour already going around the town. I mean, it's awful, though, and I don't see why the nuns couldn't just let the poor things stay where they were. You'd think it would save them money. I suppose you know Ted and Gwenda have been in with Kieran Devlin to find out if they can get them back properly?'

'Good luck with that, the poor things.'

'And Jack and Skipper are getting involved as well. It was in their house the nun and the sergeant found them. In fact it was our farm the girls turned up at in the first place.'

'Is that right?' Lena looked up in surprise as she poured two cups of tea. 'Jack didn't tell me that.'

'I suppose he thought you've had enough to deal with this past year.'

Lena set the teapot down with a cross bang. 'Ah, come on, Em, are you serious? Bad enough Mam was talking with you about sending me to St Catherine's without the rest of you starting to keep me in the dark about difficult things, like we used to do with Mam. We made her worse by doing it – it made her even more paranoid.'

'I know, Lena, but –'

'And while we're on the subject, what's on your plate, Em? And don't say nothing. I know you.'

Emily sighed and gave in. 'Fine, but I don't even know where to start.'

'The beginning?' suggested Lena rather caustically, sitting down.

'OK, OK. Well, you know Nellie's been working up at the Star of the Sea nursing home, and she really enjoys it.'

'Yes, it's great for her. Sarah says Nellie told her she was thinking of doing the nursing training?'

Emily nodded. 'Yes, she wants to be a nurse. She's spoken to the matron, Mother Bridget, and she gave her the green light, so she's all excitement. She's very friendly with this young nun, Sister Martina, and they're inseparable, it seems.'

'And you're not happy about it?' Lena was puzzled; she'd met Sister Martina and thought she was adorable. The nun had even played 'Here Comes the Sun' on the old piano in the library when she and Nellie called up to visit her a few weeks ago. She had a beautiful singing voice. So Lena couldn't help feeling kindly towards her.

'And now she's getting up so early, and I thought it was for the early shift at the nursing home, but it turns out it was early Mass. The Monsignor says one at seven for people going to work, and apparently Nellie's taken to going most mornings, and she even looks up all the obscure patron saints with Peggy.'

Lena still couldn't see what the problem was. Nellie had had an awful time, and it was taking a while to get her back to her old confident self, but she was doing so well and really seemed to be putting the last two years behind her. 'Sure, don't most parents these days complain their children aren't going to Mass enough, or devout enough or whatever it might be, and your one has a track worn up to the church.'

'I don't mind that, or I wouldn't, and the nursing part is fine, but she's not happy just to be a nurse, Lena.'

'You've lost me.' Lena's brow furrowed.

'Lena, she's insisting she wants to be a nun.'

Lena was so startled, she had to fight back the urge to laugh. Less than two years ago, Nellie had been a wild child, all make-up and cigarettes and short skirts. Admittedly she was a more subdued version of herself these days – getting pregnant by some reckless boy was bound to take its toll, not to mention the cult she'd got caught up in in California – and she was dressing much more conservatively now, quieter, more contemplative somehow. But a nun? Surely not.

'Ah, she's only pulling your leg, Em. Nellie has no more notion of joining the nuns than Pádraig does. She's just winding you up,' she reassured her sister.

Emily's face darkened, and she stopped even pretending to be calm. 'She is serious, Lena. Do you think I can't tell when my own daughter is joking around? That I'm such a terrible mother she goes off and gets pregnant, then goes to America and meets up with some weird cult, and now I'm so hopeless I can't tell the difference between messing and the truth? She wants to be a nun. She's spoken to Mother Bridget about it, and if Blackie and I agree, she can more or less enter right away. So don't patronise me and tell me I'm missing out on a joke.'

Lena was taken aback at how angry Emily was. 'I'm sorry, Em. I didn't mean that at all. You're a wonderful mother to Nellie and

Aidan. I just...' She was at a loss as to how to explain without hurting her more. 'It just seems a strange choice for her, that's all.'

'Strange? *Strange?*' Emily's voice was rising in both pitch and volume. Her rare but intense temper was, as always, something to behold. 'It's not strange. It's insane, absolutely crazy, and more of Nellie's impulsive behaviour. She never thinks, that girl, about the consequences of anything. Act first, think later. And now this. I won't allow it, Lena, I just won't.'

Lena moved her chair beside Emily's and held her hands, speaking soothingly, deliberately keeping her voice light and calm. 'I'm on your side, Em, that's the first thing. Always and ever totally on your side. But maybe if you can just take a minute and think about what it is about it that's so objectionable? Like, do you not want Nellie to be a nun because you don't want that life for her? Or do you not want it because you think she's not serious about it and it's just another fad of hers?'

'I don't know or care what her reason is – it's wrong for her,' Emily snapped, still furious, refusing to make eye contact.

'And what does Blackie think? Does he know?'

Emily kept staring towards the kitchen window, tears forming in her eyes. She looked older these days, Lena thought. Nellie's misfortunes had taken a heavy toll, and Emily's lustrous blond hair looked dank and limp, the furrows on her brow had deepened, and there were crow's feet around her eyes. 'She told him first, knowing I'd go mad.'

'Ah, Em, she just cares so much about what you think. She wants to please you, and I suppose she was scared of letting you down.' Lena longed to console her sister, who had stood by her through thick and thin.

'He's happy for her, takes it on face value that she has a vocation, but sure Blackie hasn't a clue.'

Lena was astonished, though she tried not to show it. Emily had never spoken in such a derogatory way about her husband before. Everyone in the village knew, and Blackie confirmed it every chance he got, that Blackie Crean had really struck gold the day he married

Emily O'Sullivan. And muttered under people's breath often was the sentiment that she could have done so much better. But Emily never, even as a joke, said anything of the kind. She'd built him up, helped him to shake off the shame of his family and turned him into a respected businessman in the town.

'And you think she hasn't? A vocation, I mean?' Lena asked tentatively.

'She has no more a vocation than the man on the moon,' raged Emily. 'She's all about this one Sister Martina, who is nice but a bit daft, if you ask me, and she's all Masses and saints and all the rest at the moment, but it's just because she's under the influence of this other one. I mean, it's ridiculous. Nellie used to be the kind of girl that people would worry was a bad influence, drinking, smoking, going with boys, but now she's fallen under the spell of a nun, who is leading her a merry dance of praying and saints.'

'Ah, Em...' Lena's lips were twitching, picturing the rather rotund Sister Martina spinning in a 'merry dance', but she swallowed her amusement. 'Look, maybe you're right. And if you are, well then, she'll get over it like she did the other thing –'

'Only because that Wei dragged her out of there. She liked it in the cult, did you know that? She told me so. She said, "What's so wrong with the concept of people living peacefully together, spreading love, not hate?"'

'Well, I guess there is nothing wrong with it –'

'It was a cult, Lena,' said Emily fiercely. 'I thought I reared a strong independent girl, but she clearly hasn't a mind of her own. She just wants to be told what to do. It's all because of that boy who got her pregnant and us leaving her in London, and then letting her go to America –'

'Emily, listen to me.'

'And I don't want her to make a stupid decision just because what's happened has made her afraid of life –'

'Listen to me!' This time Lena spoke so loudly and firmly that Emily did stop and look at her, woebegone, mouth trembling.

Lena then said in a kinder voice, 'Maybe you're right, Em, that this

116

decision is partly a result of what happened to Nellie in the past. But we all have things happen to us. That's what life is. And our negative experiences inform our decisions as much as the positive ones. And it doesn't make those decisions wrong, because everything that happens in our lives, good and bad, it changes us, it makes us what we are.'

'But supposing she regrets it?' Emily sighed.

'And so what if she does? It's not like she's locked up in a prison. She'll always be free to leave. So why not let her give it a go, and if she doesn't like it, well then, she can pack it in?'

For the first time, Emily looked a bit calmer and more in control of things, which was where she liked to be. 'I suppose she can.'

'And you know, when you first said it to me just now, well, it was big surprise, and I couldn't get my head around the idea of our headstrong Nellie being a nun. But now I think about it, I know she likes that sense of community, living in Kilteegan Bridge, coming from a strong family, the loving closeness of it all.'

'Do you really think so?' Emily's tears had dried. She took another drink of tea and a rather despondent bite of her cake.

'Emily, I know so. And I know as well that you're afraid of losing her. But if you ask me, Nellie's not going anywhere. I don't think she's trying to escape her life – I think this is all part of her coming home.'

And they drank tea together, and Lena finally got a bit of cake, and they talked about motherhood until the light grew dim and Emily had to go and get Aidan off Peggy, where no doubt he had the whole house wrecked and Peggy's paints splashed everywhere.

CHAPTER 13

*J*ack jumped down off the train in Heuston Station and turned to help Gwenda, but she stepped down by herself, carrying the enormous bag she brought with her everywhere; it contained screwdrivers and scissors and twine and all sorts of miscellaneous stuff, including the remains of the mountain of sandwiches she'd made for their long train ride from Cork.

'You reckon I'm some old bat, do ya?' she boomed as she batted Jack's helping hand away. Her broad Australian accent hadn't changed a bit in the year she was in Ireland. 'You'd be better off helping your Uncle Ted. He's more crook than I am, though he might not look it.'

Ted laughed as he followed her down onto the platform. Skipper jumped down next, and the four of them made their way straight to the taxi rank at the side of the station.

'Mountjoy women's prison,' requested Jack, and the driver raised his eyebrows as he put the cab into gear and drove away over the River Liffey. There he turned into the streets of old Dublin, an area of the city Ted and Jack had only rarely visited and Gwenda and Skipper never.

The large tenement squares and terraces, once home to the

supremely wealthy landlords of the eighteenth century, had fallen into disrepair and become the dilapidated tenements of the nineteenth and twentieth centuries. The ornate double Georgian doors with elaborate fanlights that once were opened to fur-clad, bejewelled guests by butlers in uniform had become the portals to the filth and depravity that only extreme poverty can create, and the incongruity was hard to reconcile.

'From Katie's description, she and Maggie were reared in one like this,' said Jack, pointing out a row of houses on Henrietta Street, where children, dressed in threadbare clothes entirely inappropriate for the sleeting rain, kicked a deflated football on the street.

'Oh, that's so sad.' Gwenda sighed, her big heart clearly breaking for her girls. 'The poor little blighters. Their mum must have been something else, seeing as they turned out so well.'

Ted nodded. 'There could be five or six families living in just one of those, no proper sanitation. Back in 1913, Dublin had the highest infant mortality rate in Europe. Things have improved but not enough.'

Skipper watched out the window, his jaw set in a determined line. Jack knew Skipper had known childhood poverty. His father was a deadbeat, and Skipper and his brother, Wyatt, had to fend for themselves entirely. He knew Skipper felt for Katie and Maggie on a level even Jack didn't understand.

The taxi soon pulled up outside the prison, and the driver advised them to go around the side of the imposing limestone building, where they would find a steel door to the public office.

The Kilteegan Bridge lawyer, Kieran Devlin, had managed eventually to secure a visiting order for the four of them to see Katie's mother; the strings and favours he'd needed to pull were incredible. Devlin hadn't been inclined to intervene at first; he'd said it would do no one any good. The State colluded with the Church in these instances, he said, hence the guard accompanying the Reverend Mother in order to retrieve the children.

He also pointed out that even if Katie and Maggie's parents both agreed to let them be fostered, well, that might work for Maggie, but it wouldn't work after Katie was sent to a laundry in the New Year because the laundries used the girls as free labour, making money for the Church, and didn't like to let them go, not even for huge sums of money.

* * *

THEY FOUND a uniformed prison officer in the small office at the side of the prison. He had a clipped grey beard and a very long narrow nose, and he was a wiry but powerful-looking man. P. Grimes was the name on his badge.

'We have a visiting order to see Olivia O'Neill.' Ted handed over the paper.

'Identification?' the officer said in a strong Dublin accent, and they each produced their passports. Ted handed him all four little books. He paused for a moment on Gwenda's blue passport with the seal of Australia on the cover before consulting a ledger that had long lists handwritten neatly. Then he looked at Skipper's American one.

'Right, Edward Hannigan, here we are...'

Gwenda smiled inwardly at the use of Ted's official name; she'd rarely heard him called Edward. Somehow 'Edward' didn't seem to fit this tall, rangy, weathered man, with silver hair and bright-blue eyes; he would always be a 'Ted' to her.

'And Gwenda Hannigan, née McCann. That's an Irish name. Well, not the Gwenda part – I never heard of that in my life – but the McCann?'

'My father's parents came from here. His dad moved to Sydney around 1910 I reckon, and his mum was one of those girls sent out from Ireland as a female convict. She was from Waterford, I think, and he was from Carlow.' Gwenda loved claiming her Irish heritage.

'Right, that's you two. And then John O'Sullivan and Skipper Malone?' He glanced up at the two men who were now in front of the desk, Ted and Gwenda having moved aside. 'Well, we're like the

United Nations here today. So, John, you're homegrown.' He ticked Jack's name off the list before turning to Skipper.

'And last but not least, our American friend. Kept the head down over here to get out of goin' to Vietnam, did ya?' He grinned. 'Don't blame ya. That's a place you'd be trying to stay away from right enough.'

Skipper glanced at Jack with the unspoken question. *Should I be worried?*

Jack gave an almost imperceptible shake of his head.

'That was not my fight, sir,' Skipper said.

'Dead right. Sure what did the Vietnamese ever do to you? 'Tis all over now, I suppose, but still, that was a right dog's dinner.'

This assessment of the Vietnam conflict didn't seem to require a response, and Skipper had no interest in getting into it.

'Well, welcome to Mountjoy so.' He handed them back their passports. 'Now if you wait here, I'll get someone to take you down to the visiting area.'

Gwenda looked around the small office, where the walls were adorned with yellowing and curling posters urging people to take care at the ports, not to bring in foot-and-mouth disease and rabies. There was a list of telephone numbers as well for various departments within the Prison Service. And incongruously a brown stuffed teddy bear was resting on the counter; it was old and battered and had only one eye. Gwenda thought it looked lonely and sad, and she wondered about the child who had mislaid it.

The officer lifted a telephone and told someone they were there. When he put the phone down, he noticed Gwenda looking at the teddy.

'A little child came to visit yesterday, and the poor lad was so upset leaving his mam, he forgot his bear. His nana is coming in tomorrow to collect it, but they're from Cork so it's a bit of a palaver. We offered to post it, but 'twould take a week at least. The small fella won't sleep without it, so Nana is coming up on the bus this evening after work and staying over in a hotel. Probably cost her a week's wages, the poor woman.'

Gwenda liked the compassion in the man's voice, not at all what she'd envisaged from a prison officer, and her heart went out to the child who was so upset his mother was in prison and who couldn't sleep without his much-loved bear. 'We could take it down. We're catching the train back to Cork once we've seen Mrs O'Neill. We could save her a trip? We could leave it at the railway station?'

The man thought for a minute. 'That might be the right job. Hang on a minute.' He checked the ledger again and dialled a number. 'Officer Grimes here. Could I speak to the Chief please?'

He paused. 'Sir, I've someone here willing to take the teddy we were taking about to Cork on the train this evening. They'll leave it at the station master's office. Save Mrs O'Callaghan the journey up. Could you let her know? Thanks, Sir...'

Another pause while he listened, then he put his hand over the receiver, addressing Gwenda. 'What train will ye get, ma'am?'

'We're booked on the five o'clock.'

'They'll be on the five o'clock leaving Heuston, and I'll wrap the bear in a brown paper parcel marked for Mrs O'Callaghan, so this lady here can drop it to the office when they get in. Lovely stuff. Thanks for letting her know. Poor woman, my heart went out to her when she rang this morning. Right so. Good luck, thanks.'

He hung up as another officer, a much younger man, appeared.

'Ah right, this is Officer Whitty. He'll take you all over, and the bear will be here ready for ye. Thanks very much for offering, ma'am. That poor woman is worn out, so it's a good thing to do her a turn.'

'No problem, sir,' Gwenda said as they were escorted away.

The visiting area was not as bad as they'd imagined. It was just a room, with a few chairs and a table. They were invited to sit at the table and wait, and the young officer left them there.

'What do you think?' Ted asked her, looking around.

Gwenda shrugged. 'It doesn't seem too awful a place. I hope it isn't anyway, for Katie's mother's sake.'

'I wonder if she'll be annoyed with us for sticking our noses in.'

'Maybe she will, maybe she won't, but –' She stopped speaking as the door opened and a thin young woman entered, followed by a short, stocky female officer.

The first woman looked very like Katie when she first arrived at the farm – nervous and rake-thin, with wary eyes, her skin an unhealthy shade of grey, her mouse-brown hair in a tight ponytail. She wore a shapeless grey jumper and dark trousers, which Gwenda assumed was the prison uniform. Even though she must have been at least thirty, she looked hardly out of her teens, and when she sat down on the other side of the table and rested her hands on the Formica, Gwenda noticed her fingernails were bitten to the quick.

The officer stood in the corner of the room, saying nothing.

Ted was looking at Gwenda, silently urging her to start off the conversation, woman to woman, so Gwenda cleared her throat and leant in.

'Hello, Mrs O'Neill. My name is Gwenda Hannigan, and this is my husband, Ted, and these men are Jack O'Sullivan and Skipper Malone. We're from Kilteegan Bridge in West Cork, and we're here to talk about your daughters, Katie and Maggie.'

The woman flinched fearfully, her eyes darting nervously to each of them and back, and when she spoke, her timid voice was barely audible. 'Are ye from the orphanage? Is something wrong with my Katie? Is she ill? Is Maggie –'

'Please don't worry,' interjected Jack hastily. 'They're not ill, they're...' He glanced towards the officer, then said in a low voice, 'The thing is, they...um...left the orphanage in Skibbereen...' He clearly didn't really want to go into the stuff about the school and the cruelty Katie in particular had suffered; it would only upset Olivia for no good reason.

Olivia's wary dark-blue eyes sprung wide open. 'The nuns let them *leave*?'

'Well...' He threw another glance towards the guard, and whispered, 'The girls didn't much like it, so they ran away, and we found them hiding on our farm. Ted and Gwenda here are relatives of mine, and they have daughters a bit older than Katie and Maggie, so the girls went to stay with them while they're waiting for you to...um...'

'Are you saying my girls are with you in Cork?' Tears fell down her cheeks now, and Gwenda handed over a handkerchief, which Olivia took and blew her nose.

'I'm so sorry,' Gwenda explained. 'I'm afraid not, Olivia. The nuns insisted on taking them back, but Katie and Maggie didn't want to go. That's why we came here to meet you, to see if there was some other way for us to keep them until you're...well, free to take them.'

'Why do you want to do that?' She blew her nose again.

The question took Gwenda by surprise. 'Well, we want to help them, both of them, if we can. We've spoken to our solicitor, and he says if you and their father allow us custody of Katie and Maggie, then there's a chance they would be given to us.'

'But what do you *want* with them?' Olivia's dark-blue eyes turned to Ted, who nodded calmly; he understood the question.

'Mrs O'Neill,' he said softly, 'I know you haven't had much luck, and you're right to be suspicious of us, but your daughters would be safe with us. As Jack said, we have two girls of our own, Sophie and Annamaria, and they've made friends with them, and there's a cousin their age, another girl, Sarah. They're all girls together. And we just couldn't do nothing when our nephew asked us if we would take them in after he found them hiding in his barn. He would have done it himself, but there's just the two bachelors in that household and it wouldn't have been right.'

'I still don't understand. Why would complete strangers go to all this trouble to help someone else's children?'

'Because I suppose I, and Skipper here too, could have done with someone to step in and look after us when we were kids ourselves.' Ted smiled, and she rewarded him with a faint upturn of her lips and a nod of growing trust. 'So we just want to help your daughters, that's all. So we've brought some papers for you to sign – it would show you give permission for my wife and I to care for the girls until you can.'

Olivia looked away then, swallowed and wiped away more tears with her sleeve. 'I don't know if there's any point me signing any papers about custody, Mr Hannigan, not while I'm in here.'

She was right, of course. Devlin had said it would most likely be meaningless, but he still thought it might help a little if they got a lenient magistrate to hear the custody case.

'Mrs O'Neill.' Skipper spoke now. 'Jack and I found the girls, but we're two single men, so the courts definitely wouldn't allow us to have them. But we live on the same farm as Ted and Gwenda here, so you consenting to them being guardians might mean we can take care of them, and we sure would like to do that. We've gotten to know them, and we care about them, our whole family does, and I know it may not work, but it's worth a try, ain't it?'

She shrugged her pitifully thin shoulders. 'They won't let me write to them even. They say I'm a bad influence. They say they'll only release them to their da, but I know he won't want Katie and I hope he don't want to have Maggie either, especially now he's living with that brasser, which I heard he was.'

'You know where the…um…where she lives?' Ted asked, taking a sheet of paper and a pencil from his pocket.

The officer raised an eyebrow, so he got up and walked over to show her it was just a blank sheet of paper. 'I want her husband's name and address, to ask him to release their daughters into mine and my wife's custody,' he explained.

The woman nodded, and Ted returned to the table.

'He's called Stephen O'Neill,' said Olivia, spitting out the name like it had a foul, bitter taste. 'And last I knew, his brasser was renting a place in Foley Street, a tenement, two rooms on the third floor of Number 26, one for living in, one for her business. I 'spect he's living off her now instead of off me.'

'And is that address near here?' Gwenda asked. 'Could we find it easily?'

'Yeh, ask anyone to tell you where Monto is. It was Montgomery Street back in the day, y'know? It's famous in Dublin for that business. The Church closed down the brothels since then, but they're not all gone yet.'

Jack drew another sheet of paper from his pocket; this one was pre-written. It was a letter from Kieran Devlin witnessing Olivia

O'Neill granting power of attorney over the affairs of her daughters to Ted Hannigan of Kilteegan Bridge.

The prison officer had her back to them now and was gazing out of the window. She seemed to be assiduously ignoring the proceedings.

Olivia signed the paper quickly, and Ted folded it and replaced it into his pocket. 'So you've three years still to serve?' he asked gently.

'Yeah, but I did nothing wrong. Not that it matters.' She was well-spoken, more refined than they'd expected.

'Tell us what happened,' Gwenda urged. 'We might be able to help if we knew the whole story. I mean, Katie told us some, but if we were sure...'

'You want me to tell you my story?' Olivia seemed amazed that anyone would be interested.

'Fair dinkum, we do. It's not right you being apart from your girls like this. We just want to help.'

She looked from one to the other, uncertain. 'Well, er, where do you want me to start?'

'Maybe when you met your husband,' Jack suggested helpfully.

'Yeah? He was from Dublin. He came to Mullingar, where I'm from. He was working on the new road...'

Mullingar, Jack noted. *So that explains why she doesn't seem to have the same accent as everyone else in Dublin.*

'And we met, and he wanted me to go back to Dublin with him. My parents had a shop. They didn't like him, but I thought they were just being prejudiced because he was from the city, so I defied them and ran away with him, and we got married. I got pregnant with Katie, and that was the first time he hit me, threw me downstairs – I almost lost her. I rang my parents from the hospital, but they said I'd made my bed so I must lie in it.'

Her voice grew raspy, choking on the emotion of it all, and Gwenda took her hand and squeezed it. The prison officer had turned back towards them and seemed to be listening.

'Well, I had nowhere to go, so I went back. He was drinking heavily in those days, no work, no money, a crying baby. We had to live with his mother, who hated me. I tried so hard to please her, but she was rotten. Then he left. Went to England, I think. His mother threw us out, but I got a job minding babies and a little flat. It wasn't much, but it was safe and dry and we had enough.' The wistful tone of her voice tugged at Jack's heart. 'Then he come back, and I got pregnant with Maggie, and then he was gone again, and this time I didn't want him back any more – he was mean and cruel. So I decided to get us out of there before he came back again – I knew he would once he needed money. I was offered night shifts at the biscuit factory, and Katie was twelve by then, so she said she could mind Maggie if I worked. I wanted to get us out of the tenement, get somewhere healthy to live down the country, get away from him.'

'So what happened?' Skipper nudged. He was obviously afraid the officer would call time on the visit.

'I was doing a day shift as well as a night shift in the end, and Katie was missing school because she was minding Maggie, but I thought it was for the best. I was trying to get us away. I'd almost all the money saved to get out of that place and somewhere safe when he came back. Drunk and looking for money.' The tears formed once more.

Gwenda stroked her hand, and Ted said quietly, 'Go on.'

'He demanded I give it to him but I refused, so he hit me a clatter and sent me flying. Katie jumped on him, and you know she's only small and light, and Maggie was screaming. And then he had his hand up Katie's skirt and he said he was going to…going to…' The tears came flooding back, and even the prison guard looked moved. 'She kicked him, and then he had his hand around her throat and was squeezing and squeezing and she went all limp, so I picked up the poker and I hit him over the head with it. It wasn't even that hard, though his head bled. The woman upstairs had called the police when he started attacking me, but when they came, they arrested me instead.'

'But surely you just told them the truth?' Gwenda clearly felt so angry on this woman's behalf.

She snorted quietly. 'Stephen has a brother in the guards who spoke against me, and he made out he witnessed it all, even though I never saw him come in until after. He was either not there or lyin', I dunno, and he said it was unprovoked, and that I was the worst mother ever, never there. And the school said Katie was missing a lot, so...' – she sighed heavily – 'I ended up in here and my girls taken away.'

'That isn't fair.' Ted was aghast.

'Life isn't, though, is it?' Olivia said sadly.

'We'll do our very best for you all, I promise,' Skipper assured her, though Jack was very afraid their best wouldn't be enough. 'We have a solicitor, a man called Kieran Devlin, working on this. We'll do all we can. We'll try and get your husband's signature now, before we go back to Cork, and maybe we can even have your case reopened too if possible.'

'Thank you, and don't worry about me – just look out for my girls. I don't know what to say except thank you so much for caring about them.' She wiped her eyes once more.

'Time is up now,' the officer said quietly.

Olivia stood up and nodded, then turned to the door. The prison officer opened it and called another to take Katie's mother back to her cell, then returned to escort the others back the way they came. As they walked, the officer muttered something under her breath, and at first Jack wasn't even sure he was being addressed, but then he turned his head and listened.

'He's a right scumbag, that Stephen O'Neill. What was done to that poor woman and her kids, terrible,' murmured the woman. Her eyes were kind, green with amber flecks, and her cheeks were round.

Jack answered in an equally low voice, 'It sure was. I just don't understand why she's in here and the girls in an orphanage, like they're getting punished for his crimes.'

'That man, Thomas O'Neill, her brother-in-law, the guard, he's been put on long-term leave pending an enquiry, dodgy dealings like. I think he's going to be chucked out soon, but on the quiet like, not to ruin the reputation of the service.'

They had reached the office, and before Jack could thank her for the information, the stocky prison guard turned on her heel and left.

In the reception area, Officer Grimes had the teddy bear wrapped in brown paper and tied up with twine. 'They got in touch with the grandmother – she'll pick him up. Thanks again,' he said, handing it over to Gwenda.

'No problem.' She smiled at him as she tucked the package into her capacious shoulder bag. 'Would you know the way to Foley Street from here?'

He looked surprised. 'What d'you want to go there for?'

'There's a man we want to see, Olivia's husband, Stephen O'Neill.'

'Ah...' He glanced around him, as if to check there was no one else in the room. 'That *scumbag*. You won't find him in Foley Street. They've run the brassers out of there now. His woman was arrested, but of course he got off scot-free again. Anyway, you'll find him living with his brother.' And with another wary glance around, he scribbled down an address and pushed it across the counter towards them.

Gwenda glanced at it; he'd drawn a map with it, and the address was only a couple of streets away. 'Right, thanks, thanks very much. That's really helpful.'

As they walked out, Jack noticed the officer whisper something in Skipper's ear. He'd ask him later, but unless Jack was very much mistaken, the officer was a man like themselves.

He then went back to writing in his ledger and drinking his cup of tea. 'Goodbye now, and good luck to ye all. And remember, some men out there are very tricky, dangerous characters, so be careful around them.'

'Stephen or Thomas?' asked Ted.

'Goodbye, Mr and Mrs Hannigan,' said the officer politely.

* * *

JACK AND SKIPPER waited over the road, keeping watch while Ted and Gwenda went up to the small terraced house with peeling paint on its front door and dirty net curtains in its windows.

Jack was tense with nerves, but Skipper seemed relaxed as he lounged against a lamppost, seemingly without a care in the world.

Jack knew he was worried about what was about to happen, but nobody could have told that by looking at him. Skipper did not wear his heart on his sleeve, and years of working with temperamental horses that could sense fear and frustration had taught him to mask those emotions well. He came across as happy-go-lucky, nothing fazing him, and he was for the most part like that. But Jack knew him better than anyone and knew when he was tense. The creases around his eyes, normally not seen because he was usually smiling, were visible now, pale-coloured lines radiating from his sapphire-blue eyes, on a face tanned from a lifetime spent outdoors. He was also, despite his languid pose, coiled like a cat, and Jack knew his reflexes were so hair-trigger, he could be fight-ready in a second.

Jack wasn't interested in fighting – he kept out of conflict as much as he could – but Skipper was different. He'd grown up needing his fists and his reflexes to survive, and he was well able to handle himself, physically as well as every other way, and he quite enjoyed it. This confrontation with the Dublin underworld would be a first for Jack, but just another fun battle for Skipper Malone.

A full minute after Ted knocked, Katie's father opened the door with his fly half-undone, his hairy bare stomach hanging over his belt and a sneer on his face. Jack could hear Ted introducing himself and Gwenda explaining they were there out of concern for his daughters, that they were hoping to foster them for a short while, that their solicitor had drawn up some papers...

Stephen O'Neill stepped out onto the pavement, and after a short inaudible exchange, he seemed to grasp the reason for their visit and bawled them out at full volume for trying to undermine his authority with his children. Apparently Katie needed the discipline of the laundry, he was glad she was going on there from the orphanage, she was a terrible influence on Maggie, and Maggie would benefit from the education in the convent until she was twelve and old enough to come home to mind her old man the way that useless wife of his should have minded him, and Katie should have minded him, only she and her mother were cut from the same cloth, useless. The nuns would have Maggie licked into shape, so they would, they'd have her trained to do what she was told, when she was told…

'Skipper, stop!' Jack raced after the cowboy as he sprinted across the road in a blinding rage. Jack just managed to grab him and restrain him from knocking Stephen O'Neill into next week. Katie's vile father yelled, 'Thomas!' and a man who was obviously his brother came storming out of the kitchen at the back of the house, wearing the jacket of a garda uniform.

'These men assaulted me,' roared Stephen, pointing at Jack and Skipper.

'Right.' The guard advanced threateningly. 'You're under arrest, and –'

But Ted intervened and stood between him and Jack and Skipper with his arms held out. 'Now, now, I'm a witness to this. No one assaulted anyone, and sure you don't want to bring attention to yourself, not while you're on long-term leave,' Ted said mildly to the guard, and as if he'd waved a magic wand, Thomas retreated into the house with dark threats and black looks, followed by the sneering Stephen.

* * *

THERE DIDN'T SEEM any point in having another go to convincing Stephen O'Neill of anything.

Gwenda raged all the way back to Heuston Station, and Ted gazed darkly out of the window. Jack was worried, though Skipper as always seemed at ease.

As the train chugged for hours to Cork between green fields, Ted and Gwenda discussed plan after plan to get the girls out of the orphanage. Ted thought the best way was to build a case to get Olivia out of prison, but Jack pointed out she wouldn't have any type of custody over her children unless she went back to her husband. Gwenda wanted to just go and physically 'drag the girls out of there', as she put it, but Ted said no, that it would only make matters worse.

'We can send them letters and food parcels and presents,' said

Gwenda, wiping away an angry tear. 'At least let them know they are loved and have people on the outside who care.'

Jack thought to himself that those food parcels and presents would end up in the wrong place altogether – only the nuns that run the orphanage would grow fatter and happier – but he didn't have the heart to tell the Australian woman, who clearly still had some faith in human kindness. He also wondered what Officer Grimes had whispered in Skipper's ear.

CHAPTER 14

*E*mmet had been working hard. He had exams coming up, and preparations had started on the site, clearing the ground while planning ahead for future landscaping, piling the topsoil in the right places, working out how to preserve some mature orange trees, deciding where to excavate the footprint of the building.

Malachy had left him mainly to his own devices, as he was busy with another job that was nearly finished, but the foreman, Johnny O'Hara, knew that it was Emmet's first-ever project and that he was there to learn. Johnny was in his sixties. He'd come over from County Mayo forty years ago, but he was still an Irish man through and through and had a soft spot for Emmet with his Cork accent. He was also a complete professional, never sending apprentices off for glass hammers or spirit-level bubbles or tartan paint, which seemed to cause such hilarity among others.

There had been some muttering from the workers at first. They'd nicknamed Emmet 'the Prince', and they obviously thought he was a little rich kid playing with money not his own, but he didn't care. He was going to do the best job he could and would take any help offered.

They had run into problems yesterday; the digger broke down and had to go in for repair, and they were behind time because there was concrete to be poured the next day. Emmet had stripped off his suit jacket, grabbed a spare pick and dug and hacked at the ground, the muscles in his back and shoulders, developed from years of horse riding, bulging under his white shirt. They worked into the late evening, and when it was finished, he got pizza and beer out of his own pocket delivered to the site for the crew that stayed on. He'd been giving his labour for free and they'd get overtime, but he knew it was important to always recognise when your workers went the extra mile. Money was a necessity, but so was the word or a gesture acknowledging the effort.

Today, the men were calling him 'the Prince' to his face, but in good-natured banter.

'Hey, your lordship,' Blue, one of the concrete layers called, 'there's a chick out there looking for you.' He jerked his thumb in the direction of the site entrance. 'I offered to help her out' – he made a lewd gesture that Emmet ignored – 'but she wants the guy with the foldin' greenbacks.'

Amid a cacophony of whoops and teasing, Emmet pulled off his yellow hat and made his way to the simple front gate, a hinged section in the chain-link fences around the site.

When he saw her, he paused in mid-stride, not sure what he should say, how he should be. It had been a month to the day since that day in the park, and he'd kept himself busy with college work and the site, trying not to give himself time to dwell on anything. Once or twice, in the late evening, he'd thought about picking up the phone, but his pride wouldn't let him, and anyway, Eli had whispered in his ear. *Let her go and see will she fly back to you, Emmet. You can't keep a wild bird in a cage.*

Today, in the fall sunshine, she looked different, more formal or something, still beautiful but he wasn't used to seeing her like this. Usually she was in jeans and a t-shirt, but today she had on a floral-print dress and a little fitted yellow linen jacket. Her hair was down, not pulled up in a messy ponytail with a pencil stuck in it, and she even wore a lemon velvet hairband. He walked towards her, stepping out of the gate. He was so glad to see her – no other girl came close to

Wei in how much he loved her company – but he didn't want to appear too eager.

'Hi,' he said laconically.

'Hi,' she said.

He tried to think of what to ask her, about what she'd been doing without him, who had she seen, what it all meant, was it over, was she back for good. In the end all he managed was, 'A hairband?'

She smiled briefly. 'Long story. Well, short story actually. Can we talk?' She glanced through the chain-link fence and saw they were a subject of intense scrutiny. There was also a torrent of expletives being yelled from inside the Portakabin that served as an office near the gate; it sounded as if someone were being killed in there. 'Somewhere else?'

He glanced at his watch. 'One minute.'

Johnny was in the Portakabin on the phone. When Emmet entered, he stopped yelling and placed his hand over the receiver. 'All OK?'

'Yeah, I just need to pop out for a while. Is that all right?'

'You're the boss, kid.' Johnny winked and went back to his call, bawling some block supplier out of it for a threatened late delivery.

'There's an Italian deli down the street. Will that do?' he asked as he came back to Wei, and she nodded. They walked beside each other, though not hand in hand. Normally she would slip her fingers into his. A terrible feeling crept up on him, that she was only there to break up with him. As he always did at bad moments, he spoke to his dad in his mind. *Please stop her dumping me, Dad. I'm mad about her*, he thought fervently.

He didn't know why he'd suggested going to a lunch place; he had no appetite now.

She said, without looking at him, 'I went to the house, and Malachy told me you were here. What is he building this time?'

'A community centre of sorts, and he's keen to get it in on time and at budget. That's why you heard the foreman just now shouting. He was just taking the head clean off someone on the phone for delays in supplying blocks. He'll be dug out of them at this rate.'

She laughed suddenly, a pleasant little peal of sound.

'What?' he asked in surprise.

'"Taking the head clean off people", "being dug out of them". I've missed your Irishisms.' Then as they reached the deli, she stopped in the middle of the sidewalk and turned to face him. 'I've missed *you*, Emmet.'

'I've missed you too,' he said, though he kept his face and demeanour neutral, as if he were just being polite. *You can't keep a wild bird in a cage.*

'I'm sorry, Emmet, about that day...on campus, dumping it on you like that without any explanation. I was... I'd been taken a bit by surprise myself and...there was someone I had to see, and I didn't want you to meet them.'

Please, Dad, don't let this be true. 'Are you saying you've been going out with someone else?' He kept his voice steady.

'No, not going out, of course not. I've been going out with you!' The way she responded was the most animated she'd seemed all conversation. 'I want to be with you, Emmet.'

He exhaled. *Thanks, Dad*, he offered up in a silent whisper. 'Me too, Wei, but I really need you to explain what has been going on because it was really weird, I was so confused. You say you don't want us to break up, and I believe you but...'

'I know, and I'm sorry, and I'll explain.' She cut across him.

'What sandwich would you like?' His appetite was back now, and the smell of hot beef as they entered the deli was delicious.

'Just a soda please,' she replied, sitting down by the window.

'You sure you don't want to eat? The sandwiches are really good here.'

She shook her head. 'No. You get something for yourself.'

He ordered a hot beef sandwich with pickles and two minerals that the Americans called sodas from the guy who owned the place, a fat bald guy who hardly ever smiled but made exquisite food.

'OK, what's the story?' he asked, sitting down opposite her.

'The reason I couldn't see you...' She stopped.

He no longer felt hungry. 'Wei, you have to tell me. Who was this someone else?'

'My father. He was in town. He arrived unannounced, and I thought...'

He nearly melted with relief. He'd never thought of it being her father, but she had said before that Ken Tan was very strict and rather dour and insisted that she obey his every instruction. When she got eighty-seven percent on a project last year, Emmet had found her in tears because her father would demand to know why she was doing so badly.

So that's all it was. She hadn't wanted her father to know she had a boyfriend, and she didn't want Emmet getting all up in a heap about it and demanding to meet him.

'You thought he wouldn't approve of me?' he surmised. He took the beef sandwich and the drinks from the man in the greasy apron with a smile that wasn't returned.

'Mm. He thinks kind of old-fashioned, like girls shouldn't date without their parents' approval, that it should be someone he has vetted beforehand, that there should be a chaperone.'

'And a red-haired Irish boy isn't what he has in mind?' Emmet finished for her, still very relieved that this was all the problem was. 'By the way, my mam would be very insulted that her precious boy isn't good enough for your father.' He chuckled, trying to cheer Wei up; she looked so morose. He took another bite of his sandwich; he was starving again. 'So chief of police or not, he better thank his lucky stars he doesn't run into Lena Kogan any day soon.'

'This isn't funny, Emmet,' said Wei quietly.

'Why isn't it? He lives thousands of miles away, you don't need to tell him about me, he visited, you did the dutiful daughter bit, and now it's business as usual, right?'

'No, not right. He's still here, and he's staying until the end of the term. You're lucky I managed to slip out at all. I had to pretend to have a class I don't have.'

'Oh, Wei... So are you telling me you have to pretend I don't exist until the middle of December?' He didn't like the sound of that. She was right – this wasn't funny at all. 'I'm beginning to think it might be better if we were introduced, give him a chance to get over himself.'

'I've already suggested that.'

He stopped with his sandwich halfway to his mouth, then lowered it again. 'What?'

'I told him about you on the first day. I said I'd love him to meet you, and he went berserk at me, telling me I should be concentrating on my studies and not being cheap with boys, and that when it was time to marry, I would come home and meet someone Singaporean, and live there and have children and all the rest of it. We had a huge fight, Emmet. It was awful. I've literally never spoken back to him, never once in my life, but he was being so horrible. And then he was shocked and said I was to go back to college but only to finish the term, that I would live with him in his hotel, move off campus, and he would supervise me until I finish this semester's exams. And then I'm to continue my degree in Singapore.' She looked at him miserably.

'What? Wei, are you joking? Supervise you? Take you home? You're a grown woman, not a child. Why are you even considering this?' Emmet was beginning to realise the seriousness of this situation.

'You don't understand.' She had tears in her eyes now. 'It's not like in your culture. I know over here we're all the same, we all live similar lives, but in Singapore things are different. The expectation of society – Singaporean ladies have to behave in a certain way…'

Emmet couldn't believe his ears. Was this really his Wei, the fearless, ruthless genius who gave no student, male or female, any quarter? Who didn't care if she looked like a show-off when she answered the professor's every question, who crowed at him if she beat him in a test by one percent?

'Ah, for God's sake, Wei, listen to yourself! Your father is from another country, and another planet, as far as I can see, if he thinks you should just become this demure little girl who does what he says.'

'Emmet, I have to.'

'Why do you?' He felt the fury blaze in him now. He hated to see her so dejected; he wanted his fiery girlfriend back. 'Why do you have to do what he says? He can't drag you by the hair of your head back there. Just stand up to him, just say you refuse. We'll be all right. And if it's your fees you're worried about, we can both work, or I can borrow it from Malachy or something – he won't mind.'

'It's not that. I just have to obey him, Emmet. My mother left him and killed herself. He needs me. I'm all he has. It's always just been him and me.'

'But he has a second wife. And he dumped you in a boarding school when your mother died, so please don't tell me he was a doting daddy, because I know he wasn't.'

Wei's mother had committed suicide when she was ten, after an unhappy affair. Her father had remarried, but the woman didn't live in Singapore with him. They met up once a month or so, but she had a business in Bangkok and another in Indonesia, so she travelled around. She had no children. Wei had only met her a handful of times and wasn't keen. She called her 'the Baroness' because she said her father's wife reminded her of the woman who was trying to marry Captain von Trapp in *The Sound of Music* – beautiful but frosty and calculating. Why would Wei want to cling to such a cold, distant family that seemed to offer her nothing but rejection?

'You don't understand,' Wei said. 'It's how we do things. He's all I have, Emmet. He's the only person in the world who is related to me, and if we are estranged... You might not understand this – you clearly don't. I can't turn my back on him. I'd be dead to the only relation I have. He would cut me off, never speak to me again if I shame him now.'

Emmet reached across the table, taking her hands in his. 'He is not all you have. You have me,' he said quietly.

'But an Irish boyfriend, no matter how much I love you...'

'You love me?'

'Yes, I do, I do love you. But maybe none of this is real. We are students, we are living here in California, it's not our real place, our families aren't here, it's a different culture. I don't know where you are going in the future, Emmet, but I think you'll go home one day and marry an Irish girl, and I'll be without anyone. I would be without love or respect or safety...' Her voice was trembling.

Emmet inhaled. His heart was beating fast. Wei had never said she loved him before. He had been tempted to say it to her, many times, but never screwed up the courage. He tried to envisage what his dad would do in this situation. And then he knew. As sure as Eli Kogan had known in that forest in Wales. He'd told Emmet the story many times, when he'd realised Lena was the one. She was facing a dire prospect, he'd said, and he wanted to rescue her, but it was more than that, much more. He'd wanted her since the first time he'd seen her, and that was his chance.

'Wei, listen to me,' he said with sudden confidence. 'Any father that could cut his child out of his life forever, for any reason, well, that's not real love. Real love is sticking by someone no matter what, knowing they are your person.'

Tears streamed down Wei's cheeks, and Emmet got a disapproving look from the wife of the café owner, another dour individual, who he imagined held all men in a very dim view. She probably assumed he was breaking up with his girlfriend.

'Maybe not, but he's all I have...' Wei repeated stubbornly.

'Stop saying that. He's not.' He took the empty soda can and detached the ring-pull.

To Wei's look of bewildered astonishment, he rose and then knelt on one knee beside her chair, the ring-pull in his hand.

'Wei Tan, I love you. And I know we're young and all the rest, but I do love you and I know there is not another person on earth like you and I...' He was stumbling over the words. 'Wei, will you marry me?'

'Emmet...I...' She opened her mouth and closed it again, no words coming out.

'We'll continue our studies, we'll find the money for fees, and we'll graduate and stay here and work, and I'll never ask you to have kids if you don't want to or cook or do any of the stuff men think wives should do. You can just be you and do whatever you want, so long as I'm by your side. What do you think?'

'Are you serious?' she asked in astonishment.

'Deadly.' He grinned. 'I love you, and I think you said that you love me too, so...'

140

'I do, I do love you,' she whispered.

'Well, then put me out of my misery.' He smiled, brandishing the ring-pull.

She offered him her hand, and he slid the metal ring, huge on her slim hand, onto her ring finger.

She gazed at him, a beam on her face now. Her mischievous side was coming to the fore. 'I would love to marry you, Emmet Kogan, and I do love you – did I not mention it before?'

'You did. So let's go and meet your father – well, let's buy a proper ring first, and then meet him and tell him the news. And we're not asking, we're telling, OK?'

'He'll go crazy,' Wei said, the uncertainty creeping in once more.

'Let him. I'm a big boy, and you are my fiancée, and if he doesn't like it, he can lump it.' He got up from his knees and kissed her, then realised they were both under the watchful eyes of the surly proprietors.

'She said yes!' he announced with delight.

'One born every minute,' the woman muttered, while the man shot her a murderous look.

Wei giggled. 'But your family, what will they make of this?'

'They'll be fine. They owe you so much. You rescued Nellie, and because of all that, Blackie and Nellie already know you and adore you. And because they do, Emily will, and if Emily does, my mam will, and all the O'Sullivans, and Skipper...'

'Skipper?'

'You'll love Skipper. He's American, a Montana cowboy in West Cork – he's a sight I can tell you, Stetson. spurs on his boots, he's the real deal. And then there's Uncle Ted and his wife, Gwenda, from Australia and –'

'Goodness, you're all very international.'

'Oh, we Irish get around, you know! I've got aunts in New Zealand as well, and my German Jewish Welsh dad is cheering us on from heaven. So you see, hanging out with someone from Singapore is nothing to us.'

He put his arm around Wei as they left the deli, and once they were on the street, he hailed a cab.

'Shreve and Company, corner of Post and Grant,' he instructed the cab driver as they settled in.

'We're really doing this?' she asked, her eyes widening at the name of the famous jewellery store.

'We really are.' He kissed her deeply then, and remembered how much he'd missed her.

CHAPTER 15

'And you're sure you don't want me to come?' Jack asked as Skipper arrived downstairs with his overnight bag packed.

'Nah. I know this horse isn't gonna be comin' here – the guy won't accept my terms. But Ollie Kavanagh asked me, and he's done me a few good turns, so I told him I'd take a look. But I can't see it happenin'.'

'And this horse is in Dublin?'

Skipper could tell by his tone that Jack strongly suspected something about this out-of-the-blue trip to Dublin wasn't right. He plastered on a big, cheeky American grin. 'Holy cow, Jack! You turnin' into my mama all of a sudden? I'm goin' to Dublin to look at a horse, and I'll be home tomorrow or the next day at the very latest.'

'OK, OK. See you so.' Jack turned to leave the house to go milking, but Skipper grabbed his hand.

'Don't be mad, Jackie-boy. I just got some business to do. I'll see you soon, OK?'

'Fine. See you when you get back.'

Skipper, feeling guilty, pulled him in for a hug and kissed his neck. 'Love you.'

'Love you too,' Jack said quietly, hugging him back for a second and then going out the door into the pre-dawn morning to milk the cows.

Skipper sighed as he made his way across the yard to the front gate. He hated lying to Jack, but telling him the truth was not an option. Wyatt always said it was easier to ask for forgiveness than permission, so that's what he was fixing to do.

He walked to the village where he caught the bus to Cork, then the train to Dublin.

The train pulled into Heuston at eleven thirty, and Skipper thought he might just get the train back that evening if he was lucky. He strolled along the quays, enjoying the fresh mid-morning. Everywhere there were people, bicycles, cars, delivery vans and lorries It felt so frantic compared to Kilteegan Bridge.

The Hungry Hare was open by the time he got there, and he went in, taking a seat at the counter. There were photos of Cary Grant and Rock Hudson on the walls, and he had a suspicion this pub might suit him. Officer Grimes had whispered to him that the Hungry Hare was a pub for 'people like them', and that he always went there for a pint and his lunch when he was off-duty, which he was for another seven days.

Skipper took a seat at the bar, and the portly barman, who had a fine head of silver hair brushed back off his high forehead, asked 'What can I get ya?' in a broad Dublin accent.

'A beer please,' Skipper said. He wasn't a big pub-goer; he normally just drank the American Budweiser beers he kept in the fridge at home.

'A pint, is it? A pint of Guinness?'

This time the barman pronounced every word carefully, and Skipper smiled; people always seemed to assume he was a little slow on the uptake when they heard his American drawl. 'Sure. Make it a Guinness.' He had still not developed a taste for the Irish black beer, but when in Rome and all of that. Besides, Jack had said whatever about Skipper refusing ever to try tea, but he wasn't allowed to keep turning his nose up at the famous black stuff.

'Ya on yer holidays?' the man asked as he reached for a pint glass.

'No, I live here – well, down south, in West Cork.'

'Go on outta that. And what in the name of God brings a cowboy from America to West Cork?' The man was definitely gay, and he beamed flirtatiously at Skipper, batting his eyelashes theatrically.

Skipper smiled again. He'd had that question many times. His jeans and belt buckle, plaid shirt and Stetson always made him stand out, but it was who he was and he wasn't about to change now. He gave the same answer he always did. 'Same reason people all over the world do crazy stuff.'

'Love, is it?' The man winked.

Skipper gave a shrug. 'Somethin' like that.'

The man had poured the pint two thirds of the way up the glass and was now watching it settle. 'Well, fair play to ya, I suppose.'

Skipper's eyes were also on the glass as the creamy brown mixture slowly separated into black and white. 'Say, you wouldn't happen to know a guy called Peter Grimes, would you?' he asked casually.

A shadow crossed the barman's cheery face. 'Not sure. What d'ya want him for?'

Skipper decided sticking close to the truth was the best option. 'Well, I was up here recently, visiting with a friend in the jail, and he was helpful to us, so I just wanted to thank him.' Skipper looked the man in the eye. 'I ain't fixin' to do him no harm or nothin'. We spoke, and I sure would like to talk to him again, and he said he came for lunch here often, so I hoped he might be here today.'

The barman nodded and relaxed. 'He'll be in for his lunch, about half twelve, I'd say.'

'Thanks.' Skipper paid for his drink. 'Have one yourself.'

'Good man,' the barman said jovially, taking the tip from the change before handing it back to Skipper.

They chatted easily for a while. The bar was still empty before the lunchtime rush. Skipper told him about Montana, and they discussed the man's sister, who'd gone on her holidays to London after the war and hooked up with a GI from North Dakota and took off for there and hadn't come home since.

'Y'all lost touch?' Skipper asked.

'Ah, not really. She writes, but I'm not much of a one for letters. She's happy out there, though, but her husband's an Indian, would you believe? American Indian, I mean. He's high up in it too, an elder or something.'

Skipper nodded. 'There's lots around those parts. What tribe, do you know?'

The man's brow furrowed. 'Sioux, I think.'

'The owners of the famous Black Hills and the mighty Missouri. They're a proud people with a long tradition.'

'Is that right? Sure all I know about Indians is what we saw in the pictures growing up, though hers don't dress much like that.' He pulled a colour photo from behind the till. 'This is them.'

Skipper looked at a middle-aged couple with four young children. The husband was definitely a Sioux, all right. He had the proud and determined set to his square jaw, a handsome face and a stocky body, and that burnished skin of the Native American.

The woman looked like she left Ireland yesterday and could have fitted in perfectly having morning tea in the Copper Kettle in Kilteegan Bridge. She had fair hair and blue eyes and a portly build like her brother; Skipper could see the resemblance clearly. With the couple were three girls and a boy, all with thick black hair and high cheekbones.

'She sends me things, souvenirs,' said the barman. 'I should send them something back, I suppose, but sure I wouldn't have a clue what an Indian child would like.'

'Well, I guess they're just like kids everywhere. I'll tell you somethin' – I'm a proud American boy, but there ain't no chocolate in the USA can touch yours here, and that's a fact.'

'Are you serious?' The barman looked unconvinced. 'Sure haven't they every kind of a sweet over there?'

Skipper nodded. 'Sure do, but trust me on this. Irish chocolate, from Irish milk, there ain't nothin' like it. It's all my little nieces want from me, my brother and sister-in-law too.'

'Just ordinary chocolate like this stuff?' he asked, pointing to a box of Cadbury Dairy Milk behind the counter.

'Yes, sir, exactly that.' Skipper took a sip of the pint now that it was fully poured and settled and found it was actually quite nice. He thought he must be finally developing a taste for it after all Jack's badgering to try it on the rare occasions they went down to the Donkey's Ears.

'And you're sure them kids would like it, and my sister wouldn't think I'd lost my marbles?'

Skipper smiled. 'They will and she won't. Why don't you write her? Send some over?'

'If you think so.' He went in the back and came out with an unopened box of chocolate bars and a blank sheet of paper. He wrote out a long note, then found some brown paper under the counter and wrapped the whole thing, the chocolate and the note in it. Then after finding his address book, he carefully wrote the address before setting down his pen with a sigh of satisfaction. 'Thanks very much. I appreciate your help. I never know what to say to her, y'see here, and I'm scared of my life I'll say the wrong thing. I don't have anything to do with kids, so I'm a bit lost and yerra...you know yourself...'

He looked so self-conscious, Skipper felt a wave of affection for him. 'Don't worry about that. I knew a lot of natives when I lived there, Choctaw, Cherokee, Chippewa. I even met an Apache once, and y'know what?' Skipper took another sip of the Guinness; it was slipping down nicely. 'They got a lot in common with y'all here, bein' oppressed and that. You ever heard of the Trail of Tears?'

The silver-haired barman shook his head.

'Was when the government forcibly removed the tribes from their ancestral lands and forced them onto reservations, where they still are, most of 'em anyway. They lost everything, their culture, their land, their traditions, languages, customs, everything.'

'Like what the British did to us.'

'You got it.' Skipper nodded. 'So maybe you and your family got something to talk about after all.'

As he took another sip of his pint, he noticed out of the corner of his eye Peter Grimes coming into the pub with a rolled-up newspaper tucked under his arm.

'The usual?' the barman called to him, and the man nodded at both him and Skipper, then took a seat over by the window, well away from the bar.

'Let me get that,' said Skipper, passing over the price of the pint, and when it was poured, he picked it up and brought it over with the remains of his own pint to the prison warden's table.

'Officer Grimes, I don't know if you remember me, but my name is Skipper Malone.'

'I remember,' Peter Grimes said cheerily as Skipper sat down.

'Well, you mentioned that you might be able to help...' Skipper was acutely aware that this contact fell firmly into the category of actions Devlin had warned them against, but the odds were firmly stacked against those little girls, so he had to take the chance.

'Tell me what's going on,' Peter said, then sipped his drink.

Skipper summarised the story, what he and Jack and the Hannigans were trying to do and what the obstacles were. Peter never interrupted but let him talk, finally speaking when Skipper had told him the entire tale.

'Well, firstly, he's a scumbag, that O'Neill, and his brother as well. He's a rotten piece of work, up to his neck in all sorts of criminality. But what they done to that poor woman and her kids, terrible.'

Skipper shook his head. 'It sure was.'

'You didn't hear this from me, right?'

Skipper nodded.

'They made up the evidence against her entirely. Thomas O'Neill said he'd witnessed her attacking his brother from behind, unprovoked. He's a liar, but he's a garda, and it was his word against a poor defenceless woman and a kid – not a fair fight. I heard him showing off to some of his cronies the day it came to court. I was there escorting a prisoner, nothing to do with this case. But I'll be honest with you – this isn't the first run-in I've had with him. Thomas O'Neill got someone I care about into very serious trouble, so I've a horse in this race too, if you know what I mean? He's holding what he knows about me over me and will want something soon, I know he will, so I've wanted him to get what's coming to him for a while, him and his brother. But it was only ever me, and I can't take on the two of them, you know, not without help from a strong man who can be relied on to lie through his teeth and say we never touched 'em.'

'Well, you've found your man,' said Skipper quietly. Though Peter was small and wiry, Skipper had known men like him all his life; he had the look of a man who could handle himself.

Peter sat back and looked him up and down. 'I'll lose me job if this ever gets out, right? So we never had this conversation?'

'Of course. It sure is a coincidence that you know the guy I'm trying to persuade, a stroke of luck.'

'Ah, Dublin's a small town really. Everyone knows everyone. And well, the criminal classes, us, the guards, we're just one big happy family.' Peter grinned.

Skipper tilted his head towards the barman with an enquiring expression.

'Don't worry about Rory,' Peter assured him. 'He's sound. I'll tell him if anyone asks that we never met, OK? He's used to covering for us.'

So much went unsaid, but Skipper knew exactly what he meant. He wondered if O'Neill had discovered Peter or his partner was gay. Clearly Peter got away with it – he was still in his government job after all – but maybe his other half didn't fare so well.

'That's good then.'

'Right, let's have another pint while we're waiting. It gets dark around four now, so we'll take our time and stroll up there after we've had a bite to eat. I've a couple of caps and scarves in my car. We can go over the back wall. Fancy a shepherd's pie? It's delicious here.'

* * *

FOUR HOURS LATER, the two men crept down the alleyway that accessed the back of Number 19, Clay Street, and scaled the garden wall. After jumping down into a flower bed full of weeds, Skipper checked in the waistband of his trousers for his Colt 45. Jack had been terrified when he came from Montana with it, but nobody had stopped them at the ferry point or searched their luggage, so he'd kept it. He almost never even took it out except to clean it once or twice a year, but he needed it now. He had a knife strapped to his leg as well, just in case. He wasn't raised in the saloons of Butte and Bozeman without learning a thing or two.

Peter landed in the flower bed beside him, wearing a pair of knuckledusters. 'A small bit on the illegal side but effective,' he whispered to Skipper with a grin.

There were no curtains at the back of the house, and there Thomas was, sitting by the fire in the kitchen, reading the paper with a bottle of something on the table beside him, his bald head sweating in the heat.

Skipper cocked his gun and held it aloft as Peter tried the back door, which was open. There was a back porch and then another door. Peter nodded, and Skipper gently opened the door to the kitchen. Katie's uncle had his back to them and never moved. The wireless was on loud, which was helpful. Skipper smelled whiskey, so it was getting better and better. He touched Peter's wrist, motioning for him to stay where he was at the door, then crept up behind Thomas O'Neill and placed the gun against the man's temple. 'Do not move, just listen.'

The man swallowed and dropped the paper on his lap. 'I don't know who –'

Skipper pressed the muzzle harder against his sweaty skin. 'Don't speak either, do you understand?'

Thomas sat in silence.

'You testified against a woman called Olivia O'Neill. Everything you said was a lie, so you're going to write a confession that will be signed by you and witnessed and signed by a guard.'

'What guard? I don't –'

Skipper hit him a blow with the butt of the gun on the side of the head, breaking the skin and causing blood to spurt. O'Neill staggered to his feet, his hand to his head, reeling, then suddenly turned and charged at Skipper. His sheer weight might have knocked the cowboy over if Skipper's reflexes weren't so fast; he leapt from the man's path, sending him crashing into the table instead.

There was a roar from the front of the house and the sound of feet running. Peter stepped to the inside door of the kitchen, waiting with fists raised.

'Stephen! Look out!' Thomas howled as his brother burst into the room. The men were very alike, both balding, both overweight, but Stephen's face bore the signs of a life hard lived.

Peter flattened Stephen with one blow and stood over him. Thomas made a dash to help his brother, but Skipper grabbed him from behind, twisting his arm up behind his back with one hand and pressing the pistol to his neck again with the other.

'Let me go, you! And you, Peter Grimes, you won't get away with it, ya dirty faggot. You'll be sacked as soon as I tell them down the station!' yelled Thomas.

'I'll shoot both of y'all any time,' Skipper hissed in the man's ear, 'if you don't keep it quiet.'

'Grimes, you're a prison officer, man. You can't let him kill me! I'm your fellow officer,' whined Thomas, scared now, and his breath made Skipper's nose wrinkle; it smelled rank of whiskey and sausages.

Peter raised his eyebrows at the disgraced policeman, standing with his foot in the small of Stephen's back, who was out cold.

'The thing is, O'Neill, your threats are meaningless. Nobody believes a word out of your mouth. You're a lowlife rat, so anything happens to you, nobody will care. Your bosses want rid of you, your colleagues hate you, half the criminals in Dublin have it in for you, so there's going to be a long list of suspects. The top brass wants rid of you – you're an embarrass-ment. And so you know as well as I do, there's not going to be some big investigation when your body is found.' Peter spoke menacingly but with conviction. Every word of what he said was true, and O'Neill knew it.

'There'll be sighs of relief all round. Too many people want you gone. Now, as for you, Stevie-boy...' He ground his boot harder into the man's spine. Stephen was still sprawled facedown on the floor, but he was groaning now, having regained consciousness. 'My friend there has some papers for you to sign, agreeing to your girls going into foster care with a lovely family until their poor mother gets out of jail. And to hurry that last part along, you're going to explain you were strangling your daughter and trying to take off her underwear and her mother came to her defence because she thought you would kill her after you'd had your way with her. And she was right.'

'Getoffmee...' the man choked, and Peter stepped harder on his back. 'Aagh, aagh, get off of me...'

'As soon as you sign,' Peter said calmly.

'I'll never...' he began, but Peter stood on his back, bouncing lightly, causing him to bellow in pain.

Peter continued pleasantly, as if this were a nice social interaction. 'You will. Because it's the truth, and telling it would be the right thing to do for one thing. But we know you don't care about that, so the reason is, this man here is going to give you money, enough to get you two fat slugs away from the law that will be coming after you both as soon as the investigation into Thomas here is complete. And I can tell you, I've seen the rap sheet myself, and it's a long one.'

'Why should I trust you?' wheezed Stephen, and Thomas asked sharply at the same time, 'How much?'

'Ah, one of you has sense, I see. I'll let my friend here tell you himself.'

'Two thousand pounds,' Skipper said calmly. A few months ago, he'd paid fifty pounds for a thin, bad-tempered horse that had been left without water in an eaten-down field; she'd been ugly and scarred and uncontrollable, but he'd turned her into a decent enough hunter and sold her on yesterday for 2500 pounds.

Skipper pulled a pre-written confession from his pocket and Peter dragged the girl's father to a seat at the table, placing it in front of him.

'Sign.' He ordered, handing him a pen.

Thomas sneered. 'You're lying. Nobody connected to a brasser living in the tenements has that kinda money.'

'Olivia has friends, O'Neill, powerful, dangerous friends, so I'd be careful and I'd take the only offer coming my way if I was you,'

Skipper said silkily into his ear, twisting the nozzle of the gun against his skin.

Thomas jerked his head to one side. 'All right, let me go. I'll write the bloody confession.'

Skipper lowered the gun but kept Thomas's arm in a deadlock as he steered him towards a chair at the other side of the greasy kitchen table from his brother. Peter took the signed confession and release order from Stephen and paused to tie his hands and feet with cable ties he'd brought for the purpose, pushing him over then with his boot, so he was facedown on the floor, he landed with a grunt and a moan, and Skipper suspected he's broken some bones. Not that he cared. Peter then came back to the table, pulling out an official garda notebook he'd found on the shelf, which he opened in front of Thomas.

'Now, I'm going to help you to tell me what really happened, Thomas,' he said. 'Because the dogs in the street around here know what went on between your brother and Katie and her mother that day. So write this. "On the seventh of April, 1975, I witnessed my brother, Stephen O'Neill, attacking his daughter Katie..."'

Thomas muttered something under his breath, but Skipper used an old trick Wyatt had showed him on how to eject an unruly customer from a bar by pinching hard both sides of the neck.

'Argh!' he yelped. 'All right, stop, stop. I'll write it.'

He still complained under his breath from time to time, but he wrote down what Peter dictated to him, about how the reason he'd lied about what happened that night was because Katie had refused him and his brother certain favours, so she was no good to them. The blood from the man's temple was oozing down his cheek, and Skipper grabbed a filthy tea towel to stop the flow; all he cared about was not getting blood on the letter.

'Sign it,' Skipper instructed, which Thomas did. Then Peter Grimes untied Stephen and allowed him to his feet.

Skipper took the notebook and tucked it into his pocket, along with the foster papers and the second confession.

The O'Neill brothers exchanged a look, both knowing they were checkmated.

When everything was done, Skipper took his wallet out of his pocket and gave Thomas twenty one-hundred-pound notes.

'Hey, half of that's mine,' Stephen exclaimed. 'Don't give it all to him – I'm entitled to my share..'

The two men turned to leave, but as they did, Peter turned back. Thomas was holding the blood-soaked tea towel to the side of his head, and Stephen was nursing the weals on his wrists where the cable ties had cut into his skin.

Without warning or word, Peter lurched at Thomas, delivering a vicious blow to his abdomen, doubling him over. As Thomas went down, Peter delivered a strategically placed kick that caught the policeman's jaw, sending him reeling backwards. Peter finished with a devastating kick to the groin, which left Thomas O'Neill groaning and howling on the floor, his hands clutching his crotch, his head pumping blood.

His brother, clearly caring nothing for him, used the opportunity to scramble for the money that had gone flying out of his hand across the floor.

'That was for Louis McGrane,' Peter spat, before following Skipper out the back door.

They heaved themselves back over the high garden wall and dropped down into the alleyway behind. There in the darkness, they shook hands warmly.

'Who's Louis?' Skipper asked.

'My version of Jack.' He smiled. 'Fell foul of that gobshite one night a few years ago, him and a few of our friends coming out of The Hungry Hare, left him in a right mess.'

'You reckon that did the trick?' Skipper asked. 'They won't give us no more trouble?'

Peter nodded. 'Oh, I know it did. They'll be on the first boat to England in the morning. I wasn't joking when I said so many people want him dead. He was running with the hares and hunting with the hounds for too long.'

'I sure hope so.' Skipper smiled.

'Next time you're in Dublin, maybe you and Jack and myself and Louis could go for a drink?' Peter suggested.

'That sounds mighty fine.' Skipper then stepped back, smiling, and they went their separate ways.

CHAPTER 16

'*R*ight, will I do?' Rosa appeared in the living room of Malachy's house wearing a midnight-blue silk sheath dress and silver sandals. Long silver and diamond earrings hung from her ears. She was breathtaking.

'You'll more than do,' Malachy said quietly, helping her into her silver stole.

'Do I make it look like Emmet is from a good family?'

'A very good family.'

The three of them were taking Wei's father out to dinner in the hopes of convincing him that Emmet was a worthy son-in-law. Tan's second wife, Liang, was going to be there as well; she had arrived from Bangkok two days ago. Rosa had announced she was going to work on her, woman to woman. Emmet warned her that according to Wei, Liang was very cold and didn't like her stepdaughter at all, but Rosa was undeterred; she said she enjoyed a challenge.

Rosa kissed Malachy's cheek lightly, careful not to get lipstick on him. 'You two look like a couple of swells.' She smiled, looking fondly at him and Emmet, who were both wearing casual trousers with open-necked shirts. 'You're like twins, you know that, right?'

'I don't know. I can see a lot of Lena in him,' Malachy said, trying to sound nonchalant and then hoping Rosa hadn't noticed the very slight crack in his voice when he said that name.

She continued smiling but changed the subject. 'And you're sure about Sam Wo, Emmet?'

Emmet nodded. 'Sam Wo is Wei's choice actually. She says her father will love it. His family moved to Singapore before he was born but his parents were from Szechuan, and he loves that sort of cuisine. And her stepmother spends a lot of time in Bangkok, so she's used to spicy food.'

'And San Francisco has the best Chinese food outside of China, as everyone knows, even better than New York, and I don't say that lightly.' Rosa winked at him.

Malachy grabbed his keys. 'Rosa doesn't allow anyone to have one up on New York on anything, Emmet, even bread stuff, so that's really saying something if she's admitting to that.'

As he drove his Mercedes towards the city, Malachy caught his son's eye in the rear-view mirror. 'What has Wei told her father about us exactly?'

'Just that she wanted him to meet me, and you and Rosa. I...em...' Emmet coloured. 'She might have let on you two were getting married, just to make it look a bit more...'

To Malachy's relief, Rosa, who was in the front seat, pealed with laughter. 'No problem, Emmet, we can do that. I and your father will do all we can to make you look respectable.' She turned to smile at him over her slim shoulder. 'But remember this. Wei is a grown woman and you are a grown man, you don't need anyone's permission to be together, and he can't drag her back to Singapore by her hair, so be polite and friendly, but you're not a schoolkid and neither is she.'

Emmet uttered a non-committal grunt, and Malachy met his eyes in the mirror again. 'I know you wish you felt as confident as Rosa says you should, Emmet, but she's right. You know I think getting married at your age is a bit premature, but if it's what you both really want, then I won't stop you. Your mother, on the other hand... Well, she'll be up to you to manage, but this guy has no right to refuse you. Wei has agreed to marry you, and that's all that matters.'

Emmet nodded. 'Yeah, I'm going to call Mam after the dinner – well, tomorrow anyway. I'm thinking I'll take Wei to Kilteegan Bridge for Christmas if it all goes OK.'

'Oh?' Malachy felt a sharp stab of disappointment and then criticised himself for being unreasonable. Of course his son was going to go home to Ireland for Christmas; he should have thought of that. Though somehow he'd imagined himself and Emmet and Rosa…

Well, Rosa was a practising Jew, so Chanukah was her holiday, but he'd thought they might all go skiing in Lake Tahoe for Christmas.

Emmet looked downcast, something Malachy noticed he always did when he was worried about something.

'It's all right, Emmet, I'll be fine,' he reassured him. 'I wasn't expecting you to keep me company.' He didn't want his son to feel like he was letting him down, and anyway, Emmet would soon be back – the boy's future was in America. Much as the boy loved his family in West Cork, the opportunities and the life he could enjoy here, and eventually inheriting the company, were enormous by comparison.

Emmet frowned at him in the mirror. 'I know, but I don't like the idea of, well, you being alone here when I'm in Ireland. So what about if I ask Mam if you and Rosa could come too? I was going to say it to her tomorrow, and I'm sure she'd love it if you did, and there's plenty of room now the attic has been turned into three extra bedrooms.'

Malachy couldn't think what to say. His son wanted him for Christmas; that was lovely. But he would have to see Lena, and introduce Rosa as his girlfriend, and that would feel so…

Rosa caught his eye as he drove. 'What do you think?' she asked. 'It sounds like a nice idea to me? I'd like to visit Eli's grave.'

He shrugged. To him it felt all wrong. 'It's an option, I suppose. Let's get this dinner done first, and we can talk about it later.'

He could sense the disappointment in the car, and not just from Emmet; he could feel it off Rosa too. He immediately felt guilty for being reluctant to share Ireland with her. Yet he liked being able to compartmentalise his life. He and Rosa spent a lot of time flying back and forth across the country. She was as busy as he was, and that was part of the reason he admired her. And he didn't just admire her, he reminded himself. He loved her. She was a wonderful woman, beautiful, brilliant. She knew who she was, where she belonged, and she was forthright and honest in her dealings.

And he'd met her halfway on most things.

She'd said she wanted more than a casual thing, and he'd agreed. She'd said she wanted them to be exclusive, and again he'd agreed. He wouldn't like to share her anyway. He'd enjoyed meeting her adoptive family very much, a loud New York Jewish brood with seemingly endless nieces and nephews, and they had welcomed him warmly. Her Great-Uncle Joachim had been an invaluable help in developing the community centre, spending hours sharing his ideas. Was she expecting him to reciprocate by bringing her into his other life, the one he'd left behind in Ireland?

He pictured being in the same house as Lena, with Rosa watching him all the time, keeping an eye on how he was reacting...

No, he decided as he drove to his office in Union Square to park the car, he would not go to Kilteegan House for Christmas.

* * *

WEI HAD MADE an effort to dress nicely for the dinner, but she was filled with dread. Her father was not going to accept Emmet, and there was no conceivable way to change his mind. And she was sure her ice-cold stepmother would be no help.

She'd been surprised enough that her father agreed to this dinner, though it seemed Ernie Considine, her father's opposite number in vice from the San Francisco Police Department, had pushed him on it a little bit. Wei's father and Considine collaborated often. There was a particular brand of gangster who liked both the equatorial Singapore and the misty Bay Area, so they often met to share information, and Considine was a good friend of Malachy's. It was after one of their working lunches that Ken Tan had finally agreed to the dinner, though he'd cautioned his daughter that he would not be changing his mind about her seeing Malachy's son.

If she and Emmet insisted on going ahead with their engagement, she knew her father would do as he threatened and walk out of her life forever, and the prospect was as terrifying as it was heartbreaking.

It was bad enough that he had barely spoken to her in the last few weeks, despite him insisting she move out of her apartment and into this expensive hotel suite with him and now his second wife.

It was the longest time she'd spent with her father in years. Her mother had run away to be with another man when Wei was ten, and then committed suicide when her lover rejected her. After that, Wei had been sent to Raffles Institution and received, according to her father, the best education money could buy. She had enjoyed school, and it was nice to be around people, but she failed to make any meaningful friendships. Everyone else had a family – a mother and father, grandparents, cousins – and that was critical to how they interacted in the world. She just had her father, and he was always working. And if he wasn't at work when she was home for the holidays, he and she sat in silence eating. He didn't invite confidences and managed to make even the most perfunctory of enquiries after his health or observations on life awkward. If she asked him about her mother, he would give her factual details – where she was from, how old she was when she'd died – but nothing about how he'd felt about her, if he'd loved her, if he'd been broken-hearted.

Coming to Stanford wasn't Wei's idea. He'd decided it was the right place for his daughter to study engineering. She'd actually wanted to do medicine – she would have loved to be a surgeon – but he wouldn't consider it. Luckily she was intelligent enough to apply herself to anything and excel at it, and she liked engineering well enough and didn't find it difficult. She really enjoyed the company of her friends in the course, and meeting Emmet Kogan had transformed her life in a way she wished she could explain to him.

She was used to feeling alone. She'd learnt self-reliance. She'd even convinced herself that she preferred to live like that, accountable to nobody, not bound by anyone else's needs. But meeting and loving

Emmet had changed all of that. She wished she had the skills to talk about it, to tell him how much he meant to her, but it was like a language she'd never learnt. She felt foolish, vulnerable, admitting how she felt about him. But Wei hadn't felt safe since her mother ran away, and she'd never felt that she wasn't alone. But with Emmet, everything had changed.

She'd heard her father telling Liang earlier today that he would be finished with his work by the end of the week and that they were all three booked on a flight to Singapore on Saturday morning, he'd decided she could study at home and come back, supervised, to do her exams. She wished she could tell her father exactly why she didn't want to go. She wished he cared about her happiness and actually asked her what *she* wanted, or why she wanted it, but he never did, and she would never start that conversation.

She put some make-up on but then took it off again, not wanting to antagonise her father further.

'Wei, are you ready?' he called.

'I'm coming.' She checked herself in the mirror one last time. Her mustard wool skirt was long enough not to cause him scandal – it stopped above her knee – and she wore pantyhose when she normally had bare legs. Her shoes were flat and dainty, and the lemon blouse was short-sleeved but buttoned up to the neck. Her dark hair was brushed and tied up in a chignon, a style appropriate for Singaporean ladies, and in her ears she wore small pearls.

She arrived into the hallway to find him there, wearing a dark suit and white shirt and charcoal-grey tie, the uniform he'd worn her whole life. He was going grey now, but his expertly cut hair had also never changed. Liang was coldly beautiful beside him, in a Thai-style dress of peacock-blue silk, straight with a high collar, and an embroidered silk jacket.

He looked Wei up and down and she assumed he approved, but he never commented.

'Will we go?' he asked. 'Do you know where this is, the place we are meeting them?'

'Yes, on Washington Street, in Chinatown.'

'Is it good?'

She smiled and nodded. 'It's not fancy, but it's the best Szechuan food in the city. Everyone goes there.'

'Am I overdressed?' he asked stiffly.

Wei smiled to herself; she liked these rare moments when her father let slip he wasn't as confident as he made out.

'It's fine,' she reassured him. 'People go there after work, so you'll see men in suits, but students go there too, and workmen, everyone really.'

Ken Tan shook his head at his wife. 'I don't understand this American way, everybody doing the same things, going to the same places. It causes confusion. When we were part of Malaysia, people knew where they stood.'

It was true about Singapore. Though Ken Tan was ethnic Chinese and Wei's mother Malaysian, the two groups were not encouraged to mix, and Wei suspected her father blamed his disastrous marriage on the fact he'd broken this social code. The Indians too made up a large percentage of the population, but likewise they mixed among themselves. And the Europeans, they were the elite.

It was the thing Wei loved most about America, that nobody cared where someone was from. She'd voiced that to Emmet one day, but he'd retorted, 'Unless you're Black.' And she knew he was right. The way Black people were treated here was appalling, but she still felt he didn't understand what she'd meant. The idea that she, a Chinese Malay Singaporean, could have an Irish boyfriend, and friends whose families had come from all over the world, was a source of excited wonder to her.

Now she dropped her eyes and said nothing; she knew better than to voice any opinion to her father, let alone a contrary one. The one time she had, when she'd argued with him about her right to see Emmet, he'd told her she was just like her mother, which in his mind was the worst insult he could possibly throw at her.

The hotel was on Nob Hill, so they had to go downtown to get to Chinatown. Normally she would have walked, but her father seemed to find everything about San Francisco distasteful, and she felt such a sense of protection towards her adopted city that she didn't want him commenting disparagingly on the graffiti or the litter. Singapore didn't have graffiti or litter or people smoking on the street because it was illegal, and people were fearful of falling foul of the authorities. Everyone kept their heads down, knew their place and followed instructions to the letter of the law. If two places could be polar opposites in terms of civil obedience, then it was Singapore and San Francisco. San Francisco was the home of the Summer of Love, of freedom of expression, of the civil rights movement, of women's liberation, of sexual freedom. All movements that exhilarated and excited her but filled her father with despair and horror; he would never understand.

'Shall I ask the doorman to get us a taxi?' she asked as they crossed the hotel lobby. Her stepmother looked at her husband, and Ken Tan nodded. Wei approached the uniformed concierge, and he stepped down onto the pavement to hail them a passing cab, which pulled up to the kerb with a screech of brakes.

'Washington please, Sam Ho,' Wei instructed as they climbed in, she and Liang in the back seat and her father in the front.

The driver grinned over his shoulder at Wei to reveal two gold teeth. 'I was there a few weeks ago. Good spot. I don't normally go for that stuff, but this chick I'm seeing, she's a fan, so she dragged me along.'

'It's very nice,' Wei said demurely, knowing her father would never approve of this kind of familiarity.

'So you visitin'?' he asked, pulling out into the traffic without looking properly, cutting off a Rolls-Royce and reacting to the honked outrage by giving them the middle finger and yelling a stream of obscenities.

'Er...no. I...I study at Stanford, but my father is visiting from Singapore.'

'That's something, eh?' He turned to wink at Ken Tan, taking his eyes off the road again. 'You must be prouda her, right? If I had a kid in Stanford, I'd be proud, but my kid is only interested in smokin' dope and sleeping with married women. Got himself beat up last week for messin' with the wrong broad, but he wasn't gettin' no sympathy from me.'

Wei's father made no effort to hide his disgust but didn't reply.

'Parents can't speak English?' asked the driver, turning his head to look at Wei again.

'Er…' Wei had no idea how to respond so decided to change the subject. 'Is the city busy today?' she asked politely.

'This place is always busy, and I came from Chicago. Had to get out in a hurry, things were getting' kinda hot there. My kid's a chip off the old block, y'know what I mean?' He winked knowingly.

Wei had no idea but assumed he was referring either to illegal drug use or extramarital affairs, subjects she had no desire to get into with him. 'San Francisco is cold today. I was in Palo Alto earlier, and it was much sunnier.'

'That's the fog, man. Chicago's cold, I'll give ya that, but this damp..nah…I live out at Sausalito. No way am I gonna stay here, breathing in that wet fog every day…' He continued for several minutes in an expletive-laden assessment of the Bay Area weather, and Wei thought they would never get to Washington Street. But finally they did, and Wei paid the driver herself so she could get her father and stepmother out of there as quickly as possible.

As the cab roared off, leaving them in a fug of exhaust fumes, he father looked distastefully at her,

'And you want to stay here, among all these filthy lowlifes who don't know their place?' She didn't reply, and they crossed the pavement to the restaurant, the one she'd thought he would love for the food but which she now realised he would hate for its lack of social segregation.

'This really is the most dreadful place, filthy, grimy, the people are so uncouth and as for their manners…

She had to say something. 'Just because people are different doesn't mean they're all lowlifes.'

He looked down his nose at her, as if she were a lowlife herself. 'You really are like your mother, Wei. She had a chance to live an honourable life among high-class people, but she chose to run off with a person from the gutter. And look where that got her – a dishonourable death and infamy for her family.'

Wei paled. Her father hardly ever mentioned her mother's demise, but to do so now, so callously, was deeply hurtful. Wei remembered her mother well, a sweet, loving woman who smiled and laughed, nothing like the cold monster she'd married. To her surprise, she felt her stepmother take her arm firmly.

'That's hardly helpful my dear,' Liang admonished him. 'And just your perspective. And anyway, I think San Francisco is charming, it's fun and vibrant and welcoming, and I can see why you like it, Wei.'

Astonished, Wei allowed her stepmother to lead her as they walked on into the bright lights of the crowded, noisy restaurant.

CHAPTER 17

*L*ena dropped the carrots she was peeling for the stew and left
the kitchen to answer the telephone.

The increasingly desperate pleas of her youngest child
followed her out into the hall. 'Mam! Wait, listen! Everyone in my
class has one, even people whose fathers are out of work, even Mrs
Canty, and she's only got a Jack Russell. Even Sammy the Post has one,
Mam, and he's nearly dead he's so old...'

Lena shut the door behind her, and as she crossed the cerulean-
blue Persian carpet towards the ringing phone, she had a mischievous
chuckle with Eli in her head; it was in those moments that she felt him
so close she could almost touch him.

Pádraig was being relentless in his campaign for a television, and
the comical thing was, he had already won. Lena had no desire whatsoever to have one, but she was getting a set as a surprise for Christmas. Meanwhile, she was letting on to the children that she thought it
was a corrupting influence and would only put unsuitable ideas in
their innocent little heads.

Still with Eli's voice in her head – he was laughing at the practical
joke – she picked up the receiver. 'Hello? Kilteegan House 35671.'

There were a few clicks, and then she knew it was Emmet. He

normally telephoned late in the afternoon, when it was first thing in the morning in San Francisco, and they chatted before he left for work, so this was an odd time for him to ring. She felt a sickening pang of dread. Had something happened?

'Emmet? Is that you?' She hated the edge of panic in her voice.

'Hello? Mam? Can you hear me?' His voice sounded tinny and far away. Sometimes the quality of the line was better than others. This was a bad one.

'Yes, love, I can hear you just about. Is everything all right?'

'...Mam, I know...' She missed the next few words and caught the end of his sentence. '...to tell you.'

'The line is awful, love. I'm only getting every third word.' She hoped he could hear her better.

'...ringing...news.'

She caught a glimpse of her furrowed brow in the oval mirror over the telephone table and realised she had better stop that if she didn't want to look ninety. Eli's death had taken a huge toll on everything about her, and the pain of his loss could still be read on her face like words in a book, though she was coping much better than before. At least now she could feel genuine emotion, love her children with a full heart and care for all her family.

She had even laughed out loud the other day at something Sarah said, such a rare occurrence that she, Sarah and Pádraig had stopped and looked at each other in surprise.

'I'm sorry, love? You have some news, is that it?' she asked, silently cursing the awful line.

'Hold...again...minute,' she heard him say, and then the line went dead. She replaced the receiver in its black cradle and waited, hoping he'd ring back. What could he have been ringing to tell her? She tried to calculate the hour in California...

The telephone shrilled again.

'Emmet?' she asked.

'Hi, Mam, is that clearer?'

'Yes, pet, a bit better. All right, now, what news have you that has you ringing me at, it must be...' – she checked her watch and tried again to do the time difference – 'almost five o'clock in the morning?'

'Well, I could have waited, I suppose, but I'm too excited. Mam, I asked Wei to marry me.'

'Wei?' Lena's mouth went dry. She knew Emmet was going out with that girl who had rescued Nellie from the cult. She was from some place in the Far East. Lena tried to remember what country – was it the Philippines? No, she didn't think so. The Philippines was a place Sarah was doing a project on in school. It had all been a blur since Eli died, and she hadn't been paying as much attention to things as she should. She had been so emotionally disengaged from all her children that she had no idea Emmet's relationship was this serious.

'Ah, Mam, you know who Wei is.' He sounded very disappointed in her. 'My girlfriend? Who saved Nellie? From Singapore?'

She could picture the girl in her mind. Emmet had sent a photo of them both on Alcatraz Island. A tiny girl, with straight black hair and beautiful eyes. Emmet dwarfed her in the photo, as she was tucked under his arm.

'Of course I remember her. Nellie said she was a great girl all right.'

'Well, I proposed and she said yes, and her father's agreed, and we're getting married!'

Lena's mind was racing, trying to make sense of all this. The girl must be pregnant. Her heart sank. Her precious boy, with his whole life ahead of him, had fallen into the same trap she had done with his father, the same trap that poor Nellie had. She couldn't be angry with him, but she was sad.

'Oh, Emmet, love.' She scrambled to gather her thoughts. 'I...em... That's... Well, I wasn't expecting that,' she managed.

'I know it's a bit of a shock, Mam, since you've never even met her, but Nellie and Blackie have, so just ask them about her.'

'So when is the baby due?'

'What baby?' He sounded confused.

'Wei's baby? Your baby?' Surely he wasn't going to pretend there was no pregnancy.

He laughed merrily. 'Mam, Wei isn't pregnant, and I won't tell her you said that. I made the mistake of thinking it myself once when she was acting all weird, and she nearly bit my head off like I'd accused her of being thick or something.'

'Well, if that's not the reason for the sudden rushed marriage, what is?' Now she was confused.

'It's not rushed, Mam, don't worry. We're not going to tie the knot any time soon now. Well, we were going to at first, but now it's going to be a long engagement. We're going to finish our degrees first – that's the deal Wei's stepmother made with Wei's father, and it's all thanks to Rosa –'

'Rosa?'

'Ah, Mam, you remember Rosa Abramson, don't you?'

She did now that he'd put a surname on her. 'Yes, of course I do, she's Eli's cousin. But what has Rosa got to do with you getting married?'

'Well, it's kind of a long story, but Wei's father is very strict – he's the chief of police in Singapore. Wei's mam died but he's remarried, and basically he arrived over here, said she wasn't to have a boyfriend, she wasn't to live on campus and that he was generally shocked at how Western she'd become. And he demanded that she just finish the semester and go back to Singapore with him and his new wife, where he could supervise her properly.'

Lena was shocked. 'But could she not just have told her father that isn't what she wants?'

'Pointless apparently,' Emmet replied cheerfully. 'He said he'd never accept me. He told Wei when he found out we were dating that he had only ever met two Irish people in his life and they were both alcoholics and that there was no way she was getting mixed up with people like that.'

'The cheek of him!' Lena couldn't help exploding.

'Calm down, Mam. Wei is nothing like him. But he said he'd cut her off, that she'd be dead to him if she defied him. She was scared to do that because she said he was all she had. And I told her that he wasn't, that she had me, and then she said that we were just dating and if we broke up and she'd burnt her bridges with her father, she'd be completely alone, so I said let's get married.'

Lena sighed. The simplicity of youth was a lovely thing, but her boy was only eighteen years old and had no idea of the reality of marriage. What would Eli say to this? She racked her brain. *Tell me what to say, Eli, please.*

'But if her father won't let her…'

'That's the thing, he wouldn't, but then Ernie Considine –'

'Ernie who?' Was this someone else she should know all about?

'The head of the vice squad here or something. Anyway, he knows Wei's dad really well and he also knows Malachy, so he persuaded Ken Tan to meet me and Malachy and Rosa for dinner –'

'Rosa?' she asked, bewildered. Never mind Considine, where did Rosa fit into all this?

Emmet carried on excitedly. 'And Ken Tan was all sour and grumpy and sneery at first, and would only talk to Malachy about work stuff, but Rosa was great. She kept talking me up. And then she and Liang – that's Wei's stepmother who Wei thought didn't like her – they went to the ladies together. Rosa told me afterwards that Liang asked her lots of questions about me, and Rosa told her great things, like I'm not afraid of hard work – she knew Ken Tan would like that – and she told her all about the community centre project and me coming top of the class in college – or I would have if it wasn't for Wei getting top marks so often – and how Malachy was going to take me on as a partner and I was going to be really rich. Rosa knows exactly how to impress a wealthy businesswoman like Liang, and she also said how she thought me and Wei were meant for each other. And it turned out Liang really likes Wei but was afraid to tell her so because she's not her real mother… I mean – you know what I mean.' He caught himself, clearly worried Lena might take this as a reflection on Eli, because Eli wasn't Emmet's biological father. 'I mean, she didn't rear Wei at all, she's just married to her father. Anyway, Liang took Ken aside and spoke to him for ages, and then when they came back to our table, Ken started saying that, well, if Rosa made sure to supervise my relationship with Wei, like – oh, I don't know, it's mad –

like she was my mam or something. It was really silly, but anyway, Rosa promised to do it. We're not to really see each other like that – you know what I mean – just as friends until we've finished college and got jobs...'

'Emmet. Emmet.' Lena's head was spinning trying to take in all this information. 'Slow down. Wait. I'm trying to get my head around this, you getting married...'

'You don't mind, do you, Mam?'

'Of course I don't mind. If it's what you both want, then I'm very happy for you, especially as you're going to wait for a while – I have to say I'm with Wei's father on that.'

'I thought you would be.'

'But it's not down to me or Ken Tan in the end. This is your life, to do what you want with.' She hoped she was saying the right things, the things Eli would have said. He was always the less impulsive of them. He would pause, allow some time to come to an opinion. She really didn't like the idea of Emmet getting married at such a young age, but then she had and it had worked beautifully until Eli was taken from her. Maybe it would be the same for Emmet and Wei. Besides, it was a couple of years off anyway, plenty of time for either of them to change their mind. And if they didn't, well, then, maybe it was meant to be...just as Rosa had said to Liang.

As if Rosa knew anything about her son.

'Listen, Emmet, I know this is not the most important thing, but what has Rosa got to do with all of this?'

'Oh, sorry, I should have said. Well, Malachy and Rosa are, you know, boyfriend and girlfriend, which sounds a bit weird at their age.' Emmet chuckled. He obviously found it hard to envisage someone in their late thirties as having any kind of relationship. 'I asked them to come to the dinner with me so Ken Tan could see I have a really good family. To him, family background is really, really important. It doesn't matter how well you do, if your family isn't a good one –'

Lena interrupted him again, still dazed. 'So Rosa was there as someone from your father's family?'

'No... Yes... What?' He sounded confused again. 'Oh, I see what you mean. No, not exactly, though that as well, I suppose. Yes, of course, she's Dad's cousin, I know, but really what I'm saying is, Rosa had to basically tell Liang she and Malachy are engaged –'

'They're *engaged*?' A strange wave of emotion crashed over Lena. She had no idea Rosa and Malachy had even started seeing each other.

'No, though they probably will be one day soon. Anyway, Rosa had to convince Liang that she and Malachy are going to be tying the knot any day now or Ken Tan definitely wouldn't have agreed to leaving her in charge.'

'Oh, well, good for Rosa,' Lena managed weakly. The wave was receding, but she felt as if it had swept her up onto a beach and left her stranded.

'So, Mam, can I bring Wei for Christmas? I'd love her to have a proper Irish family Christmas. She doesn't do Christmas because she's a Buddhist, though her mam was a Muslim, I think, so it would be lovely to show her. And you're right – it has been too long.'

Lena felt a rush of warmth. 'Oh, that's wonderful. I'd love to meet her, and I'd love to see you too, Emmet, for as long as possible. It's been a year since I saw you. I know you're busy with work and studying, but I'm sure Malachy would let you off for a month?' This was the second Christmas without Eli, but the first one was only shortly after his death so it had felt miserable and pointless. This time she wanted to make it special for all her children. Filling the house again, having everyone over for a big Christmas dinner, presents under the tree, including the television – she would make it perfect.

Emmet said kindly, 'I'll come for as long as I can, although I need to get this project finished, the community centre, so it might only be for two weeks, Mam.'

'Well, I'll be delighted to see you for however long you can come.'

He clearly heard something in her voice because he said hesitantly, 'I've been worried about you, Mam, but...em...I was hoping you're a bit brighter these days?'

She winced at his tentative tone, the exact same one she used to use with her own mother, testing the waters to see how unbalanced she might be at any given time.

'I am brighter, love.' She infused her voice with confidence. 'It was hard – it still is – but Dad wouldn't want me to be like that, no interest in anything, alone all the time. Jack and Em and everyone were trying to shake me out of it, and in the end, your granny gave me a talking to, so I just decided I needed to get my life back and look after you three as Eli would want me to, so I'm trying my best.'

'I'm so happy to hear that, Mam.' She could almost hear him exhale. 'And I'm really looking forward to seeing you. And listen, I know it might be weird, but could I invite Malachy and Rosa too? Malachy is so busy, but he needs a break, and I don't like leaving him alone for Christmas. And I know Rosa wants to come. She loved Kilteegan Bridge, and now she's promised Wei's dad to keep an eye on us. She almost seems to feel responsible for us, which is mad, I know, but still. So I was wondering, if she can persuade Malachy into it – he usually does what she wants – if they could come as well...'

Again, that wave of darkness. 'Of course. Invite them, love. It will be lovely to have them.'

'You don't mind about...' Again, the tentative voice.

'Mind about what, love?' she asked, remembering to sound cheerful.

'Rosa and Malachy?'

'Of course not! I'd be delighted to see them.'

'Thanks, Mam. They'll be delighted as well, I'm sure. Wei is going to be so excited, and you'll love her, Mam.' He paused, then said, 'She's a bit unusual. Not weird, but she's not like anyone else. Anyway, I'm not explaining it very well. You'll see in a few weeks.'

'All right, love. I'm looking forward to it so much. It will be lovely to see you.'

'You too, Mam. I'll let you know our arrival dates and all of that. Malachy's PA will arrange it for us, so it will be fine.'

Lena smiled to herself. Her son had taken to the high life like a duck to water, it would seem. 'That's great, Emmet. Talk soon, love.'

'Bye, Mam.'

'Bye, love, and congratulations.'

She hung up and stood there feeling dizzy, her mind in a whirl.

'Mam, television isn't bad for you. We can watch the news and all sorts, and there's educational programmes about nature and stuff.' Pádraig had appeared in the hall.

'I know, Podge, it's great,' said Lena, using Emmet's nickname for his little brother, before absent-mindedly taking her coat down from the hook by the door.

'You *know*? Then, Mam –'

'Pádraig, peel the rest of those carrots. I'll be back in an hour.' She hurried out of the house and ran down the gravelled driveway.

* * *

'CREAM CAKES?' asked Emily.

'Yes, and tea, right this minute.'

Emily put the kettle on her neat little range in her brand-new block-built dormer bungalow. 'Is it as bad as Nellie wanting to be a nun and moving into the convent to "get a feel for it"?'

'I don't know, Em. See what you think of this one.' Lena bit deeply into one of the cakes and said through a mouthful of fresh whipped cream, 'Emmet is only after asking that girl Wei who rescued Nellie to marry him, and apparently she said yes, though her father doesn't want it to happen until after they've finished college – thank God for him, as nobody thought to ask me about it. But anyway, Emmet's bringing her here for Christmas, and then apparently it would be too lonely for Malachy, so Emmet is bringing him too and Eli's cousin Rosa, who it seems has started a relationship with Malachy and is practically acting like Emmet's mother in America.'

'What? You're joking.' Emily was trying to take it all in, but her face was one of dismay.

Lena squinted at her cake, licking escaping cream off the side. 'Nope, not a joke, none of it. Emmet is engaged to a girl I've never met from the other side of the world, whose father thinks we're all a pack of alcoholics, by the way, and to celebrate we'll all be spending Christmas with my ex-boyfriend and his current girlfriend, my dead husband's long-lost cousin. Now that I say it out loud, it sounds like one of those awful serials in the women's magazines.'

There was a long silence, and Lena looked up at her sister, who was still standing by the range. Emily's face was completely contorted; she was obviously trying as hard as she could not to laugh.

'Oh, for goodness' sake, this is serious!' Lena said in outrage, but then the sight of Emily getting more and more scarlet in the face brought home the hilarity of the whole thing, and despite themselves both sisters collapsed into paroxysms of laughter.

'Your son...' Emily guffawed. She tried to catch her breath, but the tears of laughter and gales of mirth prevented her from speaking in full sentences. 'Is marrying a girl you've never met, and my daughter is going to be a nun... Excellent parenting there... And Malachy... And Rosa... Oh God...'

The sisters howled with laughter and were totally incapable of explaining to Blackie, who had arrived to see what was causing all the commotion.

* * *

LENA NEARLY JUMPED out of her skin as she walked past the surgery because Mike was rapping his knuckles on the window, beckoning her to come in. She retraced her steps to the front door of the gatehouse and let herself into the waiting room, which was empty. Mike called to her from his surgery, where he was sitting with the bottle of Midleton on the desk.

Lena went in and sat down, and he poured her a glass like the last time she was there. He started chatting about his day, and she wondered if this would develop into a little ritual, her popping in for a chat and a whiskey at the end of his day, and whether that would eventually erode her memories of Eli sitting at this desk.

Lena, Mike is a lovely man. He's an older brother to you. There's no one I'd prefer to have sitting at that desk, whispered Eli's voice in her mind, and it gave her an idea.

'Mike, my son Emmet is coming home for Christmas, with his

175

fiancée no less, and Malachy Berger, who is Emmet's biological father, and his girlfriend, Rosa, who is Eli's cousin, is coming as well.' It gave her a weird feeling to say it – her stomach sort of lurched – but she would have to get used to it. 'And I'm having Em and Blackie and Aidan and Nellie, and Jack and Skipper of course, and Ted and Gwenda and their girls, and Mam and Klaus as well. So I was wondering if you and Anthea would like to spend Christmas with us too? A big family Christmas, the more the merrier?'

Her 'older brother' beamed. 'I think we'd love that. Mam was asking if I was staying here for Christmas, and I said I hadn't made any plans, so she was thinking of coming down to see me anyway. But are you sure you're able for that big crowd, with the day that's in it?' He said it gently, and she realised he was speaking as her doctor now. He'd been so kind looking after her after Eli died.

'I'll be fine.' She nodded. 'Everyone will help out, so it will be grand. A bit of a free-for-all but fun. I know what you're asking, and I will miss Eli of course. But funnily enough, it's not the big days, the birthdays or Christmas, that are hardest. It's the little things. Reading something and saying, "I must tell Eli about that," or hearing something funny, knowing it would make him hoot with laughter. I miss him when the wind is howling outside and I don't have him to snuggle up to at night, or standing at the side of the pitch when Pádraig scores a goal. Those things are much harder than the big things, because they catch you unawares. I'll be going along all right, not too sad, and then bang, it hits me again.'

'Grief is like that,' Mike said wisely. 'And I know people say time heals and all of that, but I don't think it does. I think what time does is like any other wound – it scabs over to protect you so it's not raw every day, but it never goes, not when the love was as deep as it was for you two.'

They sat in companionable silence for a while, sipping their whiskey and watching the light fade outside. 'So how did you get on at your Sunday lunch with Jane Kearney?' Lena asked, trying to sound casual. She rather suspected it had gone well; Emily had been hearing a few things in the shop.

Sure enough, he was blushing, so his whole head was flaming red: hair, cheeks and beard. 'Ah, well, it's early days, but she... Well, I like her, and she seems incredibly to like me too.'

'Nothing incredible about it. Will I count her in for Christmas so?'

Mike chuckled, poured himself another glass of whiskey and topped up hers. 'Thank you, Lena. I will certainly ask Jane what her plans are. And by the way, if you need a ridiculously happy grinning Santa Claus, you know where to look.'

'You, Mike?'

'And why not? We can add a few bells and baubles and things to the wheelchair, maybe turn it into a sleigh somehow. Old Ollie the Shetland pony can be my reindeer, and I can come trundling up the drive with a big red bag over my shoulder.'

Lena laughed at the delightful vision. It was amazing how much she'd laughed today; she felt she was getting lighter and lighter by the minute. 'You know, Mike, I'm going to hold you to that. I think it's a wonderful idea.'

CHAPTER 18

*N*ellie settled herself on her bed in her tiny room in the convent to read the letter from Emmet. She hoped as she ripped the envelope that he wasn't going to be awful about her decision, or assume it was another of her madcap schemes. She'd tried to reassure him when she wrote telling him of her decision that she was sure it was the right thing, but she was worried about what he might say to her.

Mother Bridget seemed not at all surprised that she felt she had a vocation but suggested she come and live at the convent for a while before she began the process of becoming a postulant to get a better sense of what the community was like and if it was a life she would feel happy with. She would, at that stage, if she felt it was right, begin her formal nursing training as well. Nellie knew her mother was heartbroken and feared for her daughter, but Nellie also knew she was making the right decision.

She'd even told Mother Bridget about her affair with Gerard and Aidan's birth. She wanted there to be no lies, though she admitted she'd never told her parents how old her lover was, or that he was married.

The Reverend Mother had thought long about it and said she was glad Nellie had been honest with her at least. Whether Nellie told her parents was for her to decide. It had been a long conversation, and Mother Bridget said she would need time to see if Nellie was running away from life, from men and marriage and motherhood, because she'd had such a traumatic experience, or if she did genuinely have a vocation.

After that, the Reverend Mother came to speak to Emily and Blackie, and at first Nellie was worried about what she might say, but Mother Bridget didn't betray Nellie's confidence or let on she knew about Aidan. Instead she just assured them that the Sisters of Charity were not in the business of grabbing vulnerable young women from their families. Her father had seemed reassured, but her mother was yet to be convinced, Nellie knew.

Emily had a lot to say to Nellie afterwards about how cruelly the nuns at the orphanage had treated Katie and Maggie, and though Nellie was loyal to her own community, she did agree that Mother Ignatius was wrong about the way she treated children. She assured her mother that Mother Bridget had been appalled at how the two girls had been dragged back to the orphanage and that Mother Bridget and Mother Ignatius were not friendly.

The Sisters of Charity were very different from the ones that had mistreated Katie and Maggie and Nellie loved the life here.

She worked every day as normal in the Star of the Sea, but in the evenings, she came back to the convent on the grounds, attended vespers and had her evening meal with the sisters. Nobody but Mother Bridget knew of her past, not even Martina, and she felt such peace and sense of purpose, it was hard to explain. She was a different person now. The wild girl with the short skirts and make-up was gone, and while Nellie held no shame or ill will towards her, she was no longer a part of who she was. She hoped Emmet would understand.

Dear Nellie,

Wow. I honestly don't know what to say, and I know I should probably restart this letter and compose it properly and all of that, but we never spoke to each other like that and we won't start now.

You as a nun is something I'm going to need time to think about, but my first thought is that if it's what you want, and it will make you happy, then of course I'm behind you all the way.

I won't pretend to understand it, and frankly the idea of giving up the things nuns are supposed to give up (being cryptic here in case the Reverend Mother finds this – ha, ha!) is not something I could consider even for a second. But if you can, then nobody should stop you.

I know you said Auntie Em isn't keen, but as we've always said, Nel, we're only getting one life. Our parents made their decisions, and we must make ours. They won't always be popular, but I know when your mam decided she was going to marry your dad, some people thought it wasn't a good match, but they ploughed on anyway. Same for my mam and dad, and Jack and Skipper, and Ted and Gwenda and everyone. They all got to follow their own dreams, and you should follow yours too. Anyway, it's not like you're going to be leaving Kilteegan Bridge, is it? So it's not like Auntie Em will be losing a daughter.

Will I have to call you Sister Nellie, by the way? Or worse, will they give you one of those dreadful men's names? Remember Sister Stanislaus in baby infants who spat when she talked? Or Sister Columbanus who started every sentence with 'the starving children of Africa'? I hope not. To me you're my favourite cousin and my best friend, and you'll always be Nellie, no matter what name they give you.

I am listening when you say you're not having a reaction to Aidan or the cult, by the way, and I agree you're making a free choice and you know your own mind, so I'm behind you all the way.

Did Mam tell you me and Wei are coming for Christmas? Malachy and Rosa are coming too, though Malachy is being a bit weird about it. I suppose it's strange for him, going back to the house he grew up in, lots of memories and that. Him and Rosa had a bit of a fight about it. She asked him straight out if it was because he didn't want Mam to see him and her together. Rosa is sharp as a tack, and the better I get to know him, the more I realise Rosa is right – a part of Malachy will always love my mam, even though he knows there's no hope. But he and Rosa are good together, and it's nice that she's Dad's cousin. It works over here, but I think he's a bit nervous of being back. I don't know.

Wei is really looking forward to seeing you again. I think you're the biggest draw in getting her over to Ireland for Christmas. She's actually a bit nervous of meeting Mam, I think, though of course you'd never get her to admit it.

So, Nel, can I ask you a favour? Will you tell Mam how great Wei is? She's more likely to believe you than a poor boy blinded by love – ha, ha. You're the only one over there that's met her – well, apart from your dad, but that wasn't for long. And I know you two like each other, but you know how she can be, so if she comes over and is all prickly and standoffish, can you kind of pave the way by saying how nice she is really?

Wei has had such a strange upbringing. Her mam died by suicide, her dad is a cold fish, and she was in boarding schools from when she was ten. I'm just afraid when she walks into our big, noisy, loving family, she'll freeze and get overwhelmed. And overwhelmed for Wei can look aggressive. Irish culture and Singaporean are as different as chalk and cheese. They are reserved and polite, and we say the first thing that comes into our heads. I'm living in terror, to be honest, imagining all sorts.

Anyway, I know Mam is fretting, so if you can do what you can to smooth things there, I'd be very grateful.

So Wei and I are studying like mad, and I'm working on this community centre that Malachy is building. It's going to be for the Jewish people here, to tell the story of the war, and to involve the whole community, schools and all of that, so they can learn what Hitler did and hopefully not repeat it. A trust will run it, and it's going to be a success. Malachy put a really great building contractor on the job, so even though I'm supposed to be the engineer, Johnny can do this in his sleep, so I'm taking instructions from him, not the other way around. But I'm learning loads.

I can't wait to come home and see everyone. Mam seems in much better form these days, which is lovely. I realise how lucky we were to have Dad and how nobody will ever fill the hole he left, but I hate to think of Mam lost in her own sad thoughts all day.

See you soon, Sister Nellie.

Hugs. (Are you allowed to hug nuns? So much to learn!)

Emmet xx

She folded the letter and placed it back in the envelope, and lying on her back on the small narrow bed, she closed her eyes and sighed. Emmet was on her side. The relief flooded her body. For some reason, her family saw Emmet as infinitely sensible despite the Jingo catastrophe a couple of years ago, and so if he was not against her, it would be a great help to her cause.

His engagement to Wei... Well, she had been surprised when she heard. And Emmet was right – Wei was a bit emotionally cut off and could come across as aloof and a bit superior. But once you got to know her, she wasn't like that at all. She'd taken a huge risk coming into the cult, and Nellie was sure she would be good for Emmet.

She started to get ready for bed, sitting on the side of it to take off her shoes. She was absolutely shattered after a day of work and an evening of studying the lymphatic system. But then there was a knock and Martina popped her head around the door.

'Knowledge is after finding his way over to Kitty's room again and has made an indecent proposal. Sister Oliver wondered if you could go over and try to talk sense to him, because Kitty's son is going mad saying his mother is being harassed by Knowledge and is threatening all sorts, and you're the only one he listens to.'

Nellie smiled and heaved herself up. 'Of course I will.'

Her feet hurt after a long day, but Martina was right. Knowledge, as he was known around Kilteegan Bridge, a sworn bachelor all of his life, was notoriously obstinate, but for some reason, he responded to Nellie. He earned his nickname because there wasn't a subject on earth, from fly fishing to gardening to Russian literature, on which he wasn't a self-proclaimed expert. Twinkle in the Donkey's Ears had to throw him out on more than one occasion for his own safety, so annoying to the other customers was he. He'd had a fall and was no longer able to climb the stairs in his tiny cottage, so Dr Mike had decided he needed to be in the nursing home. Unfortunately, though, since being admitted to the Star of the Sea, Knowledge had fallen hopelessly in lust with poor Kitty McLoughlin, a woman who had had seven children and whose husband had recently passed away after a marriage of fifty-six years, and who had no more interest in Knowledge than the man on the moon.

Derry McLoughlin, her son, had shown patience up to this, but the amorous advances of Knowledge to his poor exhausted mother were too much, and once again Knowledge found himself within whispering distance of a box in the face. He had a morbid fear of nuns, even the kind ones, but Nellie could coax him and cajole him and get him back to his room, allowing poor Kitty to rest easy in her bed.

The only option now was to lock him in his room, but that seemed cruel. He had a bit of dementia, but that didn't mean he wasn't a sex pest.

'Apparently he tried to get into her bed,' Martina said as Nellie wrapped a warm scarf her Nana Peggy had knit her around her neck against the biting cold.

'Oh, for God's sake, we'll have to ask Dr Mike to give him something to calm his ardour,' Nellie said.

'If such a drug exists, then maybe there's more than Knowledge should be on it,' Martina said with a laugh.

'Well, it's not something we need to worry about anyway, one less problem.' Nellie chuckled as they walked across the grounds from the convent to the nursing home.

'Will that be all right for you? That part of never having a man, I mean?' Martina asked her.

Nellie had never confided in her friend that she wasn't a virgin and nor would she, though it felt a bit mean and duplicitous when her friend was so open.

'I think I'll be fine not to get married,' she answered as honestly as she could as they walked along together in the still night air. The West Cork stars twinkled overhead, and a bright silver crescent moon made the inky sky look like a painting.

'I don't think marriage and children are for me either,' said Martina, 'but sometimes I ask myself if I only think that because I wanted to be a nun so much and I had no interest in marrying anyone local. And sure I'm not the kind of girl fellas fancy anyway. I get afraid sometimes that I'll wake up one morning and it will all be too late and I'll have missed out on something big.'

Nellie linked her friend's arm. Martina was not conventionally pretty, but there was a warmth to her that radiated out, and Nellie knew she could have found a husband if it was what she wanted. She'd discovered that what women thought was beautiful and what men desired were often completely different things. Take Emmet, for example. All the Californians with their tanned skin and blond hair and big boobs did nothing for him, but Wei, who was beautiful but in a quirky rather than an obvious way, had captured his heart.

She thought hard before replying. 'Here's what I think, Martina. I think if you wanted a husband, you'd find a decent fella, no bother to you, because you are such a lovely person. I think that God didn't send anyone you liked because you wanted to enter a convent since you were a little girl, so what would be the point. And as for missing out, I think girls are brought up to believe that marriage and children is the thing to do, and for a lot of people it is, but not for everyone.' She smiled at her friend. 'You're strong enough and intelligent enough and brave enough to choose your own path, and I think you should trust your instincts. I never imagined entering a convent was in my future. I was a bit of a tearaway, to be honest, but God made sure I had those experiences, and it all led me to here. If you'd have told me three or four years ago I'd be wanting to become a nun, I'd have said you were off your head. I think there is a plan, a divine plan, for each of us, and we fight it and we think we're going wrong and all the rest, but if you relax into it, there's a plan and it's for our good.'

Before opening the door of the nursing home, Martina turned to Nellie. 'I know your family aren't mad keen – mine weren't either – but they'll see over time that this is the life for you.'

Nellie sighed. 'I hope so.'

'They will. Now let's go in there and let two young nuns calm the ardour of Knowledge.'

To the sound of their own happy laughter, they entered the nursing home.

CHAPTER 19

*T*he car pulled into the farm as Skipper was schooling a new horse in the indoor arena. Glancing towards the open doors, he was surprised to see the local solicitor's maroon Ford come to a stop in the middle of the yard and Kieran Devlin climb out.

He wondered what had brought the lawyer to their door; if there was any news to report, he'd usually just update them with a phone call. The days had been dragging by since Skipper's trip to Dublin, which he had still not told Jack the full truth of, only saying he'd gone back to see Katie's da and given him a financial inducement to change his mind about the fostering, which he did. Jack had accepted the story, though not without a suspicious stare into Skipper's innocent eyes.

The foster papers had been verified by Sergeant Flannery, then by the local magistrate, but Mother Ignatius was dragging her flat heels and making a great deal of Gwenda's lack of a Catholic baptismal certificate. 'Surely a Catholic institution is more in the children's best interests than a heathen woman from some foreign country,' she snapped whenever she was contacted by Devlin or Flannery to ask would she hand the children over.

The last Skipper had heard, Devlin was talking to the local government minister to see if he could do something to break the logjam, though as Devlin warned them, he was as likely to side with the nuns as not.

As the Montana cowboy tied up the horse and strode towards the doors, he steeled himself for yet another disappointment, another delay.

He heard their light, high voices before he even reached the open air. With a gasp of shock, he broke into a run, and as he burst out into the rainy yard, Katie and Maggie saw him and raced towards him, shrieking his name and hurling themselves into his arms.

'Holy cow! Where did you two spring from?' He swept them up in the air, one in each arm, hugging their thin warm bodies as they clung to him. 'Y'all didn't run away again, did you?'

'No!' screamed Maggie in his ear. 'We got out!'

'Well, ain't that somethin'...'

'They let me go before I was even sent to the laundry, Skipper. Mr Devlin was asked to collect me and Maggie and bring us to Auntie Gwenda's...' Happy tears were flowing down Katie's face.

'Aw, Katie, that's amazing news.' He kissed her hair, then beamed over her head at the solicitor. 'Kieran, how on earth did you manage it?'

'Chops had a word with the Mother Superior. His own cousin was in an orphanage, so it gave him a certain mindset apparently.'

Skipper, like everyone, knew the local member of the Irish parliament, he had a shop, bar and undertaker business all in the one premises outside Bandon. A man called Eoin Lambe but everyone called him Chops.

'Is Jack around? The girls wanted to come here before I took them to Ted and Gwenda's. They said you were the first ones to help them and they wanted to thank the two of you first off, fair play to them.'

'No thanks needed. Maggie, you're stranglin' me, lil' darlin'. We'll just go find Jack. He's inside poring over the accounts –'

'Do I hear squeaky voices?' Jack was grinning as he threw open the farmhouse door, and the girls immediately peeled down off Skipper's body and raced, howling with delight, towards him.

'They let us out!' shrieked Katie. 'And we're going to be staying with Auntie Gwenda and Uncle Ted until Mam has her retrial!'

'A retrial? That's wonderful!' As he stooped to hug the girls, Jack glanced at Devlin for confirmation.

The solicitor nodded briskly. 'Olivia's husband and his brother signed sworn statements that they made up their original testimony, and the Dublin guards have finally sent them up to me. And so I'm going to apply for a retrial, and any reasonable judge will give it to me, I imagine.'

'They both signed? *Seriously?*' Jack's eyes turned in amazement to Skipper, who was trying to look as innocent as possible, then back to Devlin. 'Why would they do that and risk being done for perjury?'

The solicitor shrugged. 'A change of heart? Got religion? Who knows why these things happen, but sometimes they do. Anyway, the two men have skipped the country now, according to Dublin. Oh, and I'll be representing Olivia at the retrial.'

'We'll pay you,' said Skipper immediately.

'No, you won't. This one's on me. Think of it as a Christmas present to these two young ladies.' The country solicitor was usually a man of sensible habits, but the sight of Katie and Maggie's joy had clearly addled his brain. 'Now then, we best be off to your new home. Ted and Gwenda will be delighted to see you, I'm sure, and I'm dying of the cold here.' He was right about the winter's day; the temperature was falling, and there were even a few flakes of snow circling.

'Yes, Mr Devlin, we better go. We don't want to be late,' Katie said with glee. 'We just had to stop off and tell you what happened. It's like a miracle, isn't it, Mr Devlin?'

'It certainly is.' Devlin gave one of his very rare smiles as he opened the back door of his car and ushered the children inside.

'Are you sure about this, Kieran? We can pay you?' Jack asked quietly, following him around the car to the driver's side.

'Not a bit of it, Jack. Most days my job is fairly boring, and some days it's frustrating or sad, but once in a while, things go right for someone, the law makes something better. It's rarer than you'd think, and you have to savour those days.' Before getting in the car, he shook Jack's hand and then Skipper's. 'This is one of those days.'

Then Katie insisted on jumping out of the car again and wrapped one arm around Skipper's waist and the other around Jack's. 'I love you both. You saved me life,' she whispered.

Skipper beamed at Jack over her head. 'Our pleasure, kid. Now go make Ted and Gwenda happy, and tomorrow we'll all have fish and chips for supper here at the farmhouse, huh?'

'Yes!' she screamed as she jumped back into the car. 'Bye! See you later.'

Jack and Skipper stood waving at the girls who were kneeling up on the back seat as the car pulled out of the yard.

When they were alone, Jack took Skipper by the arm and marched him into the house. He turned to face him in the kitchen, under the electric bulb. 'So when were you planning on telling me the truth?'

Skipper thought briefly about not telling him but instead confessed sheepishly, 'Mm...when and if I got caught?'

Jack sighed and shook his head. 'Well, I already guessed you must have done something more than offer their father money, and I'm assuming you took on the two of them to get them writing confessions. Just promise me they really have left the country and aren't lying dead in a ditch somewhere. And, Skipper, don't lie to me.'

'They're alive, or were the last time I saw them, I swear on my mama's grave.'

Jack's shoulders sagged with relief. 'Well, that's something, I suppose.'

The cowboy moved away, idly shifting around some of his and Jack's clutter that had built up on the kitchen table again without Katie to insist on tidying up every day. 'But what if...' He stopped.

'What if what, Skip?'

'What if something had gone wrong, like I...y'know... I mean, only in self-defence, y'know...' He glanced sideways at Jack, wondering how far the man he loved would go to save him. 'I mean, d'you think ya mighta given me an alibi if the cops came lookin'?'

Jack threw himself down on the sofa by the fire, stretching out his arm along the back of it. 'You want to know if I'd lie to keep you out of prison? Seriously?'

Skipper remained standing by the table. 'Jack, I'm not saying I'd want you to cover up for me, not about something that bad –'

'I already did cover up for you.'

Skipper stared at him. Jack was grinning.

'I know you, Skipper,' he said. 'I know how you think, and I knew there's no way you were going to let a lying devious rat like O'Neill ruin that girl's life, not if you could help it. I knew something was up when you went to Dublin – you're a terrible liar, by the way – and then the Colt was gone, so I put two and two together. I knew there was nothing I could do at that stage anyway, so I made sure that Ted and Gwenda heard me talking to you up the stairs, and I put that god-awful country music on the record player. Ted knew I'd never listen to that – he even remarked on it. And I made sure there were two dirty dinner plates on the table so we could all three of us give you an alibi if you needed one.'

Skipper plonked down beside him, throwing his arm around him and kissing him fondly. 'You're amazing, Jackie-boy.'

'I'd do anything for you, ya big eejit, you know that.' Jack sighed and kissed him back.

CHAPTER 20

Gwenda and Ted and the girls had discussed it at length, and they'd come up with a plan and spoken to Skipper about it, and now they agreed they were ready to ask Katie.

The whole family had just eaten a delicious shepherd's pie that Katie had insisted on making for everyone, and Katie was in the bedroom putting Maggie to bed and 'leaving you all alone together' as she put it shyly; she still seemed to think she and Maggie were intruding on them as a family.

The sound of her telling Maggie another exciting story about a magic door in the back of the house into a magical world with talking animals and rivers of lemonade and trees that grew chocolate leaves came to an end, and after a few minutes of silence, Gwenda stood up and went down the short passageway to her door.

'Katie!' she murmured through it. 'Could you come back down to the kitchen for a minute? Sophie and Annamaria need to talk to you.'

There was a creak of footsteps, the door opened, and the girl's white-as-a-sheet face appeared from behind it. A few days of good food, a warm bed and no violence or fear had filled out her hollow cheeks and put a shine in her hair, but despite all that, any unexpected summons still threw her into a panic, as she was so used to being torn away from the people she loved.

'It's all right. Come on. Nothing bad is going to happen,' Gwenda coaxed her gently.

Katie tiptoed behind her into the big warm kitchen, which had been tidied to levels not seen since she was living here last. Gwenda and Ted and their daughters weren't the neatest – they were used to living on a range half the size of Cork – but Katie had quietly and efficiently worked her way through the mess in between running up to the other farm to make sure Jack and Skipper had delicious food available after a hard day's farming.

Jack and Skipper always insisted on paying her, though she'd tried not to let them at first, but Gwenda had seen every coin of those wages going into a jam jar she kept beside the bed, and she'd told Gwenda it was to pay Kieran Devlin when her mother's retrial came around. 'Mr Devlin is so kind, and he'll have to go up and stay in Dublin. I want for him to stay somewhere comfortable, as I'm so grateful to him for helping my ma,' Katie had almost whispered, when Gwenda asked if she was saving up for something nice.

'Now, Katie,' she said, when they were back in the kitchen. 'The girls were sayin' that you was watching them schooling the ponies today and –'

'I wasn't! I was only goin' for the eggs and –'

'It's all right, love. I wasn't accusing you of anything,' promised Gwenda, wishing the poor child would stop being so defensive. 'They just wondered if you'd like to have a go?'

The girl looked startled. 'No... It's all right. I don't know how to. Those horses are so big and fast, I could never –'

'But, Katie, Skipper is after buying a really lovely grey-dappled mare called Polly,' explained Annamaria encouragingly, 'and she's really sweet. She would never throw you off at all. Now the one you were watching me on earlier, he's got a temper on him, but Polly's gentle, and we'd look after you.'

Gwenda smiled at how West Cork had crept into her girls' Australian accents. 'Yes, why don't you have a go tomorrow, Katie?'

she said. 'It might be fun, and the girls and Skipper would be there, so you'd be quite safe.'

Katie shook her head vehemently. 'I've the housework to do, and tomorrow I've to change all the beds.'

Gwenda sighed, placed her hands on the child's still bony shoulders and looked into her eyes. 'OK, you need to understand somethin' about this family.'

Katie's eyes widened but she held still, trembling.

'You don't work for us, OK, darling? Me and Ted here are your parents – well, I know I'm not your real mum, but I will try my best to be like a mother to you for as long as you need me to be – and Sophie and Annamaria here want to be like they're your sisters. And while I sure do appreciate all the cleanin' and cookin' and whatnot, and I don't mind any of my girls doing a few household chores, you've been doing too much, my love. You're a kid, and it's my job to make sure you have fun like a kid.'

'But I have to earn my keep...' Katie began, tears forming. Gwenda could see by her trepidation that having fun, being a child instead of spending every day slaving, was something foreign to her.

'That's what I'm tryin' to tell you – you don't. You're our daughter, for now anyway, and we don't need a housekeeper.'

'Well, that's debatable,' Ted remarked with his usual dry humour, and the girls giggled and rolled their eyes at Katie, who smiled weakly.

'Please come with us down to the river field tomorrow,' urged Sophie. 'We're planning an easy afternoon, a sort of gymkhana thing, poles on the ground, nothing scary like a hunt with big ditches to jump. Sarah is coming over too. so we're going to set up the field in the morning. Bill brought the poles down for us a few weeks ago.'

'It'll be a good way to meet people if you're not going to school,' Annamaria added encouragingly. The O'Sullivans had enrolled Maggie in Kilteegan Bridge national school, but Katie was still being home-schooled by Ted because she was so ashamed of not being able to write properly. Her letters had been improving slowly, but it was still a struggle.

'No, but...' Katie looked scared again. 'They might not like me, a girl like me. I talk different and everythin'...'

Sophie pealed with laughter. 'What about girls like us with our mad accents, half Australian and half Cork? We were worried at first too, but people think we're exotic and exciting, little do they know. We didn't know anyone when we got here first except our cousins, but loads of other young people here have horses and ponies, and we all meet up, all ages mix together here, and it's a good way to get to know people.' Sophie's infectious good humour made Katie smile slightly again.

'So what do you reckon, Katie?' Ted asked from where he was sitting in his armchair by the clay stove. 'You can't be the only one on this ranch that can't ride a horse.'

'What if I fall off in front of everybody?' she asked doubtfully.

'Then you get up, brush yourself down and get back on again straight away before you lose your nerve,' said Sophie. 'But I promise you, you won't fall off. You'll just have great fun.'

'But I only have my dress...' Though Gwenda had bought her clean undergarments, she was still wearing the same awful dress from the orphanage. And though Sophie, who was more her size, had begged her to help herself to anything in her wardrobe and Gwenda had tried to bring her shopping to Maureen's Fashions, Katie had kept on refusing, saying she was worried she might spoil something nice.

'Don't worry. I've a pair of jodhpurs that'll fit you, and an old riding jacket too, and there are boots and hats outside in the stables.' Sophie had a thought. 'Actually, will we go out now and see if we can find you a hat to fit? I know it's dark, but we can bring the old tilly lamp.'

'I...I don't –'

'Oh, come on. I've got some mints for Al. He loves them, and I swear he tries to buck me off less if I give him sweets.' Annamaria laughed, and at last Katie relented and agreed to put on an old jumper of Sophie's that was on the sofa. The three girls left, and though Katie was dubious, she went willingly.

'That was kind of our girls,' said Ted, getting to his feet and putting the kettle on.

'It was,' agreed Gwenda, 'but they love her, and Maggie as well. Sophie said to me they were already feeling sad about when the mother comes to take them back after she gets out, which she will soon enough. And I'll be delighted for her, of course, but to be honest, I reckon I'll be a bit sad as well.'

Ted put his arms around her, kissed her worn weather-beaten cheek and murmured in her ear, 'Me too, my love. They've really crept into my heart.'

CHAPTER 21

The flight from New York to Shannon was long but luxurious. Malachy had finally given in to Emmet's insistence on an Irish Christmas for them all and had booked the four of them into first class. Emmet and Wei passed the hours ordering all sorts of luxury foodstuffs, while Malachy and Rosa sipped champagne and read the free newspapers.

'You're very quiet,' Rosa remarked at one point.

'I'm fine,' he replied.

'Fine.' She turned to look at him, her perfectly shaped eyebrow arched. 'That's five times since JFK you've told me you're fine.'

'And yet you keep asking me.' Malachy sighed, shaking his newspaper pointedly.

For the rest of the flight, she didn't ask him anything at all, only chatting away to Emmet and Wei on the plane and then on the long drive down from Shannon Airport in County Clare to Cork City. There Malachy told Emmet to take the hired car and carry on to Kilteegan Bridge while he and Rosa stayed behind.

It had been one of Malachy's stipulations when he'd finally agreed to this trip, that at the beginning and end of it, he and Rosa would spend several days by themselves in the Imperial Hotel in Cork and only arrive at Kilteegan House on Christmas Eve and leave on St Stephens Day.

Emmet and Wei dropped them off, and as Malachy and Rosa walked in silence to the historic Imperial Hotel, he was sure she was annoyed at him for making her stay in Cork while Emmet went west; it was probably making her even more suspicious of his feelings about Lena. But hopefully Cork City, with its twinkling Christmas lights and old-world Irish charm, would win her over, and he did notice her looking around with interest.

At the Imperial, they checked into their suite on the top floor that exuded luxury, from the heavy damask curtains in ivory to the huge bed with its lace coverlet. His feet sank into a deep pile carpet, making no sound as he took off his jacket and went to hang it in the large Victorian wardrobe. Rosa sat on the bed and eased off her high-heeled shoes, rubbing her tired feet. Why women did that to themselves, he never could understand.

'I told you they were going to hurt.' He smiled at her, breaking the silence, trying to take some of the tension out of the room.

'You did tell me,' she said, but each word was loaded.

'Would you like a drink? Something to eat? We could get room service since it's so late.'

'No, I'm going to take a bath and go to sleep.' She stalked past him, smaller now that she was out of those vertiginous shoes.

As she passed, he grabbed her hand, pulling her back to him. He kissed her but she didn't respond.

'You're cross with me,' he stated unnecessarily.

'How astute.' She shook her hand away and swept into the bathroom with its large marble claw-footed bath. The key turned in the lock. He was definitely not welcome.

This trip was a terrible mistake, he realised glumly as he sat slumped on the end of the bed, rubbing his eyes with exhaustion. His day had begun with the flight from San Francisco to New York, where Rosa had joined them. She'd wanted to come to Ireland, and she'd taken Emmet's side – that's part of why he'd agreed to this. But now he knew he should have come alone if at all. The idea of introducing Rosa to Lena as his girlfriend just felt so wrong.

Emmet had once asked him if he was still in love with Lena. At the time, Malachy had brushed the question aside. 'It's all irrelevant now anyway, has been for years.' And he'd meant it. It was something he didn't even allow himself to think about, because it was like wishing for different-coloured eyes or to be a naturally brilliant pianist. It was an impossible dream.

But after Eli died, something had gradually changed inside him.

He couldn't help it, and he would never give Lena or anyone else the slightest indication that he felt anything for her apart from the respect and admiration due to her as his son's mother, but the fact that she was now free to have another relationship, if she ever wanted one, was something that played on his mind far more than he was ever likely to admit, even to himself. His feelings were certainly too hard and complicated to explain to Rosa, and she'd probably finish with him if she knew how often Lena still came into his mind these days, even after all the therapy.

Of course he knew he was being ridiculous. Rosa was perfect for him. She was beautiful, brilliant, kind, and she understood his world, she inhabited it. While they had stayed in America, it worked, but somehow crossing the Atlantic had made it all feel to him like the wheels were coming off.

He undressed and got into bed, his chest bare. She was a sensuous woman and made no bones about her sexual appetites, and she seemed to find him very attractive, as he did her, so maybe he could make love with her when she came out and they'd be back on track. He wished he was better at this sort of thing. He'd avoided close entanglements for years; once things looked like they were getting serious, he usually bailed. But Rosa was different. She was all he needed.

Maybe he should propose, he thought.

Lena could never be his. Emmet had often said how his mother would never marry again. So why wait? Maybe he and Rosa would find what Lena and Eli had, true love; they might even have children.

For the first time with a woman, he found the idea appealing rather than terrifying. Rosa seemed very fond of her nieces and nephews, so maybe they could have a child or two of their own. And he could probably convince her to move to San Francisco, or even move to New York himself...

He must have drifted off because he woke to her standing by her side of the bed looking at him, unsmiling.

'Nice bath?' he murmured sleepily.

'Yes.' She sat down on the edge of the bed, her slight weight depressing her side of the mattress, and he noticed she was dressed in dark-green satin pyjamas. She hardly ever wore night clothes at all, preferring to sleep naked.

He tried to sit up. 'I'm sorry, Rosa,' he said sadly. He hated her being cold like this.

She turned to him, her dark eyes glittering dangerously. 'What for?'

'For upsetting you. I know I –'

'No.' She cut across him, her voice like a whip, and not for the first time, he felt like a particularly implausible witness in the dock she was making mincemeat of. 'Why specifically are you sorry?'

'Like I said, for making you so upset...' He was foundering and he knew it.

'You haven't a clue.' She climbed into bed and turned away from him.

'So tell me.' He moved closer and leant over her. 'Tell me what I've done.'

He reached over and stroked her cheek, and to his surprise, it was wet. Rosa wasn't a crier; in fact he'd never seen her cry before.

'Ah, Rosa, darling, please.'

'You love her still,' she said belligerently, without turning back to him. 'You always will, and you're just using me. It's my own fault. I knew it all along on some level, but I thought things might change. I was wrong. I'll fly back to the States tomorrow.'

'Rosa, no, please. Please don't. I want you here, I...I...care about you...'

'You can't say it, can you?'

'Say what? That I love you? Of course I can. I do all the time. Rosa, I love you. Not anyone else – I love *you*.' He felt the panic rise up in him now. He couldn't lose the only woman who had ever come close to Lena in his heart. Anyway, what he and Lena had together was just being built up in his mind because he was a kid at the time, like the way adults remembered buildings as bigger when they were young.

'I don't believe you.' She rolled onto her back and gazed at him. Her dark hair was damp and her face clean of make-up, and she looked so young and vulnerable.

His heart lurched. 'Marry me,' he heard himself say.

'What?'

'Will you marry me? I do love you. I'm just a bit hopeless with all of this stuff, but I promise you, Rosa, I do love you, and if you'd marry me…well, we could be really happy, I think.'

She raised herself on one elbow, staring at him. 'Are you serious about this?'

'I am. I love you. I really love you.'

'And you swear to me you won't spend our life together yearning for her?'

He didn't bother to pretend he didn't know who she was talking about. 'I swear I won't.'

He reached for her then and kissed her, and the passion with which she responded to him took him by surprise. They made love furiously and passionately, and afterwards, as they lay sweating and panting beside each other, she finally spoke.

'All right, I'll marry you.'

He wrapped her in his arms and kissed her head gently, and within seconds she was asleep, her dark hair fanned out on his chest, her even breathing the only sound in the room.

And he lay there, wide awake, until the winter dawn crept across the Irish December sky. *Jet lag*, he told himself. *It's just the jet lag.* And he finally drifted off.

CHAPTER 22

*I*t was cold and dark and the roads so icy, Emmet had to concentrate on driving, and Wei, uncharacteristically subdued, just stared out the window into the dark night and barely said a word all the way down.

It was almost nine o'clock by the time they got there. As they turned up the driveway, he could see the twinkling lights of the Christmas tree in the library window, and it made him feel so glad to be home. He loved life in America, but nowhere was like Kilteegan Bridge. He just hoped Wei would love it as much as he did.

'This is the first time you've been home since your dad's funeral.' Wei spoke for the first time in over an hour.

Emmet was of course acutely aware of that fact but hadn't wanted to add to the sense of doom his fiancée clearly felt. 'Yes, and it's hard. I still expect to see him here.'

'It's like a club,' she said, almost to herself. 'You don't know about it until you're in it. The dead parent club. It's too hard to explain to anyone who doesn't have first-hand experience, and if they do, then there's no need to explain.'

'I suppose so,' he agreed. He was used to her sparse way of talking but wondered what his family would make of her.

'They're not going to want me intruding on this,' she said.

Emmet made a decision and pulled the car into the gate of the orchard, halfway up the avenue.

'What is it?' Wei turned to face him.

Emmet took her hand and, with his other hand, stroked her cheek. 'Wei, listen to me.'

'Emmet, I know you're going to say it will all be fine but –'

'Shh.' He gently placed a finger to her lips. 'Listen to me. Firstly, my family are nothing like your father, or Malachy and Rosa for that matter. They'll be a bit of a shock. They're loud and funny and argumentative and teasing, and they love me. And I love you. So even if they didn't like you, which they will, by the way, they would love you for me.'

Her almost-black eyes were still wary.

'Secondly, you and I are going to be married one day, regardless of what anyone thinks, so while it will be lovely for you to meet them all and for them to get to know you, in the end of it all, we'll go back to California and be just us, Emmet and Wei. So I don't want you thinking anything anyone here could say would make me change my mind about you.'

Her red lips twitched. 'But won't they want you to marry an Irish Catholic girl with child-bearing hips and a gold cross around her neck?'

Emmet laughed. 'Wei, as you know, my dad was a German Jew raised in Wales, my Uncle Jack lives with a cowboy called Skipper from Montana – make of that what you will – my granny is married to a former German soldier, and her brother, my Granduncle Ted, was a British spy during the war and is married to an Australian sheep farmer called Gwenda who would knock you into next week as easy as look at you. So if you're looking to be the exotic one in the family, you'll have to get in line.'

Wei started laughing. 'Well, OK. I suppose when you say it all together like that...'

'As for Blackie's father and brother, well, the less said about them, the better.' Emmet grinned and turned the key once more. 'And I'm pretty sure Auntie Emily would rather Nellie marry anyone at all than go to be a nun. So all in all, a smart, beautiful girl like you will be seen as a nice, sane, sensible addition to the family.'

'OK, that makes me feel better,' she said, with her first genuine smile since leaving Malachy and Rosa in Cork.

As he drew up next to his dad's pale-blue Rover, Eli's pride and joy, the big door at the top of the steps was flung open and his whole family erupted out to greet them. Wei was barely out of the car when his mother welcomed her with a huge hug and exclamations about how beautiful she was, and how Emmet had told her so much about her, and to please not call her 'Mrs Kogan' but instead to call her Lena. And Nellie and Blackie came crowding around her as well, and because Nellie and Wei already loved each other and Blackie was still so grateful to her for rescuing his daughter from the cult, it really broke the ice, and Emmet could see his fiancée's fears being allayed within minutes.

He himself was smothered in hugs from Sarah and Pádraig before his mother and Auntie Em, who had Aidan on her hip, could get at him, and then Blackie hugged him and Nellie, with her arm still around Wei, welcomed him home.

'Jack and Skipper are up with the cattle, but they'll be down tomorrow, and Peggy as well, and Ted and Gwenda, but we didn't want to overwhelm poor Wei at the start,' said Lena, leading them into the library, where the fire was burning merrily in the grate, the aroma of mulled wine permeated the air and the comfortable chairs and two sofas were grouped around a low table laden with Christmas cake and tangerines and mince pies.

'Mam wouldn't let me make a sandwich earlier in case I left a mess in the kitchen and Wei walked out in disgust at the state of the place, so I'm starving,' Pádraig complained, cramming one of the pies into his mouth, spitting crumbs everywhere.

'And she put a note on the towels in the downstairs bathroom saying, "Use these and I'll cut your hands off,"' Sarah added as Lena swiped at them both.

'Lies, Wei, total lies. Our house is always spotless, and my children wouldn't dream of using freshly washed white towels to wipe mucky legs after football and riding.' She laughed as she put cake and a mince pie on a plate for Wei and handed it to her, while everyone else helped themselves.

In the bay window, the huge green Christmas tree twinkled with starry lights. It was loaded with china baubles and red ribbons, and there were piles of boxed and wrapped presents beneath it. Emmet couldn't stop smiling. He was so happy to be here and even happier to see his mam laugh. The last time he'd seen her, after his father's funeral, she'd felt so far from him and all of them, he'd thought she might never again come back.

Sarah had made a beeline for Wei, who had gone to admire the tree, and by the time Emmet joined them, she was already deep in explanation about the pony she'd borrowed from a girl called Lucy Beaumont for Wei to ride since Emmet would need his mare back and she had only one other spare.

'I've never sat on a horse in my life,' Wei said, with a panicked look at Emmet.

'Ah, don't worry about that. Flash is half dead – he'll mind you,' Sarah said breezily. 'Sure our foster cousin up at Ted and Gwenda's has only been riding a short while, but she can put her pony Polly over a small jump already, so I'll give you a few lessons before St Stephen's Day and you'll be good to go.'

'St Stephen's Day?'

'It's the day after Christmas Day.' Emmet smiled, his arm around Sarah's shoulders, while Nellie, who was busy ladling out the mulled wine into glasses, handed him and Wei two steaming aromatic drinks. 'And I might have forgotten to mention you'll need to hunt on St Stephen's Day.'

'Hunt? Hunt what?' Wei looked even more stricken.

'Don't mind him, Wei. They can go off chasing over the country-side. We'll stay here by the fire. It's a mad pastime, but my children are addicted to it.' Lena looked over at them and admonished Emmet. 'You shouldn't sneak things up on the poor girl like that.'

Pádraig had sidled up to where they were standing and stood, staring at Wei.

'Pádraig, shut your mouth and stop gawking,' snapped his older sister.

'But I never met a Chinese person before,' he said through a mouthful of cake.

'Pádraig!' exclaimed Sarah.

'What?' he asked, colouring.

'You shouldn't call Wei Chinese! She's from Singapore. Wei, I'm so sorry, he didn't mean...' Sarah was puce.

Wei broke out laughing. 'It's all right. I actually am half Chinese. My father is Chinese, my mother was Malaysian, but I was born in Singapore, so I'm a bit of a mongrel.' She spoke easily and without any of her signature prickliness. She seemed delighted with everything, and Emmet breathed again and wandered off to get another mince pie.

'So, Emmet, you're giving us a day out, we hear?' Blackie asked, refusing mulled wine and accepting a bottle of stout. It was the first mention of the engagement, and Emmet glanced at his mother, but she just smiled and nodded.

'Well, not for a while yet,' he said. 'We have to finish college and everything, but yes. And don't worry, you'll all be invited, but you might have to come to California for it, because my bride isn't a fan of the rain.'

'Oh, I know what you mean then, I'm not much of a fan of the rain myself, Wei. I got nearly drowned today loading stuff into the shop,' Blackie called over to Wei, and she beamed and came over to them, sipping her mulled wine.

'I like how green everything is, though, Mr Crean,' she said warmly, 'and you can't have that without rain. California is very dry, and I miss the lushness of Singapore, so Ireland is more like home.'

'Ah, do you hear that, Lena? We've her converted in one night.' Blackie winked and everyone laughed. 'And call me Blackie. Everyone else does.'

'Is that the name your parents gave you?' Wei asked in that direct way she had.

'Ara no, but I was always black with the dirt when I was a small fella, we sold coal and I was a divil for playing in it, so everyone called me Blackie.'

'So what's your real name?' she asked with a smile.

'Aidan, I was christened Aidan but even my Mam calls me Blackie now.'

'And now your son has your name, so it's not lost.'

'That's right.' Blackie beamed, 'He's a much cleaner individual than me, and smart like his Mammy so he won't be hauling coal his whole life that's for sure.'

'Can I see the ring?' Sarah asked, following Wei over.

Wei smiled and took off the solitaire diamond Emmet had bought for her and handed it to his sister.

'Oh, Mam, look, isn't it beautiful?' Sarah showed it to Lena and Emily, who admired it, and both of them, Emmet noticed in amusement, twisted it three times round their own fingers for luck.

Everything was going to be fine.

CHAPTER 23

*T*wo days later, Christmas Eve dawned cloudy, and to everyone's delighted astonishment, by mid-morning the ground was covered in a carpet of white snow.

Lena was in the kitchen whipping up brandy butter in a blue china bowl, while Maria was making another tray of mince pies; Klaus, who had turned up that morning, was baking two German Christmas fruit cakes called stollen, and Emily was sticking hundreds of cloves into an enormous ham that she had boiled in a huge copper pot on the range. The ham would be glazed in sugar, and the caramelised fat on the meat, flavoured with cloves, would have everyone going for seconds. The festivities in Kilteegan House would start that evening, when everyone would tuck into a feast of hot ham sandwiches with mustard, followed by a slice of toasted stollen, and open one present each, which was always a pair of cosy Christmas pyjamas.

Ted and Gwenda weren't coming until tomorrow, but they had been down to the house yesterday with their four girls to see Emmet and Wei. Annamaria had given Wei a riding lesson, while Katie, who was a sturdy horsewoman already, kept telling Wei it was really easy… 'If you keep your back straight and your heels down and your elbows by your sides, though if you want, you can stand up to canter – it stops you getting bumped around, though you have to sit and stand as well with the trot, and be sure to be on the right diagonal or you'll get bounced off.'

It was all very confusing to Wei, but at least Flash didn't much like to trot or canter. She was twenty-three years old and only interested in stopping to eat grass.

Jack and Skipper had popped down for the afternoon to see how it was all progressing and were now annoying the cooks by milling around the kitchen with Emmet, Wei, Nellie, Sarah and Pádraig, grabbing for hot mince pies that scorched their mouths and begging slices of stollen and wanting to scrape out the icing and brandy butter bowls, until Lena banned them all as the place was getting dangerously overcrowded. Aidan was playing in the corner, in a playpen filled with dinky cars and blocks, and if they didn't look out, something would get dropped on him.

After some grumbling, the gathering realised the snow was deep enough now, and everyone ran outside to the front of the house. A raucous and violent snowball fight got underway, until Pádraig yelled, 'Hey, look, here comes Santa!'

It was Mike O'Halloran, wearing a red velvet dressing gown and a huge white beard made of cotton wool stuck on crookedly with surgical tape. He drove slowly up the lane in his electric wheelchair, which was wrapped around in tinsel, while Ollie the old pony walked beside him with a pair of reindeer's antlers stuck on his head. Bringing up the rear of the procession was Anthea, a red bag of presents for under the tree slung over her shoulder and a huge grin on her face.

'Happy Christmas, everyone!' yelled Mike through the falling snow.

Still fired up, Pádraig decided to lob a big snowball right down the collar of Santa's dressing gown. 'That was for the tetanus injection last month,' he yelled, taking cover behind Emmet's rented car. Ollie looked bored and went off to see if he could nuzzle his way through the snow to some grass.

'Don't worry, Mike, I'll avenge you,' Anthea roared, dropping the bag and pitching a perfect snowball, getting Pádraig on the side of the head.

Lena rushed out of the house to rescue Mike and Anthea from the assault, but she wasn't needed; the two of them pelted Pádraig in a two-pronged attack, harvesting huge snowballs off the back of Eli's car.

Nellie and Sarah joined forces with Pádraig and gave return fire, while Jack and Skipper lined up behind Mike, but to everyone's hilarity, Emmet shimmied up a tree and agitated the branch, heavy with snow, over Skipper's head, dumping an enormous amount of cold, wet snow on his cowboy hat and knocking it off altogether.

'Oh, you picked the wrong enemy now...' Skipper bore down on Emmet, his hat scooped full of snow. 'Come here, pretty boy...' He grabbed Emmet in a headlock and plonked the snow-filled hat on his head, soaking his hair. Emmet howled and pulled it off, ducking down behind the tiny Wei, fearing another attack.

'I'd think twice about this guy if I was you, Wei. He ain't nothin' but a yellow belly, hidin' behind a girl.' Skipper grinned as Emmet lobbed another feeble snowball at him, which the cowboy batted away with his hat.

'Don't let him hurt me, Wei,' Emmet squeaked theatrically as Skipper bore down on him again.

Without warning, Wei grasped Skipper and in a split second had the cowboy on his back in the snow. Emmet howled with laughter at Skipper's stricken face. Jack rushed to pull him to his feet, nearly crying with laughter himself.

'How in the name of...' Skipper said in stunned amazement as Jack dusted the snow off his broad back. 'How come a little girl like you can do that?'

'I'm Asian. Have you never seen a Bruce Lee movie? We're all able to do that,' Wei replied with a wide grin.

Emmet was astounded at how relaxed Wei was around his huge family. All his fears had been unfounded, and she was fitting in perfectly.

Only that morning, the two of them had gone for a long walk with

Nellie, hearing all about her plans for the future. Incredibly, his wild, funny, cheeky cousin was determined to be a nun, and she was so excited about it.

Despite his supportive letter to her, Emmet had had private doubts about whether Nellie was doing the right thing. But seeing the light shine out from her when she spoke about life in the convent, her work at the nursing home, the sense of peace and joy the whole experience was giving her, it removed any misgivings.

She'd spoken at length about her faith, something Emmet had never experienced before. Irish Catholicism was strange that way; he'd realised that when he went to America. People there seemed to be more vocal about their religion. A friend in his class, a Baptist from Georgia, had even asked him if he had a personal relationship with Jesus. Emmet had been so embarrassed, he'd nearly died, and just mumbled that he was a Catholic, as if that was an answer.

Irish Catholicism seemed on one hand to permeate every aspect of life in this country, like Nellie's Nana Peggy was always saying she would pray to saint this or that depending on the issue she needed help with, and people peppered their speech with 'God love you' or 'May God be good to him'. But as he'd explained to Wei, it was more an automatic way of talking. Nobody ever discussed their actual deep-down faith.

So it was a surprise to him when on their long walk, Nellie started talking about how she felt God was calling her to this life, how giving up men was no hardship whatsoever and she had no desire to be a mother and was sure she never would. She'd looked at them as she said it, knowing they both knew about Aidan.

'You've convinced me anyway, Nellie,' Wei had said sincerely.

'And me.' Emmet had given his cousin a hug.

The snowball fight was ended by Maria appearing outside with a tray of mugs full of hot cocoa to warm everyone's freezing hands, and as the adults dispersed into the house, Nellie, sipping happily at her warm sweet chocolate, joined Emmet and Wei on the steps, where they lingered for a moment to admire the beautiful snowy view, all the trees and bushes looking like white crocheted tea cosies.

'So when's the date set for?' she asked as a stray snowflake melted in her drink.

'We are in negotiations,' Emmet said with a grin. He and Wei had been joking that they made a hoo-ha about getting engaged but had yet to set a date because it was going to be so long away.

'Not getting cold feet, are you?' Wei teased him.

'My feet are absolutely bloody freezing, but that has no impact whatsoever on my wanting to marry you, Wei Tan.' He took her empty mug and with a wink handed it, along with his own mug, to Nellie. He swept Wei up in his arms and kissed her to the whoops and laughter of Sarah and Pádraig. Emmet had never in his entire life felt so happy. He could feel his dad's hand on his shoulder, his voice in his ear, encouraging and joyous for him.

It was strange. Now that he was home, he recalled the years when he felt like he didn't quite fit in; maybe all teenagers felt like that. But now among his people, with Wei by his side and Malachy and Rosa on their way here too, there was nowhere he would rather be.

'Could we do it here when it happens? In Ireland, I mean?'

'You want to get married in Ireland?' Emmet kept his arms around her, gazing down into her face, as Nellie ushered her two giddy young cousins away to give the young lovers some peace.

Wei nodded. 'I never even thought about Ireland before I met you, to be honest, but I like it here. It's like Singapore, so green and damp, though much cooler, in every sense of the word.' She gave a wry smile. 'But I think this place must be beautiful in the spring, a different beautiful to now.'

'It is. And you know, I had to leave to really see it,' he said in amazement. 'There are snowdrops carpeting our lawns in January and gold and purple crocuses in February and daffodils in March, bluebells in April. So any time in spring here is gorgeous.'

'And it's not like I'll have any big family to bring to the party, and yours are so nice and welcoming. I'd love my dad to meet them all, and Liang as well...' She stopped, and he recognised that face. Wei didn't do embarrassment as such, but when she felt insecure, she closed down.

'I'd love that, I really would,' Emmet said quietly. 'Let's do it the spring of the year after we've finished college.'

'Really?' She softened again.

'Why not?' He tucked her hand in his coat pocket, and they set off down the steps, then strolled towards the stables. 'If you want to marry here, my lovely Wei, then that's what we'll do. I don't know how it will work, me marrying a non-Catholic, but I don't care about the church part. I'm happy to get married in a registry office and scandalise the parish.'

'I would convert, if it mattered to you,' she offered sincerely, and he felt such a rush of love for his unusual, brave, sometimes spiky girl.

'It doesn't matter at all. I was baptised into the Catholic religion by Mam, but Malachy is half Protestant and Eli was a Jew, so I'm not exactly in a position to be bothered about who is what. But thank you for offering. Were you raised very religious?'

There was such a lot he didn't know about her. Their lives in California were so fast-paced, so immediate, that the past hadn't seemed to matter at all until that business with her father, when it all came crashing.

'Well, I'm a Buddhist like my father, as you know, but it's not really a religion, more a way of life. My mother was Muslim, but her family disowned her when she married my father, and he didn't like her to practise her faith.'

'She must have been very much in love with him?' Emmet found it hard to imagine the dour Ken Tan eliciting enough passion in anyone to make them abandon both family and religion.

Wei nodded. 'My grandma told me when I was little how he was a police officer on the border between Singapore and Malaysia. My uncles were members of the MNLA, it seems, Malaysian Freedom Fighters, fighting for an independent Malaysia free of the British. The British had arrested her brothers after an attack on a police station outside KL, so she had to go on the run. My mother met my father when fleeing from Johor.' She smiled at his confused face. 'Kuala Lumpur, the capital of Malaysia?'

'Oh right.' Emmet was intrigued. Wei had barely mentioned her maternal family before, maybe because talking about her mother at all was so difficult for her. It was wonderful that she trusted him enough now to open up.

'And so with my father's help, she took her parents across the border to Singapore, which was British controlled as well but not so severely. They were known to be the family of what the British deemed as terrorists, but my father offered them protection and help, and she and he fell in love. Despite him being their saviour, my grandparents refused to accept the marriage.'

'Because he was a Buddhist?' Emmet asked as they entered the stables. He could hear Second Chance, his horse, whickering at the sound of his voice; the bay mare remembered him, and he'd been glad to see how well she looked under Sarah's diligent care. Now he took four apples from the windfall box. They were wrapped in newspaper, but they'd been bruised when they fell and several were going brown and spotted and out of shape – but the horses didn't care about that.

'More because they hated the British, and they saw him as loyal to them. The British don't like to broadcast it, but they used concentration camps in Malaysia, you know?'

'I didn't,' Emmet said seriously, feeding one apple to Second Chance, who crunched it noisily. He then moved along the stalls, giving the others to Sarah's Molly and Pádraig's old Shetland pony, Ollie, who had found his own way back to his stall, and Flash, the semi-retired horse that Sarah had borrowed for Wei from the Lambkins. 'Tell me about it?'

Wei stroked Flash on the neck, and he nuzzled into her, happy in her company. 'Yes, there was a governor sent over from England, Briggs was his name, and he realised that the independence fighters in the jungles were winning – they were better at jungle warfare than the British and they had the support of the people. So he came up with the idea of "new villages", and he herded half a million Malays into compounds, surrounded with barbed wire and police posts. The whole place was floodlit, so they couldn't offer or receive help from the fighters. It's hard to believe, I know, but they did it. Malaysia was too valuable to them economically to lose.'

'You don't need to convince anyone in this country about the brutality of the British occupation. We had eight hundred years of it.'

'Maybe our cultures have more in common than we first thought.' She smiled as she rubbed Flash's nose.

'I guess they do,' he agreed. 'And what happened to your mother then?'

'Well, as you know, she married my father anyway, and they moved away from her parents, and they never spoke again. And it made her very unhappy. I think that's what went wrong between her and my father, why she ran away with another man. He was a Muslim as well, so maybe she felt that would fix things with her parents. But then the new man's parents made him reject her for being married already, and she committed suicide.'

'Religion has a lot to answer for.' Emmet sighed.

'Yup,' she agreed. 'That's why I don't bother with it.'

There was a blast on a car horn from around the front of the house. Malachy and Rosa had arrived.

CHAPTER 24

$\mathcal{T}$he Christmas Eve feast of hot ham sandwiches with mustard was a raucous affair in the library. Everyone tore open their parcel of Christmas pyjamas and declared them the nicest, cosiest ones ever. Afterwards, the men insisted that all the ladies retire to the inner sitting room with a cup of tea while they washed up and prepared the table in the dining room for tomorrow, with candles and serviettes and decorations of holly.

'Don't worry, Lena. We've had some lovely new dinner services arrive in the shop, so we'll be able to replace everything they break,' Emily joked as the men headed for the kitchen, Klaus pinching a bottle of brandy off the sideboard to take with them.

'I think I'll head up to bed,' said Rosa, clearly feeling like the odd one out among the women, but Wei took her by the arm and led her after the others towards the sitting room.

'Come and talk to the real movers and shakers,' she advised Rosa. 'The women in Ireland rule the roost, so Emmet tells me.'

Rosa smiled gratefully and followed her in.

In the library, Lena and Maria were already settled on the sofa and Emily had collapsed in the armchair on one side of the glowing fire. The logs crackled, and the aroma of pine needles from the enormous real Christmas tree and cinnamon from the biscuits just out of the oven was wonderful.

Anthea had gone with Mike to spend the rest of Christmas Eve – but before he left, he mentioned to Lena that Jane Kearney would take her up on her offer of joining them for Christmas dinner – so with all the men in the kitchen, it was just the five women.

Wei got Rosa to sit in the armchair on the other side of the fire from Emily, and then sat cross-legged on the lovely silk carpet at her feet. Sarah and Nellie had tried to coax her upstairs to play Christmas records on Eli's beloved stereo, which had somehow become a perma-nent fixture in Sarah's bedroom, but she obviously didn't like to leave Rosa alone when she was looking so tense.

'So, Wei,' said Maria, beaming at the latest newcomer to her family. 'Emmet tells me we'll have a day to look forward to, and it's going to be here in Ireland?'

Wei blushed. 'Well, yes, we hope so. We need to sort out all the legalities and stuff like that, but I'd like to do it here and I know Emmet would too.'

Lena watched the girl's eyes light up as she said Emmet's name, and she prayed that Wei and her son could make their marriage work, despite their youth.

She leant back on the sofa and went inside herself for a moment. *Is this the right thing for Emmet, Eli?* she asked. She never told anyone in her family she could hear Eli so loudly and clearly in her head – she was still a bit shaken up by realising everyone had thought she was going mad earlier in the year – but she loved that when she asked him a question, he almost always answered her.

She's a beautiful pilipala, *inside and out. She's right for our boy*, she heard him reply now, and she smiled. They'd so often sat on this sofa together, chatting like this.

'What's that about?' her mother asked, leaning closer to her.

'What was what about?' Lena asked, startled.

'You had a beam on your face. I wondered what put it there,' Maria said quietly.

Lena didn't answer right away; she didn't want to discuss it in front of everyone. But Wei was busy telling Rosa about the St Stephen's Day hunt, while Emily, exhausted from having a baby to mind, rested with her eyes closed. Aidan was sleeping peacefully in his pram in the library, worn out from all the people and fun, so she was taking her rest while she could.

Lena decided to tell her mother the truth but kept her voice very, very low. 'I was asking Eli's advice, if Emmet and Wei were doing the right thing.'

She hoped Maria would understand. She and her mother had grown much closer this past year. Maria was very stable on her medication, and she knew the pain of the loss of an adored husband taken too soon. They had recalibrated their relationship and were more like equals now, and Lena confided in her in a way she had never done all her life.

'And what did he say?' whispered Maria, not batting an eyelid.

'He said she was a beautiful *pilipala*, inside and out.'

'*Pilipala*? What...'

'It's Welsh for butterfly. Eli loved butterflies and even asked Vera Slattery to recommend some plants for the garden that attracted them. He used to call Sarah his *pilipala*, the way she was always going from one thing to the next.' Lena smiled at the memory, and though a pang of loneliness washed over her, she found to her surprise that she didn't want to cry.

'I can see that she's like a butterfly,' Maria murmured, watching Wei across the room as she chatted away to Rosa, trying to put her at her ease. 'She's resilient but fragile. But she loves him, and I know they're young, but love is all that matters in the end, Lena.'

'Rosa, you will surely be here for Emmet's wedding, won't you?' Emily asked, opening her eyes suddenly and smiling at the American woman. 'I mean, with Malachy?'

Rosa looked thoughtfully at Emily, and then for some reason, her dark eyes strayed over to Lena. The New York lawyer had been much more reserved on this trip than Lena remembered her being before, and there was an odd coolness between her and Malachy from the moment they'd arrived. Maybe they weren't as much of an item as

Emmet had said. A strange light-headed emotion washed over Lena. A sense of relief? No, it couldn't be. She crushed the feeling down hard, whatever it was.

'You should, Rosa. We'd love you to come,' she said a bit too loudly. And then more softly, 'And it's not just about you being with Malachy. You're Eli's cousin, so you're family. You should be here in your own right.'

Rosa smiled faintly, still assessing her with those dark, intense eyes, until Lena felt she was being pinned to the sofa. 'You mean, if Malachy and I break up in the meantime?' she asked calmly.

'No, goodness, I didn't mean...' She was horrified Rosa might think she'd be glad if that happened.

'No, don't apologise. I don't blame you for not knowing. He obviously hasn't told you.' She paused, seemed to make up her mind about something, then said, 'You see, Malachy and I are getting married as well.'

'Oh goodness,' gasped Wei, as Emily and Maria burst out with words of congratulations.

'It was quite a surprise. I've never been exactly keen on marriage as a concept, to be honest, but when he proposed, I found I liked the idea, so I gave in.' Rosa was smiling now, but her gaze was still locked on Lena's face; she was clearly watching for her reaction.

Lena hadn't moved or spoken. Her heart was pattering fast. It was all so unexpected, so many changes, everyone finding new love, while her own world seemed to have stopped when Eli died. But then she made an effort to pull herself together.

'Congratulations,' she said warmly, and stood up to hug the American woman. 'I'm delighted for you.' And she was, she really was. Rosa was beautiful, clever. She was family, Eli's cousin. She was a perfect match for Malachy, and Emmet loved her already.

'Delighted for Rosa with what?' asked Malachy behind her; he must have only just come into the library. 'Has she finally agreed to learn to ride a horse?'

Lena turned to face him, her dark-brown eyes meeting his green ones, a big smile on her face. 'No, she's telling us about your plans to tie the knot, and we're all very happy for you. It's high time you settled down.'

He looked startled and glanced at Rosa. 'Oh...'

'I'm sorry, did you want me to wait until you were ready to tell everyone yourself?' asked Rosa brightly.

'Well...no... It's just...' He took a deep breath and steadied himself. 'If I'd known we were making the big announcement tonight, I'd have made sure to bring some champagne.'

'There's a bottle back at our house – I can send Blackie for it,' Emily said helpfully, beginning to stand up.

'No, stay where you are, Emily,' said Lena. 'I have a case of it in the scullery that Mike brought up earlier – it was under his chair as an extra surprise. I'll go and get one of those and some glasses.' She bustled towards the door, very glad of something to do.

Malachy turned as she passed him. 'Lena, I –'

She shut the door firmly behind her.

In the scullery, she paused for a moment to steady herself. Outside the window the snow continued to fall. It was lucky Rosa and Malachy had arrived when they did. The drifts were too deep now, and they'd never have made it in time for Christmas.

Yes, it was lucky they had made it. She liked Rosa a lot. Rosa and Malachy were perfect for each other.

She took a bottle and straightened her shoulders before marching through the kitchen. 'Emmet, Jack, Skipper, Blackie, go into the library – Malachy and Rosa have some good news to tell you,' she ordered briskly, and then she went to fetch the glasses from the glass cabinet.

The men didn't need to be told twice, and she found herself alone. The snow was deep outside on the back lawn, but something made her open the back door. An icy blast of cold air tingled her arms and face, so she took an old jacket of Pádraig's from the hallstand and wrapped it around her, stepping outside.

Standing there for a moment, she looked up at the dark sky, from which the snowflakes fell twirling, illuminated like stars by the kitchen windows. *Eli, what is this?* she asked him. *Why am I all up in a heap? This is what I've always wanted for Malachy, to get himself a good woman and settle down.* Though she felt a bit guilty asking Eli for his advice about anything to do with Malachy Berger. It had taken her years, honestly years, to make him believe she hadn't married him as a kind of consolation prize, and that she didn't feel anything for Malachy any more.

She wouldn't even have blamed Eli for refusing to answer, but in fact he replied straight away. *Be happy, Lena.*

Happy? Happy for who? She was confused. *You're not being very help-ful, my love.*

The muffled sound of voices raised in chatter and congratulations seemed far away, and she stood stock-still as a vixen passed her, just ten feet away. The animal stopped momentarily and fixed her with a yellow-eyed stare before loping off.

She shuddered. It was freezing hard now.

CHAPTER 25

*C*hristmas Day dawned with a streaky pink and blue sky and the world under a blanket of snow that sparkled in the cold winter sun. Lena sprang out of bed to get the fires lit.

At nine, Emily and Blackie arrived with Nellie, Aidan and Peggy, and everyone gathered in the library and opened their stockings, which were hung from the mantelpiece. Aidan was given his own little sock with a stuffed toy pig and a miniature truck, which delighted him altogether.

After breakfast, Ted and Gwenda turned up with Sophie, Annamaria, Katie and Maggie, all four girls muffled up in brand-new woollen winter coats with hand-knitted hats and scarves all made by Maria; they were all pink in the face from having had to walk from their farm because the roads were impassable. Jack and Skipper arrived soon after on horseback. Jack rode Sophie's horse, Angel, his feet nearly on the ground, and he led the little grey-dappled Polly, while Skipper rode Annamaria's black show jumper, Al, who was enormous. All the girls greeted their horses with delight and rushed to bring them around to the stables where there was a happy and noisy reunion with the other ponies.

Mike and Jane and Anthea appeared last of all. Jane had walked in from town, and she and Anthea had imagined they were going to have to carry Mike up the avenue – his electric motor wouldn't have been able to manage it. They'd been delighted to find Joseph Murphy had popped around earlier to clear a path down the middle of the avenue for Mike, using the scoop of the small tractor he used to ferry stuff around the grounds.

The presents were piled high under the tree, and the great unwrapping began. Peggy had painted a tiny portrait of Aidan for Blackie and Emily, a picture of Kilteegan House for Lena and nice flower paintings for everyone else. Mike and Anthea handed out boxes of fancy chocolates from Clerys, and Jane gifted everyone with pots of her homemade marmalade. Maria and Klaus bought Lena exquisite leather gloves made by Jimmy Piper, the local leatherworker who had just last week married Mrs Weldon.

Jimmy's wedding had been another poignant milestone for Lena. Eli was supposed to have been his best man. The wedding had originally been planned for a little over a year ago but had been cancelled after Eli died.

After trying on her leather gloves and loudly admiring the stitching to cover her sudden fit of sadness, Lena gave Mike a very expensive bottle of single-malt Midleton whiskey, which sent him into raptures, and silver brooches in the shape of snakes to Anthea and Jane. Nellie got a copy of *The Pilgrim's Progress*, with a soft sky-blue leather cover, and Emmet gave Nellie a gold cross and chain that had been blessed at the National Shrine of St Francis of Assisi, for whom the city of San Francisco was named. This made her squeal with delight and throw her arms around him.

Emmet's present to his father was a silver hip flask with his initials on it. Lena's to Malachy was a dark-blue shirt, the colour she'd always thought went with his eyes, even though it shouldn't because his eyes were green. She gave Emmet a green silk tie, which did match his eyes exactly, and Rosa a delicate pair of gold earrings, and she received a linen tablecloth and a smart red woollen jacket in return. Wei was inundated with gifts of perfume and book tokens; nobody knew her well enough yet to be sure what she would like. But Emmet had got her two tickets to *Carmen*, to be performed at the San Francisco Opera in the spring, and she was delighted.

Malachy had bought single pearls on solid gold chains for all the women and girls, even Maggie, as usual spending far too much money for Lena's comfort. Rosa mocked him gently for his lack of imagination, but he protested that they were real pearls from the ocean, not cultured ones, and that's why they were all strange and different shapes and colours, so they weren't all the same at all.

Lena worried that despite Rosa's bright smile, she was upset to be getting the same sort of present as everyone else.

Malachy caught her eye as she tried on her pink pearl in the oval mirror over the fireplace, and she smiled back at him and mouthed, 'Thank you.' He smiled back and mouthed, 'Happy Christmas.'

For the men, Malachy had bought Longines watches, though all of them except Mike and Emmet put them away very carefully, knowing the watches wouldn't last a second if they wore them while working their farms or taming wild horses or carrying sacks of cement.

Jack and Skipper gave each of the girls a blanket for their horse, and a new football to Pádraig. Maria had knitted everyone colourful jumpers, Blackie and Emily had brought up boxes of board games from their shop, and Ted produced winter bird feeders for everyone's houses, which he'd woven of willow.

Apart from that, there were plenty of clothes for Katie and Maggie. There was an exchange of bridles and stirrup leathers between Sarah, Sophie and Annamaria.

Then Gwenda opened her enormous bag and handed around bottles of clear liquid, sealed with a brown paper twist at the top. 'This is my contribution to the party,' she boomed.

'Oh Lord, what have you now?' Klaus groaned. A few weeks ago when Klaus visited Ted, the pair had got very drunk on some kind of delicious-tasting but wildly alcoholic liqueur Gwenda had made, and Klaus had sworn to never take a drink from her again.

'Just a little tipple I made – it's not that strong,' Gwenda called, taking some little sherry glasses from the sideboard and passing them around.

'Gwenda, it's not even midday yet, and poor Klaus couldn't get out of bed after the last night in your house,' Maria warned.

'Ah, that's 'cause he had you in it with him, I reckon.' Gwenda laughed, and Maria laughed and rolled her eyes.

Maria and Gwenda were as different as it was possible for two women to be, and Maria had confided to her daughters that she had trouble at first warming to the brash, outspoken Australian married to her brother. But then she'd found out Gwenda had such a kind heart, and that had been demonstrated by her taking young Katie and Maggie O'Neill into her home, and since then Maria had warmed to her a great deal.

Gwenda had made something different for Maria. She knew her sister-in-law never drank alcohol, as to do so would upset her medication and she was so grateful for her equilibrium, she would never risk it. The drink Gwenda had made for her was a delicious ginger beer, sweet and spicy but warming.

Lena was amused to notice that Sarah and Pádraig were beginning to look a bit confused. They'd hadn't had anything at all from their mother, and the pile of presents under the tree had dwindled to nothing.

Now Lena got to her feet and stretched her arms up to the ceiling, faking a big yawn. 'Right, that's presents over for this year,' she said cheerfully as Sarah and Pádraig gaped at her. 'So I suppose I'd better go and check on the turkey.'

'But, Mam...' groaned Pádraig.

'Now nobody move! I'll be back in a moment.' She walked casually out of the library, then sprinted to the cupboard under the stairs, which she'd kept locked this last while, telling everyone she kept bleach in there for cleaning and Aidan might get in there and root around and poison himself. The real reason was that was where she had hidden the television. She dragged it out – it was resting on the serving trolley that was usually in the dining room, the whole thing covered in a white tablecloth – and trundled it towards the library.

'I hope you're watching this, Eli,' she said happily. She couldn't stop giggling – maybe it was Gwenda's liqueur – as she propelled the trolley and its cloth-covered burden through the library door.

'I thought I'd bring the turkey in here to show you all,' she announced, trying to keep a straight face as everyone turned to her in puzzlement. 'It's looking very strange. I think I've burnt it. I need your opinion...' And while her whole family looked at her in wide-eyed horror, clearly thinking she really had gone mad with the strain of Christmas, she whipped off the white tablecloth. 'Ta-da!'

'Mam!' screamed Pádraig and Sarah at the same time. Emmet cracked up, and everyone else applauded frantically.

* * *

'Oh...I'm full as a goog!' Gwenda announced with a sigh as she scraped up the last of the Christmas pudding and brandy butter.

'As full as a *what?*' Wei asked, bemused.

'An egg.' Gwenda laughed. 'In Australia we call eggs "googs" and chickens "chooks".'

Ted's Australian wife was in great form. She'd had them all in hysterics over dessert. The fact there were two engaged couples at the table had put her in mind of her own wedding, when she'd had to help an ewe in trouble lambing the morning of her wedding, so she got married in a white dress but with sheep dung in her hair and filthy fingernails.

'Thank goodness love conquers all, or so they say,' said Ted, with his usual dry humour.

'Oh, it does. It's all we need anyway.' Emmet smiled at Wei, who turned pink with pleasure and whispered something to him that made him blush as well.

Lena could see that Rosa was waiting for Malachy to murmur something equally romantic to her, but Malachy was chatting away to Nellie and didn't seem to have even noticed. The lively conversation continued around the table, and as the moment passed, Rosa crumpled up her linen napkin in her hand and drank another glass of wine.

Lena's heart went out to her.

CHAPTER 26

'*Y*ou're up early?'

He turned with a start, Lena's voice shaking him out of his reverie. She was standing there in her rose-pink Christmas pyjamas and a silvery dressing gown, her hair dishevelled and dark rings under her eyes. She looked thin and pale...and beautiful.

'You're early too.' He smiled. 'I wasn't expecting anyone for ages.' It was only a little after seven, but he'd been sitting by himself in the kitchen for the last couple of hours, a cup of coffee in his hands. 'For me it's the jet lag. What's your excuse?'

She busied around, looking for something to tidy. 'Ah, I can't sleep in any more. I wish I could, but I wake early now, so I might as well get up. Though somebody seems to have tidied the whole place last night. I went to bed while the sing-song was in full swing.'

Malachy grinned. 'I think it was Jack and Pádraig, avoiding being asked to sing.'

'Did you get any sleep at all?'

He shook his head. 'I've not been to bed, sadly. The jet lag is real. I don't know how Rosa manages to sleep, although I suppose it's a lot less of a difference between New York and here than California.' He had left her fast asleep in their bedroom, which was on the top floor in what had once been the attic but which was now partitioned into three rooms, with a spiral staircase that ran up from the second landing.

Lena looked at him in amazement. 'You've been up all night, seriously?'

'I'll probably get a couple of hours later this morning.' He shrugged. 'I was going to go for a walk to tire myself out as soon as the dawn comes up – will you join me?' The invitation was out of his mouth before he had time to think about it.

Lena took a moment to consider it. 'I will. Let me just get a cup of tea and a ham sandwich, and then I'll get dressed.'

At five to eight, as the soft dawn light came through the snow-laden trees, they were off. Lena was in an old men's work coat, several times too large, and Malachy wondered if it had been Eli's. Her dark hair was covered in a pink knitted hat with a bobble, and on her feet, she wore green wellingtons. She smiled up at him, and something in the pit of his stomach lurched. This was a mistake.

But he didn't turn back.

'If you sleep all morning, you'll miss the hunt, you know,' she said. 'Emmet and the girls are all rearing to go, and Jack and Skipper brought the horses for the girls down from the farm.'

'I don't mind. My hunting days are well behind me.' He grinned. 'I'm getting old, Lena.'

They opened the gate at the back of the house that led through a stand of trees to the walled orchard. 'Remember the photo of my dad lifting you out of that tree, with me in the background?' Lena asked as they walked.

He nodded. 'I do. I found it in the photograph album you put away in the attic, when it was still an attic, that time I...' He blushed. He was still ashamed of the way he had entered her house, unbidden, when she was away, wanting to see where his son slept, but also, if he was honest, wanting to feel her presence. 'I'm sorry.'

'I'd like to see that photo again sometime,' she replied simply.

'I'll show it to you if you ever come to America,' he said, his heart lifting again.

She pushed the gate into the old orchard. The path was covered in snow, and the apple and pear trees, devoid of leaves, held snow where the limbs joined the trunk. 'I'm delighted for you both, by the way. It's great news about you and Rosa. She's a lovely woman.'

'She is, no doubt about it,' he agreed, but he caught himself trying to analyse the tone of Lena's voice, wondering if she was genuinely happy for him or if she was just the tiniest bit sad…

Stop it, he admonished himself. *Why on earth would you want Lena to be sad?*

'And Emmet is loving life in California. I miss him terribly, but I know he's in the right place and doing the right thing. He's so happy, and now he has Wei.'

'Are you all right about them getting married, really?' Malachy asked, glad to have a different wedding to talk about.

Lena sighed. 'To be honest, they seem too young, but then we were young, and Eli and I were young, and, well…we can't stop them and she seems like a very nice girl.'

They walked around the orchard and out the other side. The snow was beginning to fall gently again, but they didn't notice as they were deep in conversation about California and Emmet and Wei's father. Lena was as outraged as Malachy that this Ken Tan had been so hard to persuade that their son was the perfect match for his precious daughter.

Then they talked about life without Eli for her and how she'd come to terms with his loss finally, or at least come to accept that he was dead.

The conversation was gentle and easy, joking sometimes, and when the ground beneath their feet was treacherous – there had been a freeze overnight, so there were layers of ice below the newly fallen snow – he caught her when she almost slipped.

Without either of them mentioning it, she kept her arm linked with his. They walked through another carefully managed woodland, where the floor was sheltered, but when they emerged on the other side, the snow was falling heavier. They soon realised the gentle snowstorm was rapidly becoming more like a blizzard.

As they struggled head down across the upper paddock, it was getting so hard to see where they were going that Malachy nearly walked into a stone wall. Lena pulled him back just in time. 'Look out! It's the old gamekeeper's hut.'

'I don't remember this?' He placed his hand on the rough stone building; it felt sturdy.

'Well, it wasn't much more than a heap of stones when we used to play here as children. But we fixed it up last year and re-thatched it with reeds. The kids love using this field for practising jumping the horses, so we store the jumps here in the winter.' She unlatched the door and went in.

He followed her. There were a lot of jumps stacked neatly against one of the gable walls and a black iron fireplace in another, as well as two old súgán chairs. Now he remembered this place; he had indeed played here with Lena as a child, when the roof had been open to the sky and the walls half tumbled down.

'Will we shelter in here till it eases?' Lena asked him, pulling off her bobble hat and shaking out her hair. 'We probably should have headed back sooner, but in the woods, you don't really notice and it kind of got worse all of a sudden.'

'I think you're right. We'll be soaked if we try to walk in it, it's so heavy. Let's see if it passes.'

Although the sun had fully risen, the snowstorm had blackened the sky again to near twilight darkness. Malachy poked around and found a box of candles. The box of matches that were with them was damp, but he had a lighter in his pocket.

There was a basket of dried logs, and using some blown-in leaves and twigs that were on the floor, he managed to kindle a small fire. Within minutes the hut was warming up. Lena sat on one of the súgán chairs, warming her hands at the flames.

He reached into his pocket and pulled out the silver hip flask Emmet had given to him and offered it to her. 'What is it?' she asked, taking it.

'A very fine brandy. Emmet had it filled up, and he gave me the rest of the bottle later.' He smiled at her.

'Ah, that was kind of him.' She took a sip but wrinkled her nose. 'That's supposed to be good? I think I prefer Midleton whiskey – Mike's really turned me on to that.'

'Well, it will warm you up if nothing else,' he said, smiling, then took a sip himself.

'You and Emmet really get along, don't you?' she asked, without rancour.

He nodded, pleased she didn't seem to mind. He often felt guilty about Emmet being in California, worried Lena might feel he'd stolen him away. 'I was delighted when he decided to come over to study, but also kind of terrified. I've no experience whatsoever with teenagers, and I was scared I'd get it wrong with him. Eli was his father in every way, and I didn't want to try to take his place. I never could anyhow, but I didn't want Emmet thinking that I was trying to, or for you to be angry at me taking him away from here.'

She smiled at the fire. 'Emmet was never going to stay here – I think I always knew that on some level. He never fitted into Kilteegan Bridge the way Sarah and Pádraig do. I can't explain it. He was so restless. He wanted to explore the world and achieve great things. But seeing him now, grown up, and so confident but still the sweet boy I've always known him to be – you're doing a good job yourself, Malachy.'

'I didn't do anything. He was reared by the time I got him. He's a credit to you and Eli, not to me.'

Lena smiled and sat with her chin on her hands, watching as the flames licked merrily up the chimney. 'Do you remember us playing house here?' she asked.

'I do,' he said with a smile, taking the other low súgán chair.

'You were kind to play it with me.'

'I liked playing it with you.'

'Really? I thought boys hated playing house with girls.'

'I think that depends who the girl is.'

'Oh...' She shot him a brief smile, both startled and amused. 'Well, here we are playing house together again.'

She went back to gazing into the flames. The snow swirled outside, and the wind was picking up. The hut was cosy and warm now, and in that moment, gazing at her face, the snow melting from her eyelashes, he felt like they might be the only two people in the world.

'Here we are,' he echoed her softly. 'Just as we used to be.'

The words hung in the still-smoky air. He was only feet from her. The only sound was the crackling of the dry wood on the fire and the wind whistling outside.

She said something very softly.

'What?' He shifted his chair a little closer.

'I said, you need to be kinder to Rosa.'

His mood fell slightly. 'What do you mean? I am kind to her.'

She turned her head and looked straight at him. 'It's not fair to marry her if you don't want to do it a hundred percent.'

'Lena, I... Where is this coming from?'

'I've been watching you.'

'*Watching* me?'

'Yes, and it's not fair. It's...well, it's a bit mean actually. Rosa is a wonderful woman. She's perfect for you. She's beautiful, she's clever, she's independent, which I know you like, and your own son thinks she's great. But you're going to lose her if you don't give her your whole heart, like Emmet does to Wei. Don't you see how he does that? Can't you do the same?'

She kept her dark eyes on him for a moment, then went back to staring into the fire. The flames were beginning to die down, and after a minute or so, he threw on another log. He'd decided he didn't want this conversation to end. He needed it.

'I used to think I had to give my full heart to a woman,' he said softly. 'That's why I've stayed single all these years. But maybe I just can't do it, Lena, even with someone as wonderful as Rosa. And it's OK. Over there, in America, it's easy. Rosa and I work better there than here. But coming back to Kilteegan

House... I don't know. It's been hard, all the memories...and everything.'

'Maybe you shouldn't have come.'

He winced. 'Well, I did think that,' he said defensively, 'but Emmet insisted, and Rosa wanted it as well, so they ganged up on me.' He threw another few sticks on the fire. 'What about you, Lena? Would you rather I'd stayed away?'

He hoped and even expected she would rush to reassure him, but instead she sat, frowning to herself, as if not knowing the right answer. 'No,' she said at last, to his relief. 'I like seeing you, Malachy. And Rosa is lovely, and I like Emmet to be happy, and I know he's glad you're here with him.' She paused, then added, 'I just wish...'

'Wish what?'

She shrugged. 'Like I said, I just feel like you're being distant with her, and I don't like...well, I don't like her thinking that's my fault.'

He sat hunched on the chair, his arms folded tightly across his heart. 'Did you give your whole heart to Eli, right from the beginning of your marriage?'

She glanced at him, frowning. The fire was reflected in her deep brown eyes, fierce sparks of gold. 'You know I did. I was all his, every bit of me.'

'Right from the beginning?'

'Yes.'

'Be honest, Lena, please. It would help me. I need to know if I can marry Rosa with a little piece of my heart still somewhere else and later make my heart whole again, like you made yours whole with Eli.'

She hesitated then, her head tilted to one side. 'I... No, I don't think I ever held any of myself back. Not like you're doing with Rosa. I mean, once I'd decided...'

'You never had doubts? I was gone, just like that?' He felt slightly cruel for pushing her, but he needed to know. 'Is that possible, after what we had?'

She was a long while about answering this time, and that was enough for him to know he was right. Her feelings for him hadn't disappeared overnight; they couldn't have done. They were real, and he'd known each time he had come back. Those rare occasions, he'd known it was true; he'd known she hadn't forgotten him entirely. She had kept a part of him in her heart; she'd never thrown it out.

Instead of answering directly, she drew the old coat around her like armour. 'I'm not the same person I was, Malachy. The girl who took you into the tack room that night, the girl you drove around in your car – that's what I was, a girl, and you were a boy. We knew nothing. I think we romanticised it in our heads, and it's all got twisted up with your father and mother, and my father and mother, and the horrible lies and secrets that we got caught up in. A kind of Irish Romeo and Juliet.'

'A tragic romance?'

'A romance, yes, but romances don't all have to end in tragedy. Ours didn't. I found my Eli. And you've found your Rosa. And you need to stick with her to have a happy ending. The past is no good for us, Malachy. It's not possible just to turn back time and pretend the years between have never happened.'

Malachy threw another few last sticks on the fire, and the sparks flew up the chimney. He leant forwards, his elbows resting on his knees and his hands clasped between them. He was so close, close enough to kiss her, but he couldn't.

Instead, he told her what was in his heart. He had to do it, once and for all, if he was ever going to move on.

'You say I've found my Rosa, and maybe you're right, and I do love her. But I fell in love with you when we were seventeen years old. And all of what you say is right – we were kids and hadn't a clue. And I let you down. I believed my father when I should have known better, and that is a decision I've regretted every day of my life since then. Every day, Lena, every single one of them. I shave in the mornings, and I wonder how you are. I hear a song, and I wonder if you've heard it, or seen a movie or eaten a meal. Everything, and I mean everything, is through the lens of Lena O'Sullivan. I love our son for himself. But I also love him because he's a solid representation that what we had was real. We might have been young and foolish, but you weren't a conquest or a fling for me. You were the one –'

'Stop it, Malachy.' She spoke sharply.

He stopped. His heart was racing. He'd said far more than he'd meant to say. He'd started this by wanting to lay a ghost to rest, but the longer he'd spoken, the more the ghosts had arisen and swirled around him, blinding him like the snowstorm that had driven them into this sheltered space. 'I'm sorry,' he said stiffly. 'I didn't mean to offend you.'

She sighed. 'You didn't offend me, Malachy. You're just addled for lack of sleep, and now you're full of romantic childhood memories. We shouldn't have stopped in here. I was silly to remind you about playing house together. All that is past. You're different, I'm different, and you have a fiancée, Malachy. She's back at the house waiting for you, and you need to go back to her now, even if it's just to sleep. You broke my heart once, Malachy, and I won't be part of you breaking another woman's heart in the same way. I just won't. I won't be blamed for it. I wouldn't wish it on anyone what you did to me...' Her voice rose in distress.

'I'm so sorry, Lena.' He was desperate to take her in his arms, but he was unable to move.

'And you're right,' she said. 'It did take me years for my heart to feel whole again, but I got there...' She hesitated, then repeated in a firmer, calmer voice, 'I *got* there. And so will you, Malachy, if you'd only try.'

She stood up and went to the door. When she opened it, a huge slab of wet snow fell in, but above them the sky was a silky pale-blue, and the frosted trees glittered in the sunlight.

They walked back across the paddock, taking huge steps through the deep snow. Lena was so much smaller than he was. She was panting and struggling through the drifts, the bobble on her hat shaking with determination, the snow often up to her knees.

He offered her his arm again, but she didn't take it.

* * *

HE WOKE beside Rosa in time for the afternoon's hunt. He could hear the huntsman's horn and the muffled sound of hooves on snow, and he opened and leant out of the attic window to see all the riders gathered below in the avenue, their red jackets magnificent against the sparkling whiteness, their glossy horses blowing out clouds of breath. Gwenda and Ted, who had stayed on the sofa bed in Eli's old dressing room, were carrying out trays of hot port to warm the riders, and Nellie was helping them, wearing her modest uniform from the nursing home where she would be working later; she looked like a nun already in her white cap and flat shoes, demure and sweet.

He could see Lena laughing and chatting down below as she adjusted Emmet's stirrups for him; their son's legs were so much longer than Sarah's, who had been the last person to ride Second Chance. Katie was sitting very upright on the grey-dappled Polly, and Wei was coming from the direction of the stables riding Flash, being led by Skipper. The two newest riders were going to follow quietly along behind the rest, with the cowboy on foot as their escort.

Another girl with a long blond plait falling out from under her riding hat brought her horse up beside Second Chance and leant across, talking to Emmet intently as her mount pawed impatiently at the snow, muscles rippling under its glossy black coat. Even from this height, Malachy thought he recognised her. Yes, she'd been hanging around Emmet at the time of Eli's funeral. She was the third of Professor Lamkin's daughters and the older sister of Pádraig's best friend, Oliver.

She was sweet on him it would seem, but Emmet had never once even mentioned her.

Now Isobel looked annoyed and moved away from his son, over to a bunch of other girls Malachy didn't recognise. Nellie came up to their group carrying a tray of port and offering it around.

And then…

For a moment Malachy thought he was seeing things, but Rosa, who had padded quietly up beside him, gasped aloud and squeezed his arm, so she must have seen it too. 'What on earth is she *doing*, Malachy?'

Isobel had bent down to say something in Nellie's ear as she took a glass of hot port, and suddenly Nellie seemed to lose her mind. She hurled the tray to the ground, grabbed Isobel by the collar of her red hunt jacket and dragged her clean off her horse into the snow. The black stallion took off with its reins flapping, and the other horses circled, snorting and stamping. The voices of the two girls rose shrilly in the cold air. Isobel was hitting at Nellie with her riding crop, while Nellie was trying to push the posh girl's face into a snowdrift.

Emmet swung down off his horse and rushed to haul Nellie back, scolding her furiously, and Malachy caught the words, 'if you ever want to be a nun'. But then Nellie faced him, speaking rapidly and pointing at Isobel. Emmet stalked over to his former girlfriend, who was still floundering in the snow, jerked her to her feet and said a few words with a very intense expression. He then turned and went to Wei, who was still seated on Flash looking bewildered, and took her hand and kissed it.

'Well, I don't know what happened there,' said Rosa in astonishment, 'but I can't wait to find out, and if Nellie needs a lawyer, I'm her woman. I don't like the look of that other one. Let's get dressed and go downstairs and find out what happened.'

Grinning, Malachy closed the window and slipped his arms around his fiancée. This was Rosa at her finest, always ready to help the underdog, a heart of gold. She was still wearing her Christmas pyjamas, dark-blue with silver stars. He had seen Emmet kiss Wei's hand, and he had listened to Lena. Lena was right – Rosa deserved his full heart. He would make the effort, and everything would be all right.

CHAPTER 27

'Is Wei not having breakfast?'

'She's been throwing up in the bathroom all morning, best not enquire,' Emmet said with a grimace as he scanned through his exam notes one last time that were scattered across the black-marble island in the Palo Alto kitchen.

'Is she ill?' Malachy felt a jolt of shock. Women being sick in the mornings was a sign of pregnancy, he knew that much. Emmet and Wei shared a room, which he suspected Lena probably wouldn't approve of. They'd not been put in the same room when they visited at Christmas but in the other two bedrooms on the top floor, beside him and Rosa. But Malachy felt they were going to do what young people do anyway. They were alone in the house much of the time, so the pretence that they wouldn't sleep together seemed a silly one.

That said, if Wei got pregnant, he would not like to be the one telling Emmet's mother.

'No, just nerves. She's always like this the morning of an exam,' his son said casually, gathering his notes into a pile and stuffing them into a folder.

'That's good.' The relief must have been evident in his voice, because Emmet looked over at him with a grin.

'We're being very careful, Malachy, don't worry.'

Malachy made a show of needing to get milk out of the fridge for his coffee, even though there was enough in the jug; he was only turning away to cover his embarrassment. Emmet had been raised by Eli and so had no problem talking about things of the body, but Malachy the Irishman still found it hard.

'Emmet, you're an adult,' he said rather stiffly, 'and so is Wei, and I'm not going to suddenly become the Victorian father figure. I wouldn't have a leg to stand on anyway, as you know, but I am glad to hear you're being...like you say. You are both at a really exciting time in your lives, and a baby wouldn't be helpful.'

'I know,' Emmet replied cheerfully. 'But more to the point, Wei knows as well, and she has a lot more to lose than me...' His voice tailed off. 'I mean...' He obviously felt like he might have insulted Malachy in some way, because of the way he had abandoned Lena when they were teenagers.

'No, you're right,' said Malachy, coming back to the table with his coffee and sitting down. 'The woman does have a lot more to lose, and no man should ever forget that.'

'I won't.'

'Good. Now, I was thinking. Johnny called me yesterday, and they are ready to punch list the community centre, so how about we go over after the exam and see what we can find?'

'Brilliant!' Emmet's eyes lit up. Malachy loved how construction excited his son as much as it did him. 'I was there last Thursday, and everything was looking good, but I told Johnny I'd be out of the picture for the days running up to this exam. We've been told it's the hardest one of the year, so I don't blame Wei for feeling queasy. But once it's done, the rest of the semester won't be too bad – it'll be more the fun bit of design and less physics and maths.'

'Great. I'll meet you at the site at three? And Wei as well if she wants to come. I'm picking Rosa up from the airport at one. She's excited to see the place too, and the trust representatives are due to visit next week to start planning the grand opening. Already they've lined up several events. Rosa's Great-Uncle Joachim – he's a great man – he came up with the idea of the talking library, where survivors of the Holocaust can sit and there's a chair opposite them. So a member of the public can just come in and sit down, and they'll tell their story.'

'That's going to be an incredible learning curve for lots of people. I can't wait to see the whole place up and running.' Emmet slipped down off the high stool to fetch his bag from the counter. 'By the way, I was thinking of inviting Mam over for the opening. Is it OK if she stays here? If you and Rosa don't mind?'

Malachy's heart turned over, but he worked hard at maintaining a neutral expression. 'Sure, why wouldn't we have her here after we stayed in her house and had such a magical time at Christmas?'

Emmet beamed. 'It was great, wasn't it? Apart from the Isobel Lamkin thing. I suppose we could have done without that.'

'I can't say I agree with you there, son,' said Malachy, grinning. 'I know it was awful what Isobel said, but Nellie's reaction actually made my entire Christmas.'

Emmet chuckled himself at the memory, his eyes crinkling like Malachy's always did. 'Yeah, I know, though she did get in awful trouble with the nuns when the story got out around the town. She wrote to me yesterday. It was all the nursing home was talking about the whole of January because Kitty McLoughlin's son Derry came in roaring with laughter and gave Nellie a big hug – his son works for the Lamkins and Isobel is always talking down to him like he's some sort of peasant, so he was delighted Nellie gave her a slap.'

Malachy laughed. 'I hope the nuns understood when she explained?'

'Not really. Mother Bridget went on about turning the other cheek and nuns not being violent and gave her a load of penances or what-ever would-be nuns do, but Nellie says it was worth it. She says she just saw red when Isobel called Wei 'Ming the Merciless'.'

'I don't even think he was Asian, was he?' Malachy laughed again.

'Now you mention it, I don't think he was. I remember reading the *Flash Gordon* comics, and he was always the baddie. Anyway, she couldn't hold a candle to Wei, so good riddance. She was always a bit of a pest, to be honest. I just told her never to talk to me or any of my family again, and thankfully she's at art college in France now, so she's not around enough to make all my cousins' lives a misery.' He stashed the folder into his bag, cramming it in between two fat textbooks. 'So it's really OK to invite Mam to stay here at the house?'

'Absolutely,' Malachy said with a determined smile. 'And does she know the whole story?'

'Nope, haven't said a word, so don't you either.'

'So she'll think she'll only be here to witness her pride and joy's moment of glory?'

Emmet just laughed. Sarah and Pádraig always teased him about being their mother's pet, and he always calmly and nonchalantly concurred that he was her favourite. He went out of the kitchen to the foot of the stairs and called up, 'Wei, come on! We need to get going!'

Moments later an ashen-faced Wei appeared, and Malachy's heart went out to her. She took everything so seriously, and getting less than top marks was something she couldn't countenance at all. He used to be the same, a perfectionist, and he'd learnt the hard way that it wasn't sustainable. But that was something she would have to figure out for herself.

'You know this, Wei. You've learnt everything inside out. You'll walk it,' he said, and he meant it. She was exceptional, even better than Emmet; she had no need for exam nerves. 'And you as well, Emmet, the best of luck with the exam today. I'm so proud of you both.'

'Thanks, Malachy.' Emmet smiled as he shouldered his bag. 'I wouldn't even be here only for you.'

* * *

AFTER THEY LEFT, Malachy sat in the sun-filled kitchen and sighed. Lena. Did he want her here in his house? No. He didn't even really want her in America. What he'd told her that day of the snowstorm, that he had never forgotten what she meant to him, was true. He didn't regret it – he'd needed to say it – but what he'd said about him and Rosa being fine over here in America was also true.

He contemplated the paradox.

Could two opposing ideas be equally valid? He loved Lena, he always would, and nobody could ever touch her. And seeing her and Rosa in the same room was unsettling and disconcerting and felt wrong. But also he loved Rosa, not less than Lena, just differently. He forced himself to ponder the question. If when he was in Ireland Lena had hinted there was even a chance for them, he would have ended his relationship with Rosa, and that made him feel like a snake. Was he only using Rosa because Lena wasn't available to him? He didn't think so. He and Rosa could be happy; they would be. Lena had said he had to work on giving Rosa his whole heart, and he was determined to do what she'd told him. He would make Rosa happy, and he would be happy too.

But Lena would always be there in his heart. He couldn't help it.

He thought about the therapist he'd gone to see when they got back from Ireland. He and Rosa had had a long talk, and she told him how left out she felt over there. He'd explained how Lena was part of his past, that he couldn't eradicate her, but that Rosa was who he loved, the woman he saw as his future. Rosa accepted him at his word but more or less insisted he see this therapist, so for a quiet life, he did.

The woman was tiny, with an Eastern European accent, and she took no nonsense. He'd explained to her he imagined he felt the way someone who was widowed might feel if they found love again, guilty but hopeful. The therapist had been scathing. She'd told him that his feelings for Lena would sour any future relationship and that he needed to resolve it, that both he and Lena had unfinished business and they were neither of them any good for anyone else while this went on.

She was wrong, of course; Malachy knew that. Lena had moved on with Eli; she had healed her heart. And he could do the same with Rosa. He would. He gathered his keys and wallet and let himself out. He needed to go to the office and would get some paperwork done before picking his gorgeous, brilliant fiancée up from the airport.

* * *

THE MORNING SPED BY, and as he waited at the arrivals gate for her, as he'd done so often, he felt a surge of excitement tinged with guilt as he saw her come through the doors. She was a wonderful woman, and she loved him. What more could he ask for? He would be a good husband to her, faithful, kind and loving. And, he promised himself as he saw her beam with delight at the sight of him, he would never hurt her again by ever giving her another inkling that there was a part of his heart, tiny as it might become over time, maybe one day to be buried beneath the cobwebs and dust of years, that would still be Lena's on his deathbed.

He kissed her and took her bag. 'How about lunch and a nice glass of wine? I told Emmet we'd meet him at the centre at three, so we've two hours.'

'I've a better idea.' She winked.

'Oh yes?' He knew what she had in mind. 'Home then?'

'Yes please,' she answered primly, and he wondered why on earth he couldn't get Lena out of his head when this beautiful, sexy woman was right here, and loved him.

After their passionate lovemaking, they lay in his huge bed, on black silk sheets in the white sun-filled room, filling each other in on what had been happening since they last saw each other three weeks ago.

'It's been so busy. Our firm has been involved with a high-profile trial in Germany. A camp guard, a vicious sadistic woman, was traced down by Wiesenthal, living in Queens and married to an American. Wiesenthal's people, finally, after a long process that we helped with, got her back to Germany to face trial. That was back in 1973, but her husband posted bail in Germany last year. He insists she wouldn't hurt a fly, by the way, and she got out. We were all horrified. The evidence against her is huge. But anyway, she could have kept her head down, but no, she was intimidating witnesses. This woman, Malachy, she's really evil, not just a kid who got caught up in the whole thing. She shows zero remorse and spouts anti-Semitic garbage at every opportunity, so in December last year, she was returned to prison. She stood trial and got a long sentence. Hopefully she'll die in jail.'

'I don't know how you do what you do, but I'm so proud of you,' he said, pulling her against him.

She lay on her back with his arm around her, staring up at the ceiling. 'I'm just part of a team, but yes, it feels good when it works out. It's slow and frustrating mostly. So how about you?' She turned her face towards him. 'Tell me you've found the perfect wedding venue, booked the band, arranged flowers and food and found hotels to fit my huge family?'

'Er...' He chuckled, and she thumped his bare chest.

'I thought you said you were going to plan the wedding, Mr Berger?'

'And I will, but I need your input, don't I? I'm a man. I'll get it wrong.'

'An excuse your entire gender has been using for years,' she grumbled. 'OK, how about we check out some venues this week then? I can stay until Friday, but I have a complicated case Monday morning, so I need to get home and prep.'

'Of course, let's do it. What do you think about a vineyard? There are some gorgeous ones in Napa. We could hold it there?'

'Maybe.' She looked doubtful.

'Do you wish it was a synagogue?'

'No, I don't mind that...'

'Or would you rather the East Coast? You're the one with the legions of relatives. Wouldn't it be easier to do it nearer them?'

'It would but... I don't know.'

'What don't you know?' he asked, picking up and dropping the strands of her dark hair that lay fanned out on his chest.

She leant up on an elbow, her intelligent brown eyes raking his face. 'Nothing. How about Vegas? We just fly up there, drag a couple of witnesses out of a casino and get it done?'

'There's talk of a Graceland chapel there now, where you can have an Elvis Presley–themed wedding. How does that grab you?' He chuckled.

'I don't care, you know?' She didn't laugh with him; she looked serious. 'I just want to be married to you. How that happens, I don't care. I'm only doing the big Jewish everyone-is-invited thing because my family would love it, but maybe we won't bother?'

'Whatever you want, Rosa. You want a big splash, we'll do that. You want a small thing, that's fine too. I don't care either,' he assured her.

'You really don't, do you?' she said, still studying his face with those shrewd intelligent eyes. 'In fact, do you even care about getting married at all?'

For a moment he thought she was saying she herself didn't mind whether they were married or not, but then he realised with a jolt that this was about him, not her. It was because he was being too casual about the wedding. He'd been acting as if it were nothing to do with him, making promises to set things in motion that he hadn't kept. Acting like it was she who wanted all the fuss, not him. And he hated that he'd made her feel so vulnerable. She did nothing to deserve that fear he'd placed in her.

'Of course I care,' he said, and he kissed her and drew her into his arms again. 'I love you, and I'm longing to marry you, and I want a full proper celebration with all your family, somewhere lovely and romantic and unforgettable.'

And he meant every word of it; he really did.

CHAPTER 28

*K*atie was as white as a sheet as they waited in the hallway of the Dublin court. She was dressed in a white blouse, grey skirt and pink cardigan, with gleaming-white ankle socks and polished black Mary Janes. Her hair was plaited neatly. Sarah was a dinger at doing the horses' tails and manes, so she'd applied her technique to Katie early this morning. Gwenda thought her oldest foster child looked immaculate but with the countenance of one heading for the gallows.

Jack had driven them to Dublin, Ted and Skipper as well, and now they were sitting on the bench outside Court Four, waiting for Kieran Devlin to arrive. They had got here much too early; they didn't want to risk being late so had left two hours before they really needed to. Seven-year-old Maggie had stayed at home with Sophie and Annamaria, who had promised not to act nervous around her or even tell her anything in case it all went wrong, which could easily happen.

Kieran had warned them that Olivia's appeal, which was finally going ahead in the Dublin courts, was not going to be an easy one to win. Reversing any decision of the court was notoriously difficult, as it set a precedent for others to try to do the same. Right might be on Olivia's side, but Kieran was adamant that justice and the law often bore no resemblance to each other. Katie's testimony would have to be very compelling, he'd said.

The poor child had been a bag of nerves in the run up to the hearing. Kieran Devlin had confided in Gwenda and Ted that she might not be convincing enough as a witness. She was so awkward and shy about telling what her father had done to her; she just wouldn't say it straight out, as if she was still afraid of it coming back on her.

'He says I have to answer all these questions about me da,' she had whispered to Gwenda one night by the fire. 'I wish they'd just let me tell the judge how good my ma is, and not say anything about him. It's like nobody cares if he comes back at me or what happens to me.'

'We care, Katie,' Gwenda had reminded her gently, or as gently as the rough woman was capable of being. 'We'll take care of you.'

'Oh, I know.' The child had looked panicked. 'And I'm so sorry for dragging you all into my mess. And I'll try to pay Mr Devlin back – I'm saving up loads. Thank you for helping, Auntie Gwenda. I'm really grateful.' Katie was always terrified that if she complained about anything, her world would come crashing down around her ears.

Everywhere around them, suited solicitors were engaged in earnest conversations with their clients and each other. The door of the courtroom opened and closed constantly with various people coming and going. A prison officer handcuffed to a defiant man waited on another bench further along. Outside on the steps that led to the street, people in small groups spoke urgently and in whispers, nervously dragging on cigarettes.

Kieran finally approached them through the crowd, and Gwenda felt relief wash over her. The country solicitor was not a man to be flustered or to act emotionally. He always remained the exact same person: calm, almost theatrically slow and so measured, it was hard to imagine him ever experiencing either a high or low mood.

'Good morning, Miss O'Neill,' he said to Katie formally, with a very slight twinkle in his eye.

Katie murmured a greeting, too overwhelmed by the situation to do more.

'Well, the good news is we're up first, so at least we won't have all day to wait.' He didn't smile, and Gwenda was glad of it. There was nothing to smile about. Poor Katie was the colour of a sheet and looked like a rabbit in the headlights.

'So what's going to happen?' the child whispered to him.

'Well, the judge and jury will hear from me, and I will be sure to mention that the conviction of Mrs O'Neill was based on the evidence of her husband, who was attacking his daughter in the most despicable way, and that the only prosecution witness was the now disgraced garda sergeant, who is his brother. And I will remind them that since then, both men have signed confessions to perjury before fleeing the country. We're really lucky this Thomas O'Neill was involved, since he's in disgrace with the guards and there's a trail of skulduggery behind all his cases. And, Katie, remember to answer all questions the state barrister will ask you as fully and honestly as you can. I know this is terrible and frightening, but your father won't be there. No one can hurt you now. You have friends and protectors whatever happens.'

Katie nodded miserably. She clung to Gwenda's hand as if she were drowning.

A tall, very handsome man in a silver legal wig and long billowing robes swept past them into Court One. A high-profile murder of a socialite and her married lover was being heard in there, and the courtroom was filled with journalists.

'That's Geoffrey D'Alton,' Kieran Devlin whispered, in what could be described as an almost giddy voice.

Neither Gwenda nor Katie had a clue who that was.

'The famous barrister?' Jack asked. 'I read a biography of him last year. There's hardly a newsworthy case anywhere in Europe that he's not involved with. Whoever is in the dock in there' – he tipped his head towards Court One – 'must have deep pockets.'

'I'm sure they do,' the country solicitor agreed. 'It's all the papers can write about. He's remarkable to watch, it would seem.'

Skipper smiled at Jack surreptitiously. Kieran Devlin was not the type to be starstruck, but he was now.

They waited, and the corridors became quieter as everyone went to their appointed court. A few minutes later, the clerk called the case, and Kieran explained it was time for everyone to take their seats, except Katie, who as a witness had to remain outside.

As they left her with the clerk of the court, her face was stricken with terror, but every adult there tried to infuse the girl with courage.

'We'll be very close, Katie, right behind you in the public gallery. Don't worry. Just tell the truth, and everything will be fine,' Ted said calmly.

Gwenda took a seat next to her husband in the public gallery and shivered to see how small Katie looked in the witness box, with her large dark-blue eyes fixed hungrily on her mother, Olivia, who was sitting between two police officers in the dock and who gave her daughter a little wave until one of the officers made her put down her hand.

Kieran stepped up to the witness box and questioned Katie very gently about what happened that day when her father attacked her, and gradually coaxed out of her what happened, where he'd put his hands, one on her throat, the other on her underwear.

'I don't want to talk about that bit in front of you all,' said Katie, her eyes filling with tears. 'But I'll talk about how he was holding me throat. I thought I was goin' to choke, and I was trying to shout for me ma, but then I couldn't shout no more because he was squeezing and squeezing and everything was going all grey. I tried to kick him, I did, but he was laughing and he was too strong for me. Then I could feel his other hand...'

She started sobbing uncontrollably, and Olivia wiped a tear that rolled down her cheek. The twelve jury members looked visibly shaken by Katie's testimony.

'No more questions, Your Honour,' said Kieran, and he turned to a small fat man in a grey legal wig and robes. He was the barrister for the state. 'Your witness.'

Gwenda sat tensely upright, and Ted took her big weathered hand and squeezed it tenderly.

The state barrister approached the witness box and stood looking coldly at Katie, like she was something he'd brought in on his shoe. 'I put it to you, Miss O'Neill, that you are lying,' he said in a bored, sonorous tone.

Katie cowered. 'I never lie! I never, ever...' she said in her high, panicked, defensive voice, the one she used every time she thought she was being accused of something by someone in authority, whether they were right or not.

'After the police arrived, you told them it was you who struck your father on the head with the household poker, isn't that true?'

'No, I never did –'

'But isn't it true that's what you *said* you did, Miss O'Neill?'

'Yes, but –'

'And it was to protect your mother from being blamed for it?'

'Course it was.'

'Are your family in the habit of lying to protect your mother? Do you think your father would lie to protect your mother?'

'No, he'd never. He was a lying rat, so he was. He wouldn't protect my ma. He battered her,' Katie said, less nervously this time, just full of bitterness.

'Well, well. So telling lies seems to run in your family, doesn't it? Because your uncle's confession is also a lie, isn't it? Your mother already said in her first trial that she wasn't even sure he was there, and he's not in the scene you describe, is he? So I put it to you, your uncle never witnessed anything that happened, either way, because he came in after the fact.'

Katie stared at him, a rabbit in the headlights, not understanding what was coming down the track at her.

'Don't you agree, Miss O'Neill?'

'I dunno...' She looked helplessly at Kieran Devlin, whose face was as impassive as ever, though from where Gwenda was sitting, she could see under the table his hands were tearing up strips of legal paper. 'I don't even know what you're saying to me, Mister.'

'What I'm saying, Miss O'Neill,' the barrister said with a show of enormous patience, 'is there seems to be a lot of lying going on around this case, and one of those liars is you.'

'I'm not! I swear!'

'I put it to you, Miss O'Neill, that you are lying to protect your mother.'

'I told a lie about that night to save my ma, but now yous all know the truth, what kind of man my da is, and his brother too.'

'Tell me, Miss O'Neill – and you are on the witness stand now and you've taken an oath to tell the truth, have you not? Yes, you have. Now my question is, Miss O'Neill, you lied once before. You've admitted it. Why should this court accept that you are not lying now?'

Katie said nothing, just stared at the barrister like she had no idea what he was saying. Gwenda held her breath. Ted squeezed her hand even tighter, so much so it hurt. Skipper was impassive, but Jack was sitting forwards in his seat and had forgotten himself enough to be holding Skipper's hand.

Katie replied, loud and clear. 'I'm not lying now.'

The barrister looked like he couldn't believe his luck. 'So you say but Miss O'Neill, you would lie to the court to get your mother out of prison?' He stepped forwards, his small piggy eyes boring into hers, his many chins resting on his white collar.

It was strange, almost electric, but Katie didn't look cowed any more, not even in the face of everything she feared – all the authority of the state that pulsed through the room, the state that didn't care about girls like her. In front of their eyes, she straightened her narrow shoulders and lifted her chin and became the tough little survivor who could take on anything: her father, the nuns, the priest in the orphanage, two days in the open as she walked from Skibbereen to Kilteegan Bridge, giving her coat and hat to her sister to keep her dry while she got soaked to the skin.

'Yeah, course I would,' she said contemptuously. 'Wouldn't you? Don't you love your mother?'

'But the law, Miss O'Neill,' he said in amazement. 'Whatever your childish emotional attachments, you have to respect the law.'

'But why? The law don't respect the likes of us, Mister. The law put my ma in jail for somethin' she didn't do, and you only have to look at her to see she didn't do it. She's five foot nothing, like me, and me da is a monster. He's huge and a brute, everyone knows it, and still me ma was brave enough to stand up to him and save me life when he was going to kill me 'cos I didn't want him doing his dirty thing to me.'

She glanced with her chin stuck out around the court, at the gallery, at the jury box, at the judge, a red-faced man with a bushy silver moustache, at the stony-faced garda officers.

'And how many of you can say your ma saved your life? I s'pose you all had mas that gave you life, but my ma gave me life twice over and...'

She turned to face her mother, and her face shone with such love and tenderness that Gwenda's heart felt like breaking. 'Ma, I know I'm probably doing no good here for ya. I'm making a right mess of it. But you know and I know I'm telling the truth now. He attacked me and you saved me. Whatever they do to you today, Ma, I want you to know I love you so much and I'm minding Maggie. We're both safe now with Gwenda and Ted, and Jack and Skipper. You never need to worry about us no more, whatever happens, and Da is gone for good, so you never need worry about us again. He can't get at me no more, nor Maggie when she's older, so even if they don't listen to me, even if they don't believe me today, you're my angel, Ma, and I love you like no one ever loved anybody and –'

'No more questions,' said the small grey barrister curtly, and waddled back to his seat.

It took the jury ten minutes.

The red-faced judge twitched his moustache and banged his gavel, and like that, it was all over.

Olivia was free.

CHAPTER 29

*L*ena had been very reluctant to accept Emmet's invitation to stay at Malachy's house at first. Her plan had been to stay at a hotel, but according to Emmet, Malachy wouldn't hear of it.

Everyone at home had insisted the trip would do her good. Mike said the California sunshine was his prescription for getting her smile back, though despite the West Cork weather, he was smiling ear to ear himself these days, now that Jane and himself had made a match. He was madly in love, and it was great to see.

Annie Gallagher and Joseph Murphy were holding the fort, and Sarah and Pádraig were up at the farm with Jack and Skipper, which they loved. All was peace and joy in Ted and Gwenda's house, where Olivia had come home to after the trial. She and her girls had soon after moved into the twins' little place while they found their feet. It was a simple conversion of one of the old stone sheds and had a tendency to cobwebs because of the high ceilings, but Olivia kept saying she'd never known such luxury. She'd even got a job working in Emily and Blackie's shop in Kilteegan Bridge, because Aidan was such a handful now that Emily was run off her feet and Nellie was living full time with the sisters at the convent and seemingly loving life.

So for the first time in a long while, everything was calm in Lena's life, and she'd realised she could actually leave them all and go.

She had flown from Shannon, her first time in an aeroplane since coming home from Strasbourg with Eli, back when Emmet was only seven. He was nineteen now, and when he came to pick her up from San Francisco airport, he looked even taller than she'd remembered, lightly tanned and the picture of health. He swept her up in his arms and lifted her off the ground when she came through the arrival gates, much to the amusement of her fellow passengers.

'Mam, you look beautiful,' he exclaimed, and she was glad she'd allowed Em and her mother to take her shopping for a whole new wardrobe. She lived in skirts and cardigans most of the time these days, but Maria, who had a great eye for fashion, had walked the legs off herself and Emily around the whole of Cork, finding perfect dresses, swimsuits in case she decided to risk Malachy's pool and even shorts and t-shirts. Lena had never worn shorts, but she was determined to give them a try out here, without the watchful eyes of the village thinking she'd lost her mind by walking around with her knees showing.

For the trip, she'd chosen a pair of cream trousers and a light cotton jumper in a mauve colour, and she had to admit she looked all right for a woman of thirty-seven. Her thick dark locks were streaked with grey, but Emily had insisted she have them touched up, so she was back to her rich dark-brown brunette. And she'd been daring and had her hair chopped short in the new wedge style. She wasn't sure at first, but everyone had admired the new style with steep angled layers sliced around the sides and back.

'Your hair! It's amazing. You look just like Dorothy Hamill,' Emmet enthused as he took her suitcase from her.

She laughed. 'I've no idea who that is, but thanks.'

'Dorothy Hamill, the ice skater? Won gold in the Olympics for America?' He seemed surprised she didn't know, but then Emmet was so American these days, she supposed he was bound to be more *au fait* with what went on over here.

'No clue, but I'll dig out a picture, and you'd better hope she looks good,' she teased.

'She looks fabulous. All the girls are trying to be like her. Anyway, you look so great, Mam. You seemed so much better at Christmas, but now with your hair and the outfit and everything, honestly, it's just lovely to see you...'

He didn't finish with 'back to your old self', but she knew what he meant. The year after Eli died, she was breathing, eating, sleeping, but just barely existing. Now, though, she still missed him like a physical pain sometimes, but other times she was happy and light and felt like she could live. This was one of those times. She knew Eli would be so proud of her for making the trip, and of Emmet for his building. She was excited to see it. It sounded like a very worthwhile project, something Eli would have been right behind.

'Malachy might not be there until tomorrow,' Emmet went on. 'Him and Rosa are in New York choosing a new venue for the wedding. Originally they were going to have it out here, but Rosa has loads of relatives and Malachy really just has me, so they finally settled on the East Coast. I'm to be his best man, and Wei and me will be the family of the groom, and if it happens in New York, it looks like we'll be all of his guests as well.' He grinned.

'Doesn't he have any friends in America?' Lena was worried on Malachy's behalf.

'Ah, he does, but they're all out here in California. It's not like Dublin to Galway, Mam. The East Coast is three thousand miles away, so he wouldn't expect anyone to make that journey. He's quiet anyway. He knows loads of people, and everyone likes him, women love him, but he doesn't really get close to anyone. Well, except me and Rosa, and Wei a bit now.'

'And the wedding is planned for...?' It felt so strange to ask about the date of her first love's wedding, and part of her suddenly realised what Malachy must have felt that night long ago when he'd come to her house in Kilteegan Bridge and seen her with baby Emmet in her arms and realised Eli was now the man in her life.

'Nine months' time, ages away. Rosa wants to get this building project up and running first.'

Nine months? It felt very soon to her. She tried to think of something neutral to say. 'But isn't the building done already? Isn't that why I'm here, for the opening?'

'The building is. That's what I'm going to show off to you like when I used to bring my art projects home from school.' He laughed, and with a rush of warmth, she realised how she'd missed him. He'd been her baby, and only for Eli he'd have been some other mother's son now. But Eli had made everything right, and for all of his childhood, her lovely boy had been exceptionally close to her. He'd struggled at school to fit in, and admittedly could be quite precocious at times, but he'd grown up to be a wonderful young man and she was so proud of him.

'I couldn't wait to see your projects then, and I can't wait to see this one now.' She beamed at him as they walked to the car park, which her son now referred to as 'the parking lot'. His car was a beautiful Chevrolet convertible in a mustard-gold colour with brown leather seats. 'Emmet, this car! It's gorgeous,' she gasped.

'Malachy bought it for my birthday. He spoils me in fear I'll go home.' He winked and opened the door for her, placing her suitcase on the back seat, and she felt a glow of happiness that he still called Ireland home. 'Will I put the roof up?' he asked. 'Wei always wants it up when she's had her hair done because she says it undoes all the work of the salon.' He rolled his eyes, but fondly.

'Don't worry. I have a scarf here somewhere.' She opened her bag and extracted a deep-purple and cream scarf, wrapping it expertly around her head.

'So from Dorothy Hamill to Audrey Hepburn, just like that.' Emmet chuckled as she put on a pair of sunglasses. 'You know nobody will believe you're my mam. They'll think I've got myself a new lady friend.'

'Go away out of that, you old charmer. Drive the car!' She mock-slapped him, but as she laughed, an image came back to her from long, long ago, and it was like remembering a pleasant dream.

She was running down the lane, and the heels of her new red shoes kept sinking into mud. She was wearing a striped polo-neck jumper and her dark hair was tied up in a high ponytail, and she hoped she looked nice. When she got to the road, his green Beetle was already parked on the grass verge. Butterflies danced in her tummy. She went up to the passenger door, and he jumped out to open it for her. Then a shadow crossed his face. 'Oh, sorry, you're Audrey Hepburn, aren't you? And I'd give you a spin, no bother normally, except I'm waiting for a cracking girl called Lena, so...'

She pushed the memory away and tried to concentrate on what Emmet was telling her about what she was seeing, though as he drove out onto the highway, heading south, it was hard to hear him over the sound of the rushing air and the traffic. All the place names seemed to be in Spanish: San Mateo, San Carlos, Palo Alto. The bay was confusingly to their left, but Emmet shouted over the wind that the Bay Area contained almost a landlocked bay running parallel to the coastline that was connected to the Pacific Ocean only by a strait called the Golden Gate, which was spanned by the famous Golden Gate Bridge.

It all felt like another world to Lena.

As they pulled up outside a palatial house with flowering orange trees in the front garden and a large tiled porch, Wei came rushing out to welcome her. 'I'm so sorry Malachy isn't here,' she apologised. 'He just called to say he and Rosa are delayed in New York for another few days, something to do with a case Rosa is working on. Anyway, they'll be back for the grand opening, of course, but in the meantime, it will be just us three and Juanita.'

Lena felt an odd mixture of relief and disappointment. 'Please don't apologise. I know they must be so busy.' She was exhausted anyway, but Wei and Emmet insisted on showing her all over the huge modern house, which struck her as a bit austere even though it was beautiful. In the kitchen, they introduced her to a charming elderly Mexican lady who showed her how to use the internal house phone if she needed anything at all, food or a glass of wine brought up to her room or her bathroom cleaned, and who wouldn't hear of Lena insisting she could do all that for herself.

Her bedroom upstairs had a balcony with chairs overlooking the garden and ornamental pond and the enormous bed was covered with something called a comforter instead of sheets and blankets; it was like a huge puffed-up cloud. The en suite had a chrome shower with a spray head as big as a serving plate and loads of fluffy towels folded on black-marble shelves, along with any number of shampoos and shower gels. Wei demonstrated how to use the shower, and Lena decided to have one to wake herself up a bit; it turned out to be a remarkable experience, like being in a hot rainstorm, and she was grateful for the rubber shower cap Juanita had provided to protect her hairstyle.

'Do you want me to ask Juanita to make us something? Or we could go out, or maybe get something delivered?' Emmet suggested when she came downstairs, refreshed but still longing for bed.

'Get what delivered?' she asked sleepily, picturing the deliveries to Emily and Blackie's shop, coal and cement.

'Dinner, Mam. We could get Chinese, Indian, Korean... Or, Wei, we could try that new Italian. Rosa told me she got cannoli from there for dessert recently, and it was to die for apparently, even by New York standards.'

'Some restaurants here make their food for delivery,' Wei explained, spotting Lena's blank face, 'so you can call them, order off the menu, but instead of eating in their place, they send it to you.'

'And you do the wash up yourself?' she asked, amused.

'Well, Juanita does usually,' confessed Emmet. He was sitting with his arm around Wei in the middle of a massive white sofa, a colour that wouldn't have lasted a second in Kilteegan Bridge; the children would have it covered with mud in no time.

'Honestly, lads, I'm kind of exhausted, so if I could have a cup of tea and maybe a slice of toast, I'd be as happy to go to bed.' A wave of weariness was threatening to engulf her as she spoke.

Emmet looked at his Longines watch, his Christmas gift from Malachy.

'I know you're going to hate me for this, but it's only 5 p.m. If you fall asleep now, you'll wake at two and be up every night for the week. Trust me – the only thing to do is try to stay awake and beat the jet lag.'

Lena's eyes batted slowly as she collapsed beside them on the enormous sofa, which could have held seven people easily. 'Then maybe I'll just rest here.'

'A swim, that's what she needs,' Wei announced. 'The pool is the perfect temperature. How about we all go swimming, and that will wake you up, Mrs Kogan, and then we'll go get some food, and by the time we've finished, you'll be ready for bed? I know it feels cruel of us, but when we came back from Ireland at Christmas, I was all wrong sleep-wise for almost two weeks.'

'Trust us, Mam, you need to stay awake.' Emmet stood and pulled her to her feet. 'Come on. Wei's right. Let's hit the pool. I'll ask Juanita to bring us up coffee and a few sandwiches for now if you're not that hungry, and you can tell us everything that's been happening in Kilteegan Bridge.'

Lena wasn't a swimmer and confined her forays into water to an occasional paddle in the sea if the summer was very warm. She had never been in a swimming pool before, but the idea that there was one on the roof of Malachy's house, purely for their use, was too extraordinary to miss out on. She'd promised herself to try every-thing, experience everything when she came out here, and so she figured she might as well start now, even if she risked drowning herself.

Twenty minutes later they were all sitting in the pool, which had seat shapes in it amazingly and bubbles and jets of water to soothe her aching muscles after the long flight. She needed her sunglasses because the glare of the sun on the water was blinding. They chatted away as Juanita brought them powerful black coffee that Emmet insisted on making Lena drink, and bacon, lettuce and tomato sandwiches, a combination Lena had never had before. After drinking the coffee and feeling slightly more awake, Lena filled Emmet in on everyone at home, and he explained patiently to Wei who everyone was and reminded her if she'd met them at Christmas.

'I'm sorry, Mrs Kogan. I had such a lovely time in Ireland, but there were so many people...' Wei looked embarrassed.

'Ah sure, you couldn't be expected to remember them all. We're like the Bible, there's so many of us.' Lena laughed. 'And for the love of God, Wei, will you please remember to stop calling me "Mrs Kogan"? I thought we'd got you out of that habit at Christmas. When I met Emmet's dad, I called his mother Sarah, and she's been Sarah to me all my life, so please call me Lena.'

'Of course, if you wish. Thank you,' Wei said politely.

'Is it very different in Singapore, the way you address each other, I mean? We didn't get to talk much when you came to Ireland, we were so crowded.'

Wei nodded. 'Very different. The rules of society are very strict. Ways of speaking, ways of behaving, who calls who what – there are many rules, not like in your country.'

'Oh, there are rules in Ireland too, and woe betide anyone who breaks them,' Lena said ruefully, thinking of Olivia and her daughters, what they'd been through, and then of Jack and Skipper. And herself, and Nellie, as pregnant teenagers. 'But what about here in America, aren't there any rules at all?' She made sure to smile to take any disapproval out of her voice.

Emmet had already shown her where his room was and where Wei's was on another floor – she'd moved in once her father had gone home to save money on rent, he said – but Lena found it hard to believe the young couple slept separately.

'No, California is pretty easy-going.' Emmet coloured slightly as he spoke, and Lena knew her suspicions were correct.

To spare him embarrassment, she changed the subject. 'And so what about your wedding in Ireland? Have you made any plans yet?'

Her son stopped blushing and smiled at her gratefully. 'Well, we'll have to graduate first, and now Wei wants to travel the world before we start saving up for the big day. We will be together forever, of course, so there's plenty of time for us to tie the knot.'

Lena watched her son smile in adoration at his girl. She was happy for him, and she was sure she could hear Eli's lovely lilting Welsh accent in her head, though rather faintly, as if it was harder for him to get through to her in America than in Ireland. *See? I told you it would be all right, didn't I?*

'Well, that's sounds very exciting,' she said encouragingly. When she was young, she and Malachy used to plan to travel the world and maybe end up living in America, just as Wei and Emmet were planning to now, and maybe if things had turned out differently... But things hadn't turned out differently, and so she'd lived almost all of her life in the village where she was born and she was happy about it. Living in America wouldn't suit her, she thought; the pace of life was just too fast.

'You're not disappointed we won't be giving you a day out sooner than that, Mam?'

'Aren't I having a day out to see this fantastic new building designed by my son?' She grinned.

'You are,' Wei said eagerly. 'And Mrs K... I mean, Lena, it's so lovely. Emmet's done such an incredible job, and the architect who notoriously clashes with engineers was really complimentary. Emmet changed almost everything he suggested, but he admitted it was for the better. It's so bright and airy, and the energy really flows in it, you know?'

Lena didn't really know; the idea of flowing energy wasn't anything she'd ever considered before.

'Tell Mam about feng shui,' Emmet urged Wei. 'Mam, this is a thing that I'd never heard of, but when Wei explained it to me, it made perfect sense. I used the principles of it in the planning, and that's why the building works so well. It was all her doing really.'

'What's...um...feng shui?' Lena asked Wei, taking a bite of her delicious BLT sandwich.

Wei said rather shyly, 'Well, it's just the Chinese way really, in designing buildings. The Chinese try to harmonise the environment with the people who will use it. It's based on the idea of there being a cosmic energy force, called qi. Feng shui literally means "wind water", because qi follows the same patterns as wind and water, and the Chinese believe if we design buildings to allow the free flow of qi, it can be used to improve life, wealth, family longevity, that sort of thing.'

'That's fascinating,' Lena said, thinking of hawthorn trees and ancient forts and fairy roads, all the mystic powers running through the Irish landscape that everyone was so careful not to disturb when farming or building new houses.

Wei shrugged. 'It's just how we think, the Chinese part of me anyway. We are a very old culture, like the Irish, and with that comes a kind of universal knowledge, I think. Your godbrother, the doctor, was telling me about a lady in Kilteegan Bridge who told him to date a person, and now they're happy because they followed the way fate was flowing for them instead of walking against the wind.'

'I know who you mean. She's called Vera Slattery. She's a *bean feasa*, a kind of spiritual woman, but not in the religious sense. More in the spirit of the ancients.'

'Yes, well, there's a respect for that kind of thing in Ireland. You all have been there for a very long time, and so you know the modern world doesn't have all the answers. The Chinese are the same.'

'I never thought of that, but of course you're right.'

Emmet was eager to bring the conversation back to more practical subjects. 'So this building will be a real community centre. We're going to have the talking human library once a month – that was Rosa's Great-Uncle Joachim's idea – and there are lecture series planned, and already days have been booked by schools to go there and see the exhibits. There's a little movie theatre too, and there'll be documentaries shown about what happened in Europe. The Jewish community are the custodians, but they are anxious that the place be used as a bulwark against all kinds of racism and oppression.'

Lena loved to hear the enthusiasm in her son's voice and was so glad he'd decided against changing his degree in favour of medicine when Eli died. Emmet was a buildings person, through and through, and Eli would have been bursting with pride.

'There's even going to be free English classes every day, no questions asked,' Wei added. She was as enthusiastic as he was.

'What do you mean, no questions?' Lena was puzzled.

'Well, a lot of people here in California, because it's close to Mexico, come over the border illegally. They have no legal right to stay, but they work the fields and do manual jobs for cash. Often, if they have children, they are afraid to send them to school in case the schools ask for social security numbers or other paperwork, so the board of trustees approved English classes for illegal immigrants, with no requirement to register or pay or have any ID.'

'That seems like a kind thing to do.' She knew America's willingness to accept immigrants had saved at least a million Irish people from starvation during the Famine.

Emmet nodded. 'The Jewish community here are so interesting. They are almost all the relatives of European survivors, or survivors themselves, but they mix with the Chinese, the Japanese, the Indians, the Irish, people from every corner of the planet, really. It's such a melting pot here, Mam. I love it. The electrician at the site is Puerto Rican, the block layers are this Italian crew, our secretary Ilse is from Finland, the architect is Kenyan, the foreman is Irish American, and the chairman of the board, a man called Dr Chaim Bergstein, is Jewish. He had dinner with Malachy and Rosa and Rosa's Great-Uncle Joachim, and they invited me along. It was fascinating.'

Emmet paused to slap some suntan lotion on his face; he'd learnt the hard way that redheads in California had to be hypervigilant if they wanted to tan instead of just peel.

'What did you learn?' she asked him as she turned her face to the late afternoon sun; unlike her pale boy, her skin went brown easily.

'Chaim said that the Shoah, as they call it – it's a Hebrew word for the Holocaust – must serve as a lesson to the world that this can happen to any group, any place, any time, not just Jews and not just Germany. So he thinks it's very important to make this centre not just about the story of the Jews alone but as a place where anyone can learn and understand, and Joachim agreed with him.'

'It sounds like it must be a very large building with loads of spaces?'

'It is. There's Joachim's talking library, and a large separate library, three lecture halls, a cinema, a social room and a coffee shop, and outside there are gardens with orange trees we preserved from the original site and a huge memorial fountain where people can have the names of their loved ones lost to National Socialism engraved in the marble. There are hundreds of names there already but room for many, many more, and it's all free. For many people it might be the only place they can go to have their person's name set in stone.'

'And the Jewish community here paid for all this?'

'Well, no...' He glanced at Wei, who nodded. 'Actually, Malachy paid for it.'

'He did what?' Lena sat upright. 'What do you mean, he paid for it?'

'He didn't want you to know, Mam, but I think you should. You see, Rosa's legal firm is relentless in pursuing anyone who benefitted from Nazi war crimes.'

'She's right to. The kind of people they were... Well, I only knew two, August Berger and his man Phillippe Decker, but' – Lena shuddered – 'they were cold to the bone. No remorse, no empathy, nothing. But what's that to do with Malachy? He had nothing to do with anything like that?'

'Well, the thing is, Rosa found out there were many Jews in Alsace who had their assets stolen by my great-grandparents...'

'Oh!' Lena was absolutely horrified. 'I knew there was a family called Loeb. Eli said something once about August Berger's parents probably being after their wine. Did they get it? Was it worth a lot of money?'

'It wasn't just the Loebs, Mam. The Bergers robbed a lot of Jews of their possessions. So Rosa worked out how much Malachy owed as a result of that, about ten percent of his personal wealth, as it happens, and that was what funded the centre. And he's put in more money of his own, much more, and he's set up a fund going forwards to have the fountain updated with more initials until it is completely covered, which will take years.'

'And he did all this because he was forced to or by his choice?' She was amazed. It gave her a whole new perspective on Malachy. His slightly withdrawn character and posh school manners had often made her wonder if maybe he didn't care that much about people in general, but she'd clearly been very wrong.

'By choice. Rosa would have pursued him if he hadn't, I suppose, but the courts would have awarded only a fraction of the money he's spent, and he says it's only right he makes reparation for what his relatives did. It's been amazing really, to see both sides, having grown up with Dad's story and Granny Sarah and Uncle Saul, and then to be involved with this.'

'I'm glad. And your dad would be very proud, I'm sure of it.'

And as the sun set over the bay, Lena sat quietly beside her son and future daughter-in-law as they chatted between themselves, and she wondered at how strange life could be.

CHAPTER 30

*S*kipper stuck his head around the back door of Olivia's little house. His eyes lit up at the sight of the cold chicken, cheese and tomatoes that were laid on the kitchen table beside a large loaf of bread. He was always hungry, and Olivia had promised him soup and sandwiches for lunch; she seemed to think it was her job to feed him while Jack was away at the mart in Galway. There was a ram breeder up there that Jack had wanted to see for a long time, so he'd gone for two nights while Skipper stayed behind to mind the farm.

Skipper washed his face and hands at the sink, but his jeans were still splattered with paint because he was redecorating their bedroom as a surprise for Jack. He was painting the walls and had put down a new carpet. He'd bought new furniture and a brand-new bed and mattress, making it even more their own precious space where they didn't have to pretend to the world or hide their feelings.

'Welcome, welcome.' Olivia beamed at him, running in from the front garden with lettuce she had just picked. 'Isn't it a lovely day for me to have off?' It was a Friday, but Peggy had insisted on taking over in the shop so Olivia could come home to feed Skipper.

'Sure is, Olivia, a blue sky and a warm breeze. And thanks so much for this fine spread.'

'Oh, don't thank me. All the food comes from your farm.' She smiled as she set about making him sandwiches.

He laughed and said that was nonsense, that she and Katie had earned it ten times over, all the cooking and cleaning they did and gathering eggs and minding the chickens.

'Skipper!' Katie came sliding down the ladder from her sleeping loft. 'I'm so sorry. The colt is still in the arena. I was schooling him when Mam called me in to make the beds, and then I was lying up there reading a book about ancient Rome that Ted gave me, and it's so interesting, and I forgot all about Jupiter...'

He smiled. 'Well, Jupiter ain't goin' nowhere. But you better get him stabled, huh? You OK to do it on your own?'

'Course I can.' She ran for the door.

'Woah there, Katie.' He stopped her. 'Take his saddle off and leave it in the arena OK? I'll use it later for the new filly. And lead him up by the halter. Don't take none of his ornery ways now, y'hear? He's a naughty boy.' He laughed. 'Nice and tight, and walk him in, and turn around in the stall with him, or else he'll kick ya, y'know?'

'I'll be fine. Will I brush him down?' Katie was anxious to prove how competent she was.

'If you like, and maybe a hose on his legs too for a few minutes.'

'No bother.' She scampered out.

''Tis far from horses and stables she was reared,' Olivia said with a smile.

'All the girls roundabout here, they're all horse crazy, and more than that, they're good. Annamaria is set to be a fine show jumper, and Sarah as well, and Sophie wants to race cross-country, though that's rare enough for a girl.' He sat down at the table, still wearing his hat, and took a huge bite out of the sandwich she'd prepared for him.

Olivia sat down opposite him, taking a very small bite of her own sandwich. She had more colour in her face now, but it was taking a while. 'My girls are so happy here. Maggie's doing so well in school, and Ted has Katie printing her letters grand now. I wasn't able to sleep in prison, worrying about them both, and I'm so grateful you all took such care of them. Katie and Maggie and me are very close. I know it might look like I failed them, but I swear I tried, I really did, and I don't know how I can ever repay you all.'

She'd made this little speech what felt to Skipper like a million times, but she was a bit like Katie, fearful that if she didn't constantly say the right things to the right people, her world would come crashing down around her ears.

'It's OK, Olivia,' he said patiently. 'Please, y'all don't got nothin' to be ashamed of. You don't have to keep saying these things. You're safe now, and no one can take your girls away again.'

She wrung her hands nervously, one thin nickel wedding band the only adornment. It was a reminder of the horrible man she was married to, who she could never be rid of, but still she kept it on her finger in case anyone accused her of being a single mother and took her children away. 'I hope not, and Emily is so good to let me work in the shop.'

'Sure, it's good to have a few bucks of your own,' he agreed.

'Yes, and Emily says I can have as many hours as I like, and I'd do more if I could between looking after the girls. A friend I made in jail, poor woman, she had her children taken away because she left her husband and the state said she hadn't enough money to support them as a deserted wife, which is why she went thieving. And so she lost them in the end anyway.'

Skipper saw the dark shadow of worry on her face. 'What's the problem?' he asked gently.

'You've been so kind, and I'm not looking for more or anything – please don't think that – but I worry. What if they think I haven't enough money? There's a social worker coming out next week, and I'm terrified. She'll see we're living on your charity…'

'Tell 'em you've savings in the bank,' said Skipper, with his usual unflappable calm.

'But if I lie and they… I mean, what if they check my bank balance and find I don't have one? They can do that, can't they?' She was panicking now; she lived in constant fear of the authorities who had treated her so badly.

'Well, don't you worry. You just go set up an account in the post office in the town – Geraldine Cronin, the postmistress, is a real nice lady – and we'll put some money in there. And so if they look at your bank details, they'll see you have plenty of money saved up.'

'What? I don't understand...'

'Please, Olivia, we really want y'all to stay reunited, you and the girls. We just want to help y'all. And don't ask why. None of us don't got no reason as such, just we all had a tough time as kids. Even Gwenda's childhood was rough enough. But her and myself and Jack and Ted, we all came out OK 'cause we stuck tight with our siblings, and we want Katie and Maggie and you to be able to do the same. So as long as you want to live here, and work here, and Maggie to go to school here and Ted help Katie with her readin' and writin', then you're welcome. The twins might come back sometime, but they've done so well in New Zealand, I don't think they'll be wanting to move back into this plain little ole house.'

'But it's so lovely!' she protested, astonished.

'But it's small, and it won't just be the two of them if they ever come home – they'll have two big ole New Zealand sheep farmers along with them, and I suspect a gang of kids afore long.'

Olivia wiped her eyes, shaking her head at the miracle of it. 'My grandmother was a Malone, a Catherine Malone from Waterford. She was so lovely, not a bit like my ma, and I dreamed of her last night. I think she sent you to us.'

'So we're kin really.' Skipper grinned. 'Us Malones have to stick together. We're a special breed.' He took up the second sandwich she'd just plonked down in front of him. 'This bread is delicious, Olivia. I haven't eaten any bread this good since I was in California the last time. It sure brings me back to there – how is that possible?'

'Well, Gwenda got a recipe from Rosa, is it? I never met her, but the girls say she's beautiful. But it's sourdough, and I thought you might like it for your sandwiches, you being American and all.'

'Olivia.' Skipper grinned, then took another huge bite and spoke through it. 'Y'all are not only welcome to stay here forever, but I'll be damned if I ever agree to let y'all leave. So welcome to Kilteegan

Bridge, whether you like it or not, and don't ever think of goin' back east.'

Her smile grew wider and wider. 'You know what else I can cook? I looked it up in the library when I heard you liked it.'

'No, go on?' He loved seeing her happy.

'Mac and cheese! Would you like it for your tea tomorrow?'

With a cry of joy, Skipper sprang up, grabbed her thin face in both hands and planted a big cowboy kiss on the top of her head. 'Olivia, I'm not likely ever to marry a girl – between you and me, I wouldn't and couldn't, no more than Jack could or would – but if I ever did, that girl would surely be you.'

'Well, thank you very much,' she said, with a laughing little curtsy. 'And if I were ever to want to look at a man that way again, which I surely don't, I'd say the same to you.'

CHAPTER 31

*L*ena took her second cup of tea to the garden and settled down at the acacia table to read a San Francisco guidebook. All around her swirled the Californian heat, the buzz of a million insects, the delicate lemon fragrance from the orange and lemon trees that blossomed in the garden, the distant but continuous hum of cars. It was all so different to her life in Kilteegan Bridge, but at least the tea was a taste of home.

Emmet, bless him, had scoured Palo Alto for a shop selling Barry's Tea and had found her some. Americans drank mostly coffee. She liked coffee, and it was helpful for the jet lag that was still playing havoc with her system, but she preferred Barry's in the mornings. She must be getting very stuck in her ways, she thought.

Emmet and Wei were out shopping for a new suit for him to wear to the big opening, and Lena had declined to accompany them. They'd barely let her out of their sights since she arrived; they were being so attentive, and she felt they needed time alone.

It was quite nice to get some time to herself as well. After they'd left, she'd brought her first cup of tea into the living room and telephoned Emily, making a note in the message book beside the phone of when the call began and finished. Everyone was fine, Emily assured

269

her. Olivia had agreed to do more hours at the shop in Kilteegan Bridge. She was clearly planning on staying around for a while, and she was so diligent and honest and punctual that Emily was thinking of making her a manager of the Kilteegan Bridge shop so she could focus on extending the Bandon one. Then Skipper answered the phone at the farm and he told her how Rosa had sent over the recipe for sourdough; apparently Olivia had made it for him, and he was over the moon about it. Pádraig and Sarah had gone to stay with her mother and Klaus for the Easter weekend, so she called there next, and Klaus assured her they were being thoroughly spoiled and were loving it; in fact, Maria had them at the cinema when she rang.

Now in the garden, she leafed through the guidebook as she drank her second tea, the nicest one of the day in her opinion, and read about the nearby nature reservation; it sounded as if it was as big as the whole of County Cork, and she thought maybe she'd like to go if there was time. Although, the opening was tomorrow night, so maybe there wouldn't be. Malachy and Rosa were expected back this afternoon, and she wasn't sure if she was looking forward to seeing them or not. She hoped things wouldn't be awkward between the three of them. But Emmet and Wei should be back by the time they arrived, and anyway, everything would be fine; of course it would.

Floating into her mind came that strange, dreamy conversation she and Malachy had had the last time they were alone, sitting together in the gamekeeper's hut in the snow, when he hinted he would always love her in some fashion.

She pushed the memory away, the same as she had the memory of that distant teenage girl running down the muddy lane in her red shoes to meet him.

They were both such different people now; they had lived such wildly different lives. What they'd had in the first love of youth was wild, passionate, intense. But it wasn't real; she was sure of that. The love she had with Eli, that was the genuine thing, the honest, raw, not always pretty but deep and powerful love that two parents share through good times and bad. Besides, she was no longer the innocent girl she was all those years ago, the seventeen-year-old Lena. That girl felt so far from the Lena of 1978 that she was surprised the two of them even shared the same name.

She heard the glass door of the living room open behind her. She thought it must be the lovely Juanita seeing if she needed anything – she was always checking in – and Lena turned with a smile to assure the housekeeper that she was fine.

It was Malachy, dressed in an open-necked short-sleeved shirt and light-coloured trousers, his feet bare, his copper hair wet and slicked back. He must have been in the house some time already and gone for a swim or a shower, or both, with Rosa.

'Lena,' he said, with his big attractive smile, coming over with a cup of coffee in his hand. 'Welcome to California.'

She stood up, hastily dismissing thoughts of him showering with his fiancée. 'Thanks for having me, Malachy.' She went to hug him; it would have been strange not to. He placed his cup on the table, and his arms folded around her, and the smell of him, a mixture of spice and lemon and just...maleness...made her heady.

Stop it, she admonished herself, feeling herself blush. This was ridiculous. Why on earth was this happening to her? It must have been the sun and the jet lag, the same jet lag that had made him so silly in Ireland.

'So how was your flight?' he asked calmly as he let her go and took a chair.

She sat back down at the table and covered her brief confusion by telling him in hilarious detail the adventure she'd had on the flight from New York to San Francisco, sitting beside a man who was an amateur aviation expert.

'I swear, Malachy, he started when we took off. "Ooh, I don't like the sound of that," and, "That's a lot of wear and tear on the server motor." Then he went on to explain about what causes crashes, the slightest thing, a tiny miscalibration.' She'd always had a good ear, and imitated the man's East Coast accent to a T. 'Hour after hour of the stats of aviation disasters. I told him I didn't want to hear it, I said I was a nervous flier, I begged him to shut up, but nothing would stop him. He did tell me he'd been divorced four times, which didn't surprise me in the slightest beyond the amazing fact that he got four women to marry him in the first place.'

'Why didn't you move?' He was laughing so much, he was spilling his coffee.

'The flight was full. I put in earplugs and that didn't even stop him. Honestly, I thought I was going to go crazy. So I hope this community centre of yours and Emmet's is worth the trip, Mr Berger.'

Malachy wiped his eyes. 'Hopefully it is. We'll look after you anyway, make sure you have a great time, so make yourself at home while you're here.'

'I have already, I'm afraid. I've been using the phone. I made a note of the times, and I'll pay for the calls obviously...'

'Don't be silly.' He waved her offer away.

'Well, thank you. And I must say, your house is amazing.'

'Emmet says it's a bit too modern and austere, not like Kilteegan House, but Rosa likes it.'

'And will you and Rosa live here? After the wedding?' she asked, relieved to get things back onto safer ground, his upcoming marriage to another woman. Then she remembered what Emmet had said about Malachy possibly having to sell this house to finish paying for the community centre. She didn't like to bring that up – Emmet had said it was a secret – so she just added, 'Or maybe you'll want to start again somewhere else?'

He shrugged; he didn't seem to care. 'I doubt it. We'll probably keep doing the long-distance thing. Her practice is in New York, my business is here, and neither one of us feels like starting all over again, so...'

'Oh?' was all she could manage. The idea of her and Eli living in different cities was absurd, so she didn't really understand that way of thinking, but then it probably worked for busy people like Malachy and Rosa. She glanced towards the house. 'Is she coming down for her coffee? I'm so looking forward to seeing her.'

He shook his head. 'No. Actually, she stayed in New York. She's got back-to-back meetings all day and I was just in the way, so I told her I'd see her at the opening.'

Again, Lena couldn't imagine not having waited to travel with Eli, but it seemed being wealthy in America was like living on a different planet. 'Well, the community centre sounds like an incredible place. I can't wait to see it.'

'Emmet did an amazing job, honestly, and I'm not saying that just because he's our son...' Malachy coloured slightly. 'Your and Eli's son. But the foreman and the architect had nothing but the highest of praise for him. He's so smart, but good with people too. He's a remarkable young man, Lena. You should be very proud.'

She nodded. 'I am. Eli would be too.'

'Yes, I hope so, because...' He stopped, then continued smoothly. 'I assume the young lovebirds are off putting the finishing touches to everything, so what are your plans for the day?'

'Nothing really. I thought I'd just laze around, read my book, generally be a terrible house guest. I'd clean something if a speck of dust existed in this house,' she teased him gently.

'Oh, Juanita takes care of the place, so no need for that, though there is a bit of grouting to be done, and Jorge and Miguel are off today, so if you wanted to have a go at fixing that...' He winked at her, and her stomach lurched. He was so handsome, it was unavoidable.

His eyes that had so mesmerised her as a girl were as green as ever, and it did him no harm at all that his boyish face had become more lived in during the intervening years. She remembered watching him play rugby when he was at college, powering through opponents, and his physique was the same now, strong and muscular. He hadn't run to fat like a lot of men his age, and she suspected a bit of hard work went into that. Emmet had showed her down to the home gym in the basement, which was full of weights and contraptions. There was no doubt he looked good.

'Ah, no bother, just give me the grout,' she said, with a careless shrug of her shoulders. 'You know me, a farmer's daughter from West Cork. Nothing fazes me.'

'Indeed it doesn't, Lena O' Sullivan, indeed it doesn't.' He raised his coffee cup to her in a salute.

'It's a long, long time since anyone called me that,' she answered lightly, and he looked embarrassed.

'I'm sorry. Lena Kogan. Force of habit...'

'No, it's nice. I miss being that carefree girl, Lena O'Sullivan, though I wonder, was I ever really carefree?' she mused. 'With my mam being sick, and my dad having to mind her and us, and then... I don't know. It all felt a bit... Like I look at my children, and, well, at least before Eli died, they hadn't a care in the world, but I don't think I was ever like that. Were you?'

He considered the question. 'Well, I remember being very happy with my mother before August Berger came back, and then it was awful. So my childhood was carefree at first, and then not.'

'You know, I think that's one of the things about you, about us, Malachy. We associate each other with the happy times, before our parents died and we used to play house together in the ruins of the gamekeeper's cottage. It all was lovely before your father came home.'

'August Berger,' he corrected her. 'I don't call him my father any more. In fact I'm having his name removed from my mother's family headstone.'

Lena nodded, glad for him. 'It's the right thing to do.'

'Rosa suggested it a while ago, but it seemed such a big step, an admission to the world of how evil August Berger was, not "a fighter for the French Resistance" or whatever nonsense he instructed the stone mason to put there. But when I came back at Christmas and went up to the cemetery and saw it... Like, I knew it was there, but seeing his name under my mother's...'

He ran his hand through his thick, coppery hair in grief as she sat and waited for him to continue. Rosa was good for him, she told herself; she was making him face his past head-on, not helping him to cover it up because it was shameful in some way.

'Well, there wasn't the time then, but I've been working on it since. The part with his name on it is going to be scraped, and his body disinterred and reburied in an unmarked grave in another part of the graveyard. It was hard to do, and Kieran Devlin had to petition the county council since they own the graveyard, but eventually it was allowed.'

'I'm glad Rosa suggested it. She seems like someone who understands about memory and the legacy of the past better than most,' Lena said. She took a sip of her tea, pleased at how easily she and Malachy had slipped into real conversation; she'd feared brittle small talk.

'Yes.' He looked at her thoughtfully for a moment, then said cheerfully, 'Anyway, how about we play tourists for the day? We could take a drive up to Napa, have lunch at a vineyard maybe?'

'Don't you have work to do?' she asked in surprise. 'Surely the big opening needs your attention. You're the main engineer, aren't you?'

'Well, I would have thought that a few months ago, but Emmet's made it his project now. It's special to him in more ways than one, so I won't get in his way. No, I'm all yours for the day, if you'll have me?'

The words were harmless, and Lena instructed her face not to blush, but of course it disobeyed. She tried to mask it by making a getaway. 'Let me just grab my things so,' she muttered, jumping up and skirting past him with her head down.

In her magnificent bedroom, she splashed cold water on her face and stared at her reflection.

Stop it, she said vehemently to herself. *You're being* insane. *Behaving like a lovestruck teenager over Malachy Berger of all people.* And she was grieving for her beloved Eli. How disloyal to be even thinking of another man in these terms. Disloyal to Rosa as well. It was wrong and stupid, and she thought she must be having some kind of widow's infatuation or something. She was lonely for Eli, and the first man that came along and she was all gooey-eyed; it was pathetic. She and Malachy were over for two decades, she was married, widowed, a mother of three, and this was just utterly preposterous and shameful.

She felt she should go downstairs, claim she had a headache or something and lock herself in the room for the day. That was the best thing, staying away from him until the opening tomorrow. Rosa would be there then, so that was fine, and the following day, she was going home. Emmet and Wei seemed in no rush to get married, so it could be years before she had to see him again. If he invited her to his own wedding, she'd say she couldn't go, and that would be that.

She steeled herself to leave the room, when a gentle tap on the bedroom door caused her to freeze. Her heart was thumping as she went to open it.

'I just wanted to say it can get cool up in the mountains, so take a sweater or a jacket.'

'Oh…right…fine. I will, right.' She knew she was babbling.

'Lena, are you all right?' he asked, looking concerned.

'Fine, absolutely fine, Malachy. Not a bother at all in the wide world. Lead on.'

And before she knew it, she was sitting in his maroon-coloured Mercury Grand Marquis.

'I thought Emmet's car was flashy.' She smiled at him, breathing normally now and relieved her attack of the bonkers appeared to have passed.

'We can't help it out here. There's a different attitude to Ireland. Back home you'd almost be ashamed of wealth or success, but here it's celebrated. It's a bit ostentatious, but I do like it.'

'Are you fully assimilated now, do you think?' she asked as they turned onto the highway. The powerful car roared to life with a speed that gently pushed her into the soft leather seat.

'Yes, ma'am, I'm fully American now,' he said, suddenly sounding like Skipper, making her laugh.

The day passed in a whirl of more laughter and reminiscences. She told him stories of Kilteegan Bridge and people he would have known, and he told her about the people he'd met through his work, some famous, some powerful. They drank wine and ate delicious food, and they sat in the courtyard of a fairy tale–like vineyard as the sun set over the Napa Valley and toasted their son.

'To Emmet, our finest achievement.' Malachy smiled.

'To Emmet, one of my three wonderful achievements,' she countered.

He nodded, unfazed. 'Sarah and Pádraig are great kids. You're lucky.'

'They are. Would you and Rosa like to have a family, do you think?'

He surprised her by laughing. 'Me and Rosa, have a child? Mm... definitely not.'

'Why not? She's not too old, not by a long way, and you're not exactly Methuselah either, you know.'

'I know. I'm sure it could happen if we wanted it to, and I did think once... But you know...' He twirled his wine glass in his hands, and Lena watched his face in profile. 'It wouldn't be right for us,' he said.

'Why not?' she repeated, her voice barely a whisper this time.

He turned to face her. The setting sun lit the copper of his hair, the curls managed by hair oil, the light hairs on his tanned arms, the freckles across the bridge of his nose, the light seeming to ignite his green eyes. He took her breath away. 'We want different things. I suppose that's why.'

Before she could get her voice back to answer him, the waiter came and told them the vineyard was closing for the day.

'We'd best get home. We've a big day tomorrow,' she said as he helped her on with her jacket.

'We do. I wish I'd been able to spend more time with you, but Rosa insisted she needed me in New York. I had to argue to get away for today even, and now you're going back after the opening and I feel like we've hardly had time...'

She turned to him, the stone courtyard empty but for them, and she shook her head and placed her finger to his lips. 'It was better this way,' she managed, not meaning a word of it.

She pretended to fall asleep in the car on the way home, and eventually she must have done, because when she woke, she was being carried inside by Malachy, in his strong golden arms. She opened her eyes to laugh and protest at him to put her down, and he did, setting her on her feet, but he wasn't laughing with her. He was expressionless and not even looking at her; his eyes were elsewhere. She turned to see what he was seeing. Standing in the hallway was Rosa.

CHAPTER 32

The crowd took their seats in the viewing stand erected for the grand opening. There were a variety of dignitaries and politicians in the front row, along with Malachy, Rosa, Emmet, Wei and Lena, and an elderly man Rosa had introduced to Lena as her Great-Uncle Joachim.

Dr Bergstein, chairman of the board, gave the address.

'Ladies and Gentlemen, distinguished guests,' he began. 'I'd like to welcome you here today for this most auspicious of occasions. The opening of this centre was made possible by the legal firm of Rosa Abramson, and the willingness of Mr Malachy Berger to make reparations, even going far beyond what was required of him.

'There is much to say, and I promise you many long boring speeches inside. However, they will be lubricated by wine and food, so that should take the edge off...' His humour caused a ripple of laughter. 'But before we go any further, I would like to invite the chief engineer – and I'm told the artistic genius as well as the practical brains behind the building – Emmet Kogan, to officially open the centre.'

Lena had thought Malachy or even Rosa might have been the one to open the building, but her heart swelled with pride when Emmet stood up to speak. Her son walked up to the podium, shaking hands with Dr Bergstein, then turning to the crowd.

'Thank you, Dr Bergstein. I'm so happy to be here sharing this day with such wonderful people. I know this centre will do such good in our community and further afield.'

There was a ripple of applause, which Lena joined. She'd had a peek inside the centre already, and it was absolutely beautiful; he was right to be so proud of it.

Emmet continued when the clapping died down. 'I'd like to thank Rosa Abramson and Malachy Berger for overseeing the entire operation, Dr Bergstein for steering the ship and being the chairperson of the board of trustees, who I know have tremendous plans in the near and distant futures. Great-Uncle Joachim was the genius behind the talking library.'

Another round of applause.

'And I would also like to thank Wei Tan, who contributed greatly to the design of the building with her philosophy of architecture. None of this would have been possible without her.'

Wei blushed as the list of thank yous went on, people Lena didn't know. She was so proud of her boy, standing up there in front of everyone, confident and warm and self-deprecating.

Isn't he marvellous, Eli? She spoke to him in her mind as she always did.

He is, every bit of that, she heard Eli reply.

But then, mid-speech, Emmet slowed right down and stopped. Lena felt a lurch in her stomach. Had he forgotten his words? Finally, he began again, his voice hoarse.

'You won't know this, but my dad was a survivor. He and my Grandmother Sarah and my Granduncle Saul escaped out of Berlin in 1940. They had to leave the rest of the family behind, and with the exception of his cousin Rosa, who is here today, they never saw them again. We now know they died, some in the death camps, others on forced marches, some like my grandfather who was shot dead in a railway station. That's why this centre is so important to me personally.

'My dad died over a year ago, but my mother made the journey out here to be here with us today, and I would like to ask her to join me here now so that we can officially open this wonderful place together.'

Lena felt the blood drain from her face as all eyes turned towards her. She steadied herself, wiping away tears as she recalled her beloved Eli's story once more, and then she went to join her son.

Hanging above a bed of beautiful flowers was a blue velvet curtain with a braided gold cord, which she assumed concealed the naming plaque.

Another round of applause erupted as she stood beside Emmet, who towered over her. She caught Malachy's eye, and he smiled reassuringly.

Emmet placed the gold cord in Lena's hand and nodded at her to pull it.

She did, and the curtains opened to reveal a large, simple, white marble stone with gold writing.

She read the words that swam before her eyes.

The Dr Eli Kogan Centre of Remembrance and Education.

Lena had no words. The tears flowed unchecked as her son held her in his arms.

* * *

THE DAY PASSED in a blur of conversations, congratulations and stories of others like Eli's family, who survived when their loved ones did not.

Finally, when everyone but the last few stragglers were gone, and Malachy and Emmet were deep in conversation with Johnny O'Hara about a new project they were going to work on together, Rosa approached Lena, a bottle of champagne and two glasses in her hands.

'Thanks, Rosa, but I'm going to head back, I think. It's been a very long day,' Lena said. She was still not over the jet lag that had knocked her out in the car yesterday and felt she couldn't keep her eyes open a moment longer. She was planning to leave Malachy and Emmet and Rosa to enjoy the rest of the evening together.

'It's not an invitation, it's a summons,' Rosa said, a small smile playing around her lips.

Since the night before, Rosa had been nothing but polite to her, really as if nothing had happened. Which it hadn't, apart from her falling dead asleep in the car and Malachy having to carry her in because he couldn't wake her. So Lena felt she should be polite to Malachy's fiancée now in return.

'All right, but just a small glass. It's been an amazing day, but I'm wiped out.'

Rosa led her to a quiet room upstairs in the centre, furnished simply with two easy chairs and a glass coffee table, and shut the door. Saying nothing, she opened the champagne with a pop and poured them each a glass. Wordlessly, she clinked hers off Lena's.

'So,' she said.

Lena had liked Rosa when they met in Ireland, first when Eli was alive and they were reunited, and a few times since, and even most recently when she reappeared as Malachy's girlfriend. But something told her this was not going to be like their other easy-going interactions. She said nothing and waited.

Rosa raised her glass to her lips, her eyes hooded. 'Mm. I've thought about this, really thought it through, and looked at it from every angle, and this is how I see it. Correct me if I'm wrong.' She paused, took a sip of the champagne and then put it on the glass coffee table.

'The man I'm about to marry assures me regularly that he loves me, that he wants to marry me and that we are good together. I agree, and tell him that I love him too, I want to marry him and that yes indeed we have a good thing going.'

She raised her eyes and looked directly at Lena, and Lena knew suddenly what it must feel like to be in this woman's clutches in the courtroom, rather like how a mouse feels being played with by a cat.

'So you might ask, what's the problem? He's very attentive, buys me thoughtful presents, shows up to things. He's endeared himself to my family effortlessly and he's not even Jewish, so that's saying something. My friends all like him, he's charming but not lecherous, and he speaks with genuine anticipation about our future.

'And this might be a bit too much information, but he's also a passionate, considerate, enthusiastic lover.'

Lena felt her cheeks begin to burn again. Not because she was scandalised at Rosa's revelations – she wished it were just that – but because she knew what was coming.

'So again, where is the problem?' Rosa spread her hands in enquiry. 'Any ideas, Lena?'

You could have cut the atmosphere with a knife. Lena knew she had done nothing wrong. She had encouraged Malachy to give this woman his full heart, and she knew he had committed to do just that. But Rosa was angry, and deep down, Lena knew she had every reason to be.

'Rosa, look, if you have some issue with Malachy, he's who you need to talk to,' she began, but the other woman's voice cut across her.

'I'll tell you, shall I? The problem?'

Lena said nothing.

'The problem is that my fiancée looks at you in exactly the same way as my cousin did before him. When I saw that look in Eli, I was warmed by it. True love does really exist, it does happen, I reassured myself. Years on the social circuit of New York has a way of knocking the romance out of a person, but then I saw you two and I believed.'

Rosa turned her eyes to the window, where a pair of scrub jays had landed beside each other on the branch of an orange tree outside, one of the many Emmet had been proud of preserving on the site, and then back at Lena.

'But now, seeing the man *I* love, the one *I* want to marry, the one who claims to love *me*, look at you the exact same way, that doesn't warm me at all. It makes me cold and resentful and hurt. But the thing is – and this is the real kicker – I have nowhere to put that anger. You haven't laid a finger on him with intent, nor him on you. I know that. He isn't that kind of man. Both of you wish this wasn't the case. I also know that. But the truth of the matter is, whether you choose to verbalise it or not, he's been in love with you since he was a kid, not just as a teenager, and you're in love with him too.'

'Rosa, that's just not true.' Lena pressed her hands to her cheeks; her face felt so hot. 'I'm leaving tomorrow. I'm going home, and Malachy and I won't have any occasion to meet. Don't ask me to the wedding. I wish you both a long and happy life together, genuinely.'

Rosa smiled sadly. 'I know you actually mean that, Lena. That's the hardest thing about this whole mess. He'll never end things. He'll marry me, and we'll live almost happily ever after, and for another woman, that might work – it probably would.' She shrugged pragmatically. 'Successful marriages work on a lot less. But I'm not that woman. I can't have less than everything – I'm not wired that way. It's all or nothing. So I'll end it, and I won't take him back.'

'No, don't do that…' Lena was horrified.

'You wouldn't settle for less either, Lena. We both know that. We're alike, you and I. Not on the outside maybe, but inside, we're similar.'

Lena sat there in an agony of guilt, longing to ease this woman's pain but having no words with which to do it.

Rosa drained her glass and stood up. 'Can I ask one thing of you, Lena, before I go?'

'Of course,' she replied in a whisper.

'When he comes to you, and he will sooner or later, don't turn him down because of what I or Eli or anyone else might think. If you want him, take him.'

Lena started to speak, but Rosa raised a hand, begging for silence.

'This place, these people, my family, Eli's, they all died. Millions of people who never got to fulfil their destiny because they were killed before they had a chance. Eli lived every day. He sucked the marrow out of life. He didn't let stupid things stop him. Honour his memory, Lena, and follow his lead on that.'

Rosa moved towards her then and bent down to kiss her cheek. '*Shmor al atzmeha*, Lena.'

Farewell, take care. Lena had heard Sarah say it to Eli so many times. It was leave-taking with love.

Lena didn't reply but just sat there, a million thoughts whirling around in her mind, as bubbles rose and burst in the beautiful expensive bottle of champagne that Rosa had left behind.

EPILOGUE

K̄ilteegan Bridge, Ireland, 1983

The church was packed as the entire community gathered for the occasion. The heady aroma of incense from the thurible filled the air, and the church organ played triumphantly, filling the cruciform church. All eyes were on Nellie Crean, soon to be fully professed as Sister Margaret by the bishop before her family and her community of sisters.

Lena squeezed Emily's hand as Nellie passed them up the aisle, the beam on her face radiating such joy and happiness, Lena felt warmed by it.

Last night, she'd sat up while Emily sobbed, knowing it was her daughter's most fervent wish but also knowing she had to give her to the sisters. Lena had comforted her that Nellie would never be far away, but then, who knew? Nuns often travelled the world to far-off countries, teaching and nursing. They would just have to cross that bridge when they came to it.

Blackie had a firm hold of Aidan's hand, who was now a cheeky but hilarious seven-year-old, wedged between himself and Pádraig, the little boy's idol, in the hopes that his son would behave. Their youngest daughter, four-year-old Sinead, was on his knee, gazing intently at the entire spectacle between poking at her brother. Aidan and Sinead were like most siblings, in equal measure best friends and archenemies, and they certainly kept Emily and Blackie on their toes.

Lena would never forget the day Em came to tell her she was four months pregnant. Aidan had been three years old, and Emily's pregnancy seemed like a miracle, but Mike confirmed it and Emily carried her daughter to full term with no complications despite what the midwife called unflatteringly 'her geriatric pregnancy'.

Beside her in the pew, Peggy was mopping her eyes.

'All right, Peggy?' Lena whispered to Blackie's mother.

Peggy nodded, clearly not trusting herself to speak. This was such a special day for her, and she felt none of the loss Emily did. She was so proud of her darling granddaughter and had secretly confided to Lena that she was relieved no man would ever again hurt her.

Sarah, Sophie and Annamaria were also wiping tears as the girl they would always see as their wild, beautiful and adorable cousin walked by, dressed in her black habit.

It was lovely having Sarah at home for a change; she was mostly in Argentina now. And while Lena missed her desperately, she was happy that her daughter was living her dream, playing polo professionally. She had signed a big contract with a sponsor recently, so she was making a name for herself in that sport.

Sophie was also getting well known in the horse world. She raced for Skipper all around the country; he had developed quite a prestigious stable of his own. But Annamaria had become more interested in livestock as she got older. The Australian girls, as they would forever be known, were both going out with local boys and were more rooted to the parish than people who'd been there for five generations. Their father, Ted, was less able for the land now – he had bad arthritis – but Gwenda was still managing the farm with ease. Katie and Maggie were growing into fine young women, and they and Olivia were still living in the twins' old house. Molly and May were both married to farmers in New Zealand and still hadn't come home, although they promised they would one day.

Jack and Skipper were sitting together, Skipper without his

Stetson for once, which was something they never saw. And when the whole congregation stood up for Monsignor Collins, Aidan was heard to remark very loudly that Skipper was so much shorter without his hat.

Maria looked beautiful, always ten years younger than her age. Klaus had got thinner after a bad dose of flu last winter, but Mike had assured Lena that he'd be fine. Maybe not as strong as he was – his years in a Russian prison had taken their toll – but he would live to fight another day.

Mike had come to the church with Jane, but their youngest baby, a little girl named Anthea after her grandmother, was, in the words of her adoring father, 'a right squawk-face', and they'd had to leave. They would be at Blackie and Emily's for the celebratory lunch afterwards, though, along with their two older boys, Brendan and Sean, who, together with Aidan Crean, were a force for untold destruction.

Emmet and Wei were sitting with Sister Martina, who'd become a close friend of all the family over the years. Wei and Emmet were on their way to Singapore to see Wei's father, who was terminally ill. Ken Tan had not been much in touch since their marriage, and Lena hoped it went well for them. Ken Tan was not an easy man, but you only got one father. He must surely be proud of his daughter, in partnership with Emmet in Malachy's firm now, and jointly responsible for some of the most iconic buildings on the West Coast.

Lena and Emily both participated in the Mass, squeezing each other's hands as Nellie answered the questions the bishop posed to her, asking her if she was sure she was willing to dedicate her life to God, to take a vow of chastity, poverty and obedience. Nellie's clear voice rang out, sure and confident, and as she lay prostrate on the ground, more prayers and intercessions with various saints were said. The final prayer was for her parents, and neither Emily nor Blackie managed to get through it without a tear.

And then it was over. Aidan and Sinead had been promised an ice cream if they behaved, so Pádraig lofted Aidan on his shoulders easily and trotted to the shop to fulfil the bribe. Lena and Eli's youngest child was a third-year college student now with a plan to become a doctor and was showing every bit of his father's talent, skill and empathy.

'Well?' her husband remarked with a grin. 'You were worried you wouldn't hold it together, but you did. Well done.'

'I still can't believe it, our Nellie, a nun,' Lena replied, taking his arm as they walked to the car.

'I know. When I think of the gorgeous but wild girl that landed up on my doorstep all those years ago…' He laughed.

'Luckily you saved her from a very different religious life that time,' Lena said as he opened the door for her to get into the car.

'I was only doing it to impress you.' He winked, and his green eyes twinkled.

'And I took a lot of impressing, I know, I know,' she said, mock wearily. It was a running joke in the family how long he'd pursued her, flying over so often from California that everyone thought it would have been cheaper for him to buy his own plane.

They had finally married eighteen months ago, to nobody's dismay and everyone's delight, even Sarah and Charlie who came to the wedding. Lena had been so touched when Eli's mother said she knew in her heart that Eli gave her his blessing to remarry, he'd have wanted her to be happy and knew that Malachy loved her, even all those years they were married. Lena had rushed to tell her mother-in-law that Eli never had anything to worry about, but she assured her that she, and he, also knew that very well.

Malachy had moved back to Kilteegan House, where they now lived together, travelling regularly to America and now Argentina as well to see Sarah. They'd even gone to New Zealand to visit the twins, who were, as far as Lena could see, running the whole South Island sheep industry between them.

Before he started the engine, Malachy Berger leant over and, in full view of whoever might be passing, kissed her fully and slowly.

'You were worth every second of that twenty-five-year wait, Mrs Berger, every single second.'

The End.

I SINCERELY HOPE you enjoyed this series and feel, like me, a bit sad to come to the end. If you would like to read other books of mine, you can find all you need to know on my website www.jeangrainger.com

Also there, you can join my reader's club, which is 100% free and always will be. As a reward for joining me I'll send you a free novel to download. Just pop over there and tell me where to send it.

If you enjoyed this book I would greatly appreciate a review on Amazon, it's a great way to connect with readers for me and for new readers to find out about my books.

If you are at a loss as to what to read next, why not try another one of my series?

Here are the opening chapters of a series set in Ireland during WW2 that you might enjoy.

The Star and the Shamrock
By
Jean Grainger

BELFAST, 1938

The gloomy interior of the bar, with its dark wood booths and frosted glass, suited the meeting perfectly. Though there were a handful of other customers, it was impossible to see them clearly. Outside on Donegal Square, people went about their business, oblivious to the tall man who entered the pub just after lunchtime. Luckily, the barman was distracted with a drunk female customer and served him absentmindedly. He got a drink, sat at the back in a booth as arranged and waited. His contact was late. He checked his watch once more, deciding to give the person ten more minutes. After that, he'd have to assume something had gone wrong.

He had no idea who he was meeting; it was safer that way, everything on a need-to-know basis. He felt a frisson of excitement – it felt good to actually be doing something, and he was ideally placed to make this work. The idea was his and he was proud of it. That should make those in control sit up and take notice.

War was surely now inevitable, no matter what bit of paper old Chamberlain brought back from Munich. If the Brits believed the peace in our time that he promised was on the cards, they'd believe anything. He smiled.

He tried to focus on the newspaper he'd carried in with him, but his mind wandered into the realm of conjecture once more, as it had ever since he'd had the call. If Germany could be given whatever assistance they needed to subjugate Great Britain – and his position meant they could offer that and more – then the Germans would have to make good on their promise. A United Ireland at last. It was all he wanted.

He checked his watch again. Five minutes more, that was all he would stay. It was too dangerous otherwise.

His eyes scanned the racing pages, unseeing. Then a ping as the pub door opened. Someone entered, got a drink and approached his seat. He didn't look up until he heard the agreed-upon code phrase. He raised his eyes, and their gazes met.

He did a double take. Whatever or whomever he was expecting, it wasn't this.

Chapter 1

Liverpool, England, 1939

Elizabeth put the envelope down and took off her glasses. The thin paper and the Irish stamps irritated her. Probably that estate agent wanting to sell her mother's house again. She'd told him twice she wasn't selling, though she had no idea why. It wasn't as if she were ever going back to Ireland, her father long dead, her mother gone last year – she was probably up in heaven tormenting the poor saints with her extensive religious knowledge. The letter drew her back to the little Northern Irish village she'd called home...that big old lonely house...her mother.

Margaret Bannon was a pillar of the community back in Bally-creggan, County Down, a devout Catholic in a deeply divided place, but she had a heart of stone.

Elizabeth sighed. She tried not to think about her mother, as it only upset her. Not a word had passed between them in twenty-one years, and then Margaret died alone. She popped the letter behind the clock; she needed to get to school. She'd open it later, or next week... or never.

Rudi's face, in its brown leather frame smiled down at her from the dresser. 'Don't get bitter, don't be like her.' She imagined she heard her late husband admonish her, his boyish face frozen in an old sepia photograph, in his King's Regiment uniform, so proud, so full of excitement, so bloody young. What did he know of the horrors that awaited him out there in Flanders? What did any of them know?

She mentally shook herself. This line of thought wasn't helping. Rudi was dead, and she wasn't her mother. She was her own person. Hadn't she proved that by defying her mother and marrying Rudi? It all seemed so long ago now, but the intensity of the emotions lingered. She'd met, loved and married young Rudi Klein as a girl of eighteen. Margaret Bannon was horrified at the thought of her Catholic daughter marrying a Jew, but Elizabeth could still remember that heady feeling of being young and in love. Rudi could have been a Martian for all she cared. He was young and handsome and funny, and he made her feel loved.

She wondered, if he were to somehow come back from the dead and just walk up the street and into the kitchen of their little terraced house, would he recognise the woman who stood there? Her chestnut hair that used to fall over her shoulders was always now pulled back in a bun, and the girl who loved dresses was now a woman whose clothes were functional and modest. She was thirty-nine, but she knew she could pass for older. She had been pretty once, or at least not too horrifically ugly anyway. Rudi had said he loved her; he'd told her she was beautiful.

She snapped on the wireless, but the talk was of the goings-on in Europe again. She unplugged it; it was too hard to hear first thing in the morning. Surely they wouldn't let it all happen again, not after the last time?

All anyone talked about was the threat of war, what Hitler was going to do. Would there really be peace as Mr Chamberlain promised? It was going to get worse before it got better if the papers were to be believed.

Though she was almost late, she took the photo from the shelf. A smudge of soot obscured his smooth forehead, and she wiped it with the sleeve of her cardigan. She looked into his eyes.

'Goodbye, Rudi darling. See you later.' She kissed the glass, as she did every day.

How different her life could have been...a husband, a family. Instead, she had received a generic telegram just like so many others in that war that was supposed to end all wars. She carried in her heart for twenty years that feeling of despair. She'd taken the telegram from the boy who refused to meet her eyes. He was only a few years younger than she. She opened it there, on the doorstep of that very house, the words expressing regret swimming before her eyes. She remembered the lurch in her abdomen, the baby's reaction mirroring her own. 'My daddy is dead.'

She must have been led inside, comforted – the neighbours were good that way. They knew when the telegram lad turned his bike down their street that someone would need holding up. That day it was her...tomorrow, someone else. She remembered the blood, the sense of dragging downwards, that ended up in a miscarriage at five months. All these years later, the pain had dulled to an ever-present ache.

She placed the photo lovingly on the shelf once more. It was the only one she had. In lots of ways, it wasn't really representative of Rudi; he was not that sleek and well presented. 'The British Army smartened me up,' he used to say. But out of uniform is how she remembered him. Her most powerful memory was of them sitting in that very kitchen the day they got the key. His Uncle Saul had lent them the money to buy the house, and they were going to pay him back.

They'd been married in the registry office in the summer of 1918, when he was home on brief leave because of a broken arm. She could almost hear her mother's wails all the way across the Irish Sea, but she didn't care. It didn't matter that her mother was horrified at her marrying a *Jewman*, as she insisted on calling him, or that she was cut off from all she ever knew – none of it mattered. She loved Rudi and he loved her. That was all there was to it.

She'd worn her only good dress and cardigan – the minuscule pay of a teaching assistant didn't allow for new clothes, but she didn't care. Rudi had picked a bunch of flowers on the way to the registry office, and his cousin Benjamin and Benjamin's wife, Nina, were the witnesses. Ben was killed at the Somme, and Nina went to London, back to her family. They'd lost touch.

Elizabeth swallowed. The lump of grief never left her throat. It was a part of her now. A lump of loss and pain and anger. The grief had given way to fury, if she were honest. Rudi was killed early on the morning of the 11th of November, 1918, in Belgium. The armistice had been signed at five forty five a.m. but the order to end hostilities would not come into effect until eleven a.m. The eleventh hour of the eleventh month. She imagined the generals saw some glorious symmetry in that. But there wasn't. Just more people left in mourning than there had to be. She lost him, her Rudi, because someone wanted the culmination of four long years of slaughter to look nice on a piece of paper.

She shivered. It was cold these mornings, though spring was supposed to be in the air. The children in her class were constantly sniffling and coughing. She remembered the big old fireplace in the national school in Ballycreggan, where each child was expected to bring a sod of turf or a block of timber as fuel for the fire. Master O'Reilly's wife would put the big jug of milk beside the hearth in the mornings so the children could have a warm drink by lunchtime. Elizabeth would have loved to have a fire in her classroom, but the British education system would never countenance such luxuries.

She glanced at the clock. Seven thirty. She should go. Fetching her coat and hat, and her heavy bag of exercise books that she'd marked last night, she let herself out.

The street was quiet. Apart from the postman, doing deliveries on the other side of the street, she was the only person out. She liked it, the sense of solitude, the calm before the storm.

The mile-long walk to Bridge End Primary was her exercise and thinking time. Usually, she mulled over what she would teach that day or how to deal with a problem child – or more frequently, a problem parent. She had been a primary schoolteacher for so long, there was little she had not seen. Coming over to England as a bright sixteen-year-old to a position as a teacher's assistant in a Catholic school was the beginning of a trajectory that had taken her far from Ballycreggan, from her mother, from everything she knew.

She had very little recollection of the studies that transformed her from a lowly teaching assistant to a fully qualified teacher. After Rudi was killed and she'd lost the baby, a kind nun at her school suggested she do the exams to become a teacher, not just an assistant, and because it gave her something to do with her troubled mind, she agreed. She got top marks, so she must have thrown herself into her studies, but she couldn't remember much about those years. They were shrouded in a fog of grief and pain.

Chapter 2

Berlin, Germany, 1939

Ariella Bannon waited behind the door, her heart thumping. She'd covered her hair with a headscarf and wore her only remaining coat, a grey one that had been smart once. Though she didn't look at all Jewish with her curly red hair – and being married to Peter Bannon, a Catholic, meant she was in a slightly more privileged position than other Jews – people knew what she was. She took her children to the synagogue, kept a kosher house. She never in her wildest nightmares imagined that the quiet following of her faith would have led to this.

One of the postmen, Herr Krupp, had joined the Brownshirts. She didn't trust him to deliver the post properly, so she had to hope it was Frau Braun that day. She wasn't friendly exactly, but at least she gave you your letters. She was surprised at Krupp; he'd been nice before, but since Kristallnacht, it seemed that everyone was different. She even remembered Peter talking to him a few times about the weather or fishing or something. It was hard to believe that underneath all that, there was such hatred. Neighbours, people on the street, children even, seemed to have turned against all Jews. Liesl and Erich were scared all the time. Liesl tried to put a brave face on it – she was such a wonderful child – but she was only ten. Erich looked up to her so much. At seven, he thought his big sister could fix everything.

It was her daughter's birthday next month but there was no way to celebrate. Ariella thought back to birthdays of the past, cakes and friends and presents, but that was all gone. Everything was gone.

She tried to swallow the by-now-familiar lump of panic. Peter had been picked up because he and his colleague, a Christian, tried to defend an old Jewish lady the Nazi thugs were abusing in the street. Ariella had been told that the uniformed guards beat up the two men and threw them in a truck. That was five months ago. She hoped every day her husband would turn up, but so far, nothing. She considered going to visit his colleague's wife to see if she had heard anything, but nowadays, it was not a good idea for a Jew to approach an Aryan for any reason.

At least she'd spoken to the children in English since they were born. At least that. She did it because she could; she'd had an English governess as a child, a terrifying woman called Mrs Beech who insisted Ariella speak not only German but English, French and Italian as well. Peter smiled to hear his children jabbering away in other languages, and he always said they got that flair for languages from her. He spoke German only, even though his father was Irish. She remembered fondly her father-in-law, Paddy. He'd died when Erich was a baby. Though he spoke fluent German, it was always with a lovely lilting accent. He would tell her tales of growing up in Ireland. He came to Germany to study when he was a young man, and saw and fell instantly in love with Christiana Berger, a beauty from Bavaria.

And so in Germany he remained. Peter was their only child because Christiana was killed in a horse-riding accident when Peter was only five years old. How simple those days were, seven short years ago, when she had her daughter toddling about, her newborn son in her arms, a loving husband and a doting father-in-law. Now, she felt so alone.

Relief. It was Frau Braun. But she walked past the building.

Ariella fought the wave of despair. Elizabeth should have received the letter Ariella had posted by now, surely. It was sent three weeks ago. Ariella tried not to dwell on the many possibilities. What if she wasn't at the address? Maybe the family had moved on. Peter had no contact with his only first cousin as far as she knew.

Nathaniel, Peter's best friend, told her he might be able to get Liesl and Erich on the Kindertransport out of Berlin – he had some connections apparently – but she couldn't bear the idea of them going to strangers. If only Elizabeth would say yes. It was the only way she could put her babies on that train. And even then... She dismissed that thought and refused to let her mind go there. She had to get them away until all this madness died down.

She'd tried everything to get them all out. But there was no way. She'd contacted every single embassy – the United States, Venezuela, Paraguay, places she'd barely heard of – but there was no hope. The lines outside the embassies grew longer every day, and without someone to vouch for you, it was impossible. Ireland was her only chance. Peter's father, the children's grandfather, was an Irish citizen. If she could only get Elizabeth Bannon to agree to take the children, then at least they would be safe.

Sometimes she woke in the night, thinking this must all be a nightmare. Surely this wasn't happening in Germany, a country known for learning and literature, music and art? And yet it was.

Peter and Ariella would have said they were German, their children were German, just the same as everyone else, but not so. Her darling children were considered *Untermensch*, subhuman, because of her Jewish blood in their veins.

. . .

Chapter 3

Elizabeth let herself in the front door. It had been a long day. The children in her class were fascinated and terrified by the prospect of war and Hitler and all of it. So many of them had lost grandparents, uncles and cousins the last time out, but she could see the gleam of excitement in the little boys' eyes all the same. She'd tried to get off the subject, but they kept wanting to return to it.

Hitler and the Nazis were absurd. He really was a most odious little man, and if the news was to be believed, his treatment of his own people was truly terrible.

She'd heard it discussed at the school, in the teacher's lounge, on the bus, in the corner shop. It was all anyone could talk about: Hitler and the Nazis and how he would have to be stopped.

She dropped her hessian bag full of exercise books and filled the kettle. She'd have a cup of tea before starting her corrections.

As she stood waiting for the kettle to boil, she saw the letter once more. Absentmindedly, she opened it, preparing to throw the entire contents in the bin. Nothing from Ballycreggan was of even the vaguest interest to her.

To her surprise, however, the envelope did not contain a letter from an estate agent. Instead, there was another smaller envelope inside, addressed to her, but at her mother's home in Ballycreggan. The post office must have redirected it. She pulled out the flimsy envelope with its foreign stamps. Intrigued, she opened it and extracted a single sheet.

Dear Elizabeth,

Please forgive my audacity at writing to you like this. We have never met, but I am Ariella Bannon. My husband, Peter, was, I believe, a cousin of yours. His father, Paddy, was your father's brother. I am a Jew.

Peter and I have two children. Liesl is ten and Erich is seven, and I am desperate to get them out of Germany. My husband is missing – I assume he is dead – and I fear for the safety of my children if I do not manage to get them away until all of this is over.

A family friend can arrange for them to leave on the Kindertransport, but I cannot bear to put them on not knowing where or to whom they would be going. I know it is a lot to ask, but I am begging you – please, please take my children. I will see that you are paid back every penny of the expense incurred by having them as soon as I can, but for now, there is nothing to do but throw myself on your mercy and pray.

I have tried to get a visa to leave with them, but I have been unsuccessful.

They are very good children, I promise you, and would do everything you say, and Liesl is very helpful around the house. They are fluent in English and can also speak French and Italian. If you can find it in your heart to help me, you will have my eternal gratitude.

Yours faithfully,

Ariella

PS. Please write back by return, and if you can agree, I will make the arrangements as soon as possible. Every day, things get worse here.

The kettle whistled, but Elizabeth switched off the gas beneath it. She sat down, forgetting all about her tea. She reread the letter.

A million thoughts crashed over her, wave after wave. The primary feeling was sympathy – poor Ariella, what a choice to be faced with; the poor woman must be out of her mind. She never knew her cousin was called Peter; in fact, she had to rack her brain to even recall a mention of either her uncle or her cousin. Somewhere in the deep recesses of her memory, she thought that her mother may have said something, but it was a vague recollection at best.

This woman wanted Elizabeth to take over the care of her children. They would be her sole responsibility for a time as yet to be determined. Could she do it? She was a teacher, but she'd never been a mother, and she knew nothing of raising children. Who would take care of them when she was at work? Where would they sleep? Her house only had two bedrooms. What if they hated her, hated life in England? What if they cried to go back? Elizabeth liked her own company and her small silent home – it was an oasis of calm after a day in school – and the idea that she would soon have to share it with two little strangers filled her with trepidation. But Ariella would not have asked if she were not desperate. Elizabeth would have to do it.

She sat at her kitchen table, trying to visualise this German family, her cousins. She thought she may have remembered a few Christmas cards as a child – they were a different shape to Irish ones, square rather than rectangular, and they were more like postcards. Pictures of snowy mountains. When her father died, even the Christmas cards stopped. Her mother was certainly not going to have anything to do with foreigners.

She had enough money to pay whatever costs would be incurred in taking care of two children. Her mother's legacy remained untouched in the bank, and her teaching salary was building up year after year. She'd paid Saul for the house, though after Rudi's death, he tried to write it off, and apart from a few groceries, she had hardly any outlay.

The irony that she was going to get a chance to be a mother, after all these years, was not lost on her.

She had hoped that she would become pregnant right away after she and Rudi got married in June of 1918, and she did. The joy of that memory was chased immediately by the horror of that child's loss. She'd never had another relationship, though there had been a few overtures from men over the years. It was like she was frozen inside. She couldn't allow herself to feel that deeply again. They say that grief is the price of love, but it was a price she could never pay again.

It took years to come to terms with the fact that not only had she lost Rudi but that she was never going to be a mother. And now here she was offering to be just that to two total strangers.

Sighing, she pulled out a notepad and pen and took note of the address in Berlin.

'Dear Ariella...' she began.

If you would like to read on, the book can be downloaded here:
    https://geni.us/TheStarandtheShamrocAL

ABOUT THE AUTHOR

Jean Grainger is a USA Today bestselling Irish author. She writes historical and contemporary Irish fiction and her work has very flatteringly been compared to the late, great Maeve Binchy.

She lives in a stone cottage in Cork with her husband Diarmuid and the youngest two of her four children. The older two come home for a break when adulting gets too exhausting. There are a variety of animals there too, all led by two cute but clueless micro-dogs called Scrappy and Scoobi.

ALSO BY JEAN GRAINGER

The Tour Series

The Tour

Safe at the Edge of the World

The Story of Grenville King

The Homecoming of Bubbles O'Leary

Finding Billie Romano

Kayla's Trick

The Carmel Sheehan Story

Letters of Freedom

The Future's Not Ours To See

What Will Be

The Robinswood Story

What Once Was True

Return To Robinswood

Trials and Tribulations

The Star and the Shamrock Series

The Star and the Shamrock

The Emerald Horizon

The Hard Way Home

The World Starts Anew

The Queenstown Series

Last Port of Call

The West's Awake

The Harp and the Rose

Roaring Liberty

Standalone Books

So Much Owed

Shadow of a Century

Under Heaven's Shining Stars

Catriona's War

Sisters of the Southern Cross

The Kilteegan Bridge Series

The Trouble with Secrets

What Divides Us

More Harm Than Good

When Irish Eyes Are Lying

A Silent Understanding

The Mags Munroe Story

The Existential Worries of Mags Munroe

Growing Wild in the Shade

Made in the USA
Las Vegas, NV
16 March 2023

69193223R00184